A LINE OF BLOOD

BEN McPHERSON

A Line of Blood

HarperCollins*Publishers*

HarperCollins*Publishers*
1 London Bridge Street, London SE1 9GF

www.harpercollins.co.uk

Published by HarperCollins*Publishers* 2015
1

A catalogue record for this book
is available from the British Library

ISBN 978 0 00 756956 4

This novel is entirely a work of fiction. The names, characters
and incidents portrayed in it are the work of the author's
imagination. Any resemblance to actual persons, living or dead,
events or localities is entirely coincidental.

Set in Sabon LT Std by Palimpsest Book Production Ltd,
Falkirk, Stirlingshire

Printed in Great Britain by
Clays Limited, St Ives plc

MIX
Paper from
responsible sources
FSC C007454

FSC™ is a non-profit international organisation established to promote
the responsible management of the world's forests. Products carrying the
FSC label are independently certified to assure consumers that they come
from forests that are managed to meet the social, economic and
ecological needs of present and future generations,
and other controlled sources.

Find out more about HarperCollins and the environment at
www.harpercollins.co.uk/green

For Charlotte

Crappy is the name given by North Londoners to the very worst parts of Finsbury Park. People start using the name ironically, but it very quickly sticks.

PART ONE

The Man Next Door

1

The precarious thinness of his white arms, all angles against the dark foliage.

'Max.'

Nothing. No response. He was half-hidden, straddling the wall, his body turned away from me. Listening, I thought. Waiting, perhaps.

'Max.'

He turned now to look at me, then at once looked away, back at the next-door neighbour's house.

'Foxxa,' he said quietly.

'Max-Man. Bed time. Down.'

'But Dad, Foxxa . . .'

'Bed.'

Max shook his head without turning around. I approached the wall, my hand at the level of his thigh, and reached out to touch his arm. 'She'll come home, Max-Man. She always comes home.'

Max looked down at me, caught my gaze, then looked back towards the house next door.

'What, Max?'

No response.

'Max?'

Max lifted his leg over the wall and disappeared. I stood for a moment, unnerved.

In the early days of our life in Crappy we had bought a garden bench. A love seat, Millicent had called it, with room only for two. But Finsbury Park wasn't the area for love seats. We'd long since decided it was too small, that the stiff-backed intimacy it forced upon us was unwelcome and oppressive, something very unlike love.

The love seat stood now, partly concealed by an ugly bush, further along the wall. Standing on it, I could see most of the next-door neighbour's garden. It was as pitifully small as ours, but immaculate in its straight lines, its clearly delineated zones. A Japanese path led from the pond by the end wall to a structure that I'd once heard Millicent refer to as a bower, shaped out of what I guessed were rose bushes.

Max was standing on the path. He saw me and turned away, walking very deliberately into the bower.

'Max.'

Nothing.

I stood on the arm of the love seat, and put my hands on top of the wall, pushing down hard as I jumped upwards. My left knee struck the head of a nail, and the pain almost lost me my balance.

I panted hard, then swung my leg over the wall and sat there as Max had, looking towards the neighbour's house. Seen side by side, they were identical in every detail, except that the neighbour had washed his windows and freshened the paint on his back door.

A Japanese willow obscured the rest of the neighbour's ground floor. A tree, a pond, a bower. *Who builds a bower in Finsbury Park?*

Max reappeared.

'Dad, come and see.'

I looked about me. Was this trespass? I wasn't sure.

Max disappeared again. No one in any of the other houses

4

seemed to be looking. The only house that could see into the garden was ours. And I needed to retrieve my son.

I jumped down, landing badly and compounding the pain in my knee.

'You aren't supposed to say fuck, Dad.'

'I didn't say it.' *Did I?*

'You did.'

He had reappeared, and was looking down at me again, as I massaged the back of my knee, wondering if it would stiffen up.

'And I'm allowed to say it. You are the one who isn't.'

He smiled.

'You've got a hole in your trousers.'

I nodded and stood up, ruffled his hair.

'Does it hurt?'

'Not much. A bit.'

He stared at me for a long moment.

'All right,' I said, 'it hurts like fuck. Maybe I did say it.'

'Thought so.'

'Want to tell me what we're doing here? Max-Man?'

He held out his hand. I took it, surprised, and he led me into the bower.

The neighbour had been busy here. Four metal trellises had been joined to make a loose arch, and up these trellises he had teased his climbing roses, if that's what they were. Two people could have lain down in here, completely hidden from view. Perhaps they had. The grass was flattened, as if by cushions.

Now I noticed birdsong, distant-sounding, wrong, somehow.

Max crouched down, rubbed his right forefinger against his thumb.

From a place unseen, a small dark shadow, winding around his legs. Tortoiseshell, red and black. Max rubbed finger and thumb together again, and the cat greeted him, stood for a moment on two legs, teetering as she arched upwards towards his fingers, then fell forwards and on to her side, offering him her belly.

'Foxxa.'

It was Max who had named the cat. He had spent hours with her, when she first arrived, whispering to her from across the room: *F, K, Ks, S, Sh*. He had watched how she responded to each sound, was certain he had found the perfect name.

'Foxxa.'

The cat chirruped. Max held out his hand, and she rolled on to her back, cupped her paws over his knuckles, bumped her head gently into his hand.

'Crazy little tortie,' he whispered.

She tripped out of the bower. Crazy little tortie was right. We hadn't seen her in days.

Max walked out of the bower and towards the patio. I followed him. The cat was not there.

From the patio, the pretentious absurdity of the bower was even more striking. The whole garden was no more than five metres long, four metres wide. The bower swallowed at least a third of the usable space, making the garden even more cramped than it must have been when the neighbour moved in.

The cat appeared from under a bush, darted across the patio. Too late I saw that the back door was ajar. She paused for a moment, looking back at us.

'Foxxa, no!' said Max.

Her tail curled around the edge of the door, then she had disappeared inside.

Max was staring at the back door. I wondered if the neighbour was there behind its wired glass panels, just out of view. Max approached the door, pushing it fully open.

'Max!'

I lunged towards him, but he slipped into the kitchen, leaving me alone in the garden.

'Hello?' I shouted. I waited at the door but there was no reply.

'Come *on*, Dad,' said Max.

6

I found him in the middle of the kitchen, the cat at his feet.

'Max, we can't be in here. Pick her up. Let's go.'

Max walked to the light switch and turned on the light. Thrill of the illicit. We shouldn't be in here.

'Max,' I said, 'out. Now.'

He turned, rubbed his thumb and forefinger together, and the cat jumped easily up on to the work surface, blinking back at us.

'She likes it here.'

'Max . . . Max, pick her up.'

Max showed no sign of having heard me. I could read nothing in his gestures but a certain stiff-limbed determination. He had never disobeyed me so openly before.

Light flooded the white worktops, the ash cupboard fronts, the terracotta floor tiles. It was all so clean, so bright, so without blemish. I thought of our kitchen, with its identical dimensions. How alike, yet how different. On the table was a pile of clean clothes, still in their wrappers. Two suits, a stack of shirts, all fresh from the cleaners. No two-day-old saucepans stood unwashed in the sink. No food rotted here, no cat litter cracked underfoot, no spider plants went short of water.

From the middle of the kitchen you could see the front door. The neighbour had moved a wall; or perhaps he hadn't moved a wall; perhaps he had simply moved the door to the middle of his kitchen wall. Natural light from both sides. Clever.

Max left the room. I looked back to where the cat had been standing, but she was no longer there. I could hear him calling to her, a gentle clicking noise at the back of his throat.

I followed him into the living room. Max was already at the central light switch. Our neighbour had added a plaster ceiling rose, and an antique crystal chandelier, which hung too low, dominating the little room. The neighbour had used low-energy bulbs in the chandelier, and they flicked into life, sending ugly ovoids of light up the seamless walls. What was this? And where was the cat?

Max found a second switch, and the bottom half of the room was lit by bulbs in the floor and skirting.

'Pick up the cat, Max-Man. Time to go.'

He made a gesture. Arms open, palm up. Then he held up his hand. Listen, he seemed to be saying, and listen I did. A dog; traffic; a rooftop crow. People walked past, voices low, their shoes scuffing the pavement.

These houses should have front yards, Millicent would say: it's like people walking through your living room. You could hear them so clearly, all those bad kids and badder adults: the change in their pockets, the phlegm in their throats, the half-whispered street deals and the Coke-can football matches. It was all so unbearably close.

But there was something else too, a dull, rhythmic tapping that I couldn't place, couldn't decipher. Max had located it, though. He pointed to the brown leather sofa. A dark stain was spreading out across the central cushion.

I looked at Max. Max looked at me.

'Water,' said Max.

Water dripping on to the leather sofa. Yes, that was the sound. Max looked up. I looked up. The plaster of the ceiling was bowing. No crack was visible, but at the lowest point water was gathering: gathering and falling in metronomic drops, beating out time on the wet leather below.

Now I could see that cat. She was halfway up the staircase, watching the tracks of the water through the air.

Max and I looked at each other. I could read nothing in my son's expression beyond a certain patient expectancy.

'Maybe you should shout up to him, Dad. Case he's here.'

Maybe I should. Maybe I should have shouted louder as I'd skulked by the back door, because standing here in his living room, looking up his stairs towards the first floor, it felt a little late to be alerting him to our presence.

'Hello?'

Nothing.

'It's Alex. From next door.'

'And Max,' said Max quietly. 'And Foxxa.'

'Alex and Max,' I shouted up. 'We've come to get our cat.'

Nothing. Water falling against leather. Another street-dog. I looked again at Max.

'You go first, Dad.'

He was right. I couldn't send him upstairs in front of me. I had always suspected overly tidy men of having dark secrets in the bedroom.

'Maybe he left a tap on,' I said quietly.

'Maybe.' Max wrinkled his nose.

'All right. Stay there.'

I saw the cat's tail curl around a banister. I headed slowly up the stairs.

A click, and the landing light came on. Max had found that switch too.

Two rooms at the back, two at the front: just like ours. At the back the bathroom and the master bedroom, at the front the second bedroom and a tiny room that only estate agents called a bedroom. The cat was gone. The bathroom door was open.

The neighbour was in the bathtub, on his back, his legs and arms thrown out at discordant angles, as if something in his body was broken and couldn't be repaired. His mouth was open, his lips were pulled back.

His eyes seemed held open by an unseen force; the left eye was shot through with blood. Blood was gathering around his nostrils too.

I did not retch, or cover my eyes, or cry, or any of the thousand things you're supposed to do. Instead, and I say this with some shame, I heard and felt myself laugh. Perhaps it was the indignity of the half-erection standing proud from his lifeless body; perhaps it was simply my confusion.

I looked away from his penis, then back, and saw what prudishness had prevented me from seeing before. Lying calmly in the gap between the neighbour's thighs was an iron. A Black and Decker iron. Fancy. Expensive. There were burn-marks around the top of his left thigh. The iron had been on when he had tipped it into the bath.

Did people really do this? The electric iron? The bath? Wasn't it a teenage myth? Surely, you would think, surely the fuse would save you? Surely a breaker would have tripped?

Apparently not.

The bath had cracked. The neighbour must have kicked out so hard that he'd broken it. Some sort of fancy plastic composite. The bath would have drained quickly after that, but not quickly enough to save the neighbour from electrocution. Poor man.

'Dad.'

Max. He was standing in the doorway, the cat in his arms. I hadn't heard him climb the stairs. Oh please, no.

'Is he dead?'

'Out, Max.' *Surely this needs some sort of lie.*

'But Dad.'

'Out. Downstairs. Now.'

'But Dad. Dad.'

I turned to look at him.

'What, Max?'

'Are you OK, Dad?' said Max, stepping out on to the landing. I looked at him again, his thin shoulders, his floppy hair, that unreadable look in his eyes. You're eleven, I thought. *When did you get so old?*

'Dad. Dad? Are you going to call the police?'

I nodded.

'His phone's downstairs in the living room.'

He was taking charge. My eleven-year-old son was taking charge. This had to stop. This couldn't be good.

'No, Max,' I said, as gently as I could. 'We're going to go back to our place. I'll call from there.'

'OK.' He turned and went downstairs.

10

I took a last look at the neighbour and wondered just what Max had understood. The erection was subsiding now; the penis lay flaccid on his pale thigh.

I heard Max open the front door. 'You coming, Dad?'

I went home and rang the police and told them what we had found. Then I rang Millicent, though I knew she would not pick up.

Max and I sat at opposite sides of the table in our tired little kitchen, watching each other in silence.

After I had called the police I had made cheese sandwiches with Branston pickle. Max had done what he always did, opening his sandwiches, picking up the cheese and thoughtfully sucking off the pickle, stacking the cheese on his plate and the bread beside it. He had then eaten the cheese, stuffing it into his mouth, chewing noisily and swallowing before he could possibly be ready to. Normally I would have said something, and Max would have ignored it, and I would have shouted at him. Then, if Millicent had been with us, she would have shot me a furious glance, refused to speak to me until Max had gone to bed, then said, simply, 'Why pick that fight, Alex, honey? You never win it anyway. You're just turning food into a *thing*. Food doesn't have to be a *thing*.'

Tonight I simply watched Max, wondering what to do, and what to tell Millicent when she came home.

A father leads his son from the world of the boy into the world of the man. A father takes charge, and does not without careful preparation expose his son to the cold realities of death. A father – more specifically – does not expose his son to the corpse of the next-door neighbour, and – most especially – not when that corpse displays an erection brought on by suicide through electrocution.

The tension in the limbs, that rictus smile, they were not easily erased. What did Max know about suicide? What could an eleven-year-old boy know about despair? I had to talk to him, but had no idea what to say. This was bad. Wasn't this the stuff of full-blown trauma, of sexual dysfunction in the teenage years, and nervous breakdown in early adulthood? And though I hadn't actively shown Max the neighbour, I had failed to prevent him from seeing him in all his semi-priapic squalor. What do you say? Maybe Millicent would know.

'Can I have some more cheese, Dad?'

I said nothing.

Maybe I should ring Millicent again. The phone would go to voicemail, but there was comfort in hearing her voice.

Max went to the fridge and fetched a large block of cheddar, then took the bread knife from the breadboard. He sat back down at the table and looked directly at me, wondering perhaps why I'd done nothing to stop him. Then he cut off a large chunk. I noticed the bread knife cut into the surface of the table, but said nothing.

The cat was at the sink. She looked at Max, eyes large, then blinked.

Max went to the sink and turned on the tap. The cat drank, her tongue flicking in and out, curling around the stream of water.

'Can I watch Netflix?'

I looked at my computer, at the light that pulsed gently on and off. *No.* Seventy hours of footage to watch, and a week to do it. *I have to work.* I really should say no.

'Dad?' said Max.

I nodded. Work seemed very distant now. Max stared.

'I'm not taking a plate,' he said at last.

'OK.'

At eleven thirty I heard Millicent's key in the lock. I was sitting where Max had left me at the kitchen table, my own sandwich untouched; the tap was still running.

I heard Millicent drop her bag at the foot of the stair. For the first time I noticed the sound of the programme on the

12

computer: helicopters and gunfire; screaming and explosions. Millicent and Max exchanged soft words. The gunfire and the screaming stopped.

'Night, Max.'

'Night, Mum.'

The sound of Max going upstairs; the sound of Millicent dropping her shoes beside her bag.

'So, Max is up kind of late.' Millicent came into the kitchen. She stopped in the doorway for a moment, and I saw her notice Max's plate, the stack of uneaten bread, the bread-knife cut in the table surface. She turned off the tap, then sat down opposite me. She made to say something, then frowned.

'Hi,' I said.

'Hey.' Her voice drew out the word, all honey and smoke. When Millicent first came to London it had felt like our word. The long Californian vowel, the gently falling cadence at the end, were for me, and for me alone. *Hey.* There was such warmth in her voice, such love. In time I realised *hey* was how she greeted friends, that she had no friends in London but me at the start; the first time she said *hey* to another man the betrayal stung me. Don't laugh at me for this. I didn't know.

'So,' said Millicent. 'I didn't stink.'

I don't know what you mean.

'In fact, I think I did OK. I mean, I guess I talked a little too much, but it went good for a first time. Look.'

A bag. A bottle and some flowers. *There's a dead man in the next-door house.*

I looked up at a dark mark in the wall near the ceiling. *Round, like a target.* Draw a straight line from me through that mark, and you'd hit the neighbour. Seven metres, I guessed. Maybe less.

Millicent looked at me, then reached out and took my hand in hers, turning it over and unclenching my fist.

'You are super-tense.'

'It's OK.'

'You're OK?'

No. I was as far from OK as I could imagine but the words I needed wouldn't form. 'Yes,' I said at last.

'You forgot.' It took a lot to hurt Millicent, but I could feel the edge of disappointment in her voice. The interview, on the radio. Of course.

'No,' I said. 'Radio.' *Why can't I find the words?*

'OK,' she said. She looked at me as if I had run over a deer. 'But you didn't listen to it. I mean, it's also a download, so I get that maybe it's not time-critical, but I guess I was kind of hoping, Alex . . .'

I breathed deep, trying to decide how to say what I had to say. From the look of Millicent, Max had told her nothing of what we'd seen. I wondered where the police were. Maybe bathroom suicides were a common event around here. *What do you say?*

'What is it, Alex?'

From upstairs I heard Max flush the toilet. I thought of the bathroom in the house next door, of the bath five metres from where he was now.

'Alex?'

'OK.' I took Millicent's hand in mine, looked her in the eye. 'OK.'

'You're scaring me a little, Alex. What's going on?'

Three sentences, I thought. Anything can be said in three sentences. You need to find three sentences.

'OK. This is what I need to tell you.'

'Yes?'

'The neighbour killed himself. I found him. Max saw.' Nine words. Not bad.

'No,' she said. Very quiet, almost matter-of-fact, as if refuting a badly phrased proposition. 'No, Alex, he isn't. He can't be.'

'I found him. Max saw.' Five words.

She stared at me. Said nothing.

'I should have stopped him from seeing. I didn't.'

Still she stared at me. She brought her right hand up to her face, rubbing the bridge of her nose in the way she does when she's buying time in an argument.

'I haven't talked to him yet about what he saw. I know I have to, but I wanted to talk to you first.' *Because you're better at this than me. Because I don't know what to say.*

Still Millicent said nothing.

The doorbell rang. Millicent did not move. I did not move. It rang again. We sat there, staring at each other. Only when I heard footsteps on the stairs did I stand up and go to the front room. Max had the door open. He stood there in his lion pyjamas, looking up at the two policemen.

'Upstairs, Max,' I said, trying to smile at the policemen, aware suddenly of the papers strewn across the floor, of Millicent's pizza carton and my beer cans on the side table. 'I'll be up in a minute, Max,' I said, guiding him towards the stair.

'It's OK. Night, Dad.' He kissed me and slipped away from my hand and up the stairs. I nodded at the policemen and was surprised by the warmth of their smiles.

We agreed that it would be easiest for them to enter the neighbour's property through our back garden. Save breaking down the front door and causing unnecessary drama. Better to keep the other neighbours in the dark for the time being.

The policemen weren't interested in explanations; they didn't care what Max and I had been doing in the neighbour's house, seemed completely unconcerned with what we had seen. That would come later, I guessed. They said no to a cup of tea, nodded politely to Millicent, who still hadn't moved from her chair, and disappeared into our back garden. I went upstairs, and found Max in the bathroom, standing on the bath and looking out of the window as the policemen scaled the wall.

'Bed, Max.'

'OK, Dad.'

When he was tucked up, I drew up a chair beside the bed.

'What are you doing, Dad?'

'I thought I'd sit here while you go to sleep.'

'I'm fine, Dad. Really.'

Three heavy knocks at the front door. A dream, perhaps?

2

Millicent's side of the bed was empty. We had lain for hours without speaking, neither of us finding sleep. Then she had reached across for my hand, encircled my legs with hers, and held me very tightly. I had felt her breasts against my back, her pubic bone against the base of my spine, and I'd wondered why we rarely lay like this any more.

After some time, Millicent's breathing had slowed and her grip loosened into a subtler embrace. I became more and more aware of her pubic bone, still gently pressing against me. But at the first stirring in my penis I remembered the neighbour's half-erection in the bath. I stretched away from her, and she went back to her side of the bed.

'Millicent?'

'Mmm.'

'Can we talk?'

'Tomorrow,' she had said.

Now I got up and dressed in yesterday's clothes. I opened the door to Max's room for long enough to see the calm rise and fall of his chest. Asleep. Clothes folded. Toys in their place. I watched him for a while, then went downstairs. Three minutes past six.

The cat tripped into the living room, tail high, limbs taut. She danced around my feet, and I reached down to her.

'Hello, Foxxa.' She sniffed approvingly at the tips of my fingers; then she pushed on to her hind legs, running her back upwards against the palm of my hand, forcing me to stroke her. For a moment she stood, unsteady, looking up, eyes bright and wide, as if surprised to find herself on two feet. Then she lowered herself on to all fours and wove a figure-of-eight around my calves, catlike again.

A mug on the living-room table: Millicent had drunk coffee in front of the television. I saw that the front door was unlocked, and found the kitchen empty. The cat followed me in, ate dried food from her bowl.

Millicent had left a folded note.

Alex,
We need to
   talk Max   *(3)*
   talk school   *(1)*
   talk shrink   *(2)*
   talk police   *(?)*
But please, none of this before we speak.
M

The coffee-maker was on the stove, still half-full. I checked the temperature with my hand. Warm enough to drink. I stood on the countertop and felt around on top of the cupboard, just below the plaster of the ceiling. Marlboro ten-pack. I took one and replaced the packet.

We had started hiding cigarettes from Max. He didn't smoke them, as far as we could tell, but a pack left lying on the kitchen table would disappear. Millicent was certain that he sold them, but Max disapproved of our smoking with such puritanical disdain that I was sure he destroyed them.

In the garden I pulled the love seat away from the wall

18

and drank my coffee, smoked my cigarette. On a morning like this, Crappy wasn't so bad. No dogs barked, no one shouted in the street, no police helicopters watched from above. We should sort out the garden though. The garden was a state.

I stood on the love seat, looked back over the wall. Poor man, with his trimmed lawn, his verdant bower and his successful suicide attempt. From here there was nothing – *nothing* – that betrayed our neighbour's sad, lonely death.

I pushed the love seat back against the wall and stood up, finished my cigarette, tried to plan the day. Quiet word with the teacher. Phone calls to the shrink. The police, I imagined, would make contact with us.

What had Max seen? When he had climbed the stairs behind me, what had he *seen*? That jolt, that first image, that's what stays with you, isn't it? Contorted face or pitiful erection? Rictus or dick? Which would be more traumatic for a boy of his age?

I flicked my cigarette butt over the wall and went back into the house. Max was in the kitchen, all pyjamas and tousled hair, rubbing sleep from his eyes. I bent down to hug him. He sniffed dramatically.

'You've been smoking.' But he threw his arms around my neck and hung there for a moment, then sat down at the table. I searched his face for some sign of something broken in him, but found nothing.

'Max.'

'Yeah.'

'I'm going to be coming with you to school today. I need to tell your teacher what you saw.'

'His name's Mr Sharpe.'

'. . . to tell Mr Sharpe what you saw.'

'You forgot his name, didn't you?'

'Max. Can you listen?'

'What? And *why* do you have to tell him?'

'Because what you saw was very upsetting.'

'It wasn't.'

'You might be upset later.'

He shrugged. 'Can I be there when you tell him?'

'Sure. OK. Why not.'

I kept expecting the police to knock on the door. Typical of Millicent to be out at a time like this.

I made a cooked breakfast to fill the time before we left. I let Max fry the eggs, which surprised him. It surprised me too. We ate in silence, then shared Millicent's portion, enjoying our guilty intimacy. Max went upstairs. I put the plates and pans in the dishwasher and set it running. Millicent didn't need to know.

Max came downstairs, dressed and ready to go. I texted Millicent to say I was taking him to school.

There was a man standing outside our house. He was casually dressed – leather jacket, distressed jeans – but there was nothing casual about his stance. Perhaps he had been about to knock, because the open door seemed to throw his balance slightly off. Max had flung it wide, and there stood the man in front of us, swaying, unsure of what to say.

'Who are you?' said Max. 'Are you a policeman?'

The man nodded, ran the back of his hand across his mouth. He carried a briefcase that was far too smart for his clothes.

'I could tell you were,' said Max. 'Are you going to arrest someone?'

The policeman ignored the question. 'Mr Mercer?' he said. I nodded, and he nodded at me again. He told me his name, and his rank. I immediately forgot both.

'You got a minute?'

'I was going to take Max to school.'

'It's OK,' said Max. 'I can just go.'

'I'd like to speak to your son actually, if that's all right. With your permission, and in your presence.'

No.

'My name's Max,' said Max.

I looked at Max. *You want to do this?* He nodded at me.

'OK,' I said.

'You're giving your consent?'

'I am,' I said, 'yes.'

'Me too,' said Max.

The policeman explained that this was not an interview, although he had recently been certified in interviewing children. He gave me a sheet of paper about what we could expect from the police and how to make a complaint if we were unhappy. Then he took out a notebook. I handed the paper to Max, who read it carefully.

First sign, I thought. First sign that this is taking a wrong turn and I end it and ask him to leave. *He's eleven.*

I brought a chair in from the kitchen for the policeman. Max and I sat on the sofa. The policeman asked me where Millicent was, and I told him she was out. He asked me where she worked, and I said that she worked from home. He asked me where she was again. I said I wasn't sure.

He made a note in his notebook.

'She often goes out,' said Max. 'Dad never knows where she is.'

'Max,' I said.

'Well, you don't.'

The policeman made a note of this too.

'Mum *values her freedom.*'

The policeman made yet another note. Then he took out a small pile of printed forms on to which he began to write.

'How old are you, Max?'

'Eleven.'

'And is Max Mercer your full name?'

'Yes. I don't have a middle name.'

'And you're a boy, obviously.'

'Obviously.'

21

They exchanged a smile; I realised that the policeman was simply nervous.

'Can I sit beside you?' said Max. 'Just while you're doing the form?'

The policeman looked at me.

'If that's OK with your dad.'

'Sure,' I said. I asked him if he wanted a coffee; he asked for a glass of water instead. I went through to the kitchen. Was he nervous, I wondered. *Or are you playing nice cop?*

'I'm white British,' I heard Max say, 'even though British isn't a race but the human race is. We're not religious or anything. And my first language is English, so I don't need an interpreter.'

He was reading from the form, I guessed, checking off the categories: so proud, so anxious to show how grown-up he could be. 'For my orientation you can put straight.'

'That's really for older children,' I heard the policeman say.

'But can't you just put straight?'

'All right, Max. Straight.'

I came back in with the water. The policeman got up and sat opposite us again in the kitchen chair, writing careful notes as his telephone recorded Max's words.

'What were you doing before you found the neighbour, Max?'

'Not much. Like reading and homework and stuff. I'm not allowed an Xbox or anything. And Mum was out, and Dad was working. He lets me borrow his phone, though.'

The policeman sent me an enquiring look. Then he made another note. I was wrong. It wasn't nervousness; it was something else. There was a shrewdness to him that I hadn't noticed at first, and that I didn't much like. 'We're good parents,' I wanted to say to him. 'We love him unconditionally. We set boundaries.' *Don't judge us.*

He was good at speaking to children, though: I had to give him that. Max told him everything. That we had been looking for our cat, that the cat had led us into the neighbour's house, that the back door had been open, and that the cat had disappeared up the stairs.

'Is it better to say *erection*, or can I say *boner*?' said Max.

'Just say whichever you feel more comfortable saying,' said the policeman.

'But what should I say in court?'

'I don't think you're going to have to speak in court,' said the policeman. 'That's very unlikely.'

'What would you say, though?'

The policeman laughed gently. 'Probably erection. It's the official word.'

'OK.' Max smiled a wide smile. 'Erection.' Then he became serious again; he made himself taller and stiffer, an adult in miniature. 'Anyway, even though Dad tried to stop me seeing, I saw that the neighbour had an erection.'

I hadn't tried to stop Max from seeing, though. At least I didn't think I had. I was suddenly unsure. Perhaps I had.

'I'm sorry, Max,' said the policeman. 'That must have been upsetting for you.'

'You don't mean the erection. You mean the dead body.'

'Yes,' said the policeman.

'It was OK,' said Max. 'I mean, it wasn't nice, but it was OK. Have you seen a dead body before?'

'No,' said the policeman, 'only pictures.'

'Isn't it your job?'

'We all have slightly different jobs,' he said.

'How long have you been a policeman?'

'Couple of years,' he said.

I had been wondering whether to send Max upstairs to his bedroom, or to ask whether I could drop Max at school and then come back. Of course, Max could have walked to school by himself, but I wanted to walk by my son's side, to see him safely there, to make sure he was OK after the questions from the police.

The policeman didn't need to speak to me. He had other children he had to speak to. Formal interviews.

'Dark stuff,' he said, and a troubled look clouded his features.

'What dark stuff?' said Max.

The policeman checked himself again. He stood up, put the forms in his briefcase, and handed me a card, told me his colleagues would be in touch to speak to me.

'What dark stuff?' said Max again.

'Not all parents love their children the way your dad loves you, Max.'

As we left the house Max slipped his fingers through mine. *Little Max, my only-begotten son.* He hardly ever held my hand these days.

'Dad,' said Max, 'Dad, Ravion Stamp had to go to the police station, and they filmed it and everything. And his dad wasn't allowed to be there.'

'That isn't going to happen to you,' I said.

'But what if they arrest you?'

'Why would they do that?'

'But Ravion's dad . . .'

Jason Stamp had violently assaulted his son. Ravion had testified by video link. I wasn't sure how much Max knew about the case.

'That won't happen to us, Max. I promise you.'

'But how could that man know that you love me?' he said.

'He could see it.'

'How?'

'OK, he was just guessing.'

'You are so an*noy*ing, Dad,' he said. But he leaned in to me and wrapped his arms around me for a moment. My beautiful, clever son. My only-begotten. Whose first word was *cat* and whose seventh was *fuck*; whose forty-fourth word was a close approximation of *motherfucker*.

Forget the swearing, though. We fed Max, we clothed him,

24

we sang him to sleep at night. We set clear boundaries, and applied rules as fairly as we could. Our house was full of love. We are the classic *good-enough* parents.

Millicent and Max would bath together; I would hear their shrieks of laughter from halfway down the street. Listen to that: that's the sound of my little tribe. Listen to that and tell me it's not real.

Yes, we swore in front of Max, and yes, we smoked behind his back. That doesn't matter. What matters is this – my wife, my son, the water and the laughter.

My little tribe.

Max let me hold his hand until we neared the school, then slipped his fingers from mine, walked beside me. On the final approach, he half-ran, putting ground between himself and me, anxious not to be seen arriving with a parent.

Millicent rang. I cradled the phone to my ear. Screams and shouts of morning break, six hundred London children giving voice.

'I was worried.'

'Hey. Sorry.' Her voice was strained.

'Where are you?'

'On my way. You at the school?'

'Yes.'

'Wait for me?'

'I'd hoped to speak to him before they go in again.'

'You've forgotten his name again, haven't you?' Her voice softened.

'I know. Bad Dad.'

'So, you going to wait for me, Bad Dad?'

'OK. All right.'

I saw Max in a dissolute huddle of boys, all oversized shirts and falling-down trousers. I caught his eye and pointed to the school building. 'See you in there,' I mouthed. He nodded and turned away.

Millicent arrived five minutes after the school bell. She was pale, the contours of her face shifted by lack of sleep. She reached up and kissed me.

Even in heels, Millicent was short. When we'd first met, it had made me want to protect her. Now I hardly noticed. I held her, grateful that she was there. She held me just as tightly. Then she ended the embrace by tapping me on the back.

'Where've you been?' I said.

'Out. Thinking. Sorry.'

It's been like this since we lost Sarah. Millicent's reaction – her ultimate reaction, after she had fallen apart – was to do the opposite of falling apart. She reconstructed herself. She became supercompetent. Make your play, she writes, then move on. Play and move on.

The classroom looked like a post-war public information film, but with more black and brown faces. Didactic posters covered the walls. The children sat in orderly rows, working in twos from textbooks. Three rows back sat Max with his friend Tarek. He looked up when we entered, but didn't acknowledge us.

Mr Sharpe too looked like a man from another age. Dark-skinned, and with close-cropped hair, dressed in a faultlessly pressed suit: like a black country schoolmaster from a time when no country schoolmaster was black. His hair was brilliantine slick, his moustache pencil thin, his hands delicate and agile.

'May we speak with you?' Millicent said. 'We're Max's parents. We wanted to explain the reason for his lateness.'

'Of course.'

'In private.' She turned towards the corridor.

'Actually, that isn't really appropriate.' He gestured towards the class. I looked around, and found Tarek and Max looking directly at me. Tarek whispered something to Max; they looked at the teacher and at us, and laughed.

26

'Unless, of course, you can wait until lunch break. Twelve fifteen. Here.'

'We'd like Max to be present.'

Mr Sharpe nodded, waved us from the room and closed the door behind us.

3

'Uh huh,' said Millicent. 'That sure went well.'

We bought bad coffee from a bad café, drank it from bad Styrofoam cups on a low wall on the baddest of Crappy's bad streets. I lit a cigarette, and we shared it like the bad boy and bad girl we weren't and never would be.

Millicent inhaled deeply, holding back some of the smoke inside her mouth, catching it as it started to wisp upwards, then sucking it hungrily down into her primed lungs. Two hits in one draw: proper film noir smoking. Even after thirteen years of marriage it suggested something unknowable, some glamorous secret that I was never quite party to.

'What is it, Alex?'

'You. Smoking in the sun. Hello.'

That same image – Millicent, backlight and smoke. It repeats itself sometimes, and it catches me off guard. It's no more than a sliver of who she is, a reminder of a moment before we began to share our imperfections with each other. The American girl I met in the pub.

'So,' said Millicent, 'the radio thing.'

'I'm sorry. I should have listened to it.'

'No, I kind of get why you couldn't do that, Alex.' She laughed gently. 'I *really* did not see that one coming.'

I laughed too, then stopped, brought up short by the flash frame of the neighbour that cut hard into my thoughts: the broken body in its broken bathtub, the blooded eye cold against the London heat. Water falling through space.

Three frames of the wrong kind of reality.

'What is it, Alex, honey?'

Erase. *Breathe.*

'Alex, are you OK?'

'Yes,' I said. *Breathe.*

Millicent looked concerned, put a hand on my arm.

'I'm fine.' I breathed.

'You're fine?'

'I'm fine.' I breathed again. 'You said you didn't suck, Millicent.'

'No, I sucked a little, but I didn't stink.'

'They gave you flowers.'

'It was an evening transmission. I guess they already bought them before the show.'

'But they liked you. Come *on.*'

'Yes.' Her eyes shone. 'Yes, I guess they did like me. Because also they gave me this. Look.' From her bag she produced an envelope.

I took it from her.

'Wow,' I said. 'A contract.'

'A letter of engagement. They emailed it to me. At four thirty this morning.'

'You can't have sucked at all, Millicent.'

'They're on summer schedule. They need cover. Tuesdays eight to ten. Four weeks.'

'Wow,' I said again.

'Yeah, wow,' she said. 'That's good, right?'

'It's brilliant, and you know it.'

My America.

We sat grinning at each other on our low wall.

Manifest destiny.

*   *   *

The meeting with Mr Sharpe lasted ten minutes. Max spent the first five looking out of the classroom window. When I described my fear that what he had seen might have trauma- tised him, *must* have traumatised him, Max looked round at me, then at Mr Sharpe. Then he yawned and went back to looking out of the window.

Mr Sharpe listened closely. When I had nothing more to say, he sat, drumming his fingers lightly on his desk, looking from Millicent to me, and back again. He opened a notebook that had been lying on the desk.

'So, Mrs . . . I'm sorry, *Ms* Weitzman.'

'Millicent.'

'Hmm. Quite so. You asked that Max be present at this meeting. May I ask why?'

'You wanted to be here,' I said, 'didn't you, Max-Man?'

'Yes,' said Max, still looking out of the window.

'And why was that, Max?' asked Mr Sharpe, closing his notebook and placing it carefully back on the desk.

'I don't know, Mr Sharpe.'

'Do you have anything to add to what your father has told me?'

'No, Mr Sharpe.'

'All right, Max. Run along and join your friends, then.'

Max left the room, closing the classroom door with exag- gerated care. Millicent and I exchanged a look. *Run along?* Still, there was something strangely comforting about this odd little man with his easy paternalism and his brilliantined hair.

Through the wired glass I saw Max linger for a moment, then he disappeared down the corridor.

'So, Millicent and . . .'

'Alex.'

'Millicent and Alex. Quite. Max seems well-adjusted, well- parented, if I may use that expression. You may be sure that I shall keep an eye open for any sign of the trauma that concerns you.'

'That's most kind of you, Mr Sharpe,' said Millicent.

'Yes, thank you,' I found myself saying. 'Really very kind indeed.' The man's formality was catching.

Mr Sharpe smiled a benign smile. 'Of course, it's summer break soon, and Max will be leaving us in a few short weeks. Was there anything else?'

'Not unless there's anything you would like us to address at home,' I said, surprised that he hadn't mentioned Max's swearing.

'No, as I said, a well-brought-up boy. Nice circle of friends, never in trouble. Studious, but not a prig. Neither a victim nor a bully. He listens in class, he does his homework, he reads well. He will settle well into secondary school life; I have no doubt of it. I'm not really sure what more I can say.'

'Well parented, you said?' asked Millicent.

'Yes, a credit to you and your husband.'

'He doesn't seem in any way odd to you?'

'Dear me, no. Why?'

We didn't see Max as we left the school.

'Shouldn't that man be a country schoolmaster somewhere in the middle of the 1950s?' I said.

'I kind of liked him,' said Millicent.

'Me too. Strange that Max likes him so much, though.'

'Kids don't like teachers who want to hang out; they don't like for adults to talk about hip hop and social networking. They want to know where the line is, and what will happen when they cross that line. Especially boys. They're kind of hardwired conservative at that age.'

'But how does that work here in Crappy?'

'So many questions, Alex. Aren't you tired?'

Seventy hours of footage sitting on my computer. Five days to view it.

4

Across the road from the neighbour's house an ambulance stood parked. Three police cars boxed in the parked cars on our side of the street.

The door of the house on the other side of ours opened. Mr Ashani, all flower baskets and civic pride. His house was freshly painted, his cream slacks smartly pleated; his smile had God on its side.

'Mr and Mrs Mercer,' he said, smiling broadly. 'We see too little of each other.'

'Hey, how are you, Mr Ashani?' said Millicent, offering up her cheek.

'French style,' said Mr Ashani. 'Nice.' He kissed her briskly, once on each cheek, then held out his hand to me. I tried to grip it as firmly as he gripped mine. 'Nice,' he said again. His right eye had the first faint suggestion of cataract clouding its surface, but his skin was flawless. I had once asked him his age, and he had laughed. 'Oh, you mean the old black-don't-crack thing, sir?' I should have asked him again, but I was afraid of appearing rude, or worse.

'Waiting for the dead man?' said Mr Ashani.

'No,' I said. 'No, not at all.'

Mr Ashani laughed, coughed a little, and laughed again.

'Not you, Mr Mercer.' He nodded towards the ambulance. The crew had the doors open in the London heat, listening to the radio, drinking water from aluminium bottles.

'I asked them, you see, but they told me nothing. The police have been there two hours. I saw men with metal cases and there were flashes coming from the house. They would not do this if this man were still alive, surely?'

'You think they're taking photographs?' I said.

'Can you think of any other reason for the flashes, sir?' he said. 'We must pray that this is not the beginning of a wave of crime.'

'No crime was committed, Mr Ashani.'

'No, my dear?'

'It appears to be a suicide,' said Millicent, her voice quiet.

'No,' he said. A look of horror passed across his face. 'What a vile and cowardly thing that would be. We must hope that you are mistaken. We must hope that this is a murder.'

'Mr Ashani, I can't believe you would say that.'

'It is not my wish to offend you, Mrs Mercer.'

'A man is lying dead in there, Mr Ashani. Surely he deserves our sympathy – your sympathy – however he died.'

Mr Ashani considered this. 'No, Mrs Mercer,' he said. 'No, suicide is the greatest of crimes. To turn one's back on redemption, to despair in such a way . . . It is . . . That you cannot see this . . . I am at a loss . . .'

He began to walk back towards his house.

Millicent made to walk after him. 'Mr Ashani. Please.'

He turned, then very deliberately walked back towards us.

'I do not wish you to think me cruel,' he said, 'but the word on this is very precise, my dear. And besides, this man was not a moral man.'

I tried to move into Millicent's line of sight. I wanted her to change the subject.

'Mr Ashani,' said Millicent, 'I respect your view, of course I do, but we disagree.'

Mr Ashani began to speak very quietly, his voice grave. 'With murder there is at least the hope of salvation. The soul of the victim may ascend to heaven, and the murderer may reflect on his crime and repent.' He turned to me, smiled the most reasonable of smiles. 'You see this, sir, do you not?'

I gave what I hope was a smile of respect. Mr Ashani nodded, as if I had confirmed his point, turned back to Millicent. 'With suicide, Mrs Mercer, a soul is forever lost to God. Forever. To choose suicide is to mark your card for damnation. No, Mrs Mercer, no, we must pray that this is a murder.'

I looked at Millicent. *Change the subject* . . .

OK. Millicent looked back at me. *All right.*

'Mr Ashani,' she said, 'my husband and I have been arguing over how old you are.'

He smiled. 'How old do you think I am?'

'So our guess was somewhere between fifty . . .'

'Fifty? Excellent.' He laughed.

'And I guess, and I hope you won't be offended, but we really didn't know . . .' She screwed up her eyes slightly, touched his hand to show that she meant no harm. 'Well, we thought upper limit seventy.'

'Upper limit? That's your upper limit?'

Millicent nodded. 'Maybe sixty-seven?'

'I'm *seventy*-seven,' he said, clearly delighted. 'Fit as the day is young.'

'My husband worries, you know, Mr Ashani. He thinks maybe you'll think badly of us for not being able to guess. You have such perfect skin.'

'No, my dear. No, I am not offended. Other things offend me, perhaps, but not that.'

'You see,' she said as I closed the front door behind us, 'he doesn't think you're a racist for not knowing his age.'

'What did he mean by other things?'

'Well, I guess maybe he *could* think that you are a little

34

racist because you don't engage with his ideas . . . I mean with anyone else you would just jump right in there, but Mr Ashani gets to believe what he wants about God and suicide and murder, unchallenged by you.'

'He's old.'

'Right . . . I'm sure that's why you don't engage with his views. And why you never invite him round. The guy likes an argument. You can see that.'

'You think I'm racist?' And suddenly I could see that she was laughing. 'So now racism is funny?'

A dull thud, as if someone in the dead neighbour's house had dropped a sledge hammer. Time stopped. Millicent winced. The air in the room was all dust and heat. Millicent laughed, as if embarrassed by her reaction. Time restarted.

'No, Alex, no. That isn't it at all. It's just . . . He's our neighbour, we have nothing in common; you don't have to invite him round to drink mineral water and talk Nigerian politics.'

Something scraped across the dead neighbour's upper floor. Millicent's eyes darted. 'Whoah,' she said. 'That was a little . . .'

'. . . unexpected,' I said.

'Unexpected.' She composed herself. 'Yeah.'

'He's from Ghana,' I said, 'and he's a nice guy.'

'Only since he found out we were married. Before that he kind of sucked. And by the way, he has *strong* opinions about Nigeria.'

'Love,' I said, and took her hand. 'Are you OK?'

'Why would you think I wouldn't be?'

I drew her to me, and she smiled weakly up at me. Because suicide terrifies you, I thought. Because you hate the idea that someone's pain might be unreachable. Because you once told me someone you knew . . .

Voices from the neighbour's house. Millicent's eyes crossed to the wall.

'So . . . This is all a little freaky,' she said. 'Why would they not take the body last night?'

35

'Being thorough,' I said. 'I mean, that would be my guess. I don't know.'

'Gross. Maybe I'm *not* completely OK with it.' She ran her tongue along the inside of her lips.

Why would you be, I thought? How could anybody be *OK* with this? I put my hand on her cheek and she held it there for a moment and looked me in the eye. Then she looked away and a shiver seemed to pass through her body.

'Hey,' I said. 'I'm here. You can tell me what you're feeling.'

'I think I just did.'

You didn't, I thought. Not really.

'The guy was OK. A little buttoned-up, but OK. I guess I liked him.' A troubled look clouded her eyes. 'I guess I'm a little freaked out also. That he would still be in there.'

'You knew him?'

'Kind of an over-the-fence thing . . .'

A shadow across the curtain in the front window; three knocks at the front door.

I looked at Millicent. She was shaking her head at me. *Police*, she mouthed. She looked small again, hunched. *No*, she mouthed. *Not now, Alex*. Defensive eyes, like an animal that was past the fight-or-flight stage. I'd almost forgotten that look.

'What else are we going to do?' I said, under my breath. 'They must have heard us in here.' I walked towards the front door; Millicent slipped into the kitchen.

The man was small and thin, in white t-shirt and long shorts, and covered in a light dust. Muscular though. A builder, I thought. A builder carrying a clipboard.

'Mr Bryce?' he said. 'Hello. Continent Containers.'

He looked at me as if I should know what he meant. I didn't.

'Skip-hire provider.' He extended a hand. His smile was warm, professional.

'Sorry,' I said. 'Not Mr Bryce.'

36

'Could I speak to Mr Bryce?'

'There's no Mr Bryce,' I said. 'I'm Alex Mercer. And I've never hired a skip in my life.'

'Strange,' said the man. He looked down at his clipboard. 'All right.' He took out a mobile phone.

'You'll have to excuse me,' I said. 'We've a lot on.'

'OK, sir. Thanks, anyway.'

I closed the door. Millicent returned from the kitchen.

'I'm sorry,' she said, 'I get that you're being brave for me, and for Max. And I hate that you guys had to see what you saw.'

'I could have stopped him from seeing and I didn't.'

'I know, honey, but I'm guessing you were in shock.'

'I laughed. I actually laughed.'

'That would be a classic shock reaction, right there. You're a good father, Alex. Your instinct is to protect. I know it. Max knows it.'

'I failed. Max saw everything.'

'OK, Alex. Yes, we do need to discuss that.' She breathed out heavily.

'My honest guess? Max is going to fall apart a little.'

I sat on the sofa, bit hard into my knuckle.

What have I done?

'Alex, honey, he's going to need to do this. It isn't the end of the world. We have the summer.' Millicent sat down beside me.

'To let our son fall apart? We sit and watch while our son has a breakdown? Have him back on his feet and ready for school by September?'

'We break his fall, Alex. There's a logic to these things. We listen to him when he needs to talk, and we help him to pick up the pieces when – if – he falls apart. It's a process. He'll be OK. We're good parents. We'll find him a good shrink.'

'That's our summer?'

'That's our summer.'

37

'What about work?'

Seventy hours of footage on my laptop. Another shoot to plan.

'You can still go,' she said.

'I can't. You're going to need me here.'

Two weeks in America. An eight-week edit. How was that going to work?

'Sure you can, Alex. Max and I always manage.'

Voices through the wall again. I could see the sinews in Millicent's neck stiffen. 'Huh,' she said. 'I thought they left already. I guess I'm still a little jumpy.'

'Who wouldn't be?'

'Why are you so sweet to me?' she said, her eyes searching my face.

'I'm not,' I said.

'You are.' She pushed me gently backwards and down on to the sofa. Then she lay down and folded herself into me, her back to my chest, legs entangling mine.

'Max will be OK, Alex. With the right support he's going to be just fine.'

'How can you know?'

'Children are resilient.'

'I should be here,' I said.

She turned, arching her back, and found my mouth with hers. Her eyes didn't flick away as she kissed me: none of that reticence now. I lay on my side and she moved to accommodate me, my body cradling hers. She lifted my hand across her breasts, pushed her thighs gently back against mine. I could feel the weight in my limbs now, feel the tension easing from her body.

We lay like this for some time. I pushed gently back against her, not wanting to break the moment.

'Millicent?' I said at last. 'Love?'

'Mmm?'

'Will this be anything like Sarah?'

'No,' said Millicent, her voice heavy with the promise of sleep. 'No, Alex, this will be nothing like Sarah.'

I woke in the middle of the afternoon, stiff of neck and leg. I had been lying on my left arm, and could hardly feel it. I flexed the hand underneath me, felt it move slightly; an alien thing, a part of me that wasn't.

When I raised my head I saw that Max was lying in front of Millicent. Her arms were tightly wound around him, and he too was asleep. He must have let himself in and climbed on to the sofa to join us. Millicent had rearranged my right arm so that I was cradling both of them. Or perhaps Max had done it himself. The three of us on our cramped little sofa. *My little tribe.* How had he managed to sleep without falling off?

I raised my feet so they were on top of the sofa back, then gently freed my arm from around Max. I pushed my back as gently as I could away from Millicent. She murmured something that I didn't understand. Sleep talk, I guessed. Probably nothing.

With my right arm I pulled the rest of my body up so that I was balanced sideways on the sofa back. I brought my left leg down to the floor behind the sofa, then my right.

I heard voices through the wall again. *Were they really not finished?*

I stood up too quickly, saw stars falling past my eyes, felt my left arm tingle as the blood returned. I stood, massaging my arm in the space behind the sofa, glad that no one could see the strangeness of the scene. Then I held my breath and slid out along the wall behind the sofa.

I brought my head down to Millicent's. 'Love?'

'Mmm? Hey.'

'You have room now.'

'Mmm,' she said, and relaxed backwards into the space I had made for her, pulling Max gently with her. Max's eyes flickered open and for a moment I thought he was awake, but he screwed himself even tighter, pulled Millicent's arm firmly about him, and slept on.

Little Max-Man, I thought. *Catch you when you fall.*

A knock at the door. The police, I thought. It could only be the police. I wondered for a moment about not answering. What would happen then? How long would they knock for before they let us alone? But this had to be faced.

Another police officer. She wore a neat two-piece suit, and carried a leather briefcase exactly like the officer who had spoken to Max.

'Mr Mercer?' she said, and held out her hand. I'm fairly certain that she told me her name, but I have no memory of what it was.

'You want to speak to me about finding the neighbour?'

'That's right. I do.'

'And in principle yes,' I said.

She looked puzzled.

'Now isn't good. Could we please schedule this?' I kept my voice as level as I could. 'That really would be much more convenient.'

'Schedule?' she said. 'I'm not really sure I understand.'

I opened the door wide so that she could see Max and Millicent asleep on the sofa.

'Oh,' she mouthed.

'He's exhausted,' I said.

'I can see that,' she said, 'but it's you I want to speak to.'

'Do you have children yourself?'

She shook her head.

'He's asleep. It's a small house. And he's already told your colleague everything.'

'We do need your side of the story, Mr Mercer.'

'And I don't want to add to his burden. He's experienced a major trauma. I'd be grateful if we could do this tomorrow during school hours.'

'It's not that I don't see,' she said. 'But you're making this difficult for me, Mr Mercer.'

'Please,' I said. 'It's stability he needs.'

She blew out her cheeks a few times, then she said, 'I'll make a call.'

She took a small Bluetooth headset from the breast pocket of her jacket and crossed to the other side of the street. I stood, watching her from the threshold. Children shouted in back yards, and the traffic on the main road was loud, but I could hear most of what she said. She reported the conversation we had had, in the words that I had used. She spoke of my concern for my son. She kept looking across at me as she spoke, one hand on her briefcase, the other on her headset.

'Mr Mercer thinks . . . Mr Mercer feels . . . Mr Mercer suggests.' If she was irritated with me she didn't let it show. Her words made me sound reasonable and adult, and I was grateful to her.

I smiled at her; she smiled weakly back.

'Eleven o'clock tomorrow morning,' she said when she had crossed back over. 'Best I could do. Ensure you're in, please.'

'Thanks,' I said. 'Sorry to waste your time. But he's only eleven.'

'Yes,' she said. 'Yes, I do understand.'

'I don't have much to say anyway. Max has told you pretty much everything.'

Millicent woke at six and gently extricated herself from Max. We ate linguine in front of the television. Millicent sat on the sofa with Max's legs in her lap, balancing the plate in one hand, her white shirt flecked red-orange from the sauce. I sat on the floor, my back to the sofa, with Millicent's legs on each side of me.

Max hardly stirred. At nine I carried him up to bed.

5

That first night the sex was drunken and good-natured. Millicent allowed me to believe I had charmed her into bed.

Later we had sat side by side and eaten breakfast at an all-night café in Holborn. I was surprised to find she was nervous. She spilled orange juice in my lap, was mortified, apologised like an English girl. I offered her my last cigarette – she'd long since finished her own pack – and she gulped the smoke down with obvious relief, her spine lengthening, her shoulders descending, balance and poise returning to her body. She took another of her double drags and handed the cigarette back to me. She liked me, I realised, and I liked her. Even when sober. So I told her.

'Why? What do you like about me?'

Why *did* I like her? I knew next to nothing about her, had told her next to nothing about myself. But something had made me say it.

'You're good at smoking. You slept with me on the second date. You have slightly inverted nipples. And you're foreign. What's not to like?'

'Don't try to charm your way past the question, Alex.'

'OK. Sorry.'

'Do you? Like me? I kind of need to know.'

'Yes, I like you.'

On the fourth day she flew back to the States without much explanation. She came back ten days later. She had broken up with her boyfriend. Moved out of their rented apartment. Sold her things and come to Europe.

'Your boyfriend? Your apartment?'

'It wasn't working out.'

A bolter, friends said. Watch yourself. But I was younger then, and I was flattered by the impulsiveness of her choices. *The girl I met in the pub.*

When I asked her where her luggage was, she pointed at her bag. She had taken a courier flight from LAX. One large leather handbag. She really had sold everything. She had a week's worth of underwear. Two t-shirts. Two skirts. One pair of trousers. She had £1,500 in cash. She would work, she said. You can't, I said, you need a permit.

'About that,' she said. 'I had a couple of thoughts.'

So we entered lightly into marriage; so, at least, it seemed to me then.

I lay still in our tiny double bed, listening. I had a memory of her sliding from the bed at first light, of her whispering something to me, tender and loving.

Birds and traffic. A family shouting on a back patio. And computer keys.

I got up and pulled on a clean pair of pants. Max's door was open, his room empty. I opened the door to Millicent's office. A desk, a chair, a computer and Millicent in her kimono dressing gown. A spare bedroom without room for a bed. Millicent didn't look round.

'That bad?' I said.

'What?' she said, typing, her fingers floating elegantly across the keys, fast and precise. Her feet twitched reflexively.

'You're typing with your feet. You're nervous. What are you worrying about?'

She turned, gave me a look of mock irritation, then turned back to her screen.

'I'm preparing a little. For this evening.'

'I thought it was unscripted.'

'It pretty much is.'

'Looks scripted to me, Millicent.'

'So kill me, I'm nervous,' she said. 'Also, a guy with a drill just fitted a lock to the neighbour's front door. Which is more than a little disconcerting. Why would they feel the need to do that, Alex?'

'I don't know.'

'He just . . . I can't believe he just . . . *went* like that.' Her eyes clouded, and for a moment I wondered if she was going to cry.

'London,' I said.

'Maybe so,' she said. 'Yeah. Maybe it's London.' She sighed. Then she drew herself together again and the sadness was gone. 'How many words is two hours, Alex?'

'Three words a second,' I said. 'Makes 180 words a minute, 10,800 words an hour. Call it 21,000 words. Minus commercial breaks, which are about a quarter of the programme. So 15,000 words.'

'Huh,' she said. 'That is a *lot* of words.'

'It isn't,' I said. 'Not really. Where's Max?'

'He fixed his own breakfast and went to school.'

'He seem OK to you?'

'So far. And yeah, I'm watching him for signs.'

She went back to typing. My wife at her desk.

I tried to distract her by cupping her breasts in my hands. She looked up at me and smiled, continued typing while she held my gaze.

'How do you do that?' I said. 'Without looking?'

'Neat, huh?' she said, and turned back to the screen, carried on typing. I kept my hands on her breasts.

'It's a conversation,' I said. 'You don't need to prepare.

They ring, they tell you their problem, you answer their questions.'

'So I'm talking, what, half the time?'

'Less,' I said.

'So, that's what, 6,000 words?'

'Forget the word count, Millicent. You can't script this. And you can't write 6,000 words in a day.'

'I never did this before, and I am *super*-nervous. Also, it's forbidden to swear. And to smoke in the studio.'

'You're allowed to be nervous. You won't swear. People will call. The station will filter out the hostile callers. You will help people who need help. The station will pay you. You can smoke outside during the commercial breaks.'

'You think? You really think all of that?'

'And as soon as you're in it, you'll remember what you know.'

Self-Help for Cynics. Millicent's books had no truck with self-pity. They didn't propose chanting, or detoxes, or relentless positivity as solutions to relationship breakdowns and bereavement. They were tough and funny, but had at their core an understanding of real emotional pain.

Make your play and move on. Books for people like us, a generation of people who layer themselves in irony, people who would never be seen buying a self-help book because that would be *absurd*. Then, suddenly, the same eternal question: what to *do*? Or, as Millicent put it:

'Which version of *you* are you planning to be, when you climb out the well you just filled with your shit? Sooner or later you're going to have to swim to the top and drag yourself out. Make your play, and move on.'

Millicent's cynicism, of course, was a well-constructed front. She could speak the language of the cynic, but she knew – and I know she still knows – that she's an idealist to the core. She believes in love, and she believes that people are redeemed through loving each other. She could never allow herself to say as much – Millicent knows it would destroy the brand if she did – but *Self-Help for Cynics* worked because it was one bruised romantic talking to other bruised romantics, using the language of the disaffected.

People began to write to Millicent. 'I don't know why they're thanking me,' she said to me when the first letters had begun to arrive. 'It's pretty obvious. Get some sleep for Chrissakes. Consider not taking drugs. Go for a walk. Try to remember sex.'

Millicent had followed *Self-Help for Cynics* with *Adulthood for Cynics* and *Parenthood for Cynics*. *Bereavement for Cynics* won a minor award and got her invited to the Hay Festival; *Marriage for Cynics* had won a major award and was sold at the checkouts of upmarket supermarkets.

I took my hands from Millicent's breasts, leaned against her chair. 'I'm married to a brand,' I said. 'What more could a modern man want?'

'I'm a moderately successful author. Of self-help books.'

'You're a brand,' I said. 'We can move to Crouch End.'

'I make forty pence a copy. I'm on probation at the radio station. We can't afford to move any time soon.'

She stood up from her chair, turned around, stretched, stood on the balls of her feet, yawned and kissed me.

I turned her around again, crossed my arms across her chest and slid a hand into her dressing gown, holding her very close. She leaned into me, asked me why I was so sweet to her.

'I'm not,' I said.

'And yet somehow you are.'

You see, I thought, she needs you too.

I sat at my computer. I logged four hours of city landscapes in ninety minutes. Maybe my workload was manageable. Maybe my work was just another logistical brick in our plan for Max. Maybe Millicent was right. Maybe this was no more than a scheduling problem.

At ten to eleven two police officers appeared on the other side of the street, watching our house. I put the man at around fifty, and the woman at thirty, maybe thirty-five. Dark suits, but definitely police. They looked different from the other officers we had met, but I couldn't immediately say why. Something about their bearing.

I pulled on yesterday's jeans and t-shirt. Millicent splashed water across her face, came downstairs in a white linen dress that came halfway down her thigh.

'Interesting choice,' I said.

'Too short?'

'I have no idea,' I said. 'How do you dress for the police?'

She beckoned me downwards, reached up and did something to my hair.

'I guess this is pretty much who we are,' she said.

'You ready?'

'You'd better believe it, you handsome fuck.' She held my hand in hers, and I could feel that she was trembling. She was trying to build me up. She was as nervous for me as I was.

I could hear the officers' voices outside the front door now.

'Are they, like . . . hovering creepily?' Millicent's voice was hushed now.

'Looks like it,' I said.

'Do you think they . . .'

'No,' I said. 'They heard nothing. You're beautiful and poised, and they're here to talk to me. And we have nothing – nothing – to hide.'

The man said something to the woman, and both laughed. How relaxed they sounded. How unlike us.

'Yeah,' said Millicent. 'Easy to forget. I don't like this at all, and it hasn't even started.'

I opened the door barefoot: this is us at home, as we always are. But as soon as the door was open it felt like a mistake.

The two officers were as neat as we were wild of hair. Their eyes scanned us up and down, this straight-backed man and this straight-backed woman in their exquisitely tailored plain clothes. They were a little older than I had realised. She was forty perhaps; he was sixty. They were different in other ways, too, from the police we had met so far: their clothes were expensive and they carried themselves with a confidence that comes with high rank. I looked past them out into the street. Probably an unmarked car. Almost certainly something fancy and German. If Mr Ashani had seen them he would have guessed what they were about.

How did we read to them? Me in t-shirt and jeans; Millicent blowsy in her short linen dress. Both of us barefoot. *Parents.* It was eleven o'clock.

Could they come in, did I think? *No.* I looked round at Millicent. *No.* I turned back to them, looked down at my feet, laughed a self-conscious laugh.

'Yes,' I said. 'Yes, of course.' *No.*

'We could give you five minutes.'

'No need,' I said.

'Right then.'

'We don't wear shoes in the house. But you are welcome to, of course.'

No reaction.

'You have to understand,' I said, 'that we're under quite a lot of stress.'

They handed me their business cards. They were detectives of some sort. I glanced at the cards and handed them to Millicent, instantly forgetting their ranks. Millicent would remember if necessary. Derek and June.

Now that I had gathered myself I was angry at the intrusion.

'Coffee?' I said. The woman shook her head.

'No, thank you, Mr Mercer,' said the older man. Derek.

'Coffee, Millicent?' I asked.

'Coffee, Alex.'

In the kitchen I unscrewed the coffee-maker. Tapped the old grounds into the sink. Filled the reservoir with water from the tap. The detectives stood awkwardly, looking around, taking in the disarray of our lives. I put coffee into the little funnel, and screwed the coffee-maker back together. I lit the gas and set it on the hob.

Millicent sat down at the table, produced a packet of Marlboro and offered me one. I watched the she-detective, enjoyed her irritation as I nodded yes. June, she was called. I was short on sleep and long on caffeine and nicotine, in no mood to apologise for the mess. *Let them wait.*

Millicent took a cigarette for herself and tossed the pack to me. I caught it, removed a cigarette, and lit it from the hob. Millicent lit hers from a lighter she'd found on the table, and we smoked silently as we waited for the coffee, owning the kitchen.

'So,' I said, 'any idea how long this is likely to take?'

'An hour. Possibly two,' said the woman. 'It depends what you tell me, Mr Mercer.'

'I really should be working.'

'I suggest you ring your employer.'

'I'm working from home this week.'

'Well, then.'

'So,' said Millicent. 'You guys don't need to speak to me, right?'

There was a long pause, and the detectives exchanged a look.

'Actually, Ms Weitzman, there is something I'd like to discuss with you,' said the man. *Derek.*

'OK.'

'We can talk about it while my colleague is speaking to your husband.'

Millicent put out her cigarette, put her hand to her face, rubbed the bridge of her nose with her forefinger.

'Sure.' She gave a stiff little smile. 'Shall we speak in the garden?'

'That would be fine, Ms Weitzman.'

Millicent stood up and opened the back door.

'Your coffee, Millicent,' I said.

'Oh. Sure. Thanks.' She sent me that same stiff little smile.

I poured her a cup, poured one for myself. Millicent and Derek went out into the garden. She shut the door with great care. She didn't once look at me.

'What's that about?' I asked.

'Just something we need to clear up with your wife, Mr Mercer.'

'Alex.'

'As you wish.'

'But what do you have to clear up with Millicent?'

'Your wife is at liberty to share the content of the discussion with you, Mr Mercer. As of course you are to share the content of *this* discussion with her. Now, perhaps we should both sit down.'

We sat facing each other across the kitchen table. I felt a sudden urge to apologise for our mess, to make some excuse for the rudeness we had just shown. It's not you, I wanted to say. We're all just a little freaked out at the moment.

We're not bad people.

We're good parents.

But that would only make me look weak now, and besides, it would change nothing.

'So, Mr Mercer, you understand why we're here?'

'The suicide of our next-door neighbour.'

'It certainly could be a suicide.'

'Could be?'

'We're keeping an open mind, Mr Mercer. Now, before we go any further, I should say that we are aware that the experience of finding a body can be a traumatic one. We can arrange counselling if you should at any time find it necessary.'

'It's my son I'm worried about. This is tough on him.'

A patient smile. 'I understand. But I'm also required to say

50

that should *you* at any point require help in regard to what you have experienced, then we can assist you in arranging that help, either without cost or for a nominal fee. These things are tough on adults too.'

Since when were the police all pinstripes and counselling? I looked out of the window, but couldn't see Millicent and the he-detective. Probably sitting down. On the love seat, I thought, and found the thought darkly funny. Millicent would be suffering spasms of social agony. She hated encounters with authority figures, especially authority figures with English accents.

'Now then.' The detective produced a small voice recorder and placed it on the table. 'May I?' Yellow-grey eyes, keen and unyielding.

I nodded. She pressed the record button, and told the machine where she was, and who she was talking to. Then she turned to look at me.

'I should just say here at the start that you are by no means a suspect at the current time.'

'At the current time? What are you saying?'

'That you are not a suspect.'

'You had me worried.'

This time there was more understanding in her smile.

'We appreciate that the form of wording we use can seem vague. I hope you understand why we have to speak in these terms.'

'Sure. Sorry.'

'I need to start by asking you a little about your professional life, Mr Mercer.'

'I'm a TV producer.'

'And you work for?'

'Myself.'

'And what does that involve?'

'It used to be said that you employed everyone else on set.'

'Is that right?'

'Now I pretty much just do what I'm told,' I said.

These were her warm-up questions; my answers didn't matter. She was establishing a pattern of question-and-answer, she was making it clear that she was in control.

'I interview people on camera, so I know how this bit of your job feels.' I smiled, but she didn't smile back. She wasn't trying to establish a rapport with me.

'Do you have any imminent travel plans?'

'I plan the shooting, and the editing. I have responsibility for the budget.'

'Thank you. Duly noted. Your travel plans?'

'There's a whole lot of other stuff too. I also direct.'

'All right, Mr Mercer,' she said. 'And do you plan to work outside the country in the next twelve weeks?'

'New York. Next week. And Chicago. And LA. And San Francisco.'

'Hmm. OK.'

'Series with Dee Effingham. Her twelve favourite men in comedy.'

'Duly noted.' If she was impressed, she didn't show it.

The real questions began. She asked me to tell her about finding the dead neighbour. She was patient and very thorough. She asked open-ended questions, never trying to anticipate my answer. From time to time she would produce a small notebook from her inside pocket, write single words in block capitals. *WATER. CRACK. ERECTION.* If I started to interpret what I had seen, she would gently lead me back to the facts. All the while, the voice recorder sat at her side, bearing witness to my testimony.

Twenty minutes into our conversation, Millicent and Derek came in from the garden. Millicent was guarded, on edge. I tried to catch her eye, but she looked away, her attention focused on the detective, who nodded to his colleague but didn't look at me.

I reached for Millicent's hand, and she let it rest in mine

for a moment. Then she was seeing the detective out of the room and to the front door.

As June and I talked, I heard water running in the bathroom upstairs, heard Millicent's footfalls on our bedroom floor. Then I heard her coming down the stairs and quietly letting herself out of the house.

'I'd really like to know what that was about now, please, if you don't mind.'

'And I've explained to you that I can't discuss that with you, Mr Mercer. I'm sorry, I really am.' She meant it, the sorry part. For the first time the professional distance dropped away; I could see something like sympathy in her eyes.

'Would you mind if I had a cigarette? I could leave the back door open.' She smiled. 'And can I make some more coffee?'

'Of course. I'll have a cup too, if I may.'

This was worse. I didn't want her pity, didn't want there to be a reason for her to feel sorry for me. My hands shook as I made the coffee, shook as I lit my cigarette, shook as I handed her a cup.

'Sorry,' I said. 'Lack of sleep. And the fags probably don't help. We both know we need to stop. For our son if nothing else.'

She gave me her sympathetic smile again, left her coffee cup untouched. I drank my own coffee and smoked in silence. I wondered where Millicent was.

'Are you all right, Mr Mercer?'

'Yeah, can we get this finished now?'

We were at it for another hour. The same patience, the same open-ended questions, the same absolute professionalism. But that edge of concern in her voice, the knowledge that she now felt sorry for me – that was unbearable.

'You haven't really asked me about Max,' I said, as I realised the discussion was ending.

'No.'

'Are you planning to question him again? Because I don't think he could take that.'

'Mr Mercer, that would be a very different kind of investigation, and I don't anticipate that.'

'Meaning?'

'You can draw your own conclusions.' She smiled, that expression of concern again.

'OK, so what happens now?'

'We'll be in touch. Unless of course you or Max wish to access any of the support services we have spoken about.'

'No. Thank you.'

'And I must ask you to remain in the country. You will need to reconsider your American trip.'

'What?'

'We'd like you to remain in the country.'

'But you just said, or heavily implied that I, or rather that the investigation wasn't . . .'

She cut across me. 'Mr Mercer, you are helping us with our enquiries.'

'But I'm not a suspect.'

'Not at this stage.'

We ended the meeting, and she left me at the kitchen table, paralysed by my thoughts.

There was a *thing*, then. Some *thing* has happened.

It was the water that stirred me. For a moment I was sure I was wrong, that the tap in the neighbour's kitchen could not be running. Then I knew that it was, and wondered why the sound troubled me.

I shook myself from my trance, became aware of my legs, rose slowly, trying to rub the sleep from them as I moved towards the wall that divided our house from the neighbour's.

Water. Definitely water.

I put my right ear to the wall. Short percussive bumps. In pairs. And the water was still running.

I moved slowly to the sink, tipped wine from yesterday's

glass, shook out the last drops, and returned to the wall that divided our house from the neighbour's. I placed the base of the glass against the wall, and put my ear in the bowl of the glass. Again those short percussive bumps. The sound was no clearer than before. I moved my head away, looked at the glass. Wasn't this the way it was done? I turned the glass around, put my ear to the base of it; the sound was still no clearer. Pairs of percussive bumps. Still the sound of the water through the pipes.

I put the glass down on the table, and returned to the wall, cupped my ear to its smooth white surface with my hands.

A bump. A metallic crash. No second bump this time.

A woman's voice. A cry of frustration.

I thought for a moment of Millicent, but why would Millicent be in the neighbour's house?

I opened the front door and went out into the street.

'Look, sir, look.'

Mr Ashani was standing on the pavement outside our house. He nodded towards the dead man's house and made to speak, but I smiled and tapped him on the elbow, walked past him to the neighbour's front door. Then I saw what Mr Ashani had meant me to see.

A locksmith had fitted two small steel plates, one to the door, one to the frame. They had buckled slightly, as if under force, and the padlock that had held them had given. Someone had placed the lock on the low wall in front of the house, as if meaning to replace it.

'Oh,' I said.

'Indeed,' said Mr Ashani.

'No yellow tape, though.' Perhaps the police weren't thinking murder after all.

'In this country, sir, police tape is blue and white.'

'Well,' I said, and folded my arms.

Mr Ashani shot me an uncertain half-smile and went back into his house.

I rang the dead neighbour's bell. The door opened. I guessed at once that she was his sister. She was tall, and a little too slight for her frame. Her skin was very pale, and her brown hair hung crisply at her shoulders: the kind of woman my mother would describe as willowy. The kind of daughter my mother's friends had. Pretty, in other circumstances.

'Alex,' I said. 'I live next door.'

I looked past her. From here I could not see the sink, though I could hear the tap running in the kitchen. I could see the source of the crash, though. She had pulled a drawer out of its mount, and the sides had come away from the base as it landed. Impractical slivers of stainless steel were strewn across the kitchen floor. I guessed that the flat ones were knives, the curved ones spoons. The forks seemed to have only two prongs.

The words Crime Scene flashed across my mind. *She doesn't know.*

'I was making a cup of tea,' she said. 'Trying to. Would you like one?'

'Thanks,' I said. 'I can't.'

She stood, uncertain, as if waiting for me to say more.

Don't go in.

'Look,' I said, 'I'm sorry to ask you this, but you have spoken to the police?'

She nodded, and pushed the corners of her mouth inwards. 'But not since the night. Not been feeling very sociable. Haven't been charging my phone.' There was a glassy look to her eyes, and I could see she badly wanted not to cry.

'I don't think you should be in there just now,' I said. 'I'm really sorry.'

'Why not?'

Because the police think I might, just possibly, have killed your brother.

'Did you force the lock?'

She nodded. Etiolated, I thought. You wouldn't think there was enough strength in those narrow shoulders.

'I think the police fitted it,' I said.

'I slightly realised after I'd done it,' she said. 'Stupid, isn't it, what grief makes you do?'

She looked at me and smiled, as if that explained it.

'I think you need to turn off the tap and leave.'

'Couldn't you just come in while I get myself sorted out?'

'I'm sorry, no. Is that your bag?'

'What are you saying?'

'You can come and sit with me, if you like.'

Mr Ashani must have been watching. He sprang from his house, and had his hand on my arm before I reached my front door.

'Mr Ashani.'

'Mr Mercer, I must speak with you.'

'I'm a little busy just now, Mr Ashani.'

'I wish to discuss with you what kind of man this was.'

Leave us alone.

'I'm expecting his sister for tea. Perhaps we could talk later?'

'This is a discussion we must have, Mr Mercer.'

For a while I didn't think she would come. I made coffee and tidied up a little. I could still hear the tap running through the wall, and I guessed from the tiny scraping sounds that she was picking up the cutlery and trying to replace the drawer. Eventually she turned off the tap, and a minute after that she was sitting at our kitchen table.

Her name was Rose, and her hands shook as she drank her coffee. Her lower left arm was covered in silver bracelets, which glinted as she moved: a soft metallic sound, like breath. Why hadn't I noticed before?

I suggested she speak to the police. I hoped they wouldn't reveal that I was under suspicion, because there was something genuine about her, and I wanted her to like me. Even in her grief she was sweet and self-deprecating and funny.

57

'Was it you who found him?' she asked after a while.

'Yes. And my son. We were looking for the cat.'

She nodded as if that explained it.

'Thanks.'

We sat and drank coffee in silence. Then she asked if I minded if she smoked. 'In the garden, I mean. Would that be OK?'

'You don't need to go in the garden.'

She produced a packet of Kensitas Club and offered me one. She took out a silver lighter and tried to light my cigarette, hand shaking.

'You're not really a smoker, are you?' I said.

'It's that obvious?'

'Girls like you don't smoke Kensitas Club.' I sniffed the cigarette in my hand. 'And these are stale. You nick them from a party?'

The sadness lifted from her, and she smiled, making light.

'Busted.' A glint in her eye. More than just a nice English girl, then.

'Want a proper cigarette?'

'Yeah,' she said. 'Thanks.'

I lit two cigarettes at the stove, handed her one. She gripped the cigarette like a pen, took a drag, watched the smoke as it curled upwards. She was nothing like Millicent but she had something of the same underlying strength, some quality that made me feel I could trust her, almost as if we shared a secret, though if you had asked me to define what I liked about her I would have struggled, would have worried that you thought I was attracted to her.

'Was it awful for you?' The aching sadness was back. 'Did it look as if he was suffering? I mean, of course he was suffering. He had to be to do that. But how did he seem?' I could feel her struggling for the words. 'Did he look all right?'

'I think it was OK. He looked OK.' I thought again about that rictus smile. Of course it was awful. The erection. The violence of it. Of course he didn't look all right. But the poor man was someone's brother. He was *Rose*'s brother.

'He looked dignified. He looked peaceful.'

He looked *murdered*.

'You're a good man, aren't you? Was it really not awful?'

'No,' I said, 'I'm not good. Other people are good. And it wasn't awful.' I was lying to soften the blow.

'You are good, you know,' she said. 'There's kindness in your voice.'

She got up, asked if she could use the lavatory. Of course, I said, of course. I hoped we had shut the bedroom door.

When she came downstairs I could tell she had been crying.

'He really wasn't a bad man,' she said. 'It's important you understand that.'

'Why would I think he was a bad man?'

'I don't know,' she said. 'You might. For what he did.'

I told her I understood, although in truth I did not.

'I have to go,' she said. 'Thank you for the coffee, and for the cigarette.'

'Coffee and cigarettes is pretty much all I'm good at.'

'Don't forget kindness.' She took my hand in hers, then stopped as if embarrassed. 'Will you come to the funeral, Alex? He didn't know so many people. Bit of a loner.'

'OK,' I said. 'Sure.'

Then she kissed me on the cheek and was gone.

I sat down at my computer at the kitchen table.

Max came home at four. He commented on the smell of cigarette smoke, made his own sandwich, and went up to his room. Then he came back down and asked me for five pounds.

'What do you want five pounds for?'

'We don't have any milk.'

'Milk doesn't cost five pounds.'

'OK, two pounds then.'

'All right, Max. Here's two pounds.'

'Thanks, Scots Dad.'

'There's nothing mean about me giving you two pounds to buy milk.'

'Do you want the change?'

'Yes.'

'OK, Dad. You're not *mean* at all.'

I ruffled his hair.

'Want me to come to the shop with you, Max?'

'No, it's OK.'

I rang Millicent again. Left the same message again. Added that I missed her and wanted her to come home, then felt foolish and tried to rerecord the message. The answering service cut me off.

Max came home with a small carton of milk and a packet of Maltesers.

'I don't remember saying you could buy those, Max.'

'You didn't say I couldn't.'

'I said I wanted the change.'

'Here.' He handed me seven pence. 'Do you want some Maltesers?'

'Yeah. All right.'

I pushed my computer to one side. We sat at the table drinking milk and dividing up the Maltesers. Max got a kitchen knife and cut his Maltesers into halves, and then into quarters. He sat dissolving them on his tongue, then sticking out his tongue to show me.

'What do you want for supper?'

'It's Mum's turn to make dinner.'

'I'm making it tonight.'

'Fish and chips. From the fish and chip shop, not home made.'

'OK.'

'Can you give me the money, and I can buy it?'

'Later, OK?'

'OK, Dad. Dad?'

'Max?'

'Aren't you going to eat your Maltesers?'

'You have them, Max.'

'OK. Dad?'

'Max?'

'Tarek said you're going to send me to a psychiatrist.'

'Why did he say that?'

'I told him what I saw.'

'Well, what you saw was pretty upsetting, wasn't it?'

Max said nothing.

'Max,' I said, 'Max, if you ever feel the need to talk about what you saw, doesn't matter where or when, we can talk about it, OK?'

'Is it because of the boner?'

'What do you mean, Max?'

'Tarek said that if you see a grown-up's willy and it's a boner then all the other grown-ups go spectrum, and you have to go to see a psychiatrist.'

I sat, trying to find an answer to this. Tarek had covered a lot of angles in one sentence.

'So do I have to go and see a psychiatrist?'

'I don't know, I think it might be a good idea.'

'Do you have to go and see a psychiatrist too?'

'No, Max, I don't think so. But Mum and I will be coming with you when you go for the first time.'

He bristled at the injustice of this.

'You saw the boner too, Dad.'

'Yes, I did.'

'So why don't you have to go?'

'Max, you're eleven.'

Max rolled his eyes in that way only eleven-year-olds do.

'In the next few years you're going to be discovering a lot about your body. And about other people's bodies. And Mum and I want to make sure that you don't find that scary.'

'I know about sex, Dad.'

61

'I know you do, Max. But Mum and I want to make sure you're OK.'

I tried to take his hand but he pushed me away.

'Are you going to tell Mr Sharpe about the psychiatrist?' There was humiliation in his eyes; his voice was very small.

'Yes, probably. But he won't tell anyone else. And if you go for a few times and Mum and I decide it's not really necessary, then you can stop. OK?'

He picked up the rest of the Maltesers and went upstairs to his room. I sat, feeling worse than ever. I'd be angry with me too if I were him.

Max and I ate our fish and chips.

The doorbell rang. My first thought was Millicent without her key, and my second thought was the police.

It was Fab5.

'Hi,' I said.

'All right, Alex,' said Fab5. He went through to the kitchen and sat in my chair, stole a large chip from Max.

'Hey,' said Max.

'Good to see you too, wee guy.'

I had hoped Millicent would love Fab5. She never did.

'Fab5? Like, we're cool and we're black and it's 1979? Guy needs to accept his reality.'

Fab5 thought Millicent lacked a sense of irony; she thought the same about him. If you forced me I would side with Millicent; she saw from the start what I did not: that he had slipped his moorings, that he was adrift.

Fab5 was my oldest friend, though. True, there was something a little faded about him now, a little stretched around the edges. It was getting harder to laugh at the stories about women and cocaine. He partied a little too hard and his hair had taken on a warm red-brown sheen that doesn't exist in nature. He knew this, though, and that's why we were still friends. Behind the laughter there was a wistfulness for a time when he and I were young together, and London, it seemed, lay at our feet: a time before Millicent, in other words. I wondered sometimes if Millicent disliked Fab5 for that reason too – he was a reminder of a younger, less faithful me.

My wife worries that I might revert to type.

Fab5 helped himself to one of my cigarettes. 'You going out like that, Lex? She'll not be pleased.'

'What?'

'Dee, you incorrigible twat.'

Dee Effingham. The Sacred Cock at seven.

'What time is it? And don't say twat in front of Max.'

Max pushed his tongue hard against his cheek and made a two-tone *mm-mm* sound.

'See, you're corrupting my wee boy, Fab5.' Twat was the right word, though.

'It's six twenty-five, Dad,' said Max.

'Run, Alex,' said Fab5. 'Run like the wind.'

It wasn't till I was on Drayton Park that I saw the scarves and the hamburger boxes, and realised it was match day at the Arsenal. Even weaving through the side streets, I couldn't avoid the football completely. I made the Sacred Cock at five to, but I'd half-run the last five hundred metres.

I ordered a pint of Flemish.

'Hello, Gorgeous. What's got you so hot and bothered?'

'Oh, Dee. Hi.'

'See, I blend in. Let me get that for you, hmm? Have you been running?' She chucked a fifty at the barman.

'Yes. You got me.'

'You've got that freshly fucked man-of-the-city thing going on. Didn't pull you out of bed, did I?'

'I wish.'

'So do I, Gorgeous. So do I.'

'Do you kiss Middle England with that mouth, Dee?'

'No, Gorgeous. First rule is never swear on the telly. And

it's *all* of England, you know. And Wales, and Northern Ireland. And, oh you know, those funny little people up north.'

'Yeah, my mum loves you.'

'Not your dad?' She mimed a hurt little pout, shaking her shoulders, and for a moment her breasts had me in their forcefield: the dangerous ravine of cleavage, the smooth milk-white vastness. She made a show of following my gaze and gave a mock-seductive sigh. 'Bad boy, Gorgeous. Caught looking.'

'I was just wondering . . .'

'Yes . . .'

'. . . whether that was part of your clothing range?'

'Nice recovery, Gorgeous. Sure that's what you were thinking?'

'Absolutely.'

'Because I could have sworn . . .'

'I'm happily married, Dee, but if I wake up single tomorrow, you're first on my list.'

'And you think that choice lies with you. That's so sweet, Gorgeous. So terribly tousled and sweet. And you would absolutely be second on my list . . .'

She insisted I match her drink-for-drink. We got quietly drunk in a corner, forgot to go upstairs to watch the comedy. I didn't want to sleep with her any more than she wanted to sleep with me, but there was something so charismatic and so pretty and so direct about her that I started to understand why Middle England loved her so much. And I was flattered that she was flirting with me over her large glass of Chenin Blanc. Flattered, too, that she wanted to work with me. It would have been bad manners not to flirt back.

On my third pint of Flemish she got me on to Max. I pulled a photo from my wallet.

'Ooh,' she said. 'Gorgeous begets gorgeous. Is his mother very beautiful?'

'I think so.'

'I'll bet. *Call* your hot wife. Get her down here. And your son, if he's still up.'

'He goes to bed at nine.'

'Not a showbiz kid, then?'

'No.'

'How very wise.'

And anyway, I thought, Millicent wouldn't like this. Whatever this is. However innocent *this* is, Millicent wouldn't like it at all. She doesn't mind, she says, the arms across the shoulders, the drinks after work, and the nuzzling goodbyes. But she's stopped coming out with me, and lies, instead, reading into the small hours. She's always awake when I come home.

'It's the industry,' I say, 'it's just what we do. No one's screwing. Not since the 90s.'

'Sure,' she says. 'I get that. Did I even say I mind? I don't mind, Alex.' But maybe this is my equivalent of *out, thinking*. Maybe it's that part of me that's unreachable to Millicent. Because she *minds*. I know she minds.

At half past eight I tried to decide what to do about Millicent's radio programme. If I left at nine thirty I could hear the end of it, and be in for when Millicent got home. Perhaps I could catch the beginning of it on the download. I could check that Max was safely asleep.

At ten past nine I explained that I had to go.

'But Gorgeous,' she said, 'we're getting to know each other. Don't you *want* us to know each other, Alex?'

'Of course I do, Dee. Of course.'

'That smile of yours,' she said. 'It's terribly beguiling. Your wife is a lucky woman. Can she really not share you with me just a *little* more? Bit harsh of her, don't you think?'

'It's not her,' I said, 'it's me.'

We're under such strain.

I had to be there.

'And after all, Alex,' said Dee. 'After all I am technically your employer. Am I not? Because no me, no show.' She put her right hand on her breastbone, and gave an ironic little pout. I laughed, but her words had a strained quality that told me I would be unwise to leave.

Over Dee's fifth glass of wine, and my fifth pint of Flemish, she asked me, 'So I'm wondering a little about your approach to fidelity, Gorgeous. How absolute is it?'

'It's very absolute. Absolutely absolute since I met Millicent. Thirteen years so far.'

'And yet you make it sound like some twelve-step programme. Each day a new day in your struggle with the demon pussy. Were you always such a gorgeous absolutist?'

'Maybe not.'

'Do you know what?' she said. 'You're going to tell me all about what a naughty boy you used to be.'

I have a memory of Dee's hand on my knee, and of five Flemishes becoming eight. I spoke of my lapses as a younger man, and of my regrets. Dee was a good listener, and I was glad to be talking about something that wasn't the neighbour. She teased, probed and massaged the information from me. I'm certain that I didn't make a pass at her, nor she at me, but I don't remember much more than the hand, the smile, and her boundless, limitless breasts. Fecund, fecund, fecund.

I did not tell Dee that I couldn't go to the States with her. I had decided that I was going. *Did June arrest me?* No. *Did June caution me?* No. *Did she politely but firmly ask me not to go?* Yes, and I would let June down just as gently. I was going to America.

I got home at twelve, offended Fab5 by trying to pay him, checked that Max was asleep, and vomited three times into the bath.

Where was Millicent?

I sat, scooping chunks from the bath into the toilet. Then I blasted the bath with the shower attachment. The smell grew worse, and I realised I had transformed my gastric fluids into an easily absorbed aerosol suspension, shrouding the bathroom in a delicate mist of puke. But at least the bath looked clean now.

I lay down fully clothed on the bed, got my phone from my pocket. I dialled her number, got voicemail, was just smart enough to remember not to leave a Flemish-amplified message. I tried to picture her; I missed her; I wanted her body beside me, around me. But the Flemish in my veins kept distorting the signal, sending me Rose's narrow shoulders and Dee's endless breasts: I couldn't find Millicent's face through the electric fog of shash, ache for her as I might.

In a small metal box in a drawer on my side of the wardrobe I keep letters from the women in my past: the letters serve as a warning; I read them when I am tempted.

6

Max was standing in the bedroom with coffee. He had chosen my favourite mug. He was dressed, he had tucked in his shirt, and he had combed his hair with water.

'Morning, Dad.'

'Morning, Max.'

'I made you some coffee because it's eight o'clock.'

'Thanks.' He handed me the cup.

I sniffed the coffee. It smelled wrong. Boiled. I put the cup down on the bedside table.

'Dad, is it true that Fab5 has a friend called Faecal Dave?'

'No, Max, no, I don't think that can be true. Can you get me some sugar?'

'You don't take sugar. And he told me what faecal meant.'

'I'd like some today, please, Max.'

Max rolled his eyes and went downstairs.

Two messages on my phone.

Gorgeous, you were and are the perfect gentleman.
Are you as turned on – creatively(!) – as I am?
DEff xx

I hadn't alienated the *Talent*. That was something.

> Twice I tried to wake you, you beautiful lame-assed
> drunken fool. And yes, I know we have to speak, and
> yes, you should call me when you wake up.

I realised that I was naked, that Millicent must have
undressed me, and rolled me and slipped me under the duvet.
That's love, I thought, in that one tiny action: my nakedness
is proof of Millicent's love. I wondered whether she had
slept.

Max came back in with the sugar. I put four spoonfuls into
the cup and stirred.

'Want me to open the blind?'

'No.'

'No what, Dad?'

'No thanks, Max. And thank you for making coffee for me.'

'That's OK. Mum said you might want some.'

'She out?'

'Yeah.'

'Say where she was going?'

'No. Do you like the coffee?'

'I love the fact that you made it for me.'

Max left the room.

I rang Millicent. She sounded lousy from lack of sleep.

'You get my SMS, Alex?'

'Yeah.'

'Meet me at the Swedish?'

'OK.'

Max and I left the house at the same time and walked the
first couple of blocks together. He hugged me when we parted,
then set off towards school at a dog-trot.

The Swedish didn't make sense in an area like ours. It
was all untreated oak and lightbulbs with complicated orange

69

filaments that hovered in front of your eyes. But the coffee was good and they left you alone to drink it. Where else were people like us supposed to go in a place like Crappy?

Millicent was sitting with her head in her hands, tiny against the vast communal table. I sat down beside her; it seemed at first as if she hadn't seen me, as if she were somewhere very private; then she sat up, looked me in the eye, and began to speak.

'I need you to understand that I have never and never would betray you, Alex.'

She hadn't slept. I could see the blood pulsing in her neck, smell the sourness on her breath.

'So I probably need to start with the really bad stuff, and then I can explain – and I hope, I really hope you're going to listen and to understand – how it isn't what it looks like. Because I know it doesn't look so good.'

She reached into her bag and produced a small white envelope; she looked at it for a moment, then handed it to me.

'So this is what the police wanted to discuss with me.'

Inside was a single photograph. An elegant metal band, very thin at the bottom, slightly thicker on the top. Soft white gold. A line of three square-cut sapphires. My grandmother's bracelet. My mother had given it to Millicent to welcome her to the family. It was so small that my mother could barely wear it, but was a perfect fit for Millicent's left wrist. On the inside of the clasp I had had it engraved. MW.

Millicent Weitzman. *My wife.*

'Alex, they found it in his bedroom.' The tiny safety chain was broken.

'His bedroom?'

'This is the bit I can't explain. The weird thing, not the bad thing. They found it between the wall and the headboard, on the floor.'

'Between the wall and the headboard?'

'That's what they said.'

70

'OK . . .'

I could think of nothing else to do, so I drank coffee. It was tepid, must have been standing for some time.

'Alex, I was never in his bedroom.'

'But you were in his house? Is that what you're telling me?'

Millicent looked past me and over my shoulder. I followed her gaze and realised I must have spoken more sharply than I'd thought. A tall Swedish girl was staring at us from behind the coffee machine. She looked away, and Millicent and I looked back towards each other.

'Christ, Millicent, what's going on?'

'Nothing, Alex. Please believe that.'

'Right. Can't be. Of course. He's dead now.'

'Sure. I probably deserve that, Alex.'

She was going to cry. That small-child voice. The redness of her eyes.

She swallowed hard. Pinched the bridge of her nose. Breathed out purposefully. Perhaps she wasn't going to cry.

'I lied to you. That's the way you're going to interpret it, and I guess it's a reasonable interpretation. It *is* a lie of omission; I didn't tell you.'

'Didn't tell me what?'

'That I knew Bryce.'

'I thought Bryce was his last name?'

Millicent gave a tiny flinch.

'You called him by his last name? Stylish.'

'I didn't betray you, Alex.' She was looking at me very directly now. I held her gaze, trying to find the lie.

'There was no sex. Just so that thought has been spoken. But I did know him. Better than I said.'

'Do you mean there was *no sex* in the American understanding of the term? You know, the Bill Clinton defence?'

'I mean there was no sex of any sort.'

'So we're talking British no sex. Just to be clear, in this country that does preclude oral.'

71

'I really hope you can understand that this is not what it looks like.'

'Funny, Millicent, because it still looks to me like what it looks like.'

'You have a right to be angry, Alex.'

'Who says I'm angry?'

'OK,' she said, uncertain.

'I'm not angry.'

'Most people would be in this situation, Alex.'

'Oh, so now you're some sort of objective voice. Instead of a wife admitting to sleeping with the next-door neighbour.'

'I did not admit to sleeping with him.'

'No. No, you didn't admit to that.' I looked around, felt eyes on me from behind the coffee machine, and for a moment caught the gaze of the Swedish girl. I tried to smile, but she looked away.

'Don't try to enlist help, Alex. We have to deal with this as a couple.'

'I'm enlisting help? Because I smiled at that pretty Swedish girl?'

'Yeah. You played that one to the gallery.'

I was shaking now. I kept my voice as quiet as I could.

'No, Millicent, I am not angry, and no, I am not trying to enlist help, and no, I was not playing to the fucking gallery. I just want to find out what you've done.'

'OK, sorry. I guess I shouldn't have said that. This isn't easy for me.'

'We're talking about infidelity – your infidelity – and you accuse me of flirting with the girl who makes the coffee?'

I made to laugh, but it came out too much like a sigh. Millicent took my hand then, and there was something so wounded and so vulnerable about her gaze that I wanted to draw her towards me and comfort her, as if she were the wronged party. Her eyes flicked towards the coffee machine, then back towards me.

'It's only because she's tall that she's even in my line of sight,' I said.

'Tall, blonde, taut and twenty,' she said. 'The antithesis of me.'

'How is twenty the opposite of thirty-five?' I said.

'So the rest of that you're not arguing with? Mother*fuck*.'

The laughter froze on my lips. 'Promise me on your life that you didn't sleep with the neighbour,' I was about to say, but the manager appeared at our side and quietly asked us if there was anything the matter. When I said no, and asked if he would mind leaving us to continue our discussion, he became very Swedish. He said that it was clear that our conversation was of a highly personal nature, that we were both highly emotional people, that this was obviously a matter about which we both felt strongly, and that once we had resolved the issue we would be welcome back any time.

At this point I became abusive. I told him that I would never again besmirch the clean white *bloody* linen of his *bloody* Swedish *bloody* cake shop.

That at least is how I remember the conversation: my use of language may have been less precise, and it's possible I used a stronger word than bloody.

'Great,' said Millicent, as we began walking home.

'What? It's a cake shop.'

'He did nothing wrong, Alex.'

'And I did? Are you trying to tell me that getting us thrown out of a café in Crappy is, like, *real bad*? Or are you telling me that what you did is *real bad, y'all*. Because right now I'm a little confused, Millicent.'

'*Y'all* is Texas, and it's a plural form, and you're being sophomoric. I'm going home. You can join me or not join me. Your choice.'

I watched her go, the anger of the righteous man coursing through me, dangerously electric. I looked down at my right hand, and saw that I'd been clenching it so tightly that the nail of my index finger had cut into the nail bed of the thumb. I brought the thumb to my mouth, and sucked at the welling blood. It too tasted electric, metallic: the air before a lightning storm.

A pair of young Somali girls walked past, staring at me, giggling. It was only when they'd gone that I realised what they'd seen: a grown man standing on the pavement sucking his thumb.

My mother called. This really wasn't the time. I rejected the call and headed home.

Pride, I thought, that's my cardinal vice; not wrath. Pride: the one sin from which all others stem. Oh, I could be the greedy man and the mean man, the envious and the enraged man, the licentious and the lazy man, but it all came down to pride; to the mortal sin of playing God, of being a complete arse, of standing in the street and passing judgment on my wife.

I married Millicent eight weeks after she moved in. A registry office, a few of my friends, and a wedding breakfast at the Rat and Pipe that flowed seamlessly into Bloody-Mary lunch and tequila supper. Neither of us had told our parents, though Millicent's younger sister Arla flew in from San Diego, got spectacularly drunk, slept with a stranger at the Troy Club, and flew back again the next day.

'Did that just happen?' I asked, as we left Arla at Heathrow.

'Like a bad version of me, right?' said Millicent.

'Don't,' I said. 'Just don't.'

So began our marriage of convenience.

For a time nothing changed. We ate, we smoked, we drank as lovers do. I would lick her to orgasm, slowly, timing the strokes of my tongue to her breathing. She would sit astride me until long after I had come, kissing and caressing me until I grew hard inside her again. We revelled in the carpet burns, the subtle bruisings, the twists and the strains that we casually inflicted upon each other. Edge of worktop, rim of bath, tiled floor and wood-chipped wall – all left their imprint upon her, upon me.

In cafés we compared our wounds: the grazes on her left wrist; on my right knee. In dark-lit restaurants she would draw my hand to her inner thigh, ask me if I could feel what she felt, that she was tender and abraded. In the aftermath of sex we found the precursor to sex. I liked her as I'd never liked anyone else.

'You like me? You *like* me?'

'I really, *really* like you.'

At this she became serious, almost formal. She took my hand and placed it in my lap.

'No, no, I think it's more than that.'

'What do you mean?'

'You love me, Alex. I actually think you love me.'

Her words lay heavy in the air: an accusation. I looked at her, made to speak, stopped myself.

'What, Alex?'

'Isn't it for me to say that I love you?'

'Well, by convention, yes, but you haven't so far. And I really think you do. You can tell me you don't, and then, of course, I won't have to tell you that I love you, which would probably be easier for both of us. But you're really very sweet to me, and although that doesn't in itself mean anything, we kind of established that being sweet to women is really not in your nature.'

'Therefore I love you.'

'Would you please drop the word therefore?'

I lit a cigarette. Tried to think. Offered her the cigarette. She snatched it from me, angry now, dropped it into the ashtray.

'You are so uptight. What's so hard about saying it?'

'Wait, please. Wait. Wait. Yes. You're right. I am uptight.'

'That's it?'

'And I do. I really do.'

'Then say it.'

'I thought I just did.'

She gave a little shake of the head. 'No. You didn't.'

'You said something just now about having to say that you loved me. Do you?'

'Love you? Yes. Yes, Alex, I really do love you. And it kind of scares me. Because I'm in your country, in your apartment – sorry, your *flat* – living on your terms, and pretty much on your money. The only friends I have here are your friends. I know no one my own age. I have nowhere to go if this screws up. Which of your friends is going to want me sleeping on their floors? Can you name just one person who'd want that? And I know you'll think I'm being unfair but I kind of wish you'd said it first, because I'm in the weaker position here.'

'I love you.'

'Say it again.'

'I love you, Millicent.'

She reached for my hand. 'And now I feel stupid again. I should not have made you say it.'

'Millicent. I love you.'

'Sorry.'

'Stop apologising.'

'Kind of English, right? I fit right in . . .'

'I love you.'

'I love you. Are we good?'

'We're good.'

At first I saw no change in Millicent, nor in myself, but other people must have seen something shift. They began to invite us out as a couple, to the pub at first, but then to parties and to weekends away.

Those friends I hadn't dropped seemed genuinely delighted when we celebrated our first anniversary with no sign of a break-up. My female friends began to make room for Millicent, to invite her to bars or to the cinema, to seek out her opinion of books. Slowly, over time, Millicent eased up. There were small changes to her wardrobe. Her breasts jutted a little less, her heels dropped slightly. She was still sharp, but the brittle quality she had had at the start was gone. I no longer had to carry her through London life, to police conversations for slurs on her age or her nationality. I didn't have to defend her against a hostile world. Millicent got life in London, and it suited her.

I loved her all the more.

Millicent handed me a cup of coffee as I entered the kitchen. I put it down by the sink, and held her in my arms. She wrapped herself around me and we clung to each other, rocking gently back and forth.

'I know you have more to tell me, Millicent.'

'I need for you to believe that I would never betray you, Alex.'

'I'm trying. I'm not finding it easy.'

'I know. And I did a bad thing. But I hope when I've finished you will see that the worst thing I have done is not to tell you about that bad thing, and that I didn't betray you. Can you let me get to the end of this?'

I took a half-step back, took her head in my hands, my palms on her cheeks, my fingers in her hair. I stared into her eyes, trying to find a sign of something — what? But she just looked strung out, a little sad.

I opened the back door and went out into the garden, sat on the patchy grass. Millicent came out with the coffee cups and sat down beside me. We drank our coffee, saying nothing, not daring to look at each other.

In the grass beside me a line of ants was dismembering a ladybird. The workers streamed back and forwards along a bare patch in the turf, carrying body parts to an unseen nest. I looked at the cigarette in my hand. My teenage self would have intervened, bringing death by fire. I flicked the ash from the cigarette, and brought the tip close to the stream of ants. It stopped. Ants stood, antennae and forelegs waving in the air, poised as if to attack. Then, perfectly synchronised, the flow of ants began again, making a small detour around the cigarette tip, paying it no mind.

My telephone rang. Work. I switched it off and put it back in my pocket.

'What are you thinking, Alex?'

'That we really should stop smoking.'

'Really? That's it?'

'Yeah.'

'OK, so the day I lost the bracelet was about six weeks ago when you were away. Bryce came round and said he'd been expecting company and been let down, and he had an open bottle of wine, and some cold cuts that needed to be eaten. And I told him that I already ate, and that Max was in bed, and that I had to be there in the house.

'And he said the wine was too good to waste, that he paid £65 for it, and he could bring the meat over, and we could eat it here in our garden, and that way I wouldn't have to leave Max; and I said sure; I mean, why not? Guy got stood up, I thought. He's lonely. He doesn't do women. He bought a $100 bottle of wine. Where's the harm?'

I turned over and lay on my back, looked up at our bedroom window. Even from here you could see the paint was peeling from the frame. Other people – my father – would notice that window and do something about it. Me, I noticed it and forgot it again. We would do nothing about it, and in five years we would have to replace the whole thing.

'So,' said Millicent, 'so we drank the wine and ate the food, and then he said he had a heater in his garden, and it was getting a little cold, so why didn't we go there and drink some more wine. And I said no, but he was really persistent. And I guess I kind of thought maybe he wanted more than company, but I was just a little drunk and I was missing you and he was kind of funny and sharp, and I still pretty much thought he was gay. And I figured if I left Max's door open, and opened the bathroom window that I would pretty much hear if anything was wrong.'

'You left Max on his own?'

'Please, Alex. Let me get to the end, and then if you want to hate me you can.'

'OK,' I said. 'Deal.'

'So I was sitting there in his garden, and he starts to say some nice things to me, about how he thinks I'm pretty and kind, and about the way I dress, and how he's always liked Americans more than English people, and how I seem like so much more to him than just a wife and mother; and I still haven't figured out that he's interested, which makes me a klutz, I know. Because as soon as I say it out loud I can see it's a pretty obvious come-on.

'And then he goes indoors and comes out with a bottle of Calvados and I ask him why he hasn't brought glasses and he says we can drink it from the bottle, and I *know* then that it's really time to leave. And I get up, and he tries to kiss me, and I step back, and I trip over, and he puts his hand out and grabs my wrist, and pulls me back to my feet. And then he tries to kiss me again, and I let him.'

I turned to look at her. She uprooted a small handful of grass. She didn't want to look at me, but I could tell she expected me to say something. I watched her pull up another handful of grass, then I turned away.

'I kissed him. Not for long. But I kissed him. That's the bad thing that I did, and for that I'm so very sorry, Alex. But I did no more. I did nothing more than kiss him. And then he touched me and I broke away from him.'

'So what sort of signal was he getting from you before this happened?'

'Alex, I don't know what sort of signal he was getting from

me. I was drunk, and confused, and he was drunk too. If I told you nothing happened, I'd be lying to you.'

I went upstairs and peed. Washed and dried my hands very precisely, trying to still the thoughts that arced across my mind. I looked out through the open bathroom window.

Bryce's bedroom and bathroom faced the back too. If he'd wanted to, he could have seen a lot of Millicent from his freshly painted windows. I wondered darkly if he had coveted his neighbour's wife, or more specifically his neighbour's wife's ass.

When I came down Millicent was sitting in exactly the same position. It looked for all the world as if nothing was wrong. She was telling me the truth: I saw that now. I wanted to take her in my arms, hold her and tell her just how much I loved her. We could get through this. A drunken kiss and a flash of flesh on flesh were tiny pricks of light in the cosmic chart of infidelity.

After some time, I said, 'You have an alibi.'

'I mean, I was at the radio station. Is that an alibi? Why would they even be thinking that way, Alex? They never once used the word alibi.'

'They asked me not to leave the country.'

'You're not serious.'

I took out the police photograph of the bracelet.

'Right there. Look. A little tag with a number on it. Looks to me like an evidence tag. I'm guessing the reason they gave you the picture and not the bracelet itself is that the bracelet is evidence in case they decide that they want to bring someone to trial. And given that they've asked me not to leave the country, I suspect the person they would be thinking of bringing to trial would be me.'

'Oh Jesus, Alex.'

'Isn't that what they call reasonable suspicion or just cause in American TV series? What do they call it here?'

'I don't know.'

'No, neither do I. So, what are you thinking right now, Millicent? Because right now I'm thinking things aren't good. Because I seem to be implicated in our next-door neighbour's suicide. How did your bracelet get there?'

She shook her head. That same sad look again.

'I'm sorry,' I said. 'I need to get a lawyer, don't I?'

'Seems weird that you can't leave the country. I guess a lawyer would be a good idea.'

I searched the bare patch in the grass. The ladybird had disappeared, and a few ants could be seen ambling around.

She moved towards me, took my hand and placed it on her thigh. I let it rest there. 'The truth is,' she said, 'the truth is I get lonely when you go away, Alex.' I let her put her head on my shoulder, reached up and rubbed the nape of her neck. 'It's like since Sarah you sublimated something,' she said, 'like your energy's all in your work.'

We went inside, climbed the stairs, failed to fuck. Millicent fell asleep nestled against my chest. I lay on my back and cradled her to me like a child, but knew that I would not find sleep.

Sarah, the little girl we almost had; Millicent, the wife who would not discuss losing Sarah.

At three fifteen someone rang the doorbell and knocked on the door. I stayed where I was; I didn't want to disturb Millicent.

We love each other: of that there is no doubt. It isn't love that's the problem here.

7

Millicent's phone rang. After four rings it stopped. I went downstairs, found the phone on the kitchen table and checked the screen. A missed call from Aileen Mercer. A bolt of guilt. Why hadn't I called my mother? I found my own phone. It was lying face down on the living-room sofa, hidden against the black leather. Two missed calls. I rang her back.

'Alexander, it's about your father.' My mother was one of those women who still had a telephone voice; her staccato formality made it hard to know how she was.

'What's happened, Mum?'

'Ach, it'll turn out to be nothing, I'm sure.'

'Mum?'

'I've some concerns about him. He's been hospitalised. Mainly tests.'

'What do you mean, mainly tests?'

'An electrocardiogram. Some blood samples.'

'Mum, that doesn't sound like nothing.'

'He took a little fall, Alexander. I'd to call an ambulance.'

'Do you want me to come up, Mum?'

'Ach, no, you're awfully busy down there, son.'

Millicent was awake when I went back upstairs. I told her about the call.

'I should ring her,' she said.

'You don't need to do that.'

'Sure I do.'

I lay on the bed. Downstairs Millicent spoke to my mother for ten minutes. I could hear the coaxing softness in her voice, the gentle laughter, the long silences she left for my mother to fill. *Why are you so good at this?*

Something deep within me had feared that Millicent and my mother would hate each other. But a year into our marriage, when I had started to trust that there was a reality to our love, that I genuinely was more than a work permit to my wife, I had rung my parents in Edinburgh to tell them my old news.

I suspected my mother minded terribly that I hadn't wanted her at the wedding, and I wondered whether her long pauses on the phone were because she was crying. She had asked to speak to Millicent, and with great formality welcomed her to the family.

Millicent was very touched, and profoundly embarrassed: even more so when my mother sent her the little gold bracelet that had belonged to my grandmother. She wrote back to her in the kind of flowing copperplate handwriting that they only teach in American schools, a long letter that she refused to let me read.

'You're really very well-brought-up, aren't you, Millicent?'

'What were you expecting, rube-face?'

'Someone less nuanced, I suppose.'

'And yet here you are with me.'

My mother called Millicent Lassie, and occasionally Girl, and Millicent called my mother Mrs Mercer. They would write each other weekly letters that again neither of them ever let me read; they even spoke regularly on the telephone, which mystified me. My mother hated the telephone. Strange that they should have this bond: what could Millicent know of my mother, or my mother of Millicent?

My father would openly disparage America at every opportunity, and Millicent would laugh gently, and quietly put him right. 'No, sir, we really are no more stupid than anyone else. Education may not be fairly distributed, but that is because wealth is concentrated in a very small number of hands, sir. Surely we can agree on that?'

They never agreed, but my father liked the fact that Millicent called him sir.

Would I have worked as hard with her parents as she did with mine? It's a question I've never had to answer: Millicent has never allowed me to meet them.

I heard Millicent end the call, heard her toss the phone on to the table, heard her feet cross the living-room floor and climb the stairs.

She came in and sat down on the bed.

'OK, so I think maybe you have to face the possibility that this situation is worse than your mother is saying, Alex. I think maybe she really needs you there. She even cried a little.'

'The timing couldn't be worse, could it?'

'Honey, listen to me: I think your dad had a stroke. That's pretty much what your mom told me. They didn't say it to her yet, I guess, because they're still doing tests, but I think she already read between the lines. She's scared and you need to be there.'

The fall. The electrocardiogram. It made sense.

'Millicent?' I said.

'Yes?'

'Thanks.'

'Sure.'

'I'd be lost without you.'

'Sure.'

The grinding sadness of that last Edinburgh train, all shouting children and glowering men, Fruit Shoots, crisps, six-packs of beer. Millicent had bought my ticket for me; she had sent me out into the London evening, an overnight bag in my hand, long before I needed to go. Now I glowered too, alone at my table, hoping no one would sit down opposite me, hoping people could read it all in my expression. *Stay away. All is not well here.*

My thoughts would not settle. My father was seriously ill – Millicent was always right about these things – and my mother would be out of her mind with worry. But when I tried to picture my mother at my father's bedside I saw only the neighbour: the swollen tongue, the red-encrusted nostril. Please, I thought, don't let that be my father's fate.

That blue-red tongue, I thought, pushing at my wife's lips. That milk-white hand seeking out her breast.

She as good as pushed you out of the front door.

I sat, trying to feel the moment again. Did she want me gone? No. No, she had held me very tightly, her cheek pressed against mine. She hadn't broken the embrace. I was the one who had pulled gently away from her.

Millicent had thrown her arms around me then, kissed me very deeply. Her eyes did not flick to some imagined lover somewhere just out of sight.

And yet, I thought. That pawing hand, that searching tongue. I worried at them; I couldn't leave them alone.

She as good as pushed you out of the door.

My mother was not at the station. I rang her. There was no answer so I took a taxi to the hospital. Millicent had written the number of the ward on the train ticket that she had printed for me. For a moment I saw myself running from one end of the building to another, hopelessly lost, but the hospital was modern and the signs were clear.

I was surprised to find two nurses at the Gerontology desk. It was almost one.

'Hi,' I said.

'Hello,' said the younger of the two.

'Alex Mercer,' I said. 'That's my name, and it's also my father's name.'

The older nurse whispered something to the younger nurse.

'Alex Mercer is a patient here,' I said. 'Just to be clear.'

The younger nurse was looking not at me but past me. She stood up, and put a hand on my shoulder. *So much kindness.* Then she put her other hand on my other shoulder and turned me. How very gentle she was.

It was then that I saw my mother, stiff-backed on a white plastic chair, immaculate in her dark blue fitted jacket and skirt. On a little table beside her was a cup of tea, two pink wafers crossed on a napkin beside it.

My mother's dark eyes were on me, and she smiled as I approached. 'The nurses have been very good,' she said. 'Tea in a porcelain cup. Hello, Laddie.'

I took her in my arms, felt her crumple a little. Then she stiffened again. She would not cry. Not yet; not here.

'I had to, you see. They told me he wasn't coming back.'

The young nurse touched my elbow gently.

'Would you like me to find you a chair, Mr Mercer? A cup of tea perhaps? And for you, Mrs Mercer?'

'Thank you,' I said. 'Yes, please.' *Why so kind?*

'I had to, Alex, son,' said my mother. 'I'm so sorry.'

My father had suffered a massive stroke. Millicent had been right. 'I didn't want to worry you unduly, son,' said my mother. 'Then they told me that he wasn't coming back. I mean, there was a theoretical chance, or some such, but it was awfully small. And I made the consultant tell me what the percentages meant, and she said your father would never return to me, not as himself. So I took a decision. I'm so very sorry, son.

'I know I could have waited until you came,' my mother said, 'but I don't think your father would have wanted you to see him like that. I could tell that the spirit was gone from him.'

*   *   *

86

My mother insisted on driving home from the hospital. It took her some time to find a parking space, and in the end we had to walk for five minutes to reach the flat. Dark sandstone loomed behind monumental trees. No chickenshops or foot pursuits here. Residents' associations and doors in approved colours. Pragmatic elegance.

My mother took the stairs briskly when we arrived, installed herself at the dining table still wearing her coat; she filled two tiny crystal glasses with gin, topped them off with vermouth, and handed one to me.

'To your father.' She drained her glass, set it back on the table. Then she exhaled heavily, seemed to become a little shorter, a little older.

'Fifty years married,' she said. 'Do you know, I thought I was too old.' She gave a sad little laugh. 'I was twenty-eight.'

I reached across and took her hand. 'I know, Mum.'

'Well, that *was* old.' She poured herself another drink. 'He was a good man, but he never loved me in quite the way I loved him.'

She gave a little half-sob, then pulled a handkerchief from her handbag and dabbed at her eye.

The walls were the same as they'd ever been: dark salmon pink and country-house green, white skirtings and door frames. It showed off the pictures, my mother always said.

'You're wrong, Mum. He cherished you.'

'No. No, Alex, I'm not wrong. I wasn't his first.'

I took her hand. 'Come on, Mum.'

She went into the living room. When she came back, she had a photograph in her hand.

'That's her.'

A woman, strikingly beautiful, her mirror-black hair in a single braid, a calligraphic downstroke across the white cotton shirt. Behind her a light grey ocean. A darker grey sky. Cloudless.

Japan, I thought. My father had been stationed in Japan

before Korea. They had sent him out in a troop ship. Taught him to drive and fire large ordnance.

'Noriko,' said my mother. 'That was her name.'

The woman's pose was Western but formal, unsmiling; all the same there was a warmth in her eyes, a secret shared with the man behind the camera.

'Did Dad take this?'

'Yes.'

I looked at my mother. She was watching me for my reaction; there was no anger, no sadness now, just a resigned patience.

'She's beautiful, is she not?' she said at last.

There was a searching look in her eyes. I fought the urge to say something soothing.

'Yes, Mum, she is beautiful.'

'Thank you, Alexander.' A little smile of satisfaction. My mother set great store by honesty. She didn't want me to protect her.

'He told me all about her. He wanted me to have all the facts at my disposal. Before I said yes to marriage.' She nodded, as if to herself. 'They were very much in love, you know. They wrote to each other, all through the war in Korea, and when he got home he kept writing, and so did Noriko. Then suddenly her letters stopped, and your father could only assume that she had ended the relationship. A terrible blow to him.'

She refilled my glass, then refilled her own. 'And of course your father's misfortune was my good fortune. He was a very handsome man, and a very honest man. He loved me, and he adored you, son. He really did. More than anything in the world.'

'Dad loved you most of all, Mum.'

'No, Alexander, no.' She took my hand in hers, catching me in the lie. 'I'm seventy-eight, son. I'm not afraid of the truth.'

'OK, Mum.'

'Anyhow, one day your father received a letter from Japan.

It was from Noriko, and it troubled him greatly. She asked why he had stopped writing. Your father showed me the letter, because he thought I ought to know; and then he burned it, because he was a good man and he had made his choice.

'And then . . . and then he went to his mother, and he asked why she had hidden Noriko's letters from him. And at first she denied it, but eventually she admitted that she had burned them. A cruel thing to have done, do you not think?' She left the question hanging for a moment. 'But I have her to thank, I suppose, because without her there would be none of this.'

My mother went to bed shortly afterwards. I wandered around the flat for a while, trying to understand what I should be feeling. My father was everywhere here: his books, his records, the rack of pipes and the stacked ashtrays; his keen eyes staring out from silver-framed photos, never less than immaculately turned-out. The sharpness of those collars.

My father's life had been a series of tickets out: the army; Edinburgh; my mother. He had entered the forces as a welder, and left as an engineer; he had taken a second degree at Edinburgh University, met my mother at a dance. He had *come up*. A sharp-looking man with quick wits and an easy charm, by the time he had left the army he had erased the Govan shipyard from his voice. He had *made good*. His parents lived an hour down the road. Tower-block folk, he called them. We never visited my grandmother. *The Noriko story, of course*. It made sense now.

My father had taken me to a war film once, at a cinema on the outskirts of town.

Later, at home, he had sat for hours, silent in his chair, smoking his pipe. And though he would often boast to his friends about having had 'a good war', I had seen him crying at the cinema.

*   *   *

89

I could hear my mother sobbing from the room that she and my father had shared. I thought of knocking on the door, of entering the room and sitting there, holding my mother's hand over the blue silk counterpane. But it would mortify my mother to know that I could hear her in her grief. It would bring her no comfort.

Now was the time I should have cried: for my father, for my mother, for what was lost. All those decisions my mother had taken, alone, in her demure desolation.

Could you not have waited, Mum?

I paced through the flat, my teenage self again, skirting the walls, trying not to cross my own path, trying not to hear my mother's sobs.

I tried to ring Millicent. Four rings, then voicemail. It was three o'clock, but she must have known that I would need to call her. I called again. Four rings, voicemail.

My parents' flat was unchanged from the day I left home twenty-two years ago. Same fridge, same photographs on the walls, same furniture. It wasn't for lack of money. They'd done well for themselves. But they had known what they liked back then, and they had never stopped liking it. Continuity. Restraint.

Where is Millicent?

I rang our home phone. It rang for the longest time.

There was a worn patch on the carpet by the side of the sofa where my mother liked to sit, and another by my father's smoking chair.

Answer the phone.

Two decades of pipe smoke had gently curled across the flat, coating every white surface in a warm sepia, damping down the pillar-box red of the living-room curtains, the cobalt blue of the silk counterpanes in the bedrooms with which my mother had, rebelliously, accented their home. *Answer the phone, Millicent.*

It was Max who answered.

90

'Max, it's Dad.'

'You woke me up. Is Grandpa dead?'

'It was peaceful, Max. He died in his sleep.'

'Oh,' said Max.

'Are you OK, Max?'

'Yes,' he said.

'I love you very much, Max.'

'I love you too, Dad,' he said dutifully.

'Can you get Mum?'

I heard him put the receiver down, could make out the sound of his footsteps as he went back upstairs to wake Millicent. *How can you sleep at a time like this?*

I looked out into the night. Large windows, wide streets, sandstone solidity. Safe, I thought. Very safe.

'Dad?'

'Yes, Max.'

'Dad, she's not here.'

'Have you checked in the garden? She could be in the garden.'

'It's raining.'

'Can you check in the garden, please, Max?'

'But why would she be in the garden? It's raining.'

'Please check the garden, Max. Now.'

'But what if she's not there, Dad? What if something's happened to her?' I was scaring him. This wasn't good.

'We'll figure it out, Max. She might have gone to the shops.'

'OK.' Max put down the receiver again. Of course Millicent hadn't gone to the shops. I shouldn't be exposing my son to my fears like this.

Where was she?

Max picked up the phone again.

'Dad, Dad, she's not here. She's not in the garden. Dad, can you come home?'

It's happening again, I thought. *Please God, don't let it happen again.* I considered ringing Fab5 and asking him to go round, but Millicent would view it as a betrayal. She would hate me for exposing her like that. Who could I ring, though? Certainly not the police.

I had to keep the fear out of my voice. 'Max,' I said. 'Max, listen to me. I want you to do something for me.' *Measure your words*. 'I want you to go back to bed, and I want you to make sure your alarm clock is set for half past seven, and at exactly half past seven I want you to wake up and go into our bedroom, and you'll find that Mum is there and everything is OK.'

'Can't I go and stay with Tarek?' said Max.

'No, love, no.' Tarek's parents might call the police. 'I need you to do what I say, Max-Man. OK?'

'I swear on my life I won't say why.'

'Max, it's the middle of the night. I need you to go back to bed. I need you to promise me that.' *There is no one to call.*

'Why should I?'

'Because in the morning this will all be OK. Trust me, Max-Man.'

'Can you come home, Dad?'

'I'll take the first train. That's a promise. Stay at home till I get there. I'll walk you to school and explain to Mr Sharpe.'

'But you said Mum would be there.'

'She will.'

'But then you said to wait until you come, so you think she might not come.'

'She will come, Max.' *Please God, let her be there.*

'Can't you take a plane, Dad?'

'The train is quicker. I'll be there as soon as I can, Max.'

'All right.'

'I love you very much, Max,' I said, but he had gone.

I sat staring at my phone for a time. Then I texted Millicent.

Max is scared. Where are you?

*   *   *

This looks bad, I know. This looks like grounds for divorce, with automatic custody awarded to the father. Believe me, it isn't that straightforward.

Max was three. Millicent was pregnant again. Six months.

We had devoted the pregnancy to a propaganda offensive. We talked about how much fun it would be for Max to have a new brother or sister, how much that child would look up to Max, how it would adore him and come to him for help and advice throughout its life. Max, we told him, was going to be a great older brother. He would love the baby, and the baby would love him.

Max and I used to lie beside Millicent on the living-room floor, each with an ear to her belly, listening, exploring with our hands, feeling for the tiny kicks and punches. We talked about the ultrasound pictures, about where the baby was lying inside Millicent, how its hands and feet were arranged, how it was fully formed now, how it looked like a proper baby now, how all it had to do was get a little bigger now. Just a little bigger.

Max wanted a sister, he told us, but a brother would probably be OK too. Guess what, we said, you're in luck: it's not a brother, it's a sister.

Max had marched around the house chanting 'baby sister, baby sister, baby sister', until he collapsed exhausted on the living-room floor and had to be carried to bed. He began to make his own preparations: he gave up drinking milk from a bottle, decided he no longer needed a nappy at night.

We bought him a baby of his own, an anatomically correct girl doll that he used to carry around the house by one arm. He would fall asleep with the doll cradled to his chest.

We had done our job well; his baby sister had become a reality for him.

One day the baby's heart stopped beating. There was no warning, and we never found out the reason; it just died there in Millicent's womb in the small hours of a Wednesday morning. Millicent woke early, felt an absence, dressed without waking me, and took a minicab to the hospital.

At seven thirty she rang me. She was talking so quietly I could barely make out what she was saying. There was no detectable heartbeat. Our little girl was gone. The hospital was going to induce a delivery. A birth that wasn't a birth.

'I'll come.'

'Don't, Alex.'

'Millicent . . .'

'To have you here would be unbearable to me, Alex. It's a parody of what it should have been.'

'I love you, Millicent . . .'

'I have to go.'

I left Max with Fab5. I bought flowers and fruit and chocolates; I bought a cream silk dressing gown; I bought a mountain of books.

I went to the hospital. I sat at my wife's side until she woke. I held her hand, wanting the first words she heard to be mine.

'I love you, Millicent . . . I love you so very much.'

My words brought her no comfort. She sat silently for over an hour. Babies screamed in nearby wards. She sent me away.

She came home two days later looking drawn and stricken. I had done what I could to prepare Max, had tried to explain what had happened, but when Millicent came through the door he looked confused. He didn't greet her, but stood watching her suspiciously.

'Where's the baby?'

'The baby isn't coming, Max,' said Millicent.

'Where's the baby?'

'Honey, sweetheart, the baby died. I'm so sorry, Max.'

Max stood for a very long time, the doll in his arms, rocking it gently back and forth. That evening he refused to speak to Millicent and insisted I put him to bed. And the next evening.

The evening after that he screamed when Millicent picked him up.

It got worse. Max would run from the room if Millicent appeared. I would find him in his bedroom, hyperventilating. Once when he seemed to have disappeared completely from our tiny house I found him under the sofa in the living room, his face streaked with snot, shaking and sobbing silently. At night he would cry for hours on end until, despairing, Millicent and I decided that I should sleep on a camp bed in his room.

Millicent found the doll in the bin under the kitchen sink, the arms and legs torn from their sockets. We sat on the sofa in the living room before Max was awake, holding each other, trying to understand what was happening to our son. *What do we do?*

I read all that I could about small children and grief. Cry with them, said the books. Don't hide your own feelings, said the magazines. They need to know it's *OK* to grieve, said the parenting sites. Have a funeral, they said. Bury a doll, they said. Yeah, we said, what a bunch of freaks.

One night, after Max had cried for six solid hours, I cried experimentally in front of him. The result was immediate, catastrophic.

Max's distress intensified. He clung to me as if I too might disappear. I tried to talk to him about why he was crying, about how that was *OK*, but he became hysterical, pushing me away, kicking and punching the mattress, screaming, 'No, no, no, no!' Then he banged his head so hard against the top rail of the bed that his nose bled for two hours. I took him to Casualty, terrified by the bruise radiating out from his left temple.

The nursery asked us to keep Max at home for a week. I called in sick.

Millicent avoided the house. She took to working as much as possible, leaving early and returning late. At home she would slink around, keeping out of the way of the boy who seemed to hate her and fear her in equal measure.

We would meet almost by chance, she and I, if I crept downstairs when Max had cried himself into catatonia: to make tea; to have a smoke; to take a telephone call. Once I stole into our bed and lay down beside Millicent for a few small minutes, only to be summoned back by my son's screams of rage from the next room.

This was unliveable. Millicent was losing weight, undone by her own grief, and by guilt at what grief was doing to her little boy.

And so Millicent's absences began. 'Out,' she would say, when I asked her where she'd been. 'I've been out. Thinking.' Out to cafés and libraries in the daytime, bars in the evening, parks at the dead of night.

'This is London,' I would say. 'Don't go to parks.'

'It's super-safe here,' she would say. 'No guns.'

Our son lies in his bedroom in our mean little house, his eyes screwed shut, alone at the dark of night.

The rain sculpts Millicent's clothes tight to her body, like cloth on to plaster of Paris. She sits on a bench at the dark of night, huddled against the cold, alone amongst the blue-black shadows of the park. *Go home.*

Do people ring Child Protection Services about parents like us? Or do they leave us alone because we look as if we know what we're doing, because we feed our son, and clothe him, and send him to school?

Four hundred miles north I pace my parents' flat. Alone at the dark of night.

Millicent is more upset about the dead neighbour than she is prepared to admit. Her absence tells me that.

I paced the flat until five, then made tea and woke my mother. Her eyes wandered around the room, then fixed on me.

'Alexander, you've not slept.'

'No, Mum.'

I sat on the bed. She ruffled my hair.

'What is it, Laddie?'

I was seven again. We were alone together, the whole day in front of us. Edinburgh Zoo, then Tantallon beach in her racy Triumph Dolomite, front seat, top down. Ice cream in Musselburgh on the way home. Vanilla or strawberry? *Both if you're good, Alexander. Both if you're good.*

I put my arm across her back.

'How was your night, Mum?'

'As expected. Alexander, son, what is it?'

'Mum, I'm so sorry. I have to go home.'

'What's wrong?'

'Nothing,' I said. Everything, I thought. Max, Millicent, Dad. Me. The police. *Everything's wrong, Mum.*

My mother looked at me, sceptical. Tell her the truth, I thought. *Tell her something like the truth.* 'It's Millicent, Mum. She needs me at home. I'm so very sorry.'

'Aye,' she said softly.

'I'll come back, Mum. I'm really sorry, but I have to go.'

'Aye,' she said again. 'Aye.'

'I can try and make the arrangements.'

'No, son. No, he'd want me to do that. I've his instructions in a letter. But you will come, will you not?'

'Yes, all of us.'

She made me chicken sandwiches, wanted to drive me to the station. While I stood by the front door, anxious to leave, she fetched a large red carrier bag from the spare bedroom. 'For Max,' she said. 'In case you can't make it back.'

'Mum,' I said, 'we'll be there. Of course we'll be there. I have to go.'

I made the five forty train with three minutes to spare.

The train came into King's Cross on time, and I was at home by ten past ten. There was Millicent at the kitchen table, looking for all the world as if nothing was wrong between us. Expensive underwear, an old white cotton shirt of mine. She smiled and got up to greet me, hands on my shoulders, flexing up to me, barefoot and tiny. I kissed the top of her head, then stepped away from her.

'Hey, honey,' she said. 'I'm so very sorry for your loss.' The right words, the right note of concern in her voice.

'Max told you.'

'How's your mother?'

'Not good,' I said. 'Where is he?'

'Max went to school. Alex, are you OK?'

'Fine. I'm fine. I *told* him to wait for me.'

'You were worried about him. There's nothing wrong with that. You're a good father, Alex.' She sat down in her chair.

Was she leaving a gap, creating a silence that I would feel compelled to fill? *You're a good mother, Millicent.* Was that what she was waiting to hear? Part of me wanted to say it so that she could contradict me.

No, Alex, I left Max alone and I feel bad. I'm a horrible, horrible mother.

Millicent sat down at the table again. I sat down on the floor, my head level with the counter top.

'So,' I said. Millicent's technique. That single word. *You fill the gap now, Millicent.*

'Oh, Alex,' she said. 'There's so much I can't tell you about my life right now.' Then she began to cry.

I watched her for a while. The anger lifted from me. It was easy to forget how vulnerable she was. I got up, tried to pull her to her feet so I could hug her to me, but she sat, balled defensively into her chair. I crouched down and held her to me. Her shoulders kept me stiffly at bay. Then her body relented and she collapsed into me.

'I'm not sleeping, Alex,' she said after some time. 'I know I never should have gone out and left Max, but I just can't seem to sleep, and you weren't here, and I was feeling stupid and ashamed about what I did, because what I did was so stupid and so shameful. So I went for a walk. I kind of destroyed my dress, and my shoes. Even my underwear.'

By the back door was a pair of black leather wedges. The heels were covered in a grey-black mud, the leather sides dulled down to a feathered salt-stained grey.

'I don't think I can save them, can I?'

'I don't know,' I said.

'I already threw my dress in the trash. And my underwear and bra. This is the second time someone I know killed themselves, Alex,' she said. 'In truth I'm struggling a little . . .'

She wiped her eyes on her shirt sleeve, and rested her cheek on my shoulder. I held her to me, rocked her gently back and forth on her chair.

'It scares me, you know, Alex. It's like, it says other people's pain is unbearable, and there's nothing you can do about it because you can't reach it. Like what if I'm wrong and they're right, and every word I write is ultimately pointless because you can't bridge that gap?'

Don't unravel, I thought. There isn't room for either of us to unravel.

'I found some stuff.' The timbre of her voice was so even, so without inflection, so studiedly calm.

She pushed me away. I sat down in the chair beside hers. She pulled away from me a little, watching my reaction.

'What stuff did you find?'

'Some letters.'

Not Caroline's letters. She didn't say Caroline's letters. She won't find Caroline's letters.

'In my sock drawer?' I said, as calmly as I could.

She nodded. 'I guess maybe you meant for me not to see them. I may have overreacted a little.'

'You overreacted?'

'I know you're not that guy.'

'No,' I said. 'I'm not. Not any more.'

'Then question,' she said. 'Why keep them?'

Because somewhere, almost out of sight now, is a darkly remembered landscape. In that landscape there is no tiny house in Finsbury Park, and no Max, and no Millicent.

'I don't know,' I said.

'Kind of funny how often the term *lack of commitment* comes up.' She gave a little laugh.

'I'm sorry, Millicent,' I said.

'It's OK, Alex, you get to have a past. I guess I was scared maybe you were feeling nostalgic for something I can't give you. Like maybe we're unreachable to each other, or something.'

'I was unhappy then,' I said.

'And you're not now?'

'Not since I met you.'

She opened her eyes very wide. Blinked hard.

'Right,' she said. 'Because life with me is just *so great*.'

'You know what I mean, Millicent.'

Don't unravel.

When we lost Sarah, Millicent had kept herself together for as long as it took to get Max back on his feet. Then she lost her job on the additives magazine.

'But I thought you'd been working crazy hours.'

'Yes. I guess I did let you think that.'

She had barely been turning up at all. She had been sitting in parks, cafés, museums and restaurants – anywhere to avoid sitting at her desk and working. There she sat for hours on end, quietly grieving, while I knew nothing of her pain.

She had been protecting me, and protecting Max, while she took the full force of the blow. She had shielded me from the horror of that birth that wasn't a birth. That tiny stiff body in the delivery room. That ward with the real living babies and the *want-some-more-gas-and-air* fathers. I was insulting her by believing I understood it.

100

I had assumed my grief matched hers, that I had the measure of her pain. I saw now that Millicent's suffering was of a different order. Gulfs, chasms, continents, voids – those are the tropes that divided her from me. I watched her suffering as though through fog: I was desperate to help; I was unable to reach her.

Millicent had begun to unravel then. If it was a breakdown, it was very controlled. She was functional when Max was around: she played with him and bathed with him, read to him and sang to him. I could feel the sadness in her then, but also the love.

But with Max asleep, or at nursery, she would lie for hours on the sofa, in our bed, in the bath, saying nothing, doing nothing.

She refused to see a doctor.

'You're depressed,' I said.

'I know,' she said. 'But please let me do this my way. I don't want it to be a *thing*.'

'It is a thing, whether you want it to be or not.'

'OK. But please, no doctor.'

And I can see now what I couldn't see then: that the seeds of her supercompetency had already been sown; that she planned the structure of her unravelment. She knew that suppressing the pain would extract a high price, that there would be a reckoning, and she planned for that reckoning.

She waited until she was sure that Max was secure. She waited until I had a break in my contract. She made sure that we were all right. As far as we could be. She even arranged extra childcare for Max.

She told me that her pain was hers to deal with, and hers alone; that I could not understand it; that I must not try. She asked me only to look after her, to wash her and to feed her, and to see to it that she did not do something stupid. Most of all she wanted me to make sure that Max was all right.

'What do you mean, do something stupid?' I said, but she never told me.

'Just make sure that Max is all right.'

Then and only then did she let herself fall; she trusted that I would catch her, and I did.

8

I woke to find Max standing in our bedroom again. He had been watching us for some time, I guessed. He seemed happy to accept that we were in bed in the late afternoon, that I wasn't at work and that Millicent wasn't at her desk. I wondered if that made us bad parents or good parents.

'OK.' He stayed where he was, all nervous expectancy. 'I'm ready.'

'What for, Max?'

'The psychiatrist.'

'The psychiatrist?'

'The psychiatrist.'

'What psychiatrist?'

'The one you think I have to go and see. Mum said it's today.'

'Is it?'

'You forgot, Dad.'

'I didn't forget. Your mum's been very tired. I'm sure she meant to tell me, but she didn't.'

'Mum doesn't forget things. You forgot.'

Normally of course that would be true, but Millicent was at the end of her strength. I tried to slide her off me without waking her, but she stirred, blinked twice, and sat up.

'Hey, Max.'

'Hi, Mum. Want me to make you some coffee?'

'I'll make some, Max,' I said, and got out of bed. 'While Mum gets ready.'

'For what?' asked Millicent.

'The psychiatrist,' said Max.

'I forgot. I'm sorry, Max.'

Max looked pained, but sat down on the bed beside her.

'You know it's not a real psychiatrist, Max,' said Millicent.

'How come?'

'Psychiatrists are doctors. This one's not a doctor.'

Max considered this.

'She's a psycho*therapist*. Lots of people go to therapists.'

'No they don't.' But he leaned in towards Millicent, who put an arm around his neck, drawing him gently to her. I pulled on a pair of trousers.

'Aren't you going to put pants on, Scottish Dad?'

'What's Scottish about not wearing pants, Max?'

Millicent and Max exchanged a look. 'The kilt thing, right, Max?' said Millicent.

Max nodded.

'What's worn under the kilt?' said Millicent.

'Nothing,' said Max with great seriousness. 'It's all in good working order.'

'Listen, small boy,' I said, 'I don't know what bothers me more: the fact that you know that joke, or the fact that you seem to understand it.'

'Mum taught it to me.'

'Yeah, Millicent, that's not good.'

Millicent made a gun with her hand, shot herself in the head. Max smirked. I put on a shirt and went downstairs to make coffee. While I waited for the coffee to boil I rang my mother.

My mother understood, she said, though in truth I hadn't explained what had happened. Her breathing sounded laboured, and I was fairly certain she was crying.

104

'I'm so sorry, Mum,' I said. 'Millicent is sorry too.'

'Aye,' she said, 'aye, son, I understand.'

'We'll be back up as soon as we can, Mum.'

'Aye, son. Aye.'

This wasn't Max's first course of therapy. After what I told you about his sister, how could it be? We have form with kiddie-shrinks.

Our very first visit to a therapist had been for 'observation'. We had agreed that Millicent would turn up fifteen minutes after Max and me, to give Max time to settle in.

'Hello, Max, hello, Alex,' said the therapist, elegant in silk slacks, her grey hair modishly shaped and highlighted. Expensive, I thought, very, very expensive. Proper oil paintings on the wall. A real bronze sculpture on the table.

Max had surprised me. He walked brightly over to the toy box in the corner and began playing quietly with a wooden train. I had expected the therapist to be watching him, but once she had decided that he was content she turned her chair to face me. I talked quietly, explaining that Max's fear of his mother was ruining our lives. We had tried everything, I said; wits' end.

Millicent entered. Max whimpered, and shrank from her.

'Interesting,' said the therapist. 'Alex, could you leave us for ten minutes?'

'I'm not sure that's a great idea.'

'Perhaps not. But could you step outside?'

I stood in the waiting area, expecting to be summoned by Max's screams. But he didn't scream. As far as I could tell, he didn't even cry.

After some time, the therapist called me back in. Max and Millicent were sitting in the corner, Max on Millicent's lap. She was reading quietly to him.

'Alex, are you aware that you flinched when Millicent walked in?'

105

'I really don't think I did.'

'It was quite distinct. And what struck me is that Max saw that you flinched. And then he flinched in his turn.'

The therapist explained that Max was *taking his cues* from me, *looking for guidance* as to how he might react to *this curious turn of events*, by which she meant the death of our little daughter. He could *read phatic signals* in my behaviour that I didn't know I was sending out. He was not the one who was angry with Millicent.

'Are you saying I am?'

'Aren't you? After all, you weren't there at the birth of your daughter.'

'But it wasn't a real birth.' *And she wasn't a real daughter.*

'But is it possible that some unconscious part of you can't forgive Millicent for sending you away? Or for not keeping her side of the deal, for not bringing *your* baby to term?'

'I'm not a chauvinist.'

'Interesting. I'm not saying you are. But many men would be angry.'

Well, it wasn't given to me to know what my *unconscious* mind was up to. Maybe I *was* sending *phatic signals* to Max that I was *angry with Millicent*. Maybe I was – unconsciously – *instructing* Max in how to behave. It seemed unlikely to me. Then again, I didn't have a better theory.

At home Max still screamed when Millicent entered the room. But at the therapist's he would sit in his mother's lap for an hour at a time, playing shyly with her hair.

We saw the therapist eight times. She explained to Max that Millicent hadn't killed the baby; that sometimes bad things in life happen over which grown-ups have no control; that we had genuinely believed he was going to have a sister; that Millicent and I were ourselves *terribly upset* at what had happened to her.

Then the therapist charged us a grand. I could have told Max the same things myself and used the cash on something useful. But we had been desperate; we hadn't known what else to do.

'Give your daughter a name,' said the therapist. 'Have a burial service. Invite other people if you want to.'

'Christ,' I said, 'what a quack.'

But Millicent insisted we do it, so we did. Just the three of us. We reassembled Max's doll, dressed it and packed it in tissue paper, and buried it in a shoe-box in the garden. Max had asked if she could be called Sarah, and we didn't have a better alternative. Max cried. Millicent cried. I cried too, hugging my wife and son so very tight.

This was ridiculous. A shoe-box and a doll called Sarah Mercer, for the love of God. Still we cried, our unhappy little tribe united in our grief.

And I hated to admit it, but the doll-burial changed something. Max was wary of Millicent, but he no longer screamed when she picked him up; he stopped crying when she tried to brush his teeth; he started to sleep through the night again. He began to let her read him stories in his bedroom; then finally he allowed her to get into the bath with him. I moved out of my son's room and back into the marriage bed.

For a long time my reaction was one of bewildered acceptance. I didn't understand what had happened to us, but knew that it had changed us all. We didn't have another child; we didn't even try.

We had come down a path at the side of a big house near Highbury Fields, rung a bell on the back door. The stainless steel plate by the door said Nora Å, PhD. After a moment, the therapist answered. Bit young to be called Nora: about my age, tall, mid-brown hair streaked with grey.

'Hello, Max,' she said, opening the door wide. 'Would you like to take a seat?'

The door opened directly into a large white-walled room.

There were three simple plywood chairs on the far wall, and another padded seat facing them.

'Is that your chair?' asked Max.

'Yes. I get the nice chair because I'm here all day.' Some very slight accent – not British, but hard to pin down.

I had expected Max to sit between us, but he chose the chair on the right. I sat on the chair on the left, leaving room for Millicent to sit in the middle. The therapist sat opposite us, and smiled at Max.

'So,' said Millicent, 'the reason we're here is that Alex and I are a little concerned.'

The therapist held up a finger.

'And I'm just going to stop you there.'

There was a long pause. The therapist smiled at Max. Max smiled at the therapist.

I tried to take Millicent's hand, let my fingers trail against hers, but she didn't seem to notice. The room was very bare. There were no curtains, and the floorboards had been painted a light grey. Behind the therapist light streamed in through the glass door and two full-height sash windows.

'Max, what would you like to talk about?'

Max looked thoughtful. 'Mum said you weren't a doctor. But you are.'

'Not a medical doctor.'

'I know that. What's the A for?'

'It's not really an A. It's got a little circle over it, and it's the last letter in the Norwegian alphabet. It's pronounced "Oh".'

'So your name is Dr N. Oh. Like Dr No?'

'If you like.'

Max smiled. 'You're not very scary.'

'Å is a place in Norway, and that's where my family's from. We're called Å. That's it.'

'Is your dad called Mr Oh?'

'Yes.'

108

'Is your mum called Mrs Oh?'

'No, she's called Dr Å. She's a proper doctor. She works in a hospital.'

'Oh,' said Max, and smiled again. 'Oh.'

'Why do you think you're here, Max?'

The smile left Max's face. 'Mum and Dad are *concerned* about me.'

'And why do you think that is?'

He sighed, looked first at Millicent, then at me. I tried to smile at him, but he frowned and turned back to the therapist.

'I don't know. I saw the neighbour's *penis*, and it was a boner.'

'OK.'

'And I know that if a man with a boner tries to touch you, then that's bad. But it's not like he was a paedo, and he was dead so he couldn't touch me.'

The therapist nodded. She looked a little taken aback.

'It would be useful to know the events leading up to this, Max. It'll help me to understand a little better.'

'We found him together, didn't we, Max?' I said. 'When I'd come out to find Max and get him into bed. You jumped down into the next-door neighbour's garden, didn't you?' I turned to the therapist. 'Max was looking for the cat.'

'And I'd like to hear about it from Max, please.' Again that raised finger.

'Sorry, Max.'

Max went very quiet. He sat looking out of the window at the trees. Millicent seemed pained. I looked at the clock on the wall behind her. Ten past six. Ten minutes we'd been here. One minute of talk, nine of pauses. At two pounds per minute that was eighteen pounds' worth of pauses.

'It's OK,' Max said at last. 'Dad can tell you.'

'He could, Max. But we all remember things in our own way.'

109

Max got up out of his chair and went to look out of the window. Eventually he turned and said, 'Can they go?'

'Do you mean that you'd like your parents to leave?'

Max nodded.

'Normally they would be here for the first session. But I can ask them if they're prepared to leave you here.'

'Sure,' said Millicent.

'Why not?' I said.

'Before you go, I should say that I normally don't tell parents the details of my conversations with their children. Because of Max's age, if there's anything I think you need to know, I will tell you. Or anything I have a legal duty to disclose. Can we proceed on that basis?'

'OK,' I said. Millicent nodded.

'Max?'

'OK, Dr Å,' said Max.

Millicent and I went for a walk around Highbury Fields. Well-heeled men and women in their forties emerged from Georgian houses with their perfectly turned-out children, walked their perfect dogs, met their perfect friends.

'What do you reckon these houses cost?' I said.

'Seven million? Twelve? I have no idea.'

'Who has that kind of money?'

'Bad people. I want to believe they're bad, bad people.'

An orange Datsun drew up on the other side of the road. As Millicent and I watched, the grey-black glass of the driver's door wound down. A child emerged through the window, naked below the waist, held firmly by stout adult arms. One arm lifted the child's feet so its legs were parallel with the road below. The child shat vigorously. The arms retracted the child, the window closed, and the car drove off.

'I guess they must not come from this neighbourhood,' said Millicent.

'I guess not.'

'That's funny, right?'

'Yes, why is that funny?'

I took Millicent's hand in mine. I wanted to tell her about everything that had happened in Edinburgh. I wanted to tell her about my mother crying through the wall, about how alone and how frail she had seemed. I wanted to suggest that we call my mother together.

I'm not sure why I didn't.

From Max's room I heard the fridge wind down and stop. The hum of the motor must have been with me for a while, pushing, gently abrasive, at the edge of my conscious mind. Following me around the house.

Only hear it when it stops.

How quiet it was in our little house now. I undressed Max and laid the covers over him. I went downstairs.

Millicent was asleep on the couch.

All the sounds that you hear but never register: all that evidence of life, all around you, and you don't feel it until it comes to an end.

Sound of nothing.

Nothing from the street.

Nothing from the neighbouring houses.

A motor cutting out.

PART TWO

Secrets, Shared with Another Girl

9

Newcomers look away from the street after nightfall. The steroidal fightdog in studded collar: *don't look*. The footfall of trainer on tarmac: *don't look*. The needled arm convulsing in the chickenshop doorway: *don't look*. Months pass, and they *don't look*, and nothing happens.

The streets hold their side of the bargain. Keep your head down and you can walk from the bus stop to your front door; don't open that door after seven, don't open your curtains after dark: don't lock eyes with the neighbourhood and the neighbourhood won't lock eyes with you. Let Crappy be Crappy, and Crappy will let you be.

With time it's not fear but minor anxiety that drives the new North Londoners: what colours are floorboards being painted this year? Why do stripped doors bleed around the joints? You could drive an armoured car through the sodium light and the dog shit, and as long as it didn't knock down the crumbling walls of their tiny front gardens, the Crappy middle classes wouldn't notice. They're passing through and they don't want trouble: let them maximise value and move on.

This is what success looks like for people like us. Seventy-three square metres, with the option of extending into the loft. This is two incomes, jobs in the media. This is me away one month in three; this is Millicent at her computer seventy hours a week.

This house is us at the top of our game. I don't know what failure would look like, but the thought terrifies me.

Three sixteen-year-olds were working the other side of the street, fingering locks on the parked cars: the North-London whiteboy's crime of choice, half-brick in hand and coat-hanger up sleeve, pockets jammed with chisels and wrenches. I guessed their only interest in me was whether I'd call the Plod.

'All right, lads?' I called out, and waved. 'How's the twocking tonight?' They clustered for a moment, then left at a slow saunter. I watched them go.

I stood for a while on the other side of the street.

I checked for anything that looked like a police car, but there was nothing, marked or unmarked. I crouched down by the kerb, looking back at our house. Yellow light from the window and door, blue light from the sky, orange light from the sodium streetlights.

My wife and son were asleep in that house: safe beds, under a safe roof. The light from our windows seemed so much warmer than the streetlight. Strange, I thought. Orange should be warmer than yellow.

There was no light from the houses on either side. No Bryce. No Mr Ashani. No one was watching.

I went back through our front door. I searched Millicent's bag. In her purse were two flat keys that I didn't recognise. Each had a hexagonal head, a stamped serial number.

I don't remember walking past Millicent. I don't remember opening our front door. All I remember is standing in the street in front of the neighbour's door.

The police locksmith had been back. There were heavy padlocks fitted top and bottom, bolted to heavy metal plates. No chance of Rose forcing her way in now. Not that it mattered.

The first of the keys slid easily into Bryce's lock. I left it where it was for a moment, went back to my own front door, looked across the threshold at my wife, saw her stir in her sleep. Had she lied? A turn of the key would tell me that. And what would I do if she had? Leave her? Forgive her?

Back. There was Millicent's key in the neighbour's front door, and there I was in front of it. I reached up and held it for a moment, then applied the gentlest of pressure. It turned, as I had known it would. Something about the way it had slid home into the lock.

I leaned gently against the door. It moved inwards, fractionally, then stopped. The padlocks, however, had not moved. It was the deadlock that had stopped it.

I didn't have the deadlock key. I thought for a moment. The other key in my hand was of the same design. What was it for?

I removed the key and went back inside our house. I closed the front door.

Millicent was still asleep where I'd left her. She looked peaceful for the first time in days. I was struck by how much I loved her, and wondered again whether I would leave or stay.

I put the neighbour's front-door key on the kitchen table and went into the back garden, sure now of what I must do.

Then I lost my nerve, and went back into the kitchen to make coffee. I smoked two cigarettes in the garden, drank down my coffee, then smoked another cigarette. *Neighbours have each other's keys all the time, don't they?*

In one possible world Millicent had been watering his plants, tending his bower while he was away. But that world didn't work. Fastidious men don't leave their deadbolts unlocked. If they trust the neighbour enough to have them water their flowers, they give that neighbour both front-door keys. Besides, there was another reason why that world didn't work: Millicent was no waterer of plants, no tender of bowers.

117

Bryce leaves his door on the latch. She lets herself in, and finds him in the bedroom. As she did last time. As she has done every time.

I fetched the love seat and was on the wall in a single clean movement. I sat, my feet on the neighbour's side of the wall, looking down into the garden. How long had it been? Four days? Already the garden had grown a little: the lawn, the bower, it all looked less precise, the lines less clean.

No lights in any of the other neighbours' windows. I jumped down. Millicent was small, but easily strong enough to get herself up on to the wall, just as I'd seen Max do it. There was a teak garden chair on the neighbour's side of the wall. I hadn't noticed it before. I sat down on the chair, rested my head in my hands. Because here's the narrative, and it's a simple one.

Perhaps the grope in the bower happened a year earlier than Millicent says, but you can be certain that it happened much as she told me it did. The first rule of lying is *tell the truth, as near as you can*. Millicent had second thoughts when the Calvados bottle appeared: we can be pretty certain of this too. She was telling me the truth, as near as she could.

But that's just the start of phase one, the beginning of my wife's seduction by the neighbour. Who knows how long that phase lasts, but it ends, and phase two begins, on the day Bryce hands Millicent a key to his front door.

Phase two happens openly. She can let herself in, but only when he's there. Max is asleep by ten thirty, and the new middle classes *don't look*. I had been away a lot, and I had trusted Millicent, so of course I had known nothing.

Perhaps it doesn't matter if there was a third phase. That front-door key tells me all I need to know – that Millicent has lied to me. But I want to know – and wouldn't you? – if there was a phase three. Because a key to the back door, that's beyond the breathless excitement of the affair, that's the foundations of a relationship.

The love seat by the wall beneath the lilac: a portal to a better, cleaner, tidier facsimile of our little house, and a cleaner, tidier version of a man.

Nothing about Bryce was frayed around the edges. Nothing about him was dishevelled. Millicent could not have chosen a lover less like me.

I was crying. It had come upon me unnoticed. I had been good at deceit once, still had it in my blood, could taste now the electric thrill of Millicent's betrayal. The older, less faithful me admired its brilliant simplicity even as silent sobs racked my body. I sat bent over in the shadows, my chest tightening, hands pressed hard against my mouth, and I let the tears come.

I counted to thirty and stopped myself from crying.

I went to the back door. There was only one lock. The key slipped easily in and turned smoothly. The lock clicked. I pushed at the key and the door swung open.

There had been a third phase then. Millicent had made a cuckold of me: not a one-time cuckold, or a sometime cuckold, but a serial cuckold. A perma-cuckold. She and Bryce had poured numberless glasses of wine, shared the flesh of countless dead animals, cracked bone, broken bread and fucked. My, how they must have fucked.

It was calm inside Bryce's house, like a cleaner, better version of ours. If I waited a few minutes my heart rate would slow. I would be calm too. I could walk around freely.

I thought of the police forensic team. They must have visited by now. And anyway, if I went in, what would they find that I hadn't already left? Wouldn't I just leave the same hairs, the same fingerprints as I already had? If I changed into the clothes I'd worn that first night I wouldn't have to worry about fibres, would I? I could slip unseen from room to room; nothing would change.

The blind was down but Bryce's kitchen was not completely dark. Shapes loomed, soft-edged and imprecise. All those tasteful shades of white bouncing the light from the doorway, picking out the edges of the furniture.

There was a low electrical hum, just at the edge of my consciousness. Fridge. I stood on the threshold and tried to find the shape of it. *I'd like to know what he eats, what he feeds Millicent. What he fed Millicent.*

If I crossed the threshold, if I opened the fridge, the light would come on. Probably none of the neighbours would notice. Under the sink I might find a box of thin latex gloves, the kind those scrupulous little English men love. I could put on the gloves, feel around the back of the fridge for the flex, and trace it back to the power point. Then I could turn off the fridge, open it, and find my way around by touch. Rack of lamb, side of beef, French cheese and German cold cuts. You can feel a lot through thin latex gloves.

Go home, Alex.

Because wearing gloves would be to trespass upon a psychological domain I didn't want to enter: the man who wears gloves is the man with something to hide; I was not that man.

My eyes had adjusted as much as they would. Seeing shapes without detail, I thought again how alike our kitchens were. Our sinks were in the same place, our cookers were in the same place, our fridges were in the same place. We sat in the same place to eat, and climbed the same stairs to the same bedroom.

For the first time I realised how odd this was. His house was next door to ours; it should have been the mirror image. That's how Victorian terraces in London were constructed: side by side, in pairs, front door by front door, corridor by corridor, all the way along the street. Mass production at its very best. Clever, fast and cheap. And now, for the first time, I realised what was wrong with our street. All the front doors were on the left-hand side, the front rooms on the right. The layout of Bryce's house was identical in every way to ours.

The map in my mind would carry me through Bryce's house in the dark. There would be no obstacles to impede my progress. I could navigate through Bryce's front room and up his stair silently and without touching a thing.

How did Bryce cope with Millicent, I wondered, with the mess that followed her everywhere? Did he fuss around her with ashtrays and dustpans, crumb vacuums and J-cloths? And how did *she* deal with that?

Alex, for the love of God, go home.

The street side of the house would be brighter. Super sodium streetlight through the living room's linen curtains. I could climb the stairs without touching anything. The only point of contact between me and Bryce's house would be my shoes. I didn't even need to change my clothes.

My blood was up. I could hear the pulse in my inner ear, feel it beating in my neck, taste metal in my mouth. I knew now what I needed to do. I needed to see the bedroom.

'Dad.'

For a moment I thought the voice had come from upstairs: Max was inside Bryce's house.

'Dad,' he said again. I took a step back, and looked up.

'Dad,' he said a third time. And there he was, leaning out of our bathroom window. 'Dad, what are you doing?'

'Nothing, Max.'

'Why are you standing so close to the neighbour's house?'

From where he was, he couldn't see the open door, or the key in the lock.

'Max, go to bed.'

'No.'

'Bed, Max.'

'You don't decide over me.'

'I do, Max. Bed.'

Max shook his head. I couldn't move away from the door. Not without closing it first.

'Max,' I said, 'I'm going to come back over the wall and

up the stairs, and if you aren't in bed and asleep by the time I get up there, there will be trouble.'

'I can't get to sleep that quickly. That isn't possible, Dad.'

'Nevertheless, Max . . .'

'No.'

I was pinned down. Someone might hear us.

I stepped towards the door.

'What are you doing, Dad?'

I reached forwards and took hold of the key. I could draw the door towards me without leaving prints, I thought.

'Why are you leaning forwards, Dad?'

I pulled on the key. Nothing happened. The door was heavier than I had realised. Perhaps the key would not be strong enough to pull it closed.

'Is the door open, Dad?'

'Shut up and go to bed.'

'No. What are you doing?'

I pulled at the key, but the door resisted and my fingers slipped uselessly off it.

'I know the door's open, Dad. I can tell.'

I gripped the key at the side just behind the head and pulled as firmly as I dared. The door began to move, painfully slow.

'Creak,' said Max.

He was right. From the hinges came a low, mocking stutter. 'Fuck,' I said. I stopped pulling.

'Fuck,' said Max, simply.

'Max.'

'Fucking fucked.'

The panic was rising in me now. 'Max . . . Be quiet.'

'OK,' he said, in a loud whisper. 'Fuck.'

'Stop that, Max.'

'I was saying it quietly. Fuck.'

'Stop it.'

'Fuckingfuckersfuckingfucked.'

'Max, I mean it. Please.'

'You shouldn't be there. You shouldn't be doing that. So I can say what I like. Fuckingfuckersfuckingfucked. You're the only one who can hear me.'

'Max, you little shit-for-brains.'

He stood in the window looking at me for a while, short, stiff and awkward. Then he began to cry silently.

What have you done?

I pulled hard at the key and this time the door slammed softly closed. I drew the key from the lock and I took a step back. 'Max,' I said, 'I'm so sorry. I didn't mean what I said.' But he just stood there, crying in the window.

I got myself back over the wall and into our house. Millicent stirred in her sleep as I passed the sofa. I took the stairs two at a time, and found Max still standing in the bathroom. When I put a hand on his shoulder he tensed, willing me gone, angling his body away from me.

'Max. Max, I'm sorry. Hey. Hey, Max-Man. Hey.'

The sobs came louder now.

'Max-Man. My little Max-Man. I'm so sorry.'

He collapsed towards me, letting me steady him, letting me pick him up and hold him tight to my chest. I could feel his tears running down my cheek, his breath hot on my neck. I stroked his back until the sobs began to subside, then set him gently down and took his hands in mine.

'Max, look at me.'

He did, and I could read anger and disappointment in him.

'You said I had shit for brains.'

'And that was a bad thing to do, and I'm very sorry.'

'I'm not stupid.'

'I know. Christ, Max, you must know how smart you are. And you must be able to see that I can see that. And yes, I know I said Christ.'

Another half-smile, quickly suppressed.

'Are you going to tell Mum what you were doing?'

I shook my head.

'Why not?'

I had no answer to this.

'You had a key,' he said at last. It wasn't a question.

'Yes, Max. Yes, I did.' There wasn't much point in lying. He had heard the door as it swung shut.

'Where did you get it? Dad?'

And this is where I should have lied. God knows I should have lied. I don't know what me made me say it, but I said it. 'From your mum's bag. It was in her purse.'

I was crying again. Max was crying again. We clung to each other, father and son, there in the bathroom, amongst the mould and the memories.

10

I made hot chocolate for Max, and we sat in silence in the kitchen as he drank it. Then I remembered the red carrier bag my mother had given me. Inside it was a canvas army-issue bag with a leather shoulder strap. Max had opened the pockets, drawn out cigar boxes filled with lead weights, with delicately tied salmon flies, with painted steel lures.

My father had promised his fishing bag to me. But as the years had passed and I'd shown no interest in catching and killing fish I suspect he'd forgotten his promise.

'Cool,' Max had said, when he had opened every pocket. 'Thanks, Dad.'

Now I lay on my back on Max's bed waiting for him to fall asleep. I was a fool, an emotional incontinent: I should never have burdened him with what I knew. As we lay, silent in the near-darkness, I dared not look at my son.

I wanted to ring my mother. I wanted to tell her how sorry I was to have deserted her, how I hadn't known what else to do. I wanted to tell her too how sorry Millicent was. I wanted her to know that I missed her, that I loved her, that more than anything I missed my father. But it was the middle of the night, and I couldn't ring.

At last Max found sleep, wheezy and restless. I got to my feet as quietly as I could and went to close the bathroom window.

I decided not to replace the keys in Millicent's bag. Let her wonder where they'd gone. I brushed my teeth and lay on my own bed. After an hour, Millicent came upstairs and undressed carefully. I feigned sleep. She touched my arm, but I did not respond. I heard her brushing her teeth in the bathroom. Then she lay down beside me and fell asleep.

I got up and rang Fab5. The phone rang twice, then went to his answering machine.

'This is Fab5. Check you.'

'Fab5, no one has said check you since 1992. Seriously, it just sounds weird in an Edinburgh accent.' I hung up.

Five minutes later he rang back.

'What's up?'

'Hello, Fab5.'

I heard a woman's voice and wondered if it was someone I knew. Then the sound went hissy and I guessed Fab5 had covered the receiver with his hand. His voice sounded distant but enclosed, as if he were shouting into a cup. 'Friend . . . touch of the old maritals . . .' The woman's voice said something I couldn't make out. Fab5 laughed. I thought I could hear the sound of a kiss. Someone said *mmm*.

'Fab5,' I shouted.

He removed his hand from the phone. 'What's up?'

'Covering the receiver with your hand doesn't work.'

'Yeah. Anyway.'

'Who's your lady friend?'

'It's three in the morning, Alex. You've not rung me to talk about me compromising my vow of celibacy. You OK?'

'No.'

'Want me to come over?'

'You're busy.'

'Break out the Courvoisier. There in ten.'

126

And ten minutes later he was sitting opposite me at the kitchen table.

'I have no Courvoisier.'

'Relax, Alex.'

'I have wine and I have good whisky.'

He looked at the labels, then tapped the whisky bottle.

'Who do you know who drinks Courvoisier anyway?'

'Figure of speech. A joke. Over your head. No big deal.'

I poured two large whiskies and offered him a Marlboro, which he declined.

'Same question, Alex. What's up? Millicent, no?'

'Why would that be?'

'Awfully highly strung.'

'I think that may just be with you. She thinks you're a little hypocritical when it comes to women. Which maybe you are. Who was that, anyway?'

Fab5 considered this for a moment. 'Displacement, Alex.'

'What?'

'You didn't call me up to pop a cap in my ass for my sex life. What's up?'

'Pop a cap in your ass? What are you, fourteen?'

'You have other friends but you called me. What's going on?'

'Wow, a real question, with real English words and everything.'

'Like I said, you have other friends.' He looked offended.

'Sorry. Sorry, Fab5.'

He nodded. 'OK.'

'I'm a judgmental twat.'

'Save it, you judgmental twat, and tell me what's wrong.'

I told him, haltingly. It took me just under half the bottle. Fab5 didn't drink much, but he did listen. At seven he put away the whisky bottle and made me drink two pints of water. At seven thirty he sent me upstairs to wash my hair and change my clothes, while he made coffee and went to the shop for orange juice. I showered and went into the bedroom for clean clothes. I was certain Millicent was awake, but she said nothing.

At eight Max appeared. He accepted Fab5's presence without explanation. Fab5 made him French toast and took him to school. I went into the garden and lay on my back smoking cigarettes. From time to time I propped myself up on my elbow to drink coffee. Mostly I smoked. I saw Millicent through the bathroom window, but she didn't come downstairs.

At nine Fab5 rang me and I went inside to let him in through the front door.

'What's happening to me, Fab5?' I said.

'Alex, friend,' said Fab5, 'right now you're drunk, and you need to be drunk. You need to switch off that right brain, sometimes. Let your left brain take over.'

'Other way round.'

'You see?' There was concern in his eyes. 'You need to decompress, mate.'

'All right. Thanks, Fab5. You're a mensch.'

'And you need to be out of this house, Habibi.'

As I was putting on my shoes I heard feet on the street outside, the sound of the gate being pushed back. Four knocks at our door.

Fab5 looked down at me, enquiring.

No, I thought back at Fab5, *no*. I shook my head.

A heavy shadow fell across the linen curtain in the front window. Someone was trying to look in. The shadow held position for a moment, then rotated gently, now to the right, now to the left. On our side of the curtain dust motes glistened, unburdened by gravity. The shadow disappeared.

Four knocks.

Fab5 looked down at me. What to do? I stood up, left my shoes unlaced, went to the door.

The stomach was slack, the shaved head puckered where it joined the neck. He weighed twice what I weighed, but behind the fat was a muscular belligerence: a strongman gone to seed. The tops of the arms, and the thighs, though, were crab-like, over-defined. There was dry skin around his mouth, but his smile was warm, and his eyes friendly.

'Yes?' *Concentrate on the smile.*

'Mr Bryce? I wondered if we could talk?'

'No,' I said.

'You're not Mr Bryce?'

'No.'

'Is this Mr Bryce?' He gestured past me.

'No,' I said. 'No, that is Mr Fab5.' I fought back the urge to laugh. Fab5 shot me a look.

I hadn't noticed the piece of paper in the man's hand when I answered the door. All I had seen was the belly – reddened and blackened from the burst veins, purplish, really, folds curling down out of his t-shirt — and the tightness of the thighs. But I was looking down at the paper now, and so was he. I took it and stared at it for a moment. Traybourne and Nephew. Scaffolding services. £23,523.

I passed the invoice to Fab5. He looked at it, then passed it back to the man.

'Is that your address?'

'Yes. But I'm Mr Mercer.'

The man frightened me, but my fear seemed theoretical, like the fear of another man. It seemed unlikely to me that the scaffolder would hit me. Where were the police when you needed them, though?

I stepped out through the door. He flexed away to let me pass, nimble on swollen ankles. *Your legs and your belly don't match.*

I pointed to the neighbour's front door.

'That's Mr Bryce's house.'

I watched as he walked out of our gate, took five steps up the street, and opened the neighbour's gate. The strength in those upper arms, those thighs. Not a man I wanted to cross. He leaned forwards and pressed the bell.

'You won't find him.'

'What, mate?'

'He's dead.'

He folded his arms across his chest. He thought I was joking.

'I found him.'

'What, mate?'

'Our neighbour, Mr Bryce, is dead. I found him.'

'Yeah?'

'Yeah. Check out the padlocks.'

He was listening to me now. He believed me now.

'What am I supposed to do about this?' He held up the invoice.

'I don't know,' I said.

'And you're nothing to do with Mr Bryce?'

I shook my head.

'This is a family business,' he said. 'Daughter's sixteen next week. What do I tell her? What do I tell the bank?'

'I don't know,' I said. 'I'm sorry. I really am.' And I was, now.

Twenty-three-and-a-half grand. That would sink you. He had a business, and a sixteen-year-old daughter. I could feel a pricking at the back of my eyes. This man was no threat to me. I could throw my arm around his heavy shoulders, and we could cry together.

'He screwed us over too,' I wanted to say. 'Life was good before he came.' God, but I was drunk.

'I'm sorry, mate,' I said. 'Wish I could help.'

I went inside. Fab5 followed me in and shut the door.

'Weird,' he said.

'Fab5,' I said. 'Fab5, I know I'm a little *reduced* right now, but did I understand that right?'

'How do you mean?'

'The guy was trading from our address.'

'Maybe.'

'Maybe?'

'Aye, maybe. And maybe it's a mistake.'

'Sure,' I said. 'A mistake that's happened twice.'

We opened the door again five minutes later; there was a police car parked across the street. Two uniformed officers watched as Fab5 and I made our way past them. The scaffolder was gone.

The manager at the Swedish seemed surprised to see me. Still he showed us to a table and took our breakfast order. We ate in silence, then Fab5 paid and left me there to meet Millicent.

'Word to the wise, friend. Try to listen to what she's telling you.'

'I'll try.'

'Good man.'

'You've been drinking,' she said as she sat down.

'I've been drinking.'

'Care to explain?'

'Fab5 came over. He made breakfast for Max, so everything's fine.'

'That's *super*.'

'Yeah.'

'It's all super.'

'Yeah.'

'Because Fratboy5's just so supergreat.'

'Actually, he was pretty supergreat. Stayed up all night. Stayed sober. Took Max to school.'

'And I thought he was some middle-aged sad-sack. Who knew?'

'Right now he's the reason I haven't left you. Yet.'

'Whoah. That came a little out of left field. Wait. What?'

'I found his keys. Bryce's, I mean. Both of them.'

She half-turned away from me, half-sniffed in the way she does when she's upset, then turned to face me again. She had rearranged her features into something calm and quizzical, but the sinews in her neck were stretched tight.

'You do this thing, Millicent,' I said. 'Your jaw makes this little side-to-side movement when you're trying to keep your composure, and it's doing it now. Sort of like you're grinding your teeth in your sleep.'

Millicent's eyes flicked away for a second, then flicked back. She was summoning her strength, steeling herself.

'You had his front-door key, but not his deadlock. Which makes me wonder, Millicent, because if it was for plant-watering, or any of the thousand other innocent reasons why people have each other's keys – letting the gas man in, say – then you'd have both.'

She turned away from me, half-sniffed again, but didn't turn back.

'And the tendons in your neck are standing right out, which isn't very you. Anyhow, one key suggests something else, doesn't it? A door readied for a special visitor. No? Feel free to interrupt me at any point.' I was calm. My world was falling apart, but there was no anger in me. Perhaps it was the alcohol, or perhaps the lack of sleep.

She looked at me, and I could read nothing in her gaze.

'You do know that I want to be wrong, Millicent.'

She met my eye, and nodded. A sad little gesture. Then she dropped her gaze and turned away, looked out into the street.

'So then at some point he gave you the key to his back door, and my guess is that your relationship entered a new phase. The run of his house. He must really have liked you. Have I got any of this wrong yet?'

She said something I didn't hear.

'What?'

'You aren't wrong. Not in any important way.'

'So Max would be at home, and when he was asleep you would leave him there, and climb the wall to the neighbour's house.'

'Alex . . .'

'Do you think this is the sort of thing an eleven-year-old boy is likely to get over?'

'Alex, listen to me . . .'

'Max knows, I'm afraid.'

'Max doesn't know.'

'I told him. I didn't mean to. I as good as told him. And he's a sensitive boy, with an agile mind. He must have figured out the rest.'

She got up, and I assumed that she was leaving. But she disappeared through the door to the lavatory.

My tongue found a sore where I'd bitten the inside of my cheek a few hours earlier. I worried at the scab with the tip of my tongue for a moment, then drained my coffee. It was cold, granular, but the familiarity of the taste comforted me.

Millicent reappeared, and went to the counter, where she exchanged words with the manager. She came back to the table and sat down opposite me.

'I ordered coffee.'

I nodded. 'How much worse is this going to get, Millicent?'

'This is pretty bad, Alex. I'm sorry.'

She took my hands in hers, turned them over. 'You always had such beautiful hands, Alex.'

'Had?'

'Would you please drop the grammar-Nazi pose for one moment? You *have always had* such beautiful hands, Alex. OK? They're beautiful.'

'The cuckold with the beautiful hands. That should be worth a compensatory shag with some pretty but slightly faded Crappy divorcée, don't you think?' I nodded towards a woman sitting alone at the long table by the till, reading the *Independent*. 'What about her over there? Great hair. Highlights and everything.'

'You said you wanted to hear what I had to say, Alex.'

I turned back to Millicent. 'You're right, and I'm still a little drunk. Sorry. Speak.'

'I ended it, Alex.'

'Did you now?'

She produced a small envelope with her name written in tidy handwriting.

'Scented,' I said. 'Classy.'

I opened the envelope and found a single sheet of paper. 'A notelet. With his address printed on and everything. Classier and classier.'

'Alex, you have the moral high ground.'

'Yes, I'd say I do. "*My America*," it begins. You let him call you *My America*?' Millicent gave a diffident little shrug.

> *My America,*
>
> *How many hours must I spend watching, seeing your shadow pass before the light, knowing you are at home, yet knowing that you will not answer? How many times must I dial your number, hear the telephone ring out through the thin wall that divides us, and know that you will not pick up?*
>
> *So it's husband before lover, duty before passion, routine before LIFE.*
>
> *I bear you no ill will. Soon I shall be gone, so that your marriage may continue, our love sacrificed on the altar of convenience and bourgeois convention.*
>
> *In eternity,*
> *Bryce*

'He loved you, Millicent. It says so here, right before the signature. That's what *In eternity* means, isn't it? And he bore you no ill will. He was grateful to you for enriching his life for those few intoxicating months – I'm reading between the lines now.'

'Alex, not so loud.'

A burst of cold adrenaline as the anger hit my heart.

'Oh, sorry, is this *humiliating* for you?' I looked around

the café. 'No one else here minds about the end of our marriage. Did you love him?'

She shook her head.

'Well, I have *your* word for that.'

'Don't.'

'Oh, and he thinks our marriage is a bourgeois sham. The little anal-retentive thinks *I'm* too middle-class. *Thought.* Sorry.'

'Alex, don't do this.'

'What do you reckon, Millicent? What's your professional hunch, as a purveyor of comfort to people in need? Are we going to be together in a year's time? Am I going to kick you out, only to realise that what I *really, really, really* need to do is to see this as an *opportunity for growth* and forgive you? Or am I going to let you stay on in the house for Max's sake? What's your guess, Millicent? Assuming, that is, you even want to stay.'

'I ended it, Alex. It won't get any worse. I promise you.'

The anger was starting to ebb from me now. I felt depleted. I longed for sleep.

'You can't promise me,' I said, 'that it won't get any worse.'

'Yes, Alex, I can promise that.'

'Millicent,' I said, 'last time we were here you *needed me to understand* that you would never betray me. And yet, you betrayed me. Repeatedly. I want to tell you to move out. But I can't because I know you'll tell me that Max has enough to worry about.' *And I'm scared that I'll end up begging you to stay.*

'I don't want either of us to move out. But I'll respect what you want, Alex.'

The phone rang. I rejected the call.

'That was Dr Å. You can ring her back. I'm drunk.' She said nothing, pressed her fingers to her temples.

The coffee arrived. I nodded at the waitress, who looked pained, even as she returned my nod.

135

'So, Millicent, why?'

'Why?'

'Yeah, why?'

Millicent rubbed the bridge of her nose. 'I don't know why Bryce killed himself.'

'That's not really one of the questions I was asking you.'

'Shut up and listen, Alex, you self-righteous asshole.' That was loud. The divorcée with the hair reacted, looked at us, intrigued. Millicent turned to her. 'Sorry, I meant arsehole,' she said, in her best Cali-girl accent. 'He's an arsehole. Did I get that right? I'm often told I lack nuance.' She turned back to me. 'You're an arsehole, Alex. You're such a freaking nihilist. You've always seen all the possibilities, decided they're meaningless, and rejected them. Bryce didn't spend our conversations pre-empting what I was going to say.'

I looked down at her hands, at her delicate wrists and slender fingers.

'What's the story with the bracelet my mother gave you?'

'I don't know.'

Millicent's phone began to ring. She ignored it, and stared directly at me.

'And I don't know why I lied, Alex. I really don't know.'

'Looking me in the face doesn't prove you're not lying now. The police think I killed him.'

'They asked you not to leave the country. That is not the same thing.'

'What did you tell them about you and Bryce?'

'The same thing I told you. First time round.' She glanced at the screen and rejected the call. 'Dr Å. We should really call her back.'

'Summoned by the shrink . . . Go right ahead.'

'Max is our joint responsibility, Alex.'

Anger like a shard of ice in my spine.

'Millicent, until four days ago I thought I was a happy nihilist. And my happy innocent state ended when Max and

I found the next-door neighbour reclining in the bath with an erection. I'm still fighting to erase the image that's imprinted on the inside of my skull, and God alone knows what Max is struggling with because he can't bring himself to talk about it. And now it turns out that it's thanks to you, and that we all three have that in common – Bryce and his penis. Whatever it is that's wrong with Max, *you* did it to him. So the shrink thing? You sort it out.

'And speaking of practicalities, a scaffolder came round with an invoice for £23,523. Made out to *your* boyfriend at *our* address. I forgot to ask for a copy to throw on the table in front of you as I walk out. Did you know he was trading from our house? Police are going to love that one.'

I got up to leave. Millicent got up too. She was close to crying.

'Alex,' she said.

'Feeling bad, Millicent? You in some sort of private hell?'

Her eyes were wet now.

'Sit down,' I said, and left, nodding to the manager on the way out.

11

On a bench in a corner of Highbury Fields I watched a mother lift a screaming baby from his pram. With her right hand she raised her top, freed her left breast, and gave suck to the child, who quietened at once.

'Sorry,' she mouthed at me.

'Don't be.'

'Thanks.'

The police would like Millicent's affair. I could argue all I wanted that I never knew, that I only became the angry husband after the neighbour was dead. But if I were the police, I would like me as a suspect.

I watched, trying not to, as the baby drank his fill and fell asleep at his mother's breast. I tried not to think about my son, and my wife. I tried not to think about Millicent feeding Max for the first time, the transcendent pleasure that I had felt in that most everyday of things.

Then I tried not to think about sex.

I failed. I thought about those things, and about what I was about to lose. I thought about them for the longest time.

Millicent was waiting outside Dr Å's door as I approached. She touched my hand, but I ignored her and pressed the bell.

Five minutes later we were sitting, miserably drinking tea, on Dr Å's straight-backed chairs. Dr Å had said little since we had arrived, and we had said even less. Her message on my answering machine had been very precise, and had left no possibility of not coming to this meeting. Millicent, I imagined, had received the same message.

Dr Å smiled her efficient Scandinavian smile, first at Millicent, then at me. Just long enough, just warm enough, entirely professional.

'Here we are,' she said.

Millicent put her cup on the floor and rubbed the bridge of her nose.

'Before we begin,' said Dr Å, 'is there anything either of you would like to tell me?'

Millicent shook her head. I spilled tea on my leg, managed not to swear, and put down my own cup. Dr Å smiled her efficient smile. I rubbed my hands together, breathed out, and steeled myself.

'So, your son strikes me as a relatively normal eleven-year-old boy. I'm really not going to tell you very much about what Max has said to me, if you don't mind. You are of course within your rights to insist that I do, given his age. But I would ask that you do not do that. OK?'

Millicent nodded.

'Sure,' I said.

'Max feels, and I don't think I'm breaking confidence here in saying this, that you are relatively good parents.'

I felt Millicent bristle.

'I should say that this is a remarkably positive assessment. Most eleven-year-olds are much less flattering about their parents' abilities. But there is one concern that Max and I share. Your relationship as a couple . . .'

'Which Max has assessed as imperfect?' I said.

'If you like, yes. Although, with children, they're often not as analytical about these things as you or I might be. But Max is deeply concerned. He rang me this morning.'

139

I stared hard at Millicent, but she stayed facing forwards, refusing the challenge.

'Did Max say what exactly it is that concerns him?'

'He believes you wish to leave the relationship, Alex.'

Still Millicent would not look at me.

'And why would I wish to do that?' I said.

'Alex, I am not here to give ammunition to your battles with your wife,' said Dr Å. 'I would ask you not to question Max about this. I doubt if you would be able to frame your questions in an appropriately neutral way. But children tend to know a lot more about the state of their parents' relationships than adults imagine. Your anger is, by the way, entirely appropriate.'

'Am I angry? And what does appropriate even mean?'

Dr Å ignored the questions. 'I cannot provide you with therapy. I can, if the two of you wish it, provide you with the names of people I can recommend, but you will understand that I do not want to find myself in a situation where the wishes of one client come into conflict with the wishes of another. As for example in the case of your perfectly natural desire to know the truth about Millicent's affair.'

'Millicent's affair,' I said, my voice flat. 'Do I even know about Millicent's affair?'

'I'm sorry,' she said. I could see that she regretted her words.

'I do know, as it happens, Dr Å. The question is, how do *you* know?'

I looked at Millicent. *Did you tell her?*

Millicent shook her head. *No.*

I looked back at Dr Å. 'Max told you.'

'Alex,' said Dr Å, 'Alex, I would ask you not to press me on this.' She looked wearily back at me, a woman burdened by the knowledge she bore.

'Could I insist that you tell me?'

The weary look passed, and she was a professional once again. 'I cannot recommend that you insist. It would not be

140

appropriate for me to discuss what Max has told me in confidence. Your son has experienced a great trauma. Alex, I feel that you too may be experiencing trauma, both from the discovery of the neighbour, and also from the discovery of the secret between Millicent and your neighbour. You will no doubt have heard of post-traumatic stress disorder. It is my job, working with Max, to help him to avoid the symptoms of which you may have heard. Flashbacks, fear of unfamiliar situations, an inability to form or maintain relationships.

'These things are severely debilitating in an adult, but imagine for a moment the devastating effect on a child. In the next few years, your son will become a sexual being. How he experiences that transition from childhood to adulthood will affect every relationship, every friendship, every professional transaction. For ever.'

'Especially when it's your mother's affair that caused the trauma.' Millicent shifted position in her chair. It was subtle, but I could read the anger in her.

'This must be very painful for you, Alex,' said Dr Å, 'but I must ask you not to confuse your own feelings with Max's feelings.'

'Max feels the same thing I do.'

'That is unlikely, is it not? After all, Millicent is his mother; she is your *wife*.'

I made to speak but she smiled and turned to Millicent.

'Millicent, you too must be suffering greatly. You are likely to be grieving both for the excitement of the affair, and for the life of a man for whom you must have had feelings.'

'She certainly spends a lot of time out of the house grieving,' I said. 'Don't you, Millicent?'

'OK,' said Millicent. 'Yes, Alex, I guess I do.'

'It's like you're breaking down all over again,' I said. I stood up. I wanted to leave.

'It wasn't a breakdown,' said Millicent, as if to herself.

'Alex, would you mind sitting down?' There was kindness in Dr Å's voice now, and the smile had lost its Scandinavian

141

precision. 'I can see that accepting Millicent's grief must be hard for you.'

I sat down, put my head in my hands, and breathed out. The room was silent, and I could think of nothing to say. Nor, it seemed, could Millicent. We sat, angled away from each other. Five minutes passed on the silent clock.

Dr Å crossed and uncrossed her legs. 'We're coming to the end of the time I had set aside. I hope you can understand that my focus has to be on Max, and on Max's needs. I will, however, say this. There is a mounting body of evidence that states that splitting up is the worst thing you could do. Unhappy parents who stay together are still better than parents who part company. For the children, that is.'

'That's your advice?' I asked. 'Don't leave?'

'That's my advice. I'm sorry I can't do more for you. I understand Max is making his own way here.'

That evening my mother rang. She was speaking so quietly that at first I could hardly make out what she was saying.

'You see, son, your father's case is what they call an automatic referral.'

'What, Mum?'

'Well, they explained that because your father's death occurred within twenty-four hours of his entering hospital, then they refer his death to the coroner. They always investigate. He's to be autopsied, and they haven't the staff.'

'Oh, Mum,' I said.

'Yes, well, it's a bind. I don't know when I can bury him.'

'Mum,' I said, 'I'm so sorry.'

'Aye, son,' she said simply. 'Aye.'

12

Max had been navigating quietly around us, sensing the fragility of the truce between Millicent and me. He made his own meals, bought fruit from the shop, and made a point of making coffee – badly – and bringing us each a cup, talking softly to me, stroking his mother's cheek, asking us whether we wanted water, or juice, or a piece of cake. He could go to the shop again, if we wanted. Max behaved, in short, impeccably. Normally, we would have teased him for this, asked him what he was planning, what terrible secret he was hiding. But now we too behaved like textbook parents.

Millicent and I did not argue in front of Max; nor did we speak much. We kept our voices low, and behaved deferentially towards each other for his sake. We ate at different times, staggered our coffee breaks and went to bed separately. Once, at the dark of night, I woke with an erection and found Millicent's arms tightly wound around my chest. I wanted to wake her, to have her witness how I recoiled from her nakedness, to have her feel my power as I shook her off; instead I unwound myself from her embrace and turned her gently on her side. I watched the tremors of her eyelids, sensed through them the darting movements of her pupils, wondered what it was she dreamed. I watched her chest rise and fall, saw words half-form on her lips, and hated myself for wanting her so badly, for craving intimacy after everything she had done.

Max spent Friday evening in his room. At eight he borrowed the lamp from Millicent's desk. At eleven I realised that his bed time had long since come and gone. His door was shut. I knocked and went in. Max was lying on his back on his bed, looking up at the ceiling. Beside his pillow lay his grand-father's fishing bag, spools of fishing line and cigar boxes around his legs.

'Hi, Dad,' he said, with studied nonchalance. I followed his gaze. In the narrow beam of Millicent's lamp was a shoal of metallic fish. Barbed hooks hung from iridescent bodies.

'Wow,' I said.

Max had created a living shoal, the larger fish at the back, chasing down the smaller fish, the very smallest fry turning and spreading as they reached the far wall. Yellow eyes, scales of blue, gold and green; the nylon fishing line almost invisible. There were at least a hundred artificial fish, steel spinners and wooden lures, rubber sand eels with red-painted gills, jointed wobblers, all brought to life by the hands of a child.

'Can you see the bubbles, Dad?'

'Those are amazing, Max.'

Max had arranged his grandfather's transparent bubble floats to enhance the drama of the scene: a cluster at the implied surface, larger bubbles rising slowly up from down below.

'Your mum needs to see this,' I said. 'You should call her.'

'Don't you think she's a fucking bitch, though? For what she did to you?' He ran the words together: *fuckingbitchthough*.

'No, Max. No, I really don't.'

'Oh,' he said.

'Don't call your mum that.'

'All right. I won't.'

144

'I don't want you to take my side. Call her in.'

'In a minute. Can you see the squid hiding from the fish?'

Subject changed. Just like that. Speed of the child mind.

'The squid are brilliant.'

'Also, Dad?'

'What, Max?'

'What's this?'

He held up a straight wooden shaft, about eight inches long, wider at the top than at the bottom. The metal core shone dully in the beam of Millicent's light.

'That's called a priest.'

'Did Grandpa use it for killing fish?'

'Yes, that's what it's for.'

'It's a bit sticky, even though it's clean.'

'I don't think that's fish blood. I guess it's probably resin from the wood.'

'Oh,' said Max. He sounded almost disappointed. 'What are the pliers for?'

'For helping you get the hook out of a fish.'

'Like if it's a big fish and it swallows the hook or something?'

'Yes, Max.'

'Yuck. Cool, though. Dad, can we go fishing together?'

'If you like.'

'I don't have a rod or anything.'

'I'll talk to your grandma, Max. I'm sure you could have one of Grandpa's old ones.'

'OK,' he said. He thought for a moment. 'I want to come to Grandpa's funeral. I don't want to see him dead or anything, though.'

'No, love, it won't be an open casket.'

'I mean, it's not like I'm not scared or anything. I know what a dead man looks like.'

'I don't think your grandpa looks anything like the neighbour did, Max.'

145

'Tarek said they put makeup on dead people.'

I looked down at my son as he lay on his bed staring up at the beautiful, twisting mass of fish that he had created.

'Move up, little man,' I said. 'Make room.'

We lay looking up at Max's shoal. I could see Max grinning to himself from the edges of my vision, feel the pride radiating from him.

'Do you like it, Dad?'

'Max,' I said, 'I think you've managed to take something that wasn't beautiful, and turn it into something that is. Send your grandma a picture.'

He turned and faced me. I stayed where I was, looking up at the ceiling.

'Do you miss Grandpa, Dad?'

'Yes. Yes, I really do.'

'I can tell, because you look quite sad.'

'I left things unsaid, you know.'

'Is Grandma really sad?'

'She is.'

'More than you?'

'More than I think I can imagine.'

'Because I don't want to send her a picture if it's going to make her cry a lot.'

'Send her a picture, love.'

He curled into me and I stretched my arm under his shoulder. We lay looking upwards for a very long time.

On Saturday morning Fab5 rang, suggesting Frisbee at the park.

'Sure,' I said, 'but I have to bring Max.'

'You got it.'

'He's going to want to play football. And I at least have to ask Millicent.'

'Whatever you need.'

I expected Millicent to refuse, but she agreed to come, and

put on a pair of running shoes that she hadn't worn in years. At the park she behaved as if she was pleased to see Fab5, let him lift her from the ground.

'Ready to get your ass kicked, hen?' he said.

'Because that's exactly what's going to happen, of course.'

'It will.'

'Who said this was sarcasm?'

We played scorer-goes-in, using trees as goalposts, every man for himself. Millicent and I hardly scored. Max and Fab5 ran rings around us, matched each other goal for goal.

I looked up at Millicent, and felt again that near-smile, the beginning of the thaw. *This*, I thought. Love expressed through the doing of stuff. We need to do more of *this*.

She reached out, rubbed my arm. 'We stink at soccer, don't we?'

I looked over at Max, as he sent the ball arcing towards Fab5. Fab5 jumped and caught it, then kicked it far off down towards the cricket pitches at the end. Max tore after it, and we watched him as he ran.

'You and I,' I said, 'stink at this. Our only hope is that.'

She leaned back against me, still watching Max, and drew my arms around her, nestled her head against my chest. 'We're not really in-the-moment people, are we?'

I kissed the top of her head. Perfume, and the shrill tone of her sweat. I crossed my arms over her breasts. 'You smell good,' I said. 'The sun is shining.'

'What is this, spontaneity 101?'

'I love you,' I said. And for a moment I felt a rush of something very pure. She looked up at me, her eyes glistening.

Then I felt foolish. I looked round at Fab5, expected him to be laughing at us, but he was watching something down by the far end of the park. I followed his gaze, saw a police car as it glided past. The car drove on. *Probably nothing.*

'What is it, honey?' Millicent drew away, looked up at me.

'Nothing,' I said. *It was nothing.* I looked back at Max,

who had turned and was racing back up the park towards us. 'Come on, Max. At him.'

Max scored twice more. So did Fab5. Fab5's forehead shone with sweat. Birds and traffic. Max tireless in the heavy sun.

This time it was Millicent who saw it. She gave a little jerk of the chin, threw a meaningful glance, then turned and kicked the ball hard at Max, who stood braced in the goal mouth. The police car. It was back now.

Max slid out a foot, and the ball spun upwards into his hands. Fab5 clapped. Millicent clapped.

The police car had drawn up in a parking space fifty metres beyond us. *Probably nothing.*

I ran a few metres towards the car, then turned to face Max. 'Max,' I shouted. 'To me!' I pointed at my head.

Max punted the ball. I missed it deliberately, then chased after it towards the police car.

'Da-ad . . .'

I recognised the officer in the front seat. A cold dread came upon me. They were going to do it now, then. *In front of my son.*

I turned and kicked the ball as hard as I could. It landed short. Millicent walked slowly over towards it. Then she turned, and kicked the ball hard towards Max, who made a point of catching it in one hand.

I walked stiffly back towards my family. *Why now? Why here?*

Max kicked the ball towards Millicent. Fab5 intercepted it, and kicked it straight at the goal. Max jumped, stretching high, but the ball passed above him.

'Ya wee beauty!' shouted Fab5.

'No way!' shouted Max.

'Is it my fault you can't reach, wee guy?'

'Mum?'

Millicent gave an exaggerated shrug. 'What do I know?'

I caught her eye and saw in her look the same fear that I felt. I nodded. She nodded. She had seen the car.

'Ice cream,' I said. 'Mum's buying.'

'Can I have a Magnum, Mum? And a Fanta?'

'You're going with her.' *Keep it light. Keep it normal.* 'One or the other, Max. Not both.'

'Why? Why can't *you* go?'

'Just go, Max.'

'But Fab5 and me are the best, so you and Mum should go.'

'Max.'

'What?'

'Do you want an ice cream or not?'

'Why do you always have to be so mean, when you're pretending to be generous?'

'I told you to go, Max.'

Max stood, arms folded, resentment and defiance. 'You don't decide over me.'

'Actually, I do, Max.'

'Honey.' Millicent slipped her arm through Max's, and whispered something to him. Max looked up at me again, then nodded. They set off together towards the corner of the park. How did she always know the right thing to say?

Fab5 and I sat on a bench. The police car waited. The door did not open. We watched Millicent and Max disappear across the grass and the drying mud. Then we watched the police car again.

'They're wrong, you know,' said Fab5.

'About what?'

'London. Like it's all bad weather and mouthy cockneys.'

A second car drew up beside the first. Unmarked. The uniformed officer opened his door and went to stand by the passenger window of the unmarked car. I wondered what would happen if I stood up and walked away. But this had to be faced.

'We haven't seen any cockneys,' I said.

'Any*how* . . .' He raised his dark glasses, looked searchingly at me.

'I'm OK,' I said. 'Thanks for asking.'

Fab5 nodded. I could see Millicent and Max crossing the street at the far end of the park. Fab5 was watching them too.

'I'm almost starting to think she doesn't hate me,' he said.

'You took Max to school.'

'And?'

'Actions count for Millicent. It's harder for her to hate you when she sees you doing right.'

The uniformed officer was still talking to his superior through the car window. What was taking them so long?

'She found some letters I maybe shouldn't have kept. What?'

'What was in the letters, friend?'

'Nothing that she didn't already know.'

The uniformed officer had turned to face us. He was staring openly now.

'I've been faithful to her from the day we met. She must know that. Why? What did you tell her?'

'I told her what you were like.'

'Cheers.'

'You slept with a *lot* of women. Truth, friend.'

They were out of the car, now, looking at us: the two plain-clothes officers who had interviewed Millicent and me. What was keeping them?

'Again, Fab5, cheers.'

'You changed. I told her that too.'

The detectives were halfway across the grass now, flanked by the uniformed officer. They would be with us in a moment.

Fab5 took off his dark glasses.

'It's going to be OK, Alex, man.'

'Is it?'

'Why wouldn't it be?'

At the far end of the park I could see Max and Millicent. Max was carrying what looked like a small cardboard box, slowly, and with infinite care.

'Fab5,' I said, 'how do you manage to be such a twat and such a *mensch* at the same time?'

150

'Practice, *Habibi*,' he said, 'practice.'

'I should stop taking you at face value.'

'You're welcome, Alex.'

Fab5 stood up and nodded at the police officers, then set off to intercept Millicent and Max.

From the back of the marked police car I watched my friend, my wife and my son. It was an interview, the police had said, nothing more.

Fab5 had caught up with Millicent and Max; they stood, easy in the sunlight, talking as if all was well with the world. Grass and trees, dogs and traffic: London pastoral.

The three police officers leaned against the car, talking lazily. Why three? And why here? Was this some sort of message to my family? To my eleven-year-old son? I felt the anger begin to rise in me.

You are not under arrest. *Breathe.*

I saw Max hand Fab5 something from his box. An ice cream? I wondered what Fab5 had said to him. Hadn't he seen the cars? The police?

'He's eleven, you evil bastards.'

I must have said it out loud. The door opened, and the female detective looked in.

'Something you wanted to say, Mr Mercer?'

I bit back my anger, smiled my most appeasing smile. 'Any sense of how long we're likely to be here?'

'Just a little catch-up between colleagues.' She returned my smile. Sympathetic and warm. She closed the door.

Fab5 produced an electric pink Frisbee. I watched the three of them, as they played one-handed, the other hand holding what must be iced lollies, catching the Frisbee on extended index fingers, spinning it away again on practised flicks of the wrist; vibrant pink against the desiccated grass.

Max never once looked towards the police car. My brave little boy.

He knows.

The uniformed policeman got in and started the engine. 'Seat belt on, sir?'

The car pulled away slowly, and I opened the window. The fear was upon me again, as if this was some sort of parting. *My wife, my child.* Behind us the unmarked car pulled out, the officers in the front seats looking relaxed and professional. The man said something to the woman, and they both laughed. They had nothing on me. They were staging this to make a point. *Breathe.*

No one reacted as the police cars passed by.

My wife could really throw. I wondered if she was faking the claps and the whoops as Fab5 threw himself to the ground, caught the Frisbee on his right index finger, jumped up and threw it to Max in a single fluid gesture. It certainly didn't look as if she was faking.

They could be any North London family. Woman, man, child. Is that what we look like when we're out together, I wondered. Do we make it look that good?

Three chairs, a table, a recording device. The walls were white and recently painted, the floor tiled in cracked slate. Across the white table were two white plastic chairs. My own chair – grey fabric – was more comfortable. A message, perhaps: this is going to take a long time.

A man in plain clothes came in with biscuits and a cup of black coffee. He asked me if I wanted a newspaper. 'Could be a bit of a wait.'

'You're Scottish,' I said. Glasgow, I thought.

'Aye,' he said, 'right enough.' Broad smile. Thirty, maybe. Close-cropped dark hair. '*Guardian*, is it?'

'How could you tell?'

He shrugged. 'You develop a sense for these things.'

'Are you even allowed to bring me a paper?'

'Nothing in the rules says I can't.'

'OK,' I said, 'sure, then. Thanks.'

152

I had made a point of not needing to make a phone call. And besides, there was no one I wanted to speak to: not a lawyer, because I didn't want the police to think that I needed a lawyer; not Millicent, because she knew where I was and if I rang it might alarm Max; I certainly wasn't going to tell my mother I was being questioned by the police.

There were graffiti scratched deep into the table. Davey S had been here. Laleh had been here, along with most of her crew. Marshall from Gorebridge had been here. So had Cookie, also from Gorebridge.

I was certain the police couldn't search the house if they didn't arrest me. I was almost certain of that.

'One *Guardian*.'

He was back with the paper. His name was Paul, and he took *The Times* himself. He'd been in London two years. He was still finding it tough down here.

'It's a great city,' I said.

'Aye, maybe we just see the wrong side of it,' he said. 'Makes a man cynical.'

'You don't project cynicism,' I said.

'Good to know, mate. Good to know.' He hovered by the door, smiling as if we were friends.

'So, Paul,' I said, 'is this all part of the process?'

'How do you mean?'

'I'm just wondering whether you're the *good cop*?'

The smile froze. 'I was just making conversation, mate.'

'You can go,' I said. 'I have everything I need. I've been offered counselling. Thanks for the paper.'

When he had left I tried to pick up the coffee cup that he had given me. My hand knocked it over; it simply missed the cup: a badly calibrated machine. I hadn't meant to sound so ungrateful; I must be more nervous than I realised.

I was alone for another hour. I picked up the paper several times, but couldn't concentrate on the stories, couldn't connect the sentences.

If the police didn't arrest me I would burn Caroline's letter. It was stupid to have kept it. Incriminating, almost: the man it described was obsessive and out of control. *I am no longer that man.*

I looked around me, as I had many times that hour. There was no camera. No one-way mirror. *They can't read your thoughts.* I was not under arrest. I was not under caution. I could leave if I wanted.

The same female detective who had interviewed me before. I asked if she could give me her card again, which she did.

She smiled at me, and I think I smiled at her. This was an interview. Nothing more. I was here to help.

Why did I struggle with her name? She was June. Of course she was June.

'I'm sorry for the wait,' she said.

'Your colleague kindly brought me a paper,' I said. *Eye contact.*

'Good,' she said.

'Good,' I said.

'Good.'

She turned on the audio recorder. Then she gave her name, and my name, and my address, and my age. She gave the date, then checked her watch, and gave the time.

Then she looked at me. I tried to look back. *Eye contact.*

'Mr Mercer, you understand, do you not, that you have the right to a lawyer?'

'Yes.'

'And you are happy to proceed without legal representation?'

'Yes.' I wanted her sympathy now, and a lawyer wouldn't help with that.

'So,' she said, 'you and your son found the body of Mr Bryce on the evening of first July, as discussed in our interview of second July.'

154

I said nothing. What was she expecting me to say?

'Do you have anything you wish to add to the recollections you gave then?'

'No.' I still remembered her kindness across the kitchen table. I hadn't wanted her to feel sorry for me then. I wanted her sympathy now, though. 'It hasn't been an easy time.' *Eye contact.*

'And we are aware that discovery of a body can be a traumatic event. You have been made aware that counselling services are available, should you wish.'

Surely she couldn't ask me whether I had seen a counsellor? Wasn't that privileged? And surely it could never count against me that I hadn't?

'Everyone has been very kind.' Her mouth smiled. There was a keenness to her gaze that I hadn't seen before, a tilt of the head that suggested distance. *Raptor.*

'Mr Mercer, what was your state of mind on the evening of the thirtieth of June?'

'You mean the first of July?'

'No, Mr Mercer, I mean the evening of the thirtieth of June. The evening before your . . . discovery of the body.'

Why the pause before the word discovery? What was she implying?

'You're asking me to account for my movements?'

'No, Mr Mercer. I'm asking you to describe your state of mind.'

'Normal. Whatever that is.'

'And what's normal, for you?'

'Nothing out of the ordinary.'

'I see.' She smiled. Then she produced a typescript from a briefcase and turned to a page marked with a Post-it.

'A neighbour of yours reports hearing raised voices in your house on the night of the thirtieth of June.'

'Raised voices?'

'An argument. Which continued from roughly eleven fifteen to eleven forty-five.'

'A neighbour?'

'Yes.'

'You're talking about Mr Ashani.'

'I'm afraid that I can't share those details with you at this point. Mr Mercer, did you and your wife argue between those hours?'

'I don't remember.' Still that professional smile. Still the keenness of the eyes. Yellow-grey, unblinking.

'Did you and your wife argue between those times?'

'I don't know. Maybe.'

'Maybe?'

'Yes.'

'That was very faint.' She gestured towards the recorder. 'Could you repeat your last answer?'

'Yes. We argued.'

The longest of pauses. Her eyes blazed. I tried to smile back. *Eye contact.* I brought the cup to my lips, realised it was empty. Smiled again. Put the cup down.

'Mr Mercer, I'm going to read from the transcript of the interview with your neighbour. All right?'

'All right.'

She read without inflection, her voice flat, like a bored clerk on a long and tedious telephone call. 'You fucking bitch. You fucking little bitch. I'm going to make you pay for that. Jesus. Next time I meet a bitch like you in a pub, the last thing I'm going to do is marry her. Christ on the fucking cross.'

The smile was gone now. Her grey-gold eyes stared. Waiting. Hungry, almost.

'It's the kind of thing I could have said.'

'Did you say it, Mr Mercer?'

'Yes. I probably did.'

'You probably did?'

'I said it.'

She closed the transcript, placed it carefully in front of her on the table. 'Well now.' The smile was back. Patient, without

156

warmth. She followed my gaze as I looked towards the door. Would she stop me if I got up to leave? Would she arrest me?

Something in me – almost a voice – told me that she couldn't search the house if she arrested me at the police station; that she could only search the place where the arrest was made. I was sure – almost sure – that I had read that somewhere. Had I read that somewhere? Why had I said no to a lawyer?

I forced myself to meet her gaze. 'You're quoting selectively,' I said.

'I'm sorry, Mr Mercer? Could you explain yourself?'

'You're taking my words out of context.' My voice sounded injured; the voice of a petulant child.

'And how would *you* contextualise your words, Mr Mercer? Let me remind *you* of what *you* said: "You fucking little bitch. I'm going to make you pay for that." We agree – do we not – that you said that?'

'Yes. Look . . .'

'Yes?'

'That's not how it was said.'

'Your voice was raised, was it not?'

'That's not what I mean.'

'Was your voice raised?'

'Obviously. Otherwise Mr Ashani wouldn't have heard me.'

'Well, quite,' she said. 'Thank you.'

'So it was Mr Ashani . . .'

'. . . a neighbour . . .'

'. . . who heard us through the wall. He's an old man, and he doesn't understand context.'

'And again, what was the context?'

'We were making up.'

She laughed. She actually laughed. She put her hand to her mouth, then composed herself. 'Go on, Mr Mercer.'

'Look at your transcript again.'

'And why would I do that, Mr Mercer?'

'Because you're leaving out what Millicent said.'

'And what did your wife say?'

'She called me motherfucker, and told me I was a jerked-up little dweeb. We were laughing. Didn't he say we were laughing?'

She leafed lazily through her transcript, made a play of not looking at me.

'We were sharing a bottle of wine; we were laughing.'

'Really, Mr Mercer? Really?'

'Really. Motherfucker is a term of affection. So's bitch.'

'Unfortunately, Mr Mercer, I have no record of your wife's reply, affectionate or otherwise.'

'I would never use the word *bitch* in anger.' I was struggling to keep the desperation from my voice. 'It's an ironic use.'

'Let's move on, shall we?'

'No,' I said, 'let's not, until we've discussed why I said it.'

'Mr Mercer,' she said, smiling broadly, 'I'm just trying to establish the facts. It's time to move on.'

They knew about Millicent's affair with Bryce. They had interviewed someone who worked at the Swedish who could only have been the manager. He had heard everything. The description he gave of my swearing didn't make it sound in any way ironic. Apparently I had used words stronger than *bloody*.

The detective made it very clear what she thought of me. It's hard to explain to a female police officer why you have used the word *cunting* in a loud argument with your wife, or why you have screamed the same word at the manager of a Swedish café. 'I didn't scream it,' I wanted to say. 'I was never that loud.' They had also spoken to someone who had seen me swearing and sucking my thumb in the street. Ranting, the description said. *Ranting*.

I tried to bring her back to my argument with Millicent the night before the neighbour died. It wasn't about the affair, I wanted to say. It was about our son. *I didn't know about the affair*. It was about vegetables, and sweets, and ice cream, and fruit. Parent stuff, and parents shout at each other about this stuff. About how much cheese is too much cheese, and how many burgers are too many burgers. My wife thinks I make a *thing* about food, and it doesn't need to be a *thing*. We were done, by the time I called her a bitch. We'd moved on. We were laughing. And anyway, who doesn't shout about this stuff?

But she kept moving the conversation forwards, never letting the subject rest for long enough for me to explain myself. I sounded lame. I sounded petulant. I sounded like a hurt child.

She left me alone. Paul came in and accompanied me to the toilet, then fetched another coffee for me. He was brisk and completely without warmth. I wondered what she had said to him.

I should have called a lawyer. I wondered what I would think, confronted cold with a man like me and a corpse in the house next door. They had spoken to a lot of people about me, and the theme that kept emerging was anger. Maybe that was me, the ranting man. A man in thrall to rage. Ranting in the home. Ranting in the café. Ranting in the street.

A small step from rage to jealous rage.

I drew myself together. So far they had nothing on me, though. Not really. Apart from the anger. And even if I was angry, there's no law against anger, is there? Not if you don't act on it. I sat for a while longer, sideways in my chair, feet on the table.

Then I took out my phone. They hadn't asked me to hand it over, and they hadn't told me not to use it. I checked that the voice recorder wasn't recording; I had seen the detective turn it off, but I wanted to be sure. As far as I could tell it was off.

I dialled a number from memory. It rang twice before she rejected the call, as I knew she would. 'I'm not here, I'm sorry to say.' Her rock-crystal voice, the careless precision of her diction. 'Leave me a message and of course I'll call you back.'

I could only hope that she would listen to my message, that she wouldn't simply press 3 and leave me to my fate.

'Caroline,' I said, 'Alex. It's Alex. And I'm sorry for this. I'm truly sorry. But if the police want to speak to you about me, I need to speak to you first. I can and will explain.'

After an hour Paul came in with a cup of coffee.

'Am I free to go?' I asked him.

'You could . . .' he said. 'You're not under arrest.'

'I can?'

'I wouldn't, though.'

'OK.' I said. 'Why not?'

He made a gesture that I couldn't read, and left the room.

I was tired now, and irritable from the coffee. I hadn't eaten in hours.

June came back in and I asked her if I could go.

'Would you *like* to leave, Mr Mercer?'

Something in her manner suggested that leaving would be a very bad idea.

'I'll stay,' I said.

'All right,' she said. She turned the recorder back on, and told the machine what time it was. 'Mr Mercer, there's a piece of information to which I'd like to know your reaction.'

'Would it be possible to have a sandwich or something?'

'This won't take long.'

That raptor smile. Those searching eyes.

'Mr Mercer, would it surprise you to know that we believe your neighbour Mr Bryce was murdered?'

'Not really.'

'That doesn't surprise you?'

'There's been a lot of police activity in the neighbour's house.'

'You surmised that from our activity?' Her head tilted gently from one side to the other, then back. The smile was gone. I met her gaze for a moment, then looked away.

'Yes. And the style of your questions suggests you think something's wrong. You asked me not to leave the country.'

160

'I see.' Some change in her, as if I had revealed a piece of myself that I should have kept hidden. She sat for a moment, consulted her papers. Then she seemed to reach a decision.

'Mr Mercer, do you know why we think your neighbour was murdered?'

'No,' I said. 'Only that you think he was.' *Breathe.*

'I see.'

She produced a colour print. A standard British three-pin plug, dismantled. She spoke an evidence number into the recorder.

'Mr Mercer is now studying the photograph. Mr Mercer, do you notice anything about this that you wish to comment on?'

'It's correctly wired.'

'It is indeed correctly wired.'

'Someone has replaced the fuse with a piece of metal.'

'Yes,' she said, '*some*one has.'

Her eyes blazed. Her smile was back.

'Mr Mercer, you will notice the cord which is attached to the plug.'

'It's from an iron, or a heater, or something.'

'Yes. It is in fact from the iron that was found in the bath beside Mr Bryce. The iron that caused Mr Bryce's death by electrocution.'

Was she accusing me? She was still smiling, and there was something more human about the smile now, a warmth, as if she were inviting me to share a confidence.

'OK,' I said, 'I suppose if you wanted to kill yourself you would modify your iron in this way.'

'If indeed you owned an iron.'

'He didn't own an iron?'

'A man of expensive tastes.'

I thought of the dry-cleaning bags on his kitchen table.

'Mr Mercer, can you account for your movements in the three hours before your discovery of the body of Mr Bryce?'

'I was working. Viewing for an edit.'

'Would that be something you were doing from home?'

'Yes,' I said, defensively.

'Can anyone verify that?'

'Max, maybe.'

She stood up, made a point of looking at her watch. She was still smiling that warm, encouraging smile. 'Useful to know.' She reached out her hand, and I shook it. 'Thank you for coming in, Mr Mercer. One of my colleagues will drive you home.'

'But . . .' I looked at the recording machine. She reached over and turned it off.

'It's been a long day for you. I'm sure you'll be glad to spend time with your wife and your son.'

While you still can, I thought. She means while you still can.

I sat in a plastic seat in the public area of the station, waiting for someone to drive me home. The desk sergeant sat reading a newspaper. Why had I agreed to be driven? I could easily walk.

They had nothing on me – I was certain of that. And yet the more I thought about the conversation with the detective, the more I admired her. She had made no threats. She had made no accusation. She had kept me waiting, but not long enough that I had reason to complain. She had seen to it that her colleagues had behaved impeccably towards me. She had the measure of people like me. She had completely done me over.

It was a brilliant piece of staging. My stomach was cramping up from the bad coffee and the lack of food. I was on edge, and desperately wanted a cigarette. But she had my measure. She had known I wouldn't get up and leave.

This wasn't about the recording. I had said nothing that would incriminate me on a transcript. I was certain of that.

No, it was all about timing, about making sure I was vulnerable, about making certain that I felt alone. It was about demonstrating her lack of empathy towards me, about timing the moment her empathy returned. It was about that one piece of information. She was working a hunch.

She wanted to know what I thought. What I felt. *'If indeed you owned an iron.'* Her eyes on my face. *Confess.*

'Alex.'

A form, all arms and shoulders and summer prints. A voice I knew. Bracelets sighing metallic on her slender arm.

'What?' I was staring at the floor.

'Alex, are you OK?'

I looked up. Rose. Pretty, etiolated Rose. Rose who didn't know her own strength.

The answer was no, of course I wasn't anything like OK, but I wasn't going to tell her that. I looked at her, and wanted Millicent. Millicent would know what to do. Millicent always knew.

'Hi,' I said. I drew myself up, sat as casually as I could, tried to project *OK*. I risked a smile. She smiled back.

'I'm waiting for a lift. This place gives me the creeps.'

'I'm waiting for a lift too.'

She nodded. She really was very pretty, in that delicate English way of hers. What did she want from me?

I picked up a newspaper. We sat there next to each other pretending to read, while the duty sergeant pretended to be busy with paperwork.

'Alex,' she said after a time, 'Alex, do you have to go straight home?'

At the Sacred Cock I bought two double whiskies. We sat at a table near the bar, said very little, stared into our drinks. Millicent thought I was still at the police station. I couldn't shake the feeling that Rose and I shared a secret, although I didn't yet know what that secret was.

I was shaken by the interview at the police station; Rose seemed shaken too. Perhaps that was all it was. Perhaps that was why I was here with her, and not at home with Millicent and Max.

'Rose,' I said.

She spoke my name just as I spoke hers.

'Jinx,' she said. 'Almost.'

'Yeah,' I said, 'almost.'

I had to ask her first. 'What were you doing there?' I needed time to decide how to explain myself to her.

'That was my question to you, Alex.'

'You first.'

She smiled. She liked me, and I didn't want to throw that away.

'They wanted to know why I walked through their crime scene. Isn't there supposed to be tape? Alex, did you know the house was a crime scene?'

'You broke their lock, Rose. Did you really not wonder?'

'Grief,' she said. She picked up a whisky and drank it down. 'Does weird things to you. I don't know what I thought that lock was doing there. They didn't like that as an answer, obviously. Though it's the truth. Cheers, by the way.'

'Cheers.'

'Alex, did they ask you about me? About whether you heard me opening drawers in the kitchen?'

'No,' I said. 'No, they didn't ask me that.'

'Well,' she said, 'somehow they knew. You would have told them if they'd asked you, wouldn't you?'

'I suppose so.'

'They were really interested in why I was opening drawers in the kitchen. I mean, *really* interested. And you really didn't tell them you heard me?'

'You have my word on that.'

'Thanks, Alex.'

'Welcome.'

Perhaps this was good. Perhaps I wouldn't have to tell her much about why I had been at the police station.

'I was trying to make a cup of tea. I was looking for tea. I kept telling them that. And they asked me all these questions. And it's all so polite and so by-the-book that it takes you a while to realise they're accusing you of murdering your brother and stealing his money. And looking for tea in his drawers is some kind of evidence of that. Although they never quite say any of that, of course. You're meant to draw the inference.'

His money? I reached across and rubbed her shoulder. A gesture of support. An innocent gesture. But she leaned back into me, took my other hand in hers.

'He didn't have any money,' she said, angry suddenly. 'Or nothing to speak of. Couldn't get a deposit together. The architect without a house.'

'He was an architect?'

'In name only. Never made a building. Just worked on other architects' buildings. Managed their projects. It's almost funny.'

'That's still an architect, isn't it?'

'No, it's an architectural project manager.' She looked around at me. I smiled awkwardly. She smiled back. 'Why are you being so kind to me, Alex?'

I thought of Millicent walking into the pub at that moment, and I patted Rose on the back and drew gently away from her.

'I'm not,' I said. 'I'm not being kind.'

'You are,' she said. She squeezed my hand. I must have made some small gesture of rejection. 'I really wasn't presuming,' she said. 'This is not a pass. Obviously.' She sighed. 'You know, they started pressing me to account for my movements.'

Before I could answer she was at the bar. I texted Millicent, said I would be home in an hour or so.

'Alex.' The pencil moustache and the brilliantined hair. It was strange to see him in t-shirt and jeans. Wrong, somehow.

'Mr Sharpe. Quick drink on the way home.' Had he seen Rose? And what if he had?

'How's Max?' he said.

'I wanted to ask you the same question, Mr Sharpe.'

'Nothing out of the ordinary.'

A text message from Millicent. My phone was lying on the table. Mr Sharpe's eyes flicked from the phone to the bag that Rose had left on her seat. I saw him register the bag, and the two empty glasses. Rose would be back in a moment.

'A friend,' I said. 'Sister of our dead neighbour.' Easier to explain now. Less embarrassing.

'A difficult time for all of you,' he said.

Rose came back with two more whiskies. I looked at Rose. I looked at Mr Sharpe.

'Good to see you, Alex.' He nodded at Rose and left us alone.

'Trebles,' said Rose. 'Sorry.'

'Nothing to apologise for.'

I picked up my phone. Millicent still thought I was at the police station. 'Courage, honey,' she had texted back. 'You have the strength.' What was I doing here?

I saw Mr Sharpe sitting at a table with a very beautiful woman in a yellow satin dress. They were looking directly at Rose, and at me. Then they looked at each other and exchanged words. Don't judge me, I thought. This is not what you think.

I drank down my whisky, then told Rose I had to go. She stood up with me, held on to my hand, and for a moment I wanted to sit down beside her again.

'Before today it would never have occurred to me that I might say this,' she said. 'I'm *embarrassed* to be saying it, but after today I slightly feel I have to.' She was holding my hand tightly now.

'I didn't kill my brother, Alex.'

'I know.'

'Surely those are words I shouldn't feel I have to say. My own brother.' She gave a bitter little laugh.

'I know,' I said. 'I know.'

Millicent was reading to Max. She was lying on her back on the sofa, book in hand. Max was stretched out on the floor, a pillow under his head. He turned gently as I came in.

'Mum said I could stay up till you came.'

My wife; my son: waiting for me to walk through the door. Love coursed through me like a feeling forgotten. *Look at that.* Love unexpected. Love intense. Love unconditional. *Look at that.*

'Hey,' said Millicent.

'Hi,' I said.

Max stood, and as I walked towards him he wrapped his arms very tightly around me. 'Oh, Max,' I said, 'oh, my little boy.' *Flesh of my flesh.* I lifted him high. Spun him around.

'You can put me down now,' he said. I lowered him to the floor. Millicent was at my side, and we clung to each other, all three of us. The mighty Alexander, weary from battle, returns to his woman and his child. Look at that, I wanted to say, to shout, to scream: look at that and tell me it's not real.

There was something in Millicent's expression, though.

'What?' I said. 'What, Millicent?'

'Mum *said* they wouldn't arrest you. *And* they didn't find anything.'

'What?'

'The police were here, honey.'

'Mum let them in. They didn't find anything though.'

'What?' I said again.

Millicent looked up at me and nodded guiltily. She hadn't wanted me to find out this way.

'All right,' I said. 'They didn't tell me they had a warrant.'

'Mum let them in anyway,' said Max.

'They were polite,' said Millicent. 'And it kind of felt like they could be *not* polite if I said they had to come back with a warrant.'

'They didn't have a warrant?'

She shook her head.

'Is that bad, Dad?' said Max.

That pleading look in Millicent's eye.

'No, Max, I think your mum probably made the right decision. She did exactly the right thing.'

Millicent looked surprised. 'Thank you,' she mouthed.

'I'm so sorry,' I mouthed back.

'Why are you sorry, Dad? You didn't do anything, did you?'

'No, Max, I didn't. But I'm sorry it happened when I wasn't here.'

A wan smile from Millicent.

'Mum made them put everything back. Especially my stuff. And she made them do my room first, so it was finished first. They were in the garden and everything. And they went through the bins even though I told them not to because they wouldn't find anything there. Like, opening the bags and stuff. It was rank.'

'I bet it was.' I looked at Millicent. *Did they?* Her eyes told me they had found nothing. Weird, I thought, but I let it pass.

'Mum said it smelled like the anus of Satan. Didn't you, Mum?'

'I may have whispered that to you, Max.'

'And three of them looked in the loft. Not at the same time, though.'

Please tell me no.

'They were there for ages on the ladder with torches – like one, and then the other one, and the other one – but they didn't go in.'

'They didn't?'

'Undisturbed dust,' said Millicent.

'Yeah,' said Max. 'Like if someone went in there you could

see it but you couldn't see it so no one did. I could hear them talking about it outside my door, even though it was closed and they were whispering.'

'Seems strange,' I said.

Unless they were looking for something very specific.

'I know, right?' said Max. 'Except then Foxxa went and hid up there and you could see all her footprints, and she wouldn't come down till they went. And then Mum had to give them her computer.'

I looked at Millicent, and she nodded, weary. She felt violated – I could see that – she was being strong for Max's sake.

'Yeah,' she said neutrally, 'they're going to want to take a look at yours too, Alex.'

'Mum said we're going to fight this together. Because we're a family.'

'Yes,' I said. 'That's exactly what we're going to do, Max. Family's exactly what we are.'

My little tribe.

'We're going to fight.'

When Max was in bed I told Millicent about going for a drink with Rose.

'Only because of the interrogation,' I said. 'There's nothing more to it than that.'

'OK,' she said.

'I guess I'm more susceptible than I thought,' I said. 'That detective: I swear, by the end of it, you want to confess to murder because she's started being nice again.'

'Psychology 101.' She smiled, and I was taken aback by the look in her eye.

'You almost want to be able to help,' I said. 'You feel as if you could confess, and everything would be just fine.'

'Honey, that stuff works. That's why it's Psychology 101. It works even when you know why it works. *Every*one is susceptible.'

'Anyway,' I said, 'Rose seemed to understand. So I went to the pub with her. I probably shouldn't have.' Still that patient look in Millicent's eye. Why was she minded to forgive me? 'There was just this weird momentary closeness between us.'

'I get it, Alex. It's OK.'

'Just . . . Sorry, it's just such a strange experience.'

'It's OK. You needed to be with someone who felt what you felt.'

'Thanks,' I said. 'Thank you for understanding that. I didn't know if you would.'

'Yeah,' she said. 'Yeah, Alex, I understand your need to be understood.'

She led me up the stairs. We undressed and sat shyly on the edge of the bed, like guilty teenagers.

'What?' we kept saying to each other. 'What?'

She had changed the sheets.

'What?'

'What?'

She got up and closed the curtains, sat a little nearer to me.

'What?' I said.

'What?'

'Stop laughing at me, Millicent.'

'Stop laughing at *me*.' She mimed hiding her breasts and pubis. 'It's most intimidating.'

'I'm not laughing at you.'

'Me neither.'

'What then?'

'I don't know.'

'And move your hands.'

She stretched her arms away from her body.

'You're very beautiful, Millicent,' I said. 'The way your breasts frame your face, and your hair frames your breasts, and your arms frame your hair.'

'Always with the framing devices,' she said, laughing.

She leaned across and kissed me very deeply.

Then she drew away and looked me up and down.

'What?' I said. 'What?'

'Well, look at you, all hard.'

I kissed her, and she kissed me hungrily back, pressed her pubic bone into mine.

'I don't think I've ever seen you more beautiful, Millicent,' I said. I drew gently away from her, pushed myself down the bed, brought my head level with the tops of her thighs.

'Really?' she said.

'Really.'

For a while I traced slow circles round her clitoris. My tongue's very tip. This way. That way. This way again. For a while she lay still, as my tongue travelled first one way, then the other. The lightest of touches, barely there.

Time passed. The tension in her body built. Time stopped.

I held her on the brink of orgasm for as long as I could. When she tilted her hips up to meet me I drew away gently and waited, kissing the tops of her thighs, resting my cheek against the springy softness of those tiny dark hairs. When the tension in her body subsided I began again.

'This isn't fair, Alex,' she said, her voice distant.

Never leave me, I thought. You must never leave me.

I held her in my arms and we dozed. When I woke she was looking down at me.

'Hey.'

'Hi,' I said.

She laughed, ran her hand through her hair. 'So this was a little unexpected. It's not like either of us had a good day.'

'No,' I said. 'No, this was not a good day.'

'Kind of helps to remember why we're together.'

'You're a great fuck.' I arched upwards, made to kiss her. She put an arm on my chest and pushed me back down.

'Don't pretend that was just about sex, Alex. You know there's more to it than that.'

'And you know that I love you.'

'Simplify, please.'

'I love you.'

'We worked together today, Alex. That's who we are. *This* was what our marriage is.'

We lay for a while, hands in each other's hair, face against face, watching each other in extreme close-up. The gold flecks in her dark eyes. The sadness in those eyes, though, even when she smiled. Always there, though I had not always known what it was. Even when we had been happiest together it had never really gone away.

'Bryce was murdered, you know.' I wished I could have found a kinder, gentler way to tell her.

'No,' she said. 'No, I don't believe that he was.'

'She said they have proof, love. I'm so very sorry.'

She had loved Bryce, after all. No matter how she had hurt me, she deserved some consideration for that.

'Alex,' she said, 'he was a little unstable. *More* than a little unstable. I can believe he would take his own life.'

'But someone put a piece of metal in the plug. In place of the fuse. They showed me pictures.'

'Believe me, Alex, it's credible that he would do that.'

'It sounded *very* credible when the detective told me,' I said, lamely. 'I'm explaining badly.'

I could see her weighing her thoughts.

'OK, Alex,' she said. 'Here it is . . .'

She made as if to speak; it was as if the thought froze on her lips.

'What is it, Millicent?'

'Bryce had some dark days.'

'He was a depressive?'

'He lost a little girl too, Alex.'

'What? What are you saying?'

'Her name was Lana. She was a year old. She died. Viral meningitis.'

'Wow,' I said.

That made a horrible kind of sense.

'His world fell apart. He lost everything, you know. His relationship with Lana's mother broke down, and he lost his job, and he had to begin again from scratch. Like he almost ended up on the street.'

'OK,' I said, 'I see.'

'He went from nothing, to this . . .' she nodded through the wall towards Bryce's house '. . . in the space of three years.'

'Wow,' I said.

'So,' said Millicent, 'I guess I'm wondering what your reaction is.'

Strangers with a common experience. A shared narrative of recovery. And a husband who was away a lot.

'I can see how that would make him attractive to you.'

'Please don't be snitty, Alex. This was not an easy thing to talk about.'

'I'm not being snitty. I can really see how that would make him attractive to you, Millicent.' I took her hand, saw surprise in her eyes. 'I mean, there's a logic to this,' I said, 'isn't there? And he was good to you.' I was fighting back the tears now. 'And people have affairs because something is missing in their lives. Don't they?'

She nodded, uncertain, as if weighing her thoughts.

'And I was missing from yours.'

'Maybe so,' she said, clutching my hand in both of hers.

'He listened. I didn't.'

She swallowed hard, and I could see that she too was trying not to cry. We sat there for a while, our hands knotted together.

'Yeah,' she said. 'He listened.'

'I'm listening now,' I said, 'if it's not too late.'

She said nothing. I cradled her to me. Five minutes later she was asleep.

*   *   *

173

At the dark of night I woke from a dream. A knife in my back, in a street very like ours. No Max. No Millicent. The more I tried to remember the dream, the more it slipped from me. Probably nothing.

That other thing: something the detective had said; or maybe Rose. Why hadn't I told Millicent the other thing? I needed her to understand the other thing. I would tell her the other thing when she woke up. I would wake her and tell her now. Perhaps she already knew.

The neighbour didn't own his house.

I lay, wanting to wake Millicent, wanting to tell her that. But as my thoughts cleared I realised that wasn't the other thing at all. The other thing was gone. All I knew now was that the other thing had been worse. Much, much worse.

I think the other thing might have been about Millicent.

13

On Sunday morning I fetched the stepladder from the back garden. It was five and already light. If Millicent asked what I was doing, I had my excuse ready.

The ladder scraped the walls on the way up. If Max woke, if he asked me what I was doing, I would answer that I couldn't sleep – that much was true – and that I was looking for photos that showed a gentler side of my father. I needed to be reminded of my father without his gun, my father without his army-issue leather belt. Max would understand that, I thought. Millicent would understand too. She knew about the beatings. She was the only person I had told.

The bulb glowed dully, pathetic in the windowless dark. The attic had lain undisturbed for years, the floor heaped with boxes and bags full of clothes. Only the cat had left her mark here, tripping teasingly about on the plasterboard floor as the police watched from the ladder, her pawprints a delicate grey-white in the grey-black of the dust.

I edged along the central beam. Above me the roof was high, though it raked so sharply down that I could touch it on both sides of me if I stretched out my hands. There was another beam above me, and I braced myself by pushing a hand hard up against it as I stepped carefully along the lower beam, careful not to step on to the plasterboard.

When I reached the middle of the room I made myself as tall as I could and curled my fingers around the upper beam. I found the envelope at once, well out of reach of Millicent or Max.

Inside the envelope was Caroline's letter. The letter was very short. She asked me to stop contacting her. Her next step, she said, would be the law.

I had made the mistake of not believing her. And there was the non-molestation order, which had been served on me that summer by a man in motorcycle leathers. The man had held my arm while he explained the terms. I must cease and desist. I must not establish contact with Caroline in any one of eleven listed ways. I felt again the strange spike of shame that I had felt then. And yes, I ceased, and I desisted.

I memorised the name and address of the solicitor. Then I put the letter and the non-molestation order back into the envelope. I was about to put them into my pocket when I heard a faint sound on the landing. Not quite a footstep, but something – a presence. Max?

I looked down at my feet on the beam. I could not move quickly from where I was. Not without making a great deal of noise, not without risking a fall.

A new noise. A faint metallic shimmer. The stepladder. I thought of Rose and her bracelets. And again, there it was, that shimmer sound. Max – I was sure of it. I slipped the envelope back on top of the beam. Burning it would have to wait. I began to move slowly to where I was sure the family photos were, somewhere in a looming mound of boxes and files. *Your granddad in happier times.*

A faint scrabbling sound at the top of the ladder.

The cat stood at the hatch, looking in.

'Foxxa, no.' At the sound of my voice she looked towards me, eager in the half-light.

I kept my voice at a half-whisper. 'Stay, Foxxa.'

The cat's ears pricked. *S*s, *T*s and *X*s, her favourite sounds. She hooked the end of her tail, ran out towards me along the beam. As I bent down to pick her up she jumped, stood for a while just out of reach, rubbing her head against a filthy wall.

'I was looking for the cat.'

'But how did she get up there, Alex?'

'I don't know.'

She spent five minutes sniffing at boxes, scent-marking their edges with the side of her head, always just beyond my grasp. Then she was satisfied, and joined me at the hatch, let me carry her down the stepladder, watched as I folded it, swearing under my breath. She walked one half-step ahead of me as I carried the ladder down our narrow wooden staircase, stopping to look up at me, as if daring me to fall over her, chirruping as she went. Then she stood, mewing by the back door, as I tried to open it while holding the ladder.

I put the ladder back in the garden. My white t-shirt and pants were covered in a thick, velvety powder. I took them off and put them into the washing machine in the lean-to. I stood naked in the garden, listening to birds and traffic. The cat sat washing in the sun, hind legs splayed. The day had barely started, and already it was too hot. I shut the back door and went upstairs to shower.

Then I went to my computer and looked up Caroline's solicitor. I wrote him a long mail in which I said that I had recently contacted Caroline directly; I acknowledged that this was unwise, and apologised. I said that I nonetheless needed to speak to Caroline about a matter of some importance. I hoped that she would forgive the intrusion. I would meet her anywhere – at his office if necessary – but I had to see her.

I stared at what I had written for ten minutes. It sounded desperate. I shortened it, and took out the offer to meet at her solicitor's office. My reason for needing to meet her seemed weak, but there wasn't much I could do about that. I added a line about having learned from the experience, and being grateful for his letter, despite the immediate pain it had brought me. Then I deleted the line about it bringing me pain, wrote that I had used the experience as an opportunity for growth, had turned my life around, was happily married now, with a son about to start secondary school.

I sent the mail before I could change my mind, then deleted it from my computer. I washed up and took out the rubbish. By the time Millicent and Max were up I had the downstairs of the house almost tidy; I had the door to the garden open, and breakfast on the table. Max fed pieces of bacon to the cat under the table and Millicent and I pretended not to notice.

I will explain about Caroline, when she contacts me. If she contacts me.

On Sunday evening as Millicent showered, I cooked a rare steak for her and a hamburger for Max, pushed a glass of Burgundy into her hand as she entered the kitchen. Max ate his hamburger in silence in front of the television. Millicent and I ate our steaks at the kitchen table, talking lightly about nothing that mattered.

Our truce was holding. There were moments where I was almost overcome by anger at what she had done. She had made a cuckold of me, and she had abandoned Max. But I understood a little better why she had done it. Bryce was a man who understood her pain. A morally unimpeachable man, who had rebuilt his life after a loss worse than ours. A man who had listened to her when her husband had not.

I thought I had been listening. Perhaps – I had to concede – perhaps after all I had not. Millicent had dealt me a bad hand, an unfair hand even. She had brought Bryce and the police crashing into my life. There had been no malice in it, though; she had been desperate. I would make the best play

I could with the cards she had dealt me, and together as a couple we would move on. This was liveable, I thought. We were getting by.

Max came into the kitchen. 'Dad,' he said, 'why don't you like Mr Ashani?'

'I do like Mr Ashani, Max.'

'So why don't you care that he's dead?'

'He isn't.'

'He didn't flush his toilet this morning. He always flushes it after breakfast.'

I laughed. 'Mr Ashani isn't dead, Max. Maybe he just hasn't been to the toilet yet.'

But Max was serious. 'He is.'

'He isn't.'

'He is.'

'He can't be.'

'Have you heard him in his house today, Dad?'

'No.'

'What about yesterday?'

'I wasn't really here yesterday.'

'He's dead.'

'Max, I know you've had a terrible shock with the death of the neighbour. But Mr Ashani isn't dead.'

Max went out of the kitchen into the front room. I glanced at Millicent; Millicent looked down at her food.

'What?' I said.

'Nothing.'

I heard the front door open, could hear traffic from the street.

'What?'

'So maybe you could not jump right in and tell him he's wrong, when we don't know if he's wrong.' She cut a strip of steak.

'Oh, come on. Of course he isn't dead.'

Through the wall I could hear Max ring Mr Ashani's

doorbell. Percussive, old, like a school bell. You could feel the vibration through the wall. Millicent chewed thoughtfully at her steak. I could hear people walking past in the street.

Millicent took a slug of wine. I heard Max ring the doorbell again. No other sound from the house next door.

'The man has a life,' I said. 'He's out.'

'Maybe so.'

'You think Max is right?'

'I just don't think he's necessarily wrong. It has been kind of quiet here.'

The bell was still ringing through the wall. Max must be leaning against the bell push now. Millicent was staring at me.

'OK,' I said. 'All right.'

I got up and went to find Max. He was standing in the street, leaning against Mr Ashani's brass bell push.

'I'm sorry, Max.'

'It's OK.' He took his weight off the bell push; the ringing stopped. 'Do you think he could be dead, though?'

'I'm sure he's fine.'

'Do you want to ring?'

'If he's in, he heard you, Max.'

Max got down on his knees, lifted the brass flap on the letterbox and looked through into Mr Ashani's front room. Then he put his lips to the gap and shouted, 'Mr Ashani!'

I had forgotten how piercing Max's shout could be. 'Max,' I said, 'don't.' I looked up and down the street.

'OK. Can you wait here, Dad?'

'Why?'

'Please, Dad?'

'All right.'

He went inside our house and up the stairs. The heat of the day lay heavy on the street even now: the sunlight dirty yellow, the air thick with car noise and pollen. In an hour the sun would be down, but the oppressive heat would remain.

Max came back downstairs with something in his hand. A thin blue shaft, ridged, slightly curved. He knelt on the mat, and pushed it through Mr Ashani's letterbox.

'What's that, Max?'

Max held the handle between his thumb and his forefinger, seemed to be adjusting the angle slightly, staring straight along it. He pushed back from the door and stood up.

'He is, Dad.'

'Is what?'

'Dead. Look.'

He handed the instrument to me. I recognised the handle of one of Max's old toothbrushes. He had cut off the bristles, and it looked as if he had used heat to angle the head upwards, then glued a small piece of mirrored glass to the head.

'Clever,' I said. 'How did you do this?'

'I used a candle to melt it.'

'Max,' I said, reflexively. 'You know you aren't supposed . . .'

'Yeah, Dad. I know. But look.'

I knelt down on the mat, pushed the toothbrush handle through the letterbox, tried to look down the shaft at the reflection in the glass.

I saw nothing. It was dark in Mr Ashani's house, and the bristles around the letterbox obscured my view. I looked up at Max.

'You're not doing it right, Dad. You have to turn it so you're looking downwards.'

I looked back in again, tried to remember how Max had held the brush. I took the handle in my thumb and forefinger, leaned my other fingers against the bristles inside the letterbox to push them out of the way, and closed my left eye. Slowly, very slowly, I rotated the handle until the mirror was angled towards the floor.

All I could see in the mirrored glass was a fraction of a whole; it was hard to form a recognisable image from the tiny pieces I could see. Then I found it. There, glistening dully, a small greyish ovoid around a smaller, darker grey circle.

It was an eye. It could only be an eye. And yet it was far too wide open, like an eye drawn by the hand of a small child.

It was as much as I could do to steady my hand. I tilted the mirrored head to where the other eye should have been, and found nothing. I tilted the mirror back, found the first eye again, and realised that its shape had confused me. It looked far too symmetrical to be real; the tiny muscles around it must be drawn tight in all directions. The slope near the temple was so steep that it matched the slope by the nose. I tilted the mirror in the other direction and this time I found the other eye. I stared at the eyes for the longest time, tilting the mirror from one to the other. They were looking straight up at me. Too open. Too alert.

I could make out details in the shadows now. I tilted the handle, followed the contours of the man, dark skin against the dark lacquered floorboards. Now that I had the eyes I knew where to look for his other features, turning the handle in tiny increments.

'Max,' I said. 'Find Mum. Get her to call an ambulance.' How long had he been there?

'But Dad, he's dead.'

'Call an ambulance, Max.'

My first kick achieved nothing. My foot stopped dead against the hardwood door. I felt the pain in my thigh, then felt it wind me like a blow to the groin. The door barely shook in its frame. I took a step back, breathing heavily. There were two locks, and I had kicked at the bottom of the door. Stupid, really, to think that would work.

This time I aimed directly between the locks, kicked out with the sole of my foot. The pain was bearable; I was ready for it. The door, however, did not move. I was getting nowhere. I didn't have the strength.

I went inside our house and fetched a claw hammer from the drawer in the kitchen.

I knocked out first the lower lock, then the upper. The door swung back against the security chain, and I leaned into it until the chain broke from its mount. The door caught again, but I forced myself through the gap, then realised that I had pushed the door hard against Mr Ashani, forcing his wrist backwards. His arm was bent out of shape. His eyes stared upwards.

I knelt down beside him, straightened out his arm. His hand was warm, but it was hot in his front room. Still, there was no smell. Didn't death have a smell?

'Mr Ashani,' I said. 'Mr Ashani?'

The sharp pleats in Mr Ashani's cream trousers looked absurd now, drooping across themselves. His stomach flopped across his fly. I put a hand on his chest, but could feel no movement.

Please, let him live.

As I was wondering how to take the pulse in his neck he blinked. 'Mr Ashani?'

I leaned forwards, pressed my nose against his. Nothing. No discernible breath. His skin was perfectly smooth, his eyes stared upwards at nothing, too wide, too awake.

I waited with him for the ambulance. People walking past in the street looked in, saw me sitting with Mr Ashani's head in my lap, and walked on. No one called out to me through the door. Perhaps I seemed to have the situation under control.

Twice more I thought I saw Mr Ashani blink. I talked, hoping my words might reach him. 'Help is coming, Mr Ashani. Emmanuel . . . Emmanuel, help is on its way.' Not once did he stir.

The ambulance crew found a pulse. They raised Mr Ashani on to a stretcher, sought out veins in his arms and legs, attached him to a clear bag of saline solution. Max was with me now, watching in fascination as the paramedics injected Mr Ashani twice in his upper thigh. Adrenaline, I guessed. Or was that something they injected into the heart?

I knew nothing about his next-of-kin, so I gave them my name and telephone number. A policewoman I didn't recognise asked me what had happened. 'It's my son,' I said. 'He knew something was wrong.'

Max stood, legs planted wide, at once proud and shy, shading his eyes in the sunlight.

'And I rang 999. By myself.'

'I think you may just have saved your neighbour's life, son,' said the policewoman.

'But what if he dies? Could he still die?'

'You did the right thing, son.'

I let Max do most of the explaining, watched as he weighed his words before speaking – slow, measured, and very adult: 'I became concerned when I realised . . . Mr Ashani's normal routine . . . My father and I felt . . .'

Later when he asked for money for a cheeseburger I said yes. 'And chips, Dad? Can I have chips?'

'Anything you like, Max.'

'Anything? Really?'

'You saved Mr Ashani's life, Max.'

'But you don't know that yet. He could still die. And I've already had a hamburger.'

'Max,' I said, 'go and buy yourself a burger.'

It was a relief to have something I could tell my mother over the phone: a heroic narrative, with Max at its centre; a narrative that made sense of our being here in London, so far from where she was. 'He saved the man's life, Mum.' A story she could share with friends over bridge: her husband's bravery, passed down the male line to her grandson. Family pride.

'Alex, get up.'

Morning light. Curtains open. Millicent at the end of the bed, fully dressed. 'Get up. Now.'

She threw underpants, a t-shirt and a pair of trousers on to the bed.

I dressed, peed, threw water on to my face. *What is this?*

Downstairs in the kitchen the lights were on. Millicent handed me a cup of coffee. 'Sit down.'

'What's going on, Millicent? Where's Max?'

'School,' she said. 'Here.'

She pushed something across the table top at me. A flat enamelled yellow tin. Gold Block Virginia tobacco.

'I mean, I guess I pretty much think that our son has a right to privacy, and that I'm a bad mother for searching in his school bag, only I didn't search it. I made him a peanut butter and jelly sandwich and put it in a brown paper bag with a note telling him I was a proud mom and that he was my boy-hero. Kind of intentionally hokey but also true, right? Because I thought maybe it would embarrass him, but in a good way. Only inside his lunchbox was this.'

I picked up the tin and turned it over in my hands. The enamel was pocked, the metal beneath rusted.

I opened the tin. A pair of pliers with pointed jaws. A small disgorger for removing fish hooks from fish gullets. Some flattened-out pieces of sheet lead. A steel penknife with a four-inch spike.

'Are you serious?' I said. 'These are fishing tools. Where's the problem, Millicent?'

'The problem is underneath.'

I lifted the tin at one end so that the tools shifted to the other side. There, underneath, was the edge of a photograph, all faded greens and blues.

There was an intensity to Millicent's eyes that I hadn't seen in years. 'Take out the picture, Alex.'

I drew it out by the edge.

The first thing I saw was the smiling faces. The next was the khaki: two men in short-sleeved shirts, short trousers, grey socks, black boots. They were standing in a clearing in the jungle, white-skinned against the dense foliage. The men looked healthy and relaxed, proud even, displaying their trophy for the camera, smiling broadly. Both were making victory signs with one hand; their other hand held their victim aloft by the ankles.

The third man's skin was darker than theirs. His clothes were torn and bloodied, his eyes forced almost shut by the bloating and the bruising on his face.

'Oh. Oh, God. What?'

Millicent's eyes bored into mine. 'That's Korea, right?'

I looked at the victim. His features were so distorted that it was impossible to guess at his ethnicity.

'It could be,' I said. 'It's hard to tell.'

'No, Alex, it *is* Korea. You didn't look closely enough.'

And then I saw it. Something about the hair, and the jawline. The white man on the right of the frame was my father. I looked up at Millicent. She nodded.

'Did you ever see this picture before?' she said.

So young he was; so fresh of face. I had never seen the picture before. I shook my head.

'Alex, did you know?'

'I suppose I knew it was a possibility.'

'But you didn't ask?'

'No. You don't ask, do you?'

'You don't ask? Really?'

'That could be anyone's father, Millicent. It was war. It could be your father.'

'Actually, no. My father burned his draft card. Pretty much the only good decision he ever made. So no, one thing this could not be is *my* father.'

I held the picture up again. How happy he looked, smiling out at the comrade-in-arms who had taken the picture. I wondered if he had shown it to my mother, passed it around during dinners with close friends, whether he had intended that Max should see it. He had certainly never shown it to me.

'New question,' said Millicent.

'I know,' I said. 'I should have checked the fishing bag before I gave it to Max.'

'OK, well, we agree on that. On Friday he took it to school and showed it to a boy called Ravion Stamp. Apparently they got in a fight.'

'I didn't know.'

'No, but you *could* have known. Why would you not check? What's the message here? Like, the men in your family solve problems by violence?'

'Don't reduce my father to this, Millicent. This . . .' I picked up the photograph '. . . is not who my father is.'

'Alex,' she said, 'I get that this is hard for you. But you *have* to protect Max from shit like this.'

'OK,' I said. 'I'm sorry.'

I could no longer tell where grief for my father began and ended; there were no clean lines around the fear that the police would charge me, nor around the gut-wrenching shock of the discovery of the neighbour's body, nor the fear that Mr Ashani too would die.

'The hard bit,' I said at last, 'has been trying to do it all without you.'

'You could let me in a little,' she said. 'We could work on things together.'

'I know,' I said, 'you have such clarity. You're better at this stuff than me.'

'*We* are better when we work together at things, Alex. You wouldn't screw up like this. And I wouldn't . . .'

'. . . seek solace in the arms of other men?'

A wounded look on Millicent's face. I was sorry as soon as I'd spoken the thought.

'I didn't mean that. Please.'

'OK, Alex. Sure. But can we at least try to work together?'

I looked at the picture of my father, smiling out at his unseen comrades-in-arms.

'OK, Millicent,' I said, 'because I do know you're right.'

Sitting in the cinema with my father: the helicopters and the flame throwers, the screams of the animals and the children.

It was my father's reaction that frightened me most. He sat rigid in his seat, as if to attention, and shook me off when my hand sought the comfort of his. The explosions lit up his face, and I could see that he was crying. I sat silently, trying for his sake to be brave.

That was the only time I saw my father cry. When we came home he sat rigid again in his comfortable chair, smoked pipe after pipe.

I should not have asked my father if he was all right. He took off his belt and made me lift up my shirt. Then he struck me eight times across the back with the leather end. I counted each blow. The beating left welts upon my skin but it did not last long, and I did not cry out.

I remember thinking how odd it was that my father had used the belt he had worn as a soldier. He confused me even more as he was putting it into his drawer afterwards; he apologised for what he had done, and told me I was a good boy. He asked me to forgive him, and said he would understand if I felt I had to tell my mother.

I never cried in front of my father. I never told my mother about the beatings, although she must have known.

I was eleven when the beatings stopped. Max's age.

For a week I worked like a dog. My boss was prepared – grudgingly – to forgive me for allowing my work to slip (he knew that Dee liked me), and I needed his forgiveness. 'These are people we can not disappoint,' he said. 'Do not disappoint them.'

'Of course not,' I said. I needed his money.

My day began at seven and ended at two. I saw Max and

Millicent over breakfast and over supper. The rest of the time I spent at the production office, dutifully ringing my mother on the walk to the station. In my lunch breaks I briefed the assistant producer, leaving her to set up the American shoot and make arrangements with Dee.

On the Monday Mr Sharpe rang. He wanted to speak to me about Max. I asked him to ring Millicent. She was better at these things, I said, and I had work to do. On Wednesday my American visa arrived, and on Thursday I handed to the edit producer my log of the footage I had seen so far, along with notes for what to do with the remaining twenty hours, which she promised to view over the weekend. If I was stressed or agitated I did not notice.

On Thursday evening I left a long message on Dee's answering machine; I told her I was sorry I'd been busy, but that I had a programme to finish, and that she could call me tomorrow at home.

On Friday, Dee's agent rang to express concern. Dee was *a little surprised* to be feeling *so neglected* after what had seemed like such a successful evening at the Sacred Cock. But there had been no feedback.

'So, I *feed back* to you about the evening I had with Dee? Is that really how this is done?'

'It's often said sneeringly, Alex, but it really is true: actors are delicate flowers. They need to be nurtured in order to bloom.'

'She's a comedian.'

'Just as delicate. Believe me.'

'So how do I bring forth blossom in Dee?'

'Orchids. Delicate flowers love delicate flowers, Alex. Send her orchids but don't spend more than a hundred pounds.'

'A hundred pounds?'

'Dee's terribly down-to-earth. But I think you already know that. She says you're very good at reading her.'

'Reading her?'

'Between you and me, she's got a bit of a creative crush on you.'

'A creative crush?'

'A creative crush.'

'Not to be confused with a crush of any other sort?'

'No, Alex, no. But creatively she says you make her all moist.'

A pause. As I wondered what to say, Millicent came into the kitchen and lit a cigarette.

'Alex, it might be useful if I could feed back something similar to Dee.'

'She's very bright, and very pretty, and very funny, and I'm really looking forward to working with her. Her charisma will really shine through the screen.' I smiled weakly at Millicent.

'Alex, don't misunderstand me and think me rude, but those things are a given. Of course you are looking forward to working with Dee. I'd like to have something a bit more to feed back to her, if you don't mind. She's terribly nervous about this trip, and it's not as if you've worked together before. She's taking a chance on you, and I think she needs to know that you are a chance worth taking . . .'

'I'm just as turned on at the prospect of working with Dee as she is at the prospect of working with me.'

'Hmm,' said Millicent. 'Interesting choice.'

'And that's great, Alex, but really you need to give a little more of yourself.'

'I'm sorry?'

'Well, with respect, you are really just repeating back to me what Dee has said about you. A bit like saying "me too" when somebody says they love you. You know?'

'You can tell Dee that I am tumescent with creativity. It's just waiting to spout forth from me.' Millicent raised an eyebrow at me.

'Really?' she mouthed.

'Yes,' I mouthed back. 'Really.'

'Yes,' said Dee's agent. 'Tumescent is a good word there. Dee will appreciate your going the extra mile. Thank you.'

'You'll tell her, then, about my creative tumescence?'

'Put it on the card you send with the orchids. Handwritten. Best if it reaches her by 4p.m. OK?'

I hung up. Millicent smiled a mocking smile. 'Let me guess. That was a business call.'

'Yes.'

'Do you think they had you on speaker?'

'I hope not.'

'You have a weird life, Alex.'

'Stop trying to make me like you.'

'Not working, huh?'

My phone rang. Rose. She had given me her number that first day, and I had stored it. I rejected the call. I didn't want to talk to Rose in front of Millicent.

Millicent offered me a cigarette. I took it, and lit it from the lighter in my pocket. We sat and smoked at the kitchen table. I could feel Millicent's eyes on me, and avoided meeting her gaze.

On the table my phone vibrated. A text message. Millicent's eyes widened. I took a drag on my cigarette, studiously avoided looking at the phone.

'Could be important,' she said, turning the phone round. 'Who's Rose?'

'The neighbour's sister. I told you that.'

'Oh yes. Sure. I'm guessing she's cute?'

'What?'

'And I'm sure she's pretty, and she's spiffy, and she's oh-so-delicate. Just your type.'

'You can't talk to me like that.'

She looked back at me, defiant. 'Alex, we have to stop walking on eggshells. I'm trying to normalise things a little.'

'Well,' I said, 'given that you slept with her brother I'm really not sure what the norms are.'

191

I rolled my cigarette around the lip of a dirty cup. 'Sorry,' I said. 'I'm trying, Millicent, really I am.'

'Alex,' she said, 'are you surprised these women feel a sense of ownership over you? Like, you have a creative hard-on for Dee. And why is . . . *Rose* . . . even texting you?'

I picked up my phone, opened the message.

> Coroner has agreed to early release of body. Funeral Saturday 2pm. St Thomas Church. Thank you for your support. Sorry for short notice. R xx

I held the phone up to Millicent.

'OK,' she said. 'I'm sorry for what I said.'

'OK.'

'You're going to go?'

I nodded. She sniffed heavily, looked pained.

'I guess they released the body. I didn't know they could do that.'

'Will you come too, Millicent?'

'Won't that be a little weird?'

'Everything's weird.' I didn't mean to spit the words at her. I was trying hard not to act on the rage that was welling inside me. But there was acid in my mouth, and it was growing harder to swallow it back.

'Alex, 'she said, 'you have a right to be angry about what I did, but I need you to listen to me.'

The fury was mounting in me. 'Bryce *listened*,' I said, 'Bryce *understood*.'

'He lost a child, Alex. Like I did.'

'Why does his loss trump mine? I feel the same pain you do, Millicent.'

'And you are so cloaked in anger since Sarah died. Alex, we grew apart. Yeah, Bryce listened. He let me talk.'

'That's *slightly* ironic.' I kept my voice as level as I could. 'Because I was trying, Millicent, I really was. But you disappeared into this weird little world of your own making, Millicent. And when you came out, you *moved on.*'

'What are you saying?'

'I held things together when you fell apart, Millicent.'

'Yes,' she said. 'Yes, Alex, you did. And I will always love you for what you did.'

'You don't want help from me, though, do you? Why wouldn't you talk to *me*?'

Millicent flinched. I realised I was holding her wrist in my right hand. I let go of her, and got up, leaned against the work surface.

'Sorry,' I said. 'That was, you know . . .'

'Inappropriate.'

'Yes. I shouldn't have done that.'

We were both fighting the tears. I hardened my resolve and looked away. I wasn't going to cry.

'Millicent,' I said, 'I'm done trying to forgive you. I've tried. I can't. And I'm sure you're right, and I'm sure some of it's my fault, but I can't accept what you've done.

'Seven years of this, Millicent. Seven years of Frisbee in the park and wordless hatred in the home. Seven years before Max leaves home. Just imagine how much we can mess each other up in that time.'

She made as if to say something, but I cut across her again.

'Your cute and adorable son,' I said, 'thinks you're a bitch, by the way. It was hard to know what to say.'

'A bitch?'

'A fucking bitch. Max's words.'

Millicent stood up, looked at me, and with great economy of movement picked up a bottle that was lying on the counter. She looked at me again, and swung the bottle at me.

'Millicent, what?'

As the bottle met my temple it shattered.

'Full,' I thought. 'Wine,' I thought. 'Red,' I said. *Dark.*

193

Millicent stood, unmoving, gulping air, the neck of the bottle still in her hand.

'Cut you, Millicent,' I said, or thought. 'You cut you.'

I nodded at her hand. There was a gash joining her lifeline to the line of her wrist. Millicent did not look down.

'Doctor you,' I tried to say. 'Mend you.'

Millicent was looking very directly at me. She dropped the bottleneck and reached towards me. I reached out for her hand, and tried to steady myself. Then Millicent went dark and the day outside went very bright.

I heard Millicent make a telephone call, and felt her hand on mine in the ambulance. I heard her whispering, 'I'm so sorry, Alex. I'm so very, very sorry.'

When she explained to the registrar she didn't try to cover her guilt. She didn't claim self-defence. She had reached the end of her tether, she said. She had run out of things to say.

Then she told the same story to the consultant, and again to the police.

'We will want to speak to your husband. He may wish to press charges. Assuming . . .'

'Assuming he's OK? Sure. I understand.'

She cried after the police had left. Then she called Tarek's mother, and asked if Max could stay over. Then she called Max, and told him that I was in hospital.

'Your dad fell over and hit his head. I'll explain when I see you.'

She instructed him on what she wanted him to pack, and when to expect Tarek's mum.

Someone tapped my arm. I felt the needle, felt nothing, then felt everything: light-shards traced from that point of singularity to the outer reaches of my body. Opiates, I thought. Good, I thought. In the absence of love, let there be opiates. Let me sleep the sleep of kings.

'No, Max, no, his eyes are open. Yes. Yes, I hope so. I think so . . . I love you too, Max. I love you too.'

My mind departed. It knew the misery of life alone in a hospital bed, and the consolation of open spaces. At some time in the middle of a dream I thought I saw Mr Ashani, sitting on the end of my bed. 'What happened?' I wanted to say. 'Are you alive?'

Mr Ashani spoke for a while. Mr Ashani told me something important. Mr Ashani was gone.

My mind returned. The light-shards dissolved from my body and I woke.

I sat up. The lamp above the next bed was on, although there was no one in it. There was a chair, on which Millicent must have sat, and a sink. The curtains were open, and there was light in the sky. I could smell old cigarettes, and guessed that Millicent had smoked out of the window.

I found something that felt like a handle and pulled it.

A person in a white uniform came in and said, 'OK, good.' She left before I could speak.

Someone had slept on top of the other bed. Or lain on it at least. The pillow was heavily indented, and the bedclothes carried the imprint of a small body. I looked at the imprint, wondered for a moment whether this would be the last I would see of Millicent.

I cupped my chin with my left hand. Wrong. Very wrong.

It took me a moment to realise what was out of balance. The thumb found stubble. The forefinger and middle finger returned the wrong data. *Nerve damage.* I changed hands. This time the forefinger and middle finger found stubble. The thumb found newly shaved skin.

I checked again with both hands. The right-hand side of my face was shaved, the left was not. The shaving had been very precise. There was a clear straight line from below my nose, past my chin, and across my Adam's apple. I could feel no pain from the right side of my face, but my fingers found what

195

must be dressings near my cheekbone. I found another shaved patch by my temple, found another dressing, and thought I could make out the shape of sutures under the dressing.

There was a mirror over the sink. But I wasn't yet ready for that.

Millicent came in. She didn't seem surprised to see me sitting up.

'Hey,' she said.

I nodded.

'So, that wasn't good.'

No, I thought, that wasn't good.

'You OK?'

I considered this. On balance, yes, I was OK. I nodded.

'Hurts, right?'

I brought my hand up to my cheek, and then to my temple.

'So, there's a doctor coming to see you. You want me to go?'

I didn't want her to go. I didn't shake my head, but she seemed to understand.

'Blink twice for no, right?'

I nodded.

Looking Millicent in the eye, I touched the left side of my face, then the right.

'I guess they were saving money,' said Millicent. 'You know, like how cancer surgeons make ugly scars because neat scars take time, and if they save half an hour every operation, they can fit in another one, right?'

I touched my face again, nodded.

'So, I guess by that logic maybe it makes sense to shave half your face, Alex. Maybe an orderly can shave a lot more half-faces than faces. If their job involves a lot of shaving.'

The doctor came in. Fifty-five, I thought, with close-cropped silvered hair. She and Millicent had a murmured conversation by the other bed. Then she shone a light in my eyes, and asked me to answer questions by raising my right or left hand.

Was I comfortable?

I raised my right hand from the sheet.

Did I remember what had happened?

I thought for a moment, then raised my right hand.

Was I in pain?

I raised my left hand.

Did I recognise Millicent?

I paused for a long time. Then I raised my left hand. The doctor looked a little concerned.

'I think he may be joking,' said Millicent. I raised my right hand.

'You see,' said Millicent. 'He's joking.'

The doctor didn't look convinced. She asked me whether, in my opinion, my body was working as it should. I raised my right hand.

The doctor began to explain something to me, but I was tiring of her. I raised my finger and put it to my lips. Millicent and the doctor looked at each other.

I touched my left cheek, then my right, then my left.

Millicent nodded. 'So, before you came in, Alex and I were discussing why you had shaved half his face.'

The doctor ignored Millicent and began to explain to me that I had suffered a blunt-injury trauma, but that there hadn't been any bleeding into my skull cavity. They would be keeping me in for observation, which might take some time.

'Ffffffff,' I said.

There was a very long pause.

'Fffffffff,' I said again.

'Mr Mercer, we need to keep you in.'

'Fffffuck.'

'Mr Mercer?'

'Offffff.'

Millicent looked as if she was about to laugh. Then she looked very serious.

I lay back on the bed.

Millicent and the doctor went to the other end of the room. I couldn't hear what they said, but Millicent was nodding.

The doctor returned.

'Mr Mercer?'

'Get . . . to fuck.'

They exchanged a meaningful look.

'Mr Mercer, we need to keep you in.'

'Away to fuck, Doctor.'

Millicent put her hand on my arm. 'Alex, the doctor is concerned. I'm concerned.'

'Why do I sound so Scottish?'

Another significant look passed between Millicent and the doctor.

'Mr Mercer, I'm pleased you are able to speak, but more than a little concerned at the content of your utterances.'

'Tell the doctor to let me go home, Millicent.'

'Mr Mercer, I don't think that's such a good idea.'

'Oh, come on, sweetchops.'

'Alex,' said Millicent, stroking my face.

'I'm fine. Tell the doctor I'm fine.'

'He says he's fine, Doctor.'

'Mr Mercer, you are not fine.'

'Millicent, ask the doctor if my face is OK to go home.'

The doctor confirmed to Millicent that there was nothing much wrong with my face.

'OK, Millicent, then I'm coming home with you.' I threw off the bedclothes and stood up.

'Mr Mercer, you are to stay here,' said the doctor.

'Away with you, hen. Millicent, where are my clothes?'

'Alex,' said Millicent, 'I need to know that you really are OK.'

'And how do I prove that to you?'

'You sure you don't want to get yourself slightly more thoroughly checked out?'

'That would be my advice, Mr Mercer,' said the doctor.

'Away to fuck, hen,' I said.

Millicent and the doctor went to the far end of the room and spoke in low voices. I heard the words *rescan him*. The doctor left the room.

'She sending for reinforcements?' I asked Millicent.

'No, Alex, they want to scan you again.'

'Fuck her.'

'Your behaviour is consistent with brain injury. Which she was trying to tell you.'

'Consistent with. But not.'

'Then what is this, Alex?'

'Displacement.'

'Displacement?'

'Displacement. This is displacement.'

'Meaning?'

'Easier to hate her than you. Doesn't hurt anyone if I hate her. Too much hurt if I hate you.'

'Isn't that transference, honey?' said Millicent. 'Anyway, I think she's a little upset, Alex. She's just doing her job.'

'Not real hurt, that. Not like what we've got. Is it?'

'I guess not. But you could be a little politer.'

'Politer?'

'Politer.'

'That's not a word.'

'It is, Alex.'

'Do I seem in any way impaired to you, Millicent?'

Millicent studied my face for a moment.

'No, not impaired, exactly. But you're being a little weird.'

'Weird how?'

'All that misdirected anger. She's only trying to help you.'

'Want me to direct it at the *appropriate* target again?'

A frown flashed across her brow. 'If I'm honest, Alex, I like this a little better.'

'You hit me with a wine bottle. I have grounds for my anger. I'm just . . . transferring it . . . to her.'

Millicent nodded.

I stood and thought. I thought of the moment just before I fell. I thought of Millicent's hand reaching out for mine. I thought of how small she had looked then, and how small she looked now.

'You reached out to me.'

'I'm not following you, Alex.'

'You reached out to me.'

'I thought you didn't do shrink talk.' She smiled up at me: an uncertain, guarded smile.

'I don't. Why did you take my hand?'

'Because in that moment I wanted to help you.'

'You wanted to help me through . . . the consequences of your hitting me in the face with a wine bottle?'

'Yes.'

'Well, I guess you did that. Thank you.'

Millicent looked apprehensive.

I took her right hand in mine. The wrist was bandaged, but there was a rust-red stain where the glass had cut into her.

'Serve you right,' I said. 'Poor you.'

'Which, Alex?'

'Both.'

A member of the hospital's Social Work team came to speak to me. She insisted that Millicent leave the room.

I told the social worker that I wanted to go home. She told me that the police had arrested Millicent, taken a statement, and released her. I told her Millicent had reached out to me and that I wanted to go home.

The hospital scanned my brain again; the machine was white and smooth-edged, and they strapped me to a gurney to keep my head from moving. Millicent could not be in the room with me and my head was filled with thoughts of executions as it hummed and glided around me.

I was achingly polite to the consultant both before and after the scan. She refused to tell me the result and insisted I stay in overnight. I may have said fuck under my breath. I'm certain she didn't hear it though.

The social worker returned after breakfast with a member of a Domestic Violence team. They brought coffee and muffins, and made Millicent leave the room. Then they asked me a series of questions about my marriage. I put it to them that the worst thing for Max would be a separation; they put it to me that witnessing violence between parents was harmful to children. I told them that Max had not witnessed the bottle striking my face; they refined their definition to include the effects of violence. I asked if they had any power to keep me in the hospital, and they told me they did not. I ended the meeting.

The consultant released me into Millicent's care with a prescription of morphine. Millicent took it to the hospital pharmacy to have it made up. We drank coffee in silence in the tiled canteen, eating the Domestic Violence muffins. Then we collected my prescription and went home by taxi.

14

I woke in the late afternoon. Max was lying beside me on the bed, playing a game on my phone.

'Hi, Max.'

'Hi, Dad.'

'Where did you find my phone?'

'In your pocket. You left your trousers on the floor.'

'Did Mum tell you what happened?'

'Yeah.'

'What did she say?'

'You fell over in the kitchen.'

'I fell over in the kitchen?'

'I didn't believe her. So I made her tell me what really happened.'

'And what did she say really happened?'

'You got hit in the head by a bottle.'

'Did she tell you who hit me in the head with a bottle?'

'She didn't want to. But I already knew.'

Max went back to his game. I watched him for a while, but could not read his expression.

'Did she do it so you wouldn't go to the funeral?'

'Max, I'd like you to save the game and give me back my phone.'

Max looked up at me, then continued playing.

'Now, Max.'

He handed me back the phone.

'How did you know Mum hit me?'

'No one else would have.' His voice was very small.

He took a folded card from his jeans pocket. He handed it to me, watching my reaction. The card was from the police. It said that they had called to speak to Millicent and to me at 15.30, but that there had been no reply. They would like me to call them back at my earliest opportunity. I wondered if not using envelopes was a deliberate policy.

'You have two missed calls on your phone too. Are they going to arrest Mum?'

'No.'

'How do you know?'

'Because I'm pretty sure they could only arrest Mum if I pressed charges. Anyway, maybe they just want to speak to us again about the neighbour.'

'Could you make them arrest Mum?'

'I don't want them to.'

'But what if you did? Could you?'

'I never would.'

Max considered this for a moment.

'Do you want to go out and get some ice cream? I have some money.'

'You don't have to buy me ice cream, Max.'

'OK. But can we go and get some ice cream?'

'All right.'

I dressed with care, and put on a clean white shirt because I didn't want to pull anything over my head. The skin beneath the bandages burned and itched, but from what I could tell in the mirror, and from feeling through the dressings, I was much less badly hurt than I had expected. My balance wasn't good on the stairs, but I decided that was the morphine.

Millicent was on the sofa in the living room, reading a book.

'You're up,' she said.

'I'm up.' I tried to smile, but it hurt.

'Dad and I are going out, Mum,' said Max, with great formality.

'Sure, honey.'

We ate our ice creams. Max had chosen the same for both of us – strawberry, blueberry and double chocolate, with fudge sauce. It was more ice cream than I wanted, and far sweeter than I wanted ice cream to be, but I was hungry and I ate it all. The coffee was surprisingly good, and cut through the cloying sweetness. I wondered if I could face going outside for a cigarette.

'That was a big thing you did, Max, bringing me here, and buying me ice cream and coffee. Makes me proud to be your dad.'

'It's good that Mum didn't come.'

'What do you mean, Max?'

'She didn't even ask to come. And if she had I would have said no, and I think she knew that, because she . . .' He was searching for the words. 'She wouldn't have had a leg to stand on. Would she, Dad?'

'What do you mean?'

'What she did to you.'

I touched my cheekbone involuntarily.

'It's not the worst thing that's ever happened, Max.'

'I don't just mean that. That's only the bit people can see.'

He left this hanging for a moment.

'What do you mean?' I asked at last.

'The neighbour.'

'It doesn't have to be the end of the world. Or the end of our marriage. And I shouldn't have told you. Not the way I did.'

'It's OK. Can I have a shake?'

'Sure.'

'Do you want some more coffee?'

'Great.'

He looked down at the coins on the tray. Not enough for both coffee and milkshake. I gave him a fiver, and he scooped up the coins.

'I'm going to have a cigarette, Max. Watch that no one takes our place.'

He rolled his eyes and joined the queue. I got to my feet. Everything hurt. I took my coffee cup and went outside.

There was a missed call on my phone. Rose. I had not made it to her brother's funeral.

Who's Rose?

Had there been an edge to Millicent's question? For a moment a dangerous thought lurked at the edges of my mind. But no, Millicent had struck me because I had forced her into a corner.

He thinks you're a bitch.

I had used Max against her. There was nothing more to it than that. I should never have used Max against her.

When I'd finished smoking I went back in and carefully arranged my body on the slick mattressed seating of the booth. Max was waiting; he hadn't started his milkshake. He picked up my coffee in two hands and gave it to me.

'Hello, Man-cub,' I said.

'Hello, Wolf-man.' Max slurped his milkshake. 'Mum took my picture of Grandpa. Can I have it back?'

'I don't know, Max. I don't think so.'

'Why? It's mine.'

'Because I don't think Grandpa meant you to have it.'

'I promise I won't take it to school again.'

'It's a very private picture, Max. You didn't tell me you'd taken it to school.'

205

'But you can tell he meant for people to see it.'

'I don't think that man's family would want you to have it. Especially not if you're showing it to people at school. He deserves some respect, Max, and some privacy.'

'But that man was our enemy.'

'He isn't any more.'

Max rolled his eyes. 'That's only because he's dead, Dad. Korea's still our enemy.'

I reached for a cigarette from the packet in front of me, then realised I couldn't smoke it. 'North Korea,' I said, 'and it's complicated.' I put the cigarette behind my ear. 'Max,' I said, 'who did you show the picture to?'

'Only Ravion Stamp. But he said Grandpa was a murderer, and I got angry, and he went spectrum and told on me to Mr Sharpe for punching him.'

'You punched him?'

Max sniffed. 'Didn't Mum tell you I punched him?'

'I assumed he punched you.'

'Maybe she didn't know. But you have to go to a meeting with Mr Sharpe. Sorry.'

Millicent hadn't told me about the meeting, either. We were all of us so strung out; we were barely getting by. Maybe I would have punched Ravion Stamp if I had been Max.

'Why did you hit him, Max?'

'I don't know.' The child's response to the adult question. But he meant it. I could see in his eyes that he didn't know why he had punched Ravion Stamp.

'You found a dead body, Max.'

'So?'

'Max, that kind of shock can make people very angry. And very sad. It can make them do things they wouldn't normally do.'

Max slurped at his milkshake. 'But Grandpa wasn't angry when he came back from the war,' he said. 'And people were trying to kill him.' He blew back down the straw. A

206

huge viscous bubble rose gently through the uniform pink liquid.

'I think he was, you know. I think your grandfather suffered a great deal more than he told people.'

'So why didn't he tell anyone?'

'I don't know,' I said. 'Men don't, always.'

'Anyway, that's not why I get angry. Not the only reason. Dr Å says it isn't.'

'Oh?' I said.

Max shook his head. 'I heard them. Mum and the neighbour in the garden. What they called each other.'

'What did you hear, Max?'

Max went very quiet. What did he know? I wanted to push him, but wasn't sure I could keep my feelings to myself. Instead I took the cigarette from behind my ear and examined it. Perhaps I shouldn't be upset that Max was angry. Perhaps Millicent would say it was entirely appropriate. *What did you hear, Max?* I put the cigarette in my mouth and reached for my lighter. Max put his hand on mine, stopping me.

'You can't smoke here, Dad.'

I looked up at him. His eyes glistened, and his lower lip curled.

'This must all have been very hard for you Max,' I said.

Max began to cry. I reached over to embrace him, but he shook me off. He covered his eyes with his hands, and sat as still as he could, his body spasming in silent, racking sobs. I looked around, not knowing what to do. I got to my feet, and moved to his side of the booth, sliding in along the slicked leather; I put my hand on his shoulder and tried to hold him to me. I wanted so badly to push him on what he had seen, what he had heard. But I had already said too much to him about Millicent's affair. When all this was over, he needed to be able to respect his mother, whether or not we were still together.

After perhaps ten minutes, Max took his hands from his eyes. I hugged him very tight.

'People can see, Dad.'

'Does that matter?'

'Yes. You can sit over there again.'

I stayed where I was. We sat there for some time. I toyed with my cigarette, and Max toyed with the last of his milkshake.

'Dad,' he said at last, 'Dad, you know how you never hit me, but you said Scottish Grandpa used to hit you with a hairbrush, and you were really afraid of him?'

'He didn't use a hairbrush. Where did you get that from, Max?'

Max shrugged. 'Grandpa liked being a gunner.'

'I'm not really sure he liked it.'

'He did, Dad. He told me. But he also shot people with a rifle, and stabbed them with knives.'

I thought of my father standing proudly there with his comrade, thought of the bruising on the face of the dead man. There was no attempt to prettify the scene. I wondered if they had beaten the Korean man before they had killed him. I wondered how many other photos he had posed for like that.

'Is it bad that Grandpa hit you?'

'I don't know, Max, those were different times.'

One night my mother used the term *shell shock* at dinner in front of guests. Although she had not been talking about him, my father became very quiet. He waited until the guests had left. He waited until he was sure that I was asleep; he even came into my room to check. But I was awake, and I heard my mother's pleas through the wall: she had not been talking about my father.

Afterwards I heard him apologise to her, as he used to apologise to me. He was ashamed of his trauma, ashamed of the trauma he was visiting upon us.

If my father had lived a little longer I could have asked him. I could have tried to understand what made a good man pose with his beaten enemy: what made a loving father beat his only son with his army-issue leather belt?

He was a good man, though. That's what complicates things. My mother and I loved my father, and eventually the beatings stopped.

'Dad,' said Max on the bus home. 'Do you think sometimes the police arrest people even though they didn't kill someone, because they can tell they're glad they're dead?'

'The police aren't going to arrest me, Max. Is that what you're talking about?'

Max brightened. 'Did they tell you that?'

'No, Max, no, they didn't tell me that. And I'm not glad that the neighbour's dead. It's a terrible thing.'

15

When we got home Arla opened the door.

'Oh, yeah, Dad, Arla's coming to stay,' said Max. 'The reason I didn't tell you was I forgot.'

Arla laughed and kissed Max, and he let her take his hand and draw him across the threshold.

'Well, this should complicate things in interesting ways,' I said. 'How's the life promiscuous?'

'I guess right now it beats the life monotonous,' she said, reaching up to be kissed.

Arla still had that West Coast sheen. She had cut her hair into a long bob and looked polished and poised in a knitted vest and knee-length skirt. Even in high shoes she was tiny: a smaller, sleeker near-facsimile of her older sister.

Millicent came in from the kitchen.

'So, why are you here, Arla?' I said. 'What can we help you with this time?'

'I asked her to come,' said Millicent. 'I figured *we* could use the help.'

I looked from Millicent to Arla to Max, then back to Millicent.

'You were unconscious, Alex,' said Millicent.

'Right enough,' I said. 'The house is yours, Arla. London

is yours. But I'm not unconscious any more so we don't need any help.'

'All good,' said Arla, voice light as spun sugar.

'Alex,' said Millicent simply, 'I'm going to need you to get Max ready for bed.'

'But I want to talk to Arla,' said Max.

'Bed,' said Millicent.

'Mum . . .'

'Max, what say tomorrow you skip school and we hang out?' said Arla.

'I'll get into trouble.'

'Not if I ring your principal and say I'm your mom.'

Max stared at Millicent. Arla stared at Millicent. Millicent looked appalled but she nodded gently.

'Can I have twenty-four hour 'flu?' asked Max.

'Sure, Max. 'Flu is good.'

'Can you say I'm delirious?'

'Sure, Max. Delirious is super-good.'

I sat on the edge of the bath as Max brushed his teeth.

'Dad, why did you call Arla promiscuous?'

'I didn't call her promiscuous.'

'You said, "how's the life promiscuous?" And then she said you were boring. Because really you were saying she's a slut.'

'We were both joking. And don't say slut.'

'Girls call girls sluts.'

'Max, don't say slut any more. OK? I don't think she's a slut, and she doesn't think I'm boring. OK?'

'If you say so, Boring Dad.'

He spat and rinsed.

'Max, you haven't really brushed your teeth.'

'Because I was talking to you, Dad. Dad, *is* Arla promiscuous?'

'Max, drop it.'

'Is she, though?'

'Bed.'

I sat on Max's bed and watched him fall asleep. He looked so very young, and so very beautiful. He stirred slightly when I ruffled his hair, and I watched him from the doorway for a long time. Millicent touched my arm; I realised I hadn't heard her come upstairs.

She nodded at Max. 'We made that.'

'Yes, we did, didn't we?'

I held her to me, felt her breath on my neck.

'It's fiendishly clever, whatever it is,' I said.

I held her very tight and we stood, watching the rise and fall of Max's torso; I found myself without anger for the first time in days. *Sleep of the innocent.*

'I need to apologise to Arla, don't I?'

I asked Arla to forgive my thoughtlessness. She hugged me, told me it was all good, and that I was being far too English about things. I corrected her by pointing out that I was Scottish. She hugged me again, and said that sort of confirmed her point. I apologised again.

Arla had bought two bottles of good island whisky at the airport. Millicent opened Max's bedroom window so that we'd hear him if he woke, and we sat on the grass drinking and talking. Arla drank her whisky with ice. Millicent and I drank it the Scottish way, dripping water from our fingers into the glasses.

'Three drops of water. No more.'

'You're freaking kidding me, right, Alex?'

'No, Arla, I'm deadly serious. You're killing it with ice.'

'So three drops of water? What's with that?'

'Releases the esters. Which for some reason improves the flavour.'

'Ooh. Science,' she said, valley-girl style. 'You Brits sure are smart.'

'Wow. Irony,' I mimicked, falsetto. 'You Americans sure do learn fast.'

'Yeah, I guess we made it as far as sarcasm.'

She picked up my drink and tasted it.

'You see?' I said. 'Much better.'

'No. Icky.'

'Please yourself.'

'I do.'

We lay on our backs, drinking whisky and looking up at the sky. Say what you will about light pollution, but I swear we saw stars.

'This place is actually pretty cool,' said Arla. 'Why do you call it Crappy?'

'Crappy Rub Sniff,' said Millicent. 'If you spell Krapy with a K and one P, and Sniff with one F.'

'Backwards, you mean?' said Arla. 'K-R-A-P-Y-R-U-B-S-N-I-F?'

'Max figured it out. Don't know why we didn't.'

'Huh,' said Arla. 'Smart kid.'

A police helicopter appeared and hovered for ten minutes, the beam from its searchlight twitching nervily, cutting white steel swathes into the blue-brown sky. For a moment the beam strayed into our garden, and Millicent and Arla raised their glasses to it.

'Feel like home?' I asked.

'Sorta kinda no,' said Arla. 'I live in a real nice neighbourhood.'

Millicent kissed me, got up and went upstairs. Arla watched her go.

'Millicent never asked me for help before,' said Arla. 'Guess she decided I finally grew up, or something.'

Millicent closed Max's window. The light in the bathroom came on, and I could see her outline on the frosted glass as she brushed her teeth.

Arla turned over and lay on her front, looked at me appraisingly. 'You guys OK, Alex?'

The words were out before I could stop them. 'Was she planning to leave me?'

'Cute question, Alex.' Arla laughed her spun-sugar laugh. 'Do you even *know* my sister?'

'What do you mean?'

'Does it seem to you like she likes to *share*?'

'She talks . . .'

'Really? With me she sure locks the hell down.'

Water trickled down the drainpipe. Millicent never turned off the tap when she was brushing her teeth.

'You know how she left *us*, Alex?' Arla turned to look at me. 'Oh, she didn't tell you? Like, on her fricking prom night she tells Mom she's going to the store.' She drained her glass. 'I mean, I guess at the time I thought it was kind of funny when her doofus boyfriend Thaddeus came round in his tux, and he's standing there sweating in the kitchen trying to make conversation with my dad, and Dad's being *super*-mean to him, like he offers him a t-shirt to change into, which obviously he can't say yes to, but does not ask him to sit down. But by ten thirty even my dad's starting to get a little agitated. And Millicent rings three days later to say she's in fricking Providence, Rhode Island.'

She paused, looked at me, made it clear she expected a reaction. 'That's like 3,000 miles.'

'No,' I said, 'no, she didn't tell me that.'

'And two days after that Thaddeus dies. At the funeral his parents present it like it's an unfortunate accident, like he mixed alcohol and painkillers by mistake. And my parents want to act like nothing's happened. And Millicent doesn't come back for the funeral. And there are all these rumours about what really happened. And she *never* comes home.'

The lightness of her voice. I've got you wrong, I thought. There's nothing flighty about you at all.

'Guess why Millicent left, Alex?'

'I don't know.'

'Neither do I. Because she never once told me. She never talked about it to you?' The disappointment was tangible.

'Like some kind of boy-trouble thing, or maybe, I don't know, an abortion, or something? There was this weird ridiculous rumour that she gave birth to a baby in a beet field. Ha.'

'I'm sorry,' I said. 'That must all have been hard for you.'

'Yeah, Mom and Dad got even more sucky after that. Kept pointing out there were no beet fields for hundreds of miles. They heard the rumours too.' She smiled brightly.

'You're right,' I said after a while. 'Leaving is her default response. She goes into lockdown with me too.'

Millicent stopped brushing her teeth. The light in the bathroom went out. The water carried on running in the drainpipe.

'I don't know what I was expecting,' I said. 'It's not as if Millicent was handing out group hugs and candy kisses. I never thought she was that kind of Cali-girl. She called me motherfucker on our first date.'

'That's that thing you do, isn't it, Alex? You know, where you try to mask what you're feeling with irony.' She drained her glass again, picked up the whisky bottle, pulled out the cork with her teeth, and poured herself another whisky. 'Kinda English.'

'I'm . . .'

'. . . Scottish. I heard ya.'

I stood up.

'Where are you going, Alex?'

'Get you some ice.'

'No need.'

'And Millicent's left the tap on.'

We drank. I smoked. The helicopter reappeared. Its beam cut violently through the garden. Arla was silhouetted against the wall for a moment. Then she was fission-bright. I lost her form in an aftershock of blur and shadows. I put my hand to my eyes. When at last I could see again, I saw that Arla was rubbing her eyes.

'Oucho,' she said.

'Yeah,' I said. 'Oucho.'

'So,' she said, 'who's the perp?'

'Sixteen and white in this area. Statistically speaking. Twocker.'

'And for those of us who don't speak Brit?'

'He takes cars without the owners' consent.'

'He's been under-parented,' she said, grinning. 'Statistically speaking.' Her mouth, I thought, it's Millicent's mouth. It has the same wry twist when she smiles. But her voice is light and air, where Millicent's is darkness and smoke.

The helicopter had fixed in one position. It was low now – perhaps sixty metres – and its beam was pointed straight down into the nearby mews. We heard sirens, then car brakes, then boots on cobblestones. There was a lot of shouting.

'Are they . . . beating on him?' asked Arla.

She was right. Cries of pain, and cries of righteous anger. It sounded bad.

'We should do something, right?' said Arla.

'Yes,' I said. 'We should.'

We put down our drinks and went running to the front door. I flung it open, and we set off towards the mews. At the end we turned left, then left again. The engine note of the helicopter grew louder, then more urgent. We turned into the mews but the cars, the men and the boy had gone. The helicopter was slowly rising. As we watched, it turned off the searchlight and headed east.

'So what do we do?' said Arla.

I looked around. There were a few tyre marks but no trace of the boy's presence in the street, no trace of his arrest, nothing that bore witness to a beating. 'Not much, I guess. I could write a concerned letter, but I probably won't.'

'I guess you gotta be cautious.' *Cau*-tious. Those long Californian vowels. Millicent was losing them now.

'Actually, they've been incredibly polite with me. Lucky I'm not a sixteen-year-old boy.' For the first time in days the fear was lifting. Alcohol helped, I decided. Alcohol and Arla.

'Alex, I think I got a shard in the sole of my foot.'

I hadn't noticed, but she had taken off her shoes, had run barefoot through the streets. I bent down. A glint of glass almost level with the skin, the blood dull brown in the orange sodium glare. The glass was ugly and uneven, and I didn't think I could get it out here. I needed better light.

She held my arm and hopped gently back to the house. I fetched antiseptic, a saucepan of hot water, and two large towels. I sat Arla on the sofa, and turned all the lights on.

'Wow,' I said. 'Even in this light you are tanned.'

'Yes,' she said. 'I am tan in any light. It's a California thing.'

'I look a little more Scottish than you, obviously.'

'Yes,' she said. 'Pleasingly Scottish. Kind of Byronic pale.'

'Byron wasn't Scottish.'

'Take the compliment, Alex,' she said.

'OK,' I said. 'You have beautiful arms, Arla. Beautiful tanned Californian arms.'

'What kind of a dolt even cares about arms?'

'Take the compliment, Arla.'

I bathed her foot, and patted it dry with a towel. Then I looked again at the glass. It seemed to be a wedge-shaped sliver, pushing a long way into the sole of her foot. Really a hospital was the place for this. I touched the edge of the glass very lightly with the tip of my finger. Arla winced.

I took a thumbnail on each side of the shard, and tried to draw it out of her foot. Nothing happened, but Arla inhaled sharply and bit her lip. I tried again, and this time the right side lifted a fraction. Blood was pooling again where the shard had shifted. I looked up at Arla. She had tears in her eyes and was clearly in pain, but she nodded at me. I tried again, and the other side of the sliver shifted. Arla put her hand on my head, stopping me. She took three deep breaths.

'OK,' she said. 'Go.'

This time the shard slipped out easily. I held her foot for a moment, and felt the stiffness in it start to ebb away.

'The doctor gave me a bottle of morphine,' I said. 'Want some?'

'Uh uh. Whisky.'

Arla washed her foot while I put coffee on the stove and fetched cigarettes and whisky. I went to the bathroom to find her a plaster, and took a large swig of morphine.

When I came down Arla had filled the glasses and was sitting with a lit cigarette in her mouth. I went to the kitchen and fetched the coffee, and found a candle on top of a cupboard.

I lit the candle, and turned off the lights in the living room. Then I gave Arla her coffee, sat beside her on the sofa.

'You smell of perfume and half-metabolised whisky,' I said.

'You also,' she said. 'Minus the perfume.'

We locked eyes for a moment. Then she patted my arm and looked away.

'Arla, I used to sleep with a *lot* of women. Before I met Millicent.'

'Why did you stop?'

'I met Millicent.'

'So again, why did you stop?'

'I couldn't get it right.'

This amused her. 'You sucked at promiscuity?'

I took her hand in mine. She turned towards me, looked down at her hand, then looked very directly at me. Those eyes. Untainted California green. A better version of Millicent, I thought. Like Millicent before me, before Max, and before Bryce. *A Millicent without the betrayal.*

'So, Arla,' I said, 'do you want to show me how it's done?'

She laughed. 'You want me to show you how to do promiscuity?'

'Yes,' I said, looking her steadily in the eye. Her face was very close to mine, and I could feel her breath on my cheek.

'You're making a pass at me?'

'Yes.'

'You'd like for us to have sex, and you'd like for us to do it without emotional involvement or hurt?'

'Yes.'

'And do you think that's possible for you, Alex?' She said this with great simplicity.

'You manage it,' I said.

'Yes,' she said. 'But I don't think you would.'

'You think I'm vulnerable.'

'Your son and your wife are asleep upstairs. I'd say that makes you vulnerable. And it makes *them* vulnerable. And she's my sister, which makes *me* vulnerable. Page one of the book is you do not screw your sister's husband. Also every other page. In capital letters and a super-easy-to-read typeface. This would not be right, Alex, for you or for me.'

'Really?' I said.

'I do promiscuity. I do *not* do cheating. I do *not* do revenge. Especially not on my sister. She adulates you, you know.'

'I know.' I pinched the bridge of my nose and thought of Millicent. 'I mean, I don't know.'

'What are you trying to say, Alex?' The perfection of those eyes, locked on to mine now, endlessly green. *Look away, Alex.*

'Yeah,' I said. 'Sorry. Thank you.'

'You're thanking me? Why are you thanking me?'

'For looking after me. And for turning me down with such charm and such kindness. Are you sure you don't want any morphine?'

'Uh uh,' she said, 'no. No morphine. But thank you for liking my arms.'

'You have beautiful arms,' I said.

'I'll try to remember that.'

We fucked there on the floor of the living room. I don't know what it was that changed in Arla, or in me, but I remember her drawing me gently down to the floor. I remember falling backwards. Arla cradled my head, made sure I wasn't any more hurt than I already was. Then she ran her hands under my shirt and over my chest, then down to my belt buckle, kissing me all the while.

We fucked with wordless intensity. I tried not to think about Millicent, then tried not to think about Arla, then tried not to think about coming.

It didn't last more than a few minutes and I don't think Arla came. It has no meaning. I told no one about it, and shouldn't be telling you.

16

Abruptly and from nowhere I was awake.

Millicent wasn't in bed, and the light from the window told me that I had overslept. The curtains were open. I wondered whether Millicent had opened them to make a point.

I had slept the sleep of the dead drunk, fully clothed, on top of the bedclothes. My mouth should have been dry, and my head should have ached. I lay for several minutes, waiting for the dizzy fug of regret and hopelessness that would surely come; nothing came.

I sat experimentally for a minute or two, expecting to be crippled by a nauseous wave of remorse, to be sent rushing to the toilet bowl or the medicine cabinet. But I was clear of head, and untroubled by guilt. My hand did not shake, nor did my vision blur. I craved neither water, nor orange juice, nor ibuprofen. I felt, in short, absolutely, gloriously, abnormally – fine.

Millicent came in with two cups of coffee. She opened the window and offered me a cigarette, which we shared, sitting up on the bed and listening to the sounds of a London morning. An operatic tenor was practising with his own window open. A mother was shouting at her children. A helicopter passed overhead but didn't stay. I took her hand and drew her towards me, certain that last night's whisky and cigarettes masked the smell of sex.

221

Millicent kissed me, then sat upright on the bed, and looked as if she had something to say.

'What?'

'I'm sorry,' she said. 'Truly sorry. I haven't been much of a wife recently. Short on domestic duties, long on domestic violence. What I did . . .'

'You don't have to explain, Millicent. I know I pushed you over some sort of threshold.'

'No. I think it might be the worst thing I ever did. That's how it felt when I did it, and that's how it feels now.'

'You didn't kill me, Millicent. And you have my attention.'

'I hate myself for what I did to you.'

I held her head in my hands. 'I'm trying to look at this as an *opportunity for growth*,' I said.

'You hate that expression.'

'I'm tired of being angry with you.'

'It's the second-worst thing I ever did.'

'Let's have breakfast. Do you want me to make breakfast for you, Millicent?'

'They're fixing breakfast,' she said. 'Arla and Max. We should go down.'

'Give me ten minutes.'

I drank down the last of my medicine.

I ran a bath, and washed all trace of Arla from me. Then I lay on my back for a while listening to the sounds of domestic life coming from downstairs. Low conversation, laughter, pan on stove and coffee pot boiling over. I sank my head under the water and the sounds disappeared. I lifted my head, and they returned, distorted for a moment as the water ran from my ears. I washed my hair, and submerged my head again. Again, domestic life disappeared.

I rinsed and repeated.

I went downstairs. Arla and Max had made pancakes with bacon and proper American maple syrup. There was orange juice, there were croissants from the market. There was no *atmosphere*. I was surprised to find myself so glad to see Arla, and surprised at how very strange the idea of sleeping with her now seemed, how very far away.

Arla had rung Max's headmaster and pretended to be Millicent. She had allowed Max to film the call on my phone, but made him promise not to show it to anyone outside the room. Max showed me the clip. Arla made a very convincing Millicent. She had deepened her voice, and even got Millicent's strange combination of short London and long Californian vowels.

'Nice touch calling the principal "head teacher",' said Millicent. 'Very London. Very me.'

'Well, head teacher,' mimicked Max, 'we'll just have to see how Max is feeling tomorrow, but right now he has a fever of 102. That's thirty-nine degrees Celsius.'

'Not bad, Max,' I said. 'Really a very good impression.'

'Who of? Arla, or Mum?'

'Both.'

'Next time I'm going to ring myself.'

'Don't even think about it. There isn't going to be a next time.'

'Dad, Arla told me she doesn't like being called Aunt Arla.'

'I'm not surprised, Max. It makes her sound like a silverwig.'

'Yeah,' said Arla. 'Aunt Arla sucks.'

'Some people say Aunt Arla sucks,' said Max. 'Some people say Aunt Arla f—'

'Don't even think of it, Max,' I said.

'You don't know what I was going to say.'

'Enough of the wide-eyed innocence, Max,' I said. 'No more poetry.'

'What rhymes with promiscuous?' said Max.

I kicked him gently under the kitchen table.

'Ow,' said Max. '*You* said it yesterday.'

'Max,' said Arla. 'I *was* thinking dinosaurs at the Natural

223

History Museum. But I guess now I'm thinking royal fashion at the Victoria and Albert Museum. Princess time for you.'

'OK,' said Max. 'Sorry, Aunt Arla.'

'It's Arla, you jerked-up little douche-canoe,' she said. 'And *you* are going to be seeing a *l-o-t* of wedding gowns.'

'OK. Arla.'

'Better, Max.'

When it was over Arla had begged me not to tell Millicent. 'What have we done,' she kept saying, 'what have we done?'

Was this revenge?

What *have* we done?

Arla and Max left for the museum and Millicent washed up.

I went into the living room. Voices through the wall.

I opened the front door and looked out into the street. There was a marked car, and another that looked like the one driven by June and Derek. The police must be interviewing Mr Ashani. I wondered whether they were asking him about us, or whether the investigation had moved on. I could not make out what they were saying, but the voices sounded calm, civil. It did not sound as if they were accusing Mr Ashani of anything.

Three very bad things happened. I rang Dee to talk about America and she put the phone down on me. I rang Dee's agent to talk about Dee and she put the phone down on me. I rang my boss and explained that it looked as if there might be a problem with Dee. He put the phone down on me.

I rang my boss again and told him, politely but firmly, that I had always thought he was a cunt. He hung up on me. Five minutes later he rang back to tell me he had put the word out about me. No one who mattered would employ me now. I was as good as blacklisted. I told him this confirmed me in my view that he was a cunt. He hung up on me for the third time.

I stood with the phone in my hand. *Millicent did this to you*, I thought. *How do you feel?* Millicent had made a cuckold of me. She had neglected our son. She had assaulted me. As a result of her assault I had lost Dee, and as a result of losing Dee I had lost my job, and most likely my career. How did I *feel*?

Fine, I thought, I felt fine. No, better than fine.

'Millicent!' I shouted. 'Millicent!'

'What?' There she was, nervous in the doorway to the kitchen. 'Alex, are you OK?'

'I've lost my job. I feel great.'

'Oh, Alex, no.'

'And I'm not angry. Not in the least.'

I wasn't *angry*. Angry was an older, stupider version of me. Arla wasn't about anger. Arla wasn't about revenge. Arla would never happen again.

I loved my wife. I knew that with perfect clarity now.

During supper Mr Ashani came round. He wanted to thank Max and me for saving his life. He handed Max an envelope with £200 in it. I stood on the doorstep watching the whole thing happen. Wrong to be accepting his money, I thought. But I was nauseous and shaky, and Millicent took charge.

I sweated the painkillers out of my system. It took three days. Millicent changed the sheets morning and night.

On the second evening Max placed on the pillow beside me a small radio tuned to Millicent's show. There was comfort in the gentle modulations of her voice, as she softly chided people for their broken lives. 'Climb out of your well of excrement, Susan.' *Make your play. Move on.* 'Chris, the good news is you get to choose *not* to be an asshole. Can I say that? Well, I said it.' For two hours I drifted calmly in and out of sleep. That was my wife out there.

Pick up your shitty hand of cards.

Make your play.

Bluff a little.

Move on.

225

The fever became intense. A coldness descended upon me, and I lay beneath the covers, clothed, drenched in sweat. I thought about hell, and about Satan in a lake of ice, and I became fearful that I might freeze to death.

When the fever was over I felt cleansed. My eyes were bright. My fingers tingled. I was clear of voice and pure of heart.

Still the expected guilt did not come. Perhaps I had not betrayed Millicent after all: perhaps Arla was simply the cosmos rebalancing after Millicent's affair; perhaps Arla had been a necessary step. Were we not now moving forward?

Karma, I murmured to myself. Surely this was karma. My job was gone, and with it my career. So what? I'd find something else to do and become a better person with it.

I knew now what I wanted: Millicent and Max, my wife and my son, my little tribe; I would become a better version of me; we would become a better version of us.

That's karma. Isn't it?

My mother called. The hospital was releasing my father's body. He would be cremated next Wednesday at nine.

'Mum,' I said, gently, 'could you not have rung me to talk about times?' We hadn't spoken since I had been in hospital, I realised guiltily. Perhaps I had been afraid to ring her; afraid of what I might say about what we had become.

I explained to my mother about Millicent's radio show, told her that Millicent might not be able to come to the service. My mother was mortified, but Millicent found us tickets on the sleeper. She could do her show, and meet Max and me on the platform at Euston. We would travel up together on the night train.

My mother didn't need us in Edinburgh before the cremation – she was insistent about this – and we had no work. Millicent wanted to go to the travel agent's.

226

'Travel agent?' I had said. 'Really?'

'Yeah, I want to go spend some money. In a real shop with a real glass window and real peeling paint. With brochures and dust and models of old airplanes. I want to pay a real person with real paper money I just got given by a real teller in a real bank. And I want them to count the money with one of those rubber thimbles, and put an elastic band around the bills, and slip them into an envelope with a window in it. And then I want to take you away, Alex.'

'Why?'

'I don't know. I need to feel that this is . . . That it isn't . . . I realise that I'm sounding stupid right now . . .'

'Real. You want it to feel real.'

'Stupid.'

'Real.'

'OK, so I'm embarrassed to say it. But yes, I want to feel that this is real. And I already checked with Arla. She's good to look after Max. We can go.'

We would go away, Millicent and I. We would reforge our union. When we returned we would be a family once more.

Arla, though.

17

We are London people. We did not seek the melancholy of the ocean liner, nor cold awakenings under canvas; we did not seek to know the terrifying power of landscape and ruin, nor the bitterness of sympathies interrupted.

We wanted a city break and a two-hour flight.

'Norway is popular,' said the travel agent, handsome in his floral shirt and fashionable glasses.

'Norway's cold,' I said.

'Yes, exactly, Norway,' said Millicent, cutting across me. 'Why not?'

'Actually, it's warm in July,' said the travel agent. 'High season.'

'Sounds perfect,' said Millicent. 'We never went there.'

I looked at her, then looked at the travel agent. 'There's always Scotland.'

Millicent grimaced. The travel agent stared back through the fashionable glasses. 'It's very unlike Scotland, I can assure you.'

'And so is Rome.'

'Alex,' said Millicent, 'could we please, just for once, do something we didn't do before?' There was a pleading look on her face. 'Also Norway has the world's happiest people. It's like they're the opposite of us.'

I shot her a look.

She smiled, rueful. 'I looked it up.'

'You looked it up?'

'I *may* already have been thinking Norway,' she said. 'Please?'

'OK,' I said. 'Norway,' I said. 'Why not?'

I wondered casually if the police might stop us at the airport, if some electronic marker would have been added to our passport records. But I had rung June and told her I was going away and she had not tried to stop me. I was starting to wonder if I was no longer a suspect.

We drifted easily through Security at Heathrow and slept like children on the plane. The world was in balance. The world was on our side.

Millicent insisted we take a taxi to the hotel. 'I want to see the countryside,' she said.

'You don't like countryside.'

'I do now.'

The countryside was flat. We saw Tommy Sharif's tyre warehouse and an IKEA superstore.

The journey cost £120. Millicent paid the taxi driver by credit card. We checked into the Grand Hotel, admired the pictures of President Obama on the balcony, and marvelled at the opulence of our room, its silken-gold carpet, its seductive bed.

'You sure we can afford this, Millicent?'

'If you keep asking that our trip is going to get very sucky indeed.'

We ate, fucked and slept out the day.

When I woke, Millicent was asleep with her head on my chest, cradled into my body. 'Millicent,' I whispered, 'have we finished betraying each other now?' She stirred and seemed to smile, but didn't wake from her sleep.

18

I woke again at eight, and found Millicent already up, staring out of the window. Shift dress and sandals, black straps and skin.

'Hey,' I said.

Without turning she said, 'There's something cleansing about the light here, like it resets a part of you that's got corrupted or confused. And yes, I think we're through betraying each other.'

'I thought you were asleep.'

She looked around at me. The brittle quality that she had carried with her was gone. 'I was drifting. I did hear what you said though, Alex. And I'm through betraying you.'

I made to speak. No words came.

'That's good, right?' she said.

I nodded.

She drew her dress up over her thigh. I looked down, and realised she was naked under it.

'Really?' I said. 'Again?'

'Yes, really.'

We made each other come with the efficiency of thirteen years of marriage, quietly, and with gentle intensity.

*　　*　　*

There were two missed calls on my phone, both from our home number. I rang back, but there was no answer. Arla was probably dragging Max through some edgy East London artspace. Max would be pretending to like it to impress Arla.

We took a ferry to an island and swam naked, surprised to find the water warm against our bodies. The Norwegians on the rocky beach paid us no mind, immaculate in their newly bought swimwear, bodies gym-firm and proud. Their children fished for crabs with baited strings, or scooped glass jellyfish from the water and arranged them in geometric shapes upon the rocks.

We swam out beyond the beach to where a line of yellow buoys marked the end of the safe area. We trod water and kissed, laughing.

Millicent raised her hands above her head and disappeared below the surface. I felt the water eddying from her body as she kicked downwards, saw her pale shape slide out of view.

I saw a small white yacht round the point, cutting close along the shoreline, sail edges quivering white against the sky. Two figures on board, spindly and slight. Children, I thought. Surely they can't be children?

Millicent reappeared beside me, and we watched the yacht as it came at us.

'That *is* going to turn, isn't it?' said Millicent.

'I'm pretty sure it has to.'

The yacht went about and the young girl at the helm waved. We waved back, felt the bow-wave gently lift us, then drop us back.

'How old do you figure those kids were?' I said.

'Eleven? Twelve?'

'Yeah, that's what I thought. Weird.'

'Swim down with me, Alex. I want to show you something.'

'Under the water? Do I need to keep my eyes open?'

'It's kind of salty, but yeah, you need to keep your eyes open. Join me.' And she disappeared again below the surface.

I took two deep breaths, then followed her down, found her shadow clinging to the chain that tethered the nearest buoy; I swam towards her, brought my face near to hers. Sudden shock of white against clear-green water. The salt stung my eyes, and the water distorted Millicent – all eyes and mouth, her body far away. She pointed up and around, and for a moment together we watched the sunlight shafting through the green. Then I looked back down. I saw her breast pass my face, then the shock of dark hair between her thighs, and she was gone. I looked up and saw her silhouetted at the surface, radiant in the light.

I let go of the chain. The water carried me up, and as my head reached the surface I sucked the air greedily down.

'Kind of transcendent, no?' said Millicent.

'It was beautiful. You are beautiful.'

We kissed, and she put her hands gently on my shoulders, nuzzled against my neck.

She inhaled deeply and held the air in her lungs, turned over in the water, raised a leg and slipped away from me. I breathed in and followed her downwards.

I found her at the same place on the chain. We brought our faces close to each other and kissed. Bubbles leaked from the side of Millicent's mouth. Don't laugh, I thought. We don't want to drown.

Millicent pulled herself down the chain, kicking with her feet. Then she wasn't there.

I didn't panic. I followed her on down the chain, hand over hand.

Sharp bolts of cold water to chest, face and groin. Everything mud-dark. Everything winter. Calm, I thought, you must be calm. I looked up and could not see the surface.

I pulled myself further down the chain. Calm hand over calm hand. Slow, I thought, be very slow. You cannot breathe deeply because you cannot breathe, but you can remain calm. Millicent is there. She is there, and she is waiting for you.

My hand found her hand before I could see her, an edgeless form in the darkness. I brought my face very close to hers, found the outline of her eyes and read in them that all was well. She smiled, brought her fingers to my face, kissed me. I held her very tight for a moment and she wrapped a leg around mine. Then I felt her uncurl from me and her shadow passed before me and disappeared.

The sounds: metal chainlinks tightening; distant cracks and clicks; an alien pressure against my eardrum. A wave, I thought. Is that what a wave sounds like this far under?

I let go of the chain. I was light, I had no up, no down. For a moment I wondered, should I kick? Calm, I thought, you must be calm.

Then the pressure against my eardrums lessened, and the coldness of the dark water was below me. I saw again the sun through the surface. There was Millicent too, and then there was I, my head above the water, breathing again, laughing again.

'You OK?' said Millicent.

I nodded. 'You?'

She smiled, and set off for the shore.

We sat naked on the rocks, drying ourselves in the strange Nordic sunlight. People swam and played in the water. A small boy fished. Light-skinned Norwegians cooked sausages on portable barbecues. Dark-skinned Norwegians grilled lamb over charcoal.

'We should have brought towels,' I said.

'This is better,' said Millicent. 'I like us naked together.'

There was a missed call on my mobile from a number I didn't recognise. There was a voicemail from the same number, which I didn't listen to, and a text from Max, sent from Arla's phone.

Arla told me she's eaten ice cream every day since she was fourteen. She says you and Mum probably think

233

that is immature, but it's actually mature, because that's when she says she started being an adult. Instead of ice cream, can I have a PlayStation, and can I have it now? Also, Mr Ashani was looking for you.

'Your son is weird,' said Millicent when I showed her the text.

'*My* son.'

'The weirdness he gets from you, Alex,' she said, resting her head on my shoulder. 'Obviously.'

'Yes, because nothing about you is weird, Millicent. *Obviously.*'

'None of the kids here seem weird,' she said after a while. 'They all seem remarkably well-adjusted.'

'That's because it's the middle of the summer, and we're at the beach. And you don't see the ones sitting at home with the curtains closed.'

'It's a low-crime society. And if you go to jail, they give you time off in lieu of holiday.'

'You think I should serve out my sentence here?'

'You aren't going to jail, Alex. No one is. Get real.'

'So why bring it up? I thought we'd come away to forget. Live in the moment, or something. Jesus.'

'We did.'

'How was the funeral, by the way?'

'The funeral was very formal. Sad.'

She was quiet, and looked out over the fjord again. I felt bad and apologised, and we let it drop.

The small boy caught a fish. We watched as he put his hand into its gill opening and twisted its head back, breaking the spinal cord. He dropped the fish gently on to the rock beside him, where it lay flicking randomly, its nerves firing their last useless volleys, its body twitching uselessly, like a last brief memory of life.

The boy cast out his line again, waited for his lure to sink.

'How old do you think that kid is?' asked Millicent.

'Seven? Eight?' I said.

'Max couldn't do that when he was eight. He can't do it now. These kids are so . . . attuned.'

'Max doesn't have to know how to kill fish. He needs to know how to stay out of fights and entertain girls at parties. He's good-weird, not bad-weird. He doesn't smoke crack and he hasn't got anyone pregnant. He's perfectly attuned to London life.'

'He's eleven.'

'You know what I mean. He's not stupid, and he's not easily led. He's his own person.'

'Do you think he'd like it here?'

'There's a leading question,' I said.

'It's just a question, Alex.'

I turned to look at her. Her eyes were shining. She tilted her head, half-raised an eyebrow.

'The answer's no,' I said. 'Absolutely, definitely not.'

'No, what?'

'We are not moving to Norway.'

'I wasn't suggesting that,' she said, but there was hurt in her voice.

'You sort of were, Millicent.'

'Oh, OK, look . . . I'm not seriously suggesting . . .' The muscle in her cheek twitched, and her nostrils flared slightly. 'Alex, can't you just go with the idea for a moment? Be a bit playful? Humour me, and not go all dark?'

'I like it here too,' I said.

'Maybe we could give him a bit more of what these kids have?'

'Maybe you could teach him how to trap and skin a rabbit?' I said. 'Pass on the fieldcraft you learned growing up in LA.'

She laughed and touched my arm. 'So we're city people. These people are city people too. But they have this.'

Grey-blue woodsmoke carried whispers of grilled lamb and

235

grilled fish. The fjord shimmered, electric and unreal. I thought of looking up through the water, breath held, thought of Millicent in a thousand brilliant shafts of light.

'Ineluctable modality of the visible,' I said.

'What?'

'I love you, and I'm glad we came here. It's making me want to be a better person.'

'Maybe that's what I'm trying to say,' said Millicent. 'Maybe it's that simple.'

'Let's stop smoking,' I said.

'Just like that?'

'Just like that.'

'OK,' she said. 'Sure.' And just like that, we stopped.

We found a pub that made its own beer and served it in pint glasses. We stood and watched the cigarette smokers in the doorway, backlit, beautiful in the haze.

'How do you feel?' I asked Millicent.

'Like an outsider.'

'Missing it?'

'No . . . Yeah. A little. But this is surprisingly OK.'

'It is, isn't it.'

We drank more. Winter-dark Steamer. Unfiltered IPA.

Max rang.

'Hey, Max.'

'Where are you, Dad?'

'In a bar.'

There was a disapproving pause. 'Are you and Mum drunk?'

'No, Max, no, we're not drunk. We're just out having a good time.'

'Why?'

I looked at Millicent. She shrugged, went to the bar. 'We've been sorting a lot of things out, Max.'

'What things?'

'We're better friends again, your mum and I.'

Another pause.

'I thought you'd be glad, Max.'

Max said nothing, although I thought I heard him sigh heavily.

'And we've decided to stop smoking.'

'Really stopped, or just decided?'

'Stopped. Completely stopped. Aren't you proud of us?'

'Dad, are you drunk?'

'I'm not drunk.'

'You don't sound drunk, but what you're saying is manipulative.' He stretched out the word, as if he were testing it. *Man-i-pu-la-tive.* I wondered if this was shrink-talk, something from his sessions with Dr Å.

'Manipulative *how*, Max?'

'You're trying to make me say good things to you. You think instead of talking about how you are making me feel bad I should be nice to you, because you *say* you've stopped smoking.'

'I have stopped. We both have. I thought you'd be pleased.'

Millicent returned with beer.

'I've decided something too.'

'What, Max?'

'I've got something to show you. It's about Mum, and what she did. Bye.'

'Max,' I said, 'are you OK?'

'I'm *fine*.' A complex accusation in a simple platitude.

'I'm glad you're fine, Max.'

Max sighed. 'Bye, Dad.'

'Bye.'

Max hung up.

'So, what did they do today?' said Millicent.

'He's fine. He told me.' Millicent looked pained. 'That's good news,' I said. 'Isn't it? Given how things could be?'

'I guess,' she said.

Is there any more, I wanted to say to her, anything that I

don't yet know? Because I don't think I can take any more revelations. I need *this* to be our new beginning and our new reality. Because I'm happy now, and couldn't bear to lose that happiness for a second time.

'What is it?' she said. 'Alex?' But I shook my head and raised my glass.

On we drank, and on: Oslo Pils and summer beer; honeyed ale and stout; porter – a very creditable porter; another round of IPA. We did not smoke. We did not once consider smoking. But we did watch the smokers; we watched, nostalgic, as strangers became friends over a cigarette in the impossible Nordic light.

The voicemail was from Caroline – I checked when Millicent was at the bar. Caroline didn't say much: she could hear from the ringtone that I was abroad; she would call back. But there was a warmth to her voice that I hadn't expected. Perhaps she isn't going to be a problem for me after all.

Caroline, then.

Somewhere, almost out of sight now, is a remembered landscape. In that landscape there is no tiny house in Finsbury Park, and no Max, and no Millicent. It's a younger, more vital me that picks his way through the bars of this desolate landscape: and in that looming, infinite London I am a charmer and seducer of women.

Caroline brought me up short, though. I had met her at a vodka party in a small brick-built country house in Somerset. Friend of a friend of a friend.

'I do love to see the English upper-middle classes at play,' I said. 'Hello, by the way, I'm Alex.'

'Caroline. My party. And I am *not* an upper-middle.' Ringlets and freckles, small breasts: *very* posh.

'Aristocrat?'

'Not that it should matter.'

'It's all right, Caroline, I'm a bohemian,' I said, trying to kiss her.

'Does that line work with other girls?'

'Only the real nobs,' I said, pulling her to me.

'You're a disgrace,' she said, biting my lower lip. 'And you have those big, sad, beautiful eyes. Are you sure you're a real bohemian?'

We had spent the rest of the night in the cornfield, fully clothed. I remember my surprise as she came, my tongue in her mouth, her cunt pressed hard against my belt buckle through her bias-cut dress. Caroline had shown no embarrassment afterwards, had invited me back the next weekend. I had declined. London, I had said. Much more my kind of place.

I was an idiot. I courted Caroline, I slept with her, and I dumped her. I liked her well enough: she was pretty and funny and clever, and she knew how to behave around my London friends. She hadn't turned her nose up at my squalid little flat. But I wasn't looking for a girlfriend, and didn't want to be weighted down. She went home one weekend to her brick-built house in the country, and I brought home a Daisy, or a Mirabelle, or a Chloe.

I didn't hide the evidence from Caroline. I didn't change the sheets. It was time she knew. She had silently and with great deliberation put her clothes back on, staring at me all the way. Then she collected her shoes from beside the door and returned to sit on the bed.

'The trouble with you, Alex, is that there's something broken in you. And you think, because of your brokenness, that you can behave like a complete shit, and that I'm fair game. And that brokenness is a real problem for me, because unfortunately it makes you something close to irresistible. And I don't know what wrong you think you're righting by hurting me, but I don't deserve this.'

'No, Caroline, you deserve a viscount.'

'Oh, piss off. Grow up. I'm not the one with a problem.'

'Because you're slumming it here with me?'

'No. Because you behaved as if you liked me, and that has moral consequences. I liked you back.' She gave an angry little laugh. 'It was more than that, actually, Alex. Much, much more than that.' She was willing herself not to cry. But it was only later that I realised she was telling me she loved me.

'How dare you, you know? You use the accident of my birth as a stick to beat me. I'm just English and stuck-up, and so are my friends, and that gives you free rein. Whereas I had thought, stupidly as it turns out, that you could see past that to something more like who I was. I thought you liked me, Alex. But really you don't, do you?'

'I do like you, Caroline.'

'Your actions suggest *my* reading over yours, don't you think?'

She pulled on her shoes and crouched down, negotiated the complex strapwork by touch, staring directly at me. I made to speak, but she stopped me with a shake of the head.

'Don't, Alex. Please don't talk because you're too good at it and I can't let myself listen to you. The truth is that I'm nothing like the person you seem to think I am. I'm just as lost as you are. And I thought because you seem vulnerable and sensitive underneath that prickly Scottish carapace that you were sensitive to me and had seen something of yourself in me, and you aren't, and you didn't, and I'm completely and utterly heartbroken.'

She had walked out of my flat then.

I wondered for a long time what had made me treat her so badly. I didn't much like her friends, but I liked her, far more than I'd realised. And she loved me. She had as good as told me so.

Caroline politely answered my phone calls, and just as politely refused to meet me. After a month I understood that she meant it, that she really was telling me no. I had humiliated her, and she would not forgive that.

I waited for Caroline on the street at the end of the working day. She asked me to leave, and went back inside the gallery where she worked. I could see her making a phone call, and shortly after that she came out and stepped straight into a taxi.

The non-molestation order stopped me cold. No one wants to be the man who is cruel to women. I spent months in desperate isolation. I slept with two women. One Claire, one Janet: both firmly within my class. Both times we agreed in advance that it was sex and nothing more. Clear boundaries, no expectations, from the start. For the first time in years I was honest with the women I slept with. I had never felt less fulfilled in my life.

And yes, I sought out a shrink, though it didn't much help.

I will say this for myself, though: when Caroline forced me to face what I had done I stopped in my tracks. I paid attention. And I realised that I had allowed some angry and resentful shadow in my troubled Scottish soul to blind me to a simple truth: that Caroline had loved me, and that I had loved her.

And then came Millicent, and she was the saving of me.

PART THREE

Manifest Destiny

19

No police officer ever explained to me why they had to make the arrest in the middle of the night. We're obedient people: we do what we're told. There was no flight risk.

But I'm getting ahead of myself.

Max hugged me as I walked in through the door. He gave Millicent a dutiful kiss, then returned to the kitchen. Arla was letting him cook fish, and he stood quietly, spatula in hand, turning the fillets over in the hot oil. He looked up at Arla, who glanced down at the pan.

'You did good, Max.'

Max nodded, and smiled. Arla put a hand on his shoulder. There was an intimacy between them that surprised me.

'You've tidied up,' I said.

'We did. We tidied up. A little,' said Arla.

'It was rank,' said Max.

'It looks good,' I said. 'Thanks.'

'That's OK. Have you really stopped smoking?'

'Yes. Yes, I really have.'

'Mum too?'

'Don't we smell a little better, honey?'

Max ignored Millicent. 'Can we have wine with the food, Dad? Arla lets me.'

Millicent and I looked at Arla.

'A half-glass,' said Arla. 'Fifty-fifty with water.'

'Like in France,' said Max.

'Do you even *like* wine?' said Millicent.

'Yes,' said Max, 'I really do.'

Fried fish with rice. A tomato salad. 'This is great, Max,' I said as we ate. 'Thank you.'

'Arla helped,' he said, but I could see the pride in him. As I smiled at Arla I sensed something angular and brittle in Millicent, some slight stiffening on the edge of my vision. Arla smiled back, and by the time I turned to Millicent, she was smiling too.

The doorbell rang. I got up to answer it, wineglass in hand.

'What if it's the police, Dad?'

Yes, I thought. What then? I put my glass down on the table.

'Do you think it is, Dad?' said Max.

'I don't know.'

I felt Millicent's eyes on me. I nodded back at her. *Courage, love.* We fight this as a family.

It was Mr Ashani.

'Sir,' he said. 'I heard you through the wall.'

'Mr Ashani.' Relief coursed through me.

'Nice,' he said. He reached out his hand. I took his hand in mine. His grip was as firm as ever. 'Nice,' he said again.

'Nice,' I said, then felt embarrassed and wished I hadn't.

'Sir,' he said, 'I wish to thank you from the bottom of my heart. I owe you my life.'

'I didn't do much,' I said. Hadn't he already thanked me?

'Sir, but you did.' He had not yet released my hand. 'And your son, of course.'

'Of course.'

'A fine boy.' His eyes darted towards the kitchen, and I had for a moment a sense of a man playing to the gallery. 'He is a credit to your wife, and to you.'

'Thank you,' I said. 'What happened? Are you all right?'

He looked again towards door to the kitchen. I could hear voices, laughter. Millicent, Arla and Max were still sitting at the table. Mr Ashani leaned in close, across the threshold, still shaking my hand. He dropped his voice. 'I must speak with you.'

'That's not terribly convenient,' I said, lowering my voice to meet his. 'Could we do it tomorrow?'

'It is a matter of some urgency. And some delicacy.'

'If it's about my wife, I forgive her.'

A shrewd look passed across his features. He let go of my hand. 'It is not about your wife. Not directly.'

He invited me loudly for a sherry, and I accepted just as loudly.

I sat waiting for Mr Ashani to return from the kitchen, worrying at a piece of nail on my right thumb, foolish and out of place. Mr Ashani's front room was scrupulously tidy. Everything was old; everything immaculately preserved. There were few pictures; a small number of leather-bound books. A large Bible dominated the bookshelf, and a small wooden cross hung from a chain above the mantelpiece. The fireplace had been boarded up, and a small gas fire installed against the plasterboard.

I guessed Mr Ashani had bought his furniture when he moved in. It was upholstered in muted greens and blues. Clear plastic strips protected the arms of the chairs; the legs sat in shallow plastic cups; more plastic preserved the area of carpet around the door.

Mr Ashani returned with a glass, which he placed on a small table beside me. Cut crystal.

'Aren't you having one?'

'Kind of you, sir, but no.'

I sat, looking at the sherry.

'May I ask you an impertinent question, sir?'

'Mr Ashani,' I said, 'it makes me uncomfortable when you call me sir.'

'But we hardly know each other, sir.'

'Mr Ashani, I'm sitting here, drinking your sherry. Would you *please* call me Alex?'

He leaned over and slammed his palm down on my knee. 'Nice! Alex! Why not? But you must call me Emmanuel.'

'And will you please join me in a drink?'

'Why not?'

'OK. Emmanuel. Thank you.'

He went back into the kitchen, and returned with another cut crystal glass, which he stroked gently as he sat, nursing it like a small and delicate animal.

'Your good health, Alex.'

'Cheers, Emmanuel.'

'I am grateful for what you did, sir.' He took an appreciative sip. 'Exquisite.'

I said nothing. I took a slug of sherry. It was bitter, though I was certain that it was good sherry.

Mr Ashani leaned forwards and grasped my knee with his right hand, his eyes very close to mine. 'I owe you my life, sir.'

'I didn't do much.' I tried not to blink. There were small grey rings around his dark pupils. 'It was Max who realised you'd been very quiet.'

'A transient ischemic attack, sir.' He relaxed his grip and sat back in his chair. 'A mini-stroke, if you will. The doctors, they told me to avoid salt, and alcohol.' He looked wryly at the glass in his hand. 'But I believe the cause to be stress, so perhaps a little sherry cannot hurt. The death of our neighbour has caused me not a little distress. Now, what is it about your wife that you have forgiven?'

I said nothing.

'You may know, Alex, that Mr Bryce was not the man he

248

appeared to be.' He eyed me levelly, measuring my response. I put my glass down as carefully as I could.

'I'm aware of that.'

'You are aware of that?' His dark eyes were keen and alert, now; I wondered what he knew about Millicent and Bryce.

'I found out very recently. I know that he didn't own his house.'

'You know about his financial embarrassment?'

'He was trading from our address.' And of course, he seduced my wife. That last thought lay heavy in the air, though neither of us spoke it.

'Well,' said Mr Ashani, 'that is one of many things, Alex, that were not as they appeared to be.' Mr Ashani stood up, and opened a drawer in the dresser that stood under the stairs. He produced a small pile of envelopes, which he handed to me. 'I was of course delighted when he told me he was an architect.'

The thought surprised me. Delighted? I looked down at the envelopes. Credit-card statements, and a number of plain white envelopes. All were addressed to Mr D. Bryce.

'One wishes to find such tenants, does one not? And when the man asked if he might make a number of small improvements – at his own expense – well, it seemed too good an offer to pass up.'

'You own Bryce's house?'

'I do, sir. And when I saw the quality of the work I was rendered speechless. I assumed, foolishly I must now concede, that he was using his own money. But you hold in your hand at least £70,000 of personal debt, sir, of which £11,745 is for work on my house. Not inclusive of VAT.'

I looked down at the envelopes. They had all been neatly opened. Mr Ashani was the kind of man to own a letter knife.

'You have a key?'

'Of course. I made regular daytime inspections. The last was a day before his death. Check my arithmetic, sir: £70,000. That I know of. There may be more.'

I looked at the envelopes in my hand. Hadn't Mr Ashani committed some kind of crime by taking them?

'Take a look.'

'I'm not sure.'

I handed the envelopes back to Mr Ashani.

'You think I was not within my right to take them? They were lying unopened, in a cupboard. There are court orders here. Distraint proceedings.'

I didn't know what distraint proceedings were. Something must have shown on my face, because he said, 'Bailiffs, sir. Seizure of possessions. And I knew nothing, sir, nothing. Smiling from behind *my* net curtains, as if all was well, when he had not paid his rent for seven months. Seven months, sir! Big contract, he would say. Money coming soon. He played me like a fish, sir. Like a fish.'

He laughed bitterly to himself, then leaned in to me and took my arm in his. 'The man was so plausible. So very plausible! He convinced me that he was merely suffering a temporary embarrassment, financially. He was after all an architect. He showed me contracts, sir, for buildings costing millions.' He shuffled through the pile and selected a windowed envelope, which he tried to hand to me. 'This tells most of the story,' he said. 'About the bailiffs and the court proceedings.'

'I'm sorry,' I said. 'That's a line I don't want to cross.'

'Well, well,' he said. 'You must do as you consider right.' He was still holding out the envelope.

'I do believe you,' I said.

'Well, well.' He put the letters down on the table beside him. 'After four months I was obliged to give him notice. I have a key, as I told you, and the things I found you would not believe. The man shopped at Selfridges.' He said this as if it removed all doubt.

He must have noticed my discomfort, because he said, 'Of course, you may say that a landlord must not spy on his tenant, and technically I was in breach of our contract, but please, sir, put yourself in my shoes. When you see that the man shops at Selfridges you know this is not a *moral* man. A man in arrears does not shop at this store, sir, not until he has dealt with his embarrassment. Nor Fortnum and Mason. Nor Waitrose. And yet he did. But there was never the money to pay the rent. A squatter, sir, nothing better than a squatter! And a trained architect too. Do you understand how hard it is to evict a man like that, sir? Do you?'

'I can see it's a problem.'

'Alex, sir, I must ask you: what have the police asked you about me?'

'Nothing,' I said.

'The police have said nothing to you?'

'No,' I said. 'No, they didn't say anything to me about you.'

What did they ask you about us, I wanted to say. What more have you told them?

'I am an honest man, Alex. I was driven to this. But I would never commit an act of violence of this sort. You believe me, do you not?'

'Of course.'

'When I bought that house it was going for a song. A song, Alex. I charge a reasonable rent. A fair market rent. And now I find, to my bemusement, that *I* am a millionaire. On paper. But I have no cash flow, sir, only costs. Can you imagine how difficult it is for me to live without cash flow? My pension, it doesn't come close.'

For a moment I actually wondered if he had done it. I found myself anxiously staring at the pleats in his trousers. He clearly made regular use of an iron, and he had reasons, financial and moral, to dislike his tenant. But the thought was absurd, and I put it from my mind.

'Why are you telling me this, Emmanuel?'

'Who else can I tell, Alex, sir? I have no one.' A change came upon him. The muscles in his face sagged and his shoulders dropped; he looked diminished, beaten: a seventy-seven-year-old man who lived alone and worried about the future. I reached across and put a hand on his arm. He nodded, patted it with his free hand.

'You are lucky you have your beautiful wife. What is it that you have forgiven her for?'

'Nothing,' I said. 'She did nothing wrong.'

'And yet you have forgiven her?'

'Yes.'

When he showed me to the door a little later I realised he had not once mentioned God.

I went home and made calls.

My mother was finding it hard to sleep. Edinburgh was unseasonably hot and the flat was like an oven. She was all right, she said; she was getting by. She had a fan in the bedroom, but it wasn't much use. I sensed that she did not want the call to end. But neither of us is good at smalltalk, so we spoke instead about forgiveness. My mother believed forgiveness brought relief to the person who had been wronged, more than to the wrongdoer. She wanted to speak about forgiveness as part of God's plan for mankind. I did not.

Neither of us spoke about my father, though he hovered at the edges of our conversation like a shadow. You're wrong, I thought, Mum. He craved your forgiveness; he never dared ask because he thought himself unforgivable.

I called my boss and apologised for calling him a cunt. I had, I explained, been under the influence of morphine at the time. I did not think he was a cunt, and deeply regretted the offence I had caused him. I did not expect him to give me my job back. It had been reasonable of him to sack me.

'There's something we can agree on,' he said, and hung up.

I rang Dee. She rejected my call, so I left her a short message apologising for my lack of engagement and explaining that my family had been under a lot of pressure, that someone close to us had died, and that I deeply regretted that she and I were no longer working together.

Half an hour later Dee's agent rang to tell me that Dee accepted my apology. She wished me well. There were no hard feelings.

Relief flooded my body; I was shocked to discover that Dee's words could mean so much. It's not as if we were friends.

'Dad,' said Max later, as we sat on his bed, 'Dad, what did Mr Ashani tell you about Mum?'

'Nothing, Max. That's not what we talked about.'

'You didn't ask him about her?'

'No.'

'So what happened in Norway then?'

'We stopped smoking. I think you'd like it there.'

'That's not what I meant. What did she *say* to you in Norway?'

'What do you mean?'

'You said you were going away to talk about what happened. But now you're all loving again. Why didn't you say you know the neighbour *did* her?'

'It wasn't like that. Mum knows I know about her affair.'

'It's like *you* keep forgetting, though.'

'People make mistakes, Max.'

'You can't just let her get away with it.' There were angry tears in Max's eyes now. 'You can't just *forgive* her.'

'Actually, I can.'

'Why?'

'Because bad things happen when you don't forgive people.'

'You think she wouldn't have hit you with the bottle if you forgave her?'

'Nevertheless, Max, I have forgiven her.' I could feel a pricking in my own eyes. I swallowed hard, put thumb and forefinger to my forehead, and breathed deeply.

'What do you want, Max? Do you want us to split up? Because the consequences if I don't forgive her are . . . you know, it would be bleak.'

'You don't have to split up. But you shouldn't just . . .' said Max. 'I mean, look.'

He reached into his trouser pocket, then held out to me a cheap black notebook. The cover was worn and striated. I looked down at it but didn't take it.

'It's about what happened when the neighbour did Mum.'

'A diary?' Max nodded and pressed it into my palm. 'Max, listen to me. Your mother made a mistake. It's over, and I am going to forgive her. You need to understand that. I am not looking for new reasons to be angry with her. If you want me to read your diary, those are my terms.'

'OK,' he said, after thinking for a while. 'I still think you should read it.'

We sat on his bed, not speaking. Max picked up a comic book. The defiance in him belonged to someone much older. 'OK, boy-man,' I said. 'I will read your diary.'

'Don't talk to me like that.' The slightness of that body – too small, too angular, too breakable. I ruffled his hair. He pushed me off, suppressed a smile, became serious again.

'Max, you're eleven,' I said.

'I know.'

'For your age, you're the most grown-up person I know.'

'I know, Dad.' Another suppressed smile. 'So are you.'

'Cheeky wee bastard,' I said.

'Same to you.'

At eleven I left Millicent and Arla talking downstairs. I brushed my teeth, undressed, and lay on top of the bed.

Inside the scuffed covers of Max's diary the pages were yellowed, uneven; something seemed to have spilled and dried, fading and separating the black ink into diffuse blues and reds. I looked again at the covers and the spine. The coarse fibres were unevenly spread, stained: watermarked.

I saw now that the whole book had been wet. Max must have dried it, then prised the pages apart; he seemed to have gone over the faded text with a fresh pen. There were pencil drawings too which had smudged a little where the pages had rubbed against each other in his trouser pocket.

The smudging and the rewriting gave Max's book a childish, incomplete feel. I half-closed my eyes, and the water damage and the smudges faded away. The diary became much more workmanlike: evenly spaced text, small images placed where the eye naturally fell.

A shift in the shadows on the far wall. I opened my eyes. The door was open, and Millicent was standing there watching me.

'What are you doing?'

'Max's diary,' I said.

'That isn't how you read a diary.'

'I was looking at the composition.'

'An excellent avoidance strategy.'

'Avoidance?'

'Yeah, that way you get to not engage with it. Do you think maybe you'll read it and decide that you don't forgive me for what I did?'

'Max doesn't want me to forgive you.'

'Think you *can* read it and still forgive me?'

'Obviously. Yes.'

'So I was thinking I would come to bed now. But I guess Arla is planning to be up for a while. I could go downstairs again.'

'No,' I said. 'Lie here.'

'You sure?'

'I've forgiven you, Millicent. That's the spirit in which I'm going to read it.'

She took off her shoes and lay on her back. 'Alex,' she said, 'you're in the process of forgiving me, which is not the same thing.'

After a time she closed her eyes. I watched her, beautiful in her white cotton shirt and black fitted skirt. I caressed her hair with my hand. *Mine*, I thought: *I really need you to be mine.*

When I was certain Millicent was asleep I began to read. Max's diary began on the evening Bryce had seduced Millicent. Max had known instantly. He had heard her take off her shoes and lay them gently on the landing, had seen her shadow cross the gap beneath his door; he had felt as much as heard the boards as they shifted beneath her. Some permanent change in the chemical structure of the house, I thought: old bonds broken, new bonds forged.

Max had crept to the bathroom. From beneath the open window he had heard his faithless mother emerge from the kitchen into the garden, heard her feet tracking low across the uncut grass. He had heard the love seat creak as she jumped easily up on to the wall. He had heard her footfalls on the other side as she landed and walked on, there to open bottles and crack bone with next-door neighbour Bryce.

The acuity of Max's hearing was a torment all its own. He had heard the flick and snap of cigarette lighter, the chink of coffee pot on china cup, the mangling of daisies under foot and under thigh.

He had not looked out of the window; once his mother was in the neighbour's garden she was hidden by the trained foliage of the hated neighbour's verdant bower. But he had heard the neighbour's terms of endearment: 'sweetest', 'loveliest', 'darlingest': they sickened him; they made him want to drench Bryce's front room in angry shards of glass, to throw a chair through his perfect little bay window, to knock out his perfect white teeth.

Then came the sex. From his room at the front of the house Max would hear the insistent rhythm of Bryce's lust, could feel, almost, the scrape of bed leg on ancient board. He would slink from his room unheard, senses raging. Crouched in our bathroom he discerned his mother and her seducer, their voices, their every whisper and moan.

It was summer. His mother had left the windows open: of course Max heard the sex.

According to Max, Bryce had <u>intercoursed</u> Millicent eleven times. He had recorded it all using the words he had learned from the books we had given him; he had counted the number of <u>orgasms</u> (for some reason he had underlined the word each time it appeared), and the number of <u>strokes</u> that had led to each <u>orgasm</u>; he had written down the words that Bryce had shouted as he had got there. Five Oh Gods, two Oh Jesuses, three Fucks and one Christ.

If Millicent had achieved orgasm, her son had not recorded the fact. I looked across at her but felt no anger now. Instead I felt a strange kind of fear. What was this knowledge doing to our son?

Max had been awake and had documented each occasion in words that betrayed no emotion. I supposed it made it easier. But against each record of sex he had drawn an illustration of a man. In each drawing the man was dressed in a polo shirt but naked from the waist down, with little round glasses and a tiny childlike penis. It was Bryce. It could only be Bryce.

The drawings were dated. Max had scratched the day, month and year on to the neighbour's flaccid penis. The first showed only Bryce, frontally, shouting 'Oh God', his eyes represented by crosses behind the lenses of his glasses. The next drawing showed him shouting 'Fuck!' with a giant noose around his neck. The third showed Bryce walking over a cliff, cartoon-like, the noose around his neck suspended from an unseen point in the sky. Then came Bryce in a forest, the noose slung around a high branch, as he shouted 'Oh Jesus'.

This was cartoon violence, no more. What eleven-year-old boy wouldn't want to see his mother's seducer punished? Be a devoted son, turn sex into death: *process* your rage. Here in this book Max could be anyone he wanted and what he wanted to be was this: Max the vengeful deity, tormenting the man who

257

had cuckolded his father and defiled his mother. Really, who could blame him? No child should be exposed to that.

The scenarios became more elaborate: Bryce suspended from a crane on a construction site; Bryce on a buffalo with a rope tied to a giraffe; Bryce jumping from a burning building, the rope tied to a window ledge. 'Oh Jesus!' ejaculated Cartoon Bryce, 'Oh fuck!', 'Oh Christ!'

My poor, poor son. Max could not have known that Bryce would take his own life. You wish him dead, you draw it in cartoon form, over and over, and presto, the neighbour is gone. A parody of magical thinking. Who wouldn't be crippled by that guilt? The thing you most desire, but the last thing you actually want: the reality of death so much worse than the fantasy. And yet my son still seemed surprisingly sane. Angry, but sane.

I looked up at Millicent, watched for a while as her chest rose and fell, thought how strange it was that we were together after all this, that we'd found a way back to each other in the midst of so much betrayal. I wondered why I felt so little anger now. Perhaps, I thought, we are evolving. We had begun repairing our marriage: perhaps we could repair Max too.

I turned the page.

I had to turn the book on its side. This was a completely different kind of drawing, using the full width of the double page, still childlike, but far more detailed than the cartoons: Bryce in a bedroom with a noose over the door handle, his crumpled body slumped beside the door, dead, no speech bubble, a book splayed open on the floor beside him, spine up. Max had used colour this time, reddening the cheeks and the lolling tongue.

Bryce was completely naked, and completely, believably dead. I thought of how Bryce had looked on the evening we'd found him in the bath. That was the Bryce in the picture. I could feel the blood pulsing in my ears now, slow but loud, a strange rushing sound.

Another description of sex followed, two minutes and forty-seven seconds of Bryce <u>intercoursing</u> Millicent, one hundred and fifty-seven strokes, at the end of which Bryce had shouted 'Ah, yes!' Very loudly, according to Max.

I could hear the blood pumping in my ears. The book on the floor – it was one of Millicent's. Max hadn't completed the title, but the words 'for Cynics' were very clear, and you could just make out the faint shape of Millicent's first name on the cover. *Millicent for Cynics*. A message, I thought. My clever, angry son: old beyond his years.

'What is it, Alex?' said Millicent.

'Sleep, Millicent,' I said. *Breathe*, I thought.

'You're so restless. What is it?'

'It's nothing,' I said. 'Sleep.'

Millicent propped herself up on an elbow. 'You think I've been asleep? Are you out of your mind?' She reached for the notebook. 'You are so crazy-tense, Alex.'

'He probably doesn't want me to give you this.'

Millicent looked at me, paused for a moment, then took the notebook.

'Well, OK,' I said.

'Make coffee, Alex,' she said softly.

I nodded and went downstairs.

Arla was in the kitchen, reading. I nodded at her too, and looked in the cupboard for the coffee-maker.

'You OK, Alex?' she said. 'You seem a little . . .'

'Tense? Yes, I'm a little tense.'

'Agitated would be the word.'

'Yes. I'm a little agitated.'

'Tell me you did not tell her.' A half-whisper; still the spun-sugar Californian lightness.

I looked at her.

'Alex, I need to know you did not tell Millicent.'

'You know, Arla, you and Millicent share a lot of the same mannerisms,' I said. 'Which might explain why I . . .'

'Why you . . . why you what, Alex?' she said.

'Did . . .' I said.

'Me?' she said. 'Why you did me?'

'Not the way I was trying to say it,' I said. 'But yes. I want you to know I feel OK about what we . . . did.'

'Yeah, we already had that conversation, Alex. I'm glad to know you feel OK about doing me. Because I *really* do not feel *OK* about what we did. Not at all. I need for you to tell me that you are not going to tell Millicent. You know, in some get-it-all-off-my-chest-and-start-afresh douchey husbandy kind of a way.'

'Your voice,' I said. 'So full of light and air.'

'Alex,' she said. 'You need to tell me you will not unburden.'

'That wasn't why I came downstairs. But all right. I am not going to tell Millicent. I will not *unburden*.'

'So then this is . . . What is this conversation?'

'Millicent sent me downstairs to make coffee.'

'You and my sister are equally weird,' she said. 'You know that, right?'

I could feel tears gathering at the edges of my eyes. I nodded and tried to smile. 'How has Max been?' I said.

'Eleven-year-old boys smell of urine and cheap candy,' she said, all Pacific Coast again. 'Max doesn't. You guys did a good job. Sure, he swears a little, but really he's a nice, smart kid. He's super-well housebroken.'

'Thank you,' I said. I swallowed hard. 'I have coffee to make.'

I stood at the stove, my back to Arla, sobbing silently as I measured coffee into the coffee-maker. Then I realised I'd forgotten the water. I lifted the aluminium filter out with my thumbnails, spilling coffee on the work surface. Arla got a cloth and wiped up the grounds. 'Sorry,' I said. She shook her head gently, took the coffee-maker from me and filled it at the sink. I stood uselessly beside her as she dropped the filter back in and screwed on the top. She lit the gas and put the coffee-maker on the stove.

Then she turned and looked very directly at me. 'You know,' she said, 'I really do not do this shit.' Then she stood on tiptoe and held me very tight in her arms. I began to sob again, silently but uncontrollably.

I didn't know why I was crying. I only knew that it had something to do with my son, and with his drawings. *Talk to him.* There was a rage and a pain in Max's drawings of his mother's seducer – and God knew, Millicent's betrayal had brought me both rage and pain too – but there was something more frightening as well, like a great beast slowly unfurling its wings, loosening the terrifying coils of its tail.

I knew I was holding Arla too tight, but couldn't relax my grip. Please God, I thought, let Max come through this in one piece.

When the water bubbled through the coffee-maker I broke away from Arla and turned off the gas. Arla opened the cupboard and got out two cups.

'You don't want any?' I said.

'I really do *not*,' she said, and I was surprised by the warmth in her smile. I stared at her for the longest time.

'What?' she said.

'People are kinder than you realise. Or kinder than I realise. Or at least, you are. And really Millicent is.'

She raised a mocking eyebrow. 'Always the comparisons, Alex.'

'I'm sorry.'

'I'm joking,' she said. 'I like that you think I'm kind.'

'OK. What do *we* do now?'

'Nothing, Alex. We do nothing at all. Please. We did a bad thing. There is *nothing* we can do to make it better. Nothing. And now your coffee is made and you can go back upstairs.' She guided me towards the living room. As I climbed the stairs, I thought I could feel her eyes on me, but wasn't certain if I had imagined it.

Millicent and I sat in silence on the bed drinking coffee.

'So,' she said after a time, 'I guess this kind of annihilates a whole lot of the good stuff we did in Norway.'

I drank down the rest of my coffee, held my hand beside the bedpost and let the cup slide through my fingers on to the floor. The sound of china on wood was bright, metallic. I looked down. The cup had landed upright.

'Are you going to leave me, Alex?' said Millicent. I reached out and took her face in my hands, turned her so she was facing me.

'No,' I said quietly.

'I had no idea that he had heard everything. You have to believe me.'

'I believe you, Millicent,' I said.

I wondered whether we had any cigarettes left downstairs. Millicent flicked distractedly through Max's book, saying nothing. Then she made a show of closing the book and placing it on the bed directly between us. 'You're going to leave me,' she said, matter-of-factly. 'You actually have to.'

'I'm not going to leave you, Millicent.'

Millicent spoke as if she hadn't heard me. 'I thought we started to mend our family,' she said. 'I actually started to feel like I could be a good person again. When you and I were alone. And now it looks like things are way more broken than I knew, and I'm the one who broke them. And whatever I do I don't get to be the good person again because look at what I did to our son.'

I said nothing. I wanted to tell her that we needed to fix ourselves if we were going to fix Max, but as soon as the words formed they felt misshapen, self-justifying. *Happy parent, happy child. I'm OK, you're OK.* Mantra of a generation of bad parents.

The sound of the doorbell cut across that thought, brought me back into the now. Someone was ringing the bell. Someone was standing on our doorstep. Someone wanted us to open the door.

I looked at Millicent. A fight? A stabbing? A deal gone wrong? *Don't open it.*

Millicent's eyes registered confusion, then concern, then something very like panic. Still the bell rang.

I picked up my phone. Two thirty. *Go away.*

The bell stopped ringing. I was on my feet. 'Millicent,' I said.

Millicent sat up, swung her feet across the bed as if about to get up. Then she froze.

'Millicent?' *What do we do?*

She looked at me and shook her head.

Four heavy knocks. Bottom of the fist. Arm extended upwards.

'Millicent?' I said again. *What do I do?*

Still Millicent sat transfixed.

Perhaps it was Mr Ashani. Perhaps he could not sleep.

The landing light came on. I heard small footsteps on the stairs.

'Max, wait!'

I was out of the bedroom and down the stairs but he had the door open.

The pinstriped suit. The apologetic smile. It was June.

'What?' I said. 'It's the middle of the night.'

'I'm sorry, Mr Mercer,' she said. She tipped her head to one side, and I saw, behind her in the street, two uniformed officers.

'Max,' I said, 'go back inside.'

'What is it, Dad?' said Max.

'Just go back inside.'

'But where, Dad?'

'Upstairs,' I said. 'Now.'

'Alex,' said June, 'Alex, I'm sorry.'

'In front of my own kid, June? Really?'

'Orders from above. This is not the way it should be. That's why I came along. I'm sorry . . .'

'Are you in the police?' said Max, defiant in his lion pyjamas.

'Yes, son. Do as your dad says, son.'

'He didn't do anything to the neighbour.'

'Max,' I said, 'go upstairs. Now.'

'But you didn't, did you, Dad?'

'Max,' I said, 'I know you're trying to help, but go upstairs. Find Mum.'

Max turned and with the slowness of the sullen child walked back up the stairs. Everyone else stayed where they were. The uniformed officers hung back in the street, the detective stood hard against the threshold, looking in, and I stood, framed in the doorway.

I realised I was naked. I looked down at my penis, thought how odd it looked, how out of context.

'Give me five minutes to get dressed and explain to Millicent,' I said.

'No, Mr Mercer,' said the detective.

'What do you mean, no?'

'We're here for your wife.'

20

The police arrested Millicent for the murder of the neighbour at a little before three in the morning. June was sorry. No, she couldn't explain to me why it had to happen then, why they couldn't simply invite her down to the station during working hours and quietly make the arrest when she arrived. It was far from ideal, she said. She agreed that Millicent was not a flight risk.

I invited the officers into the front room. Max came back downstairs carrying a pair of pants, which he handed to me. I put them on and he held my hand.

We stood in silence as Millicent went back upstairs and dressed, the door to the street open. I thought about Mr Ashani, wondered what he would think if he could see us now: me in my pants, Max in his pyjama bottoms, watching the police officers with suspicion. I could hardly bring myself to look at the detective.

Millicent came downstairs in a white shirt and dark skirt, with the training shoes she had worn in the park.

'I'll find you a lawyer,' I said.

She shook her head, asked me to bring her a list of local solicitors. She wanted to decide herself who would represent her, I realised. She wanted to retain the illusion of control.

She whispered a few words to Max, then left with the officers. They didn't handcuff her, though one of them rested a hand on her arm as they walked to a police car parked across the road. The detective hung back, reluctant to leave.

'What?' I said.

'Come in the morning, Alex. Not much you can do while she's being processed.'

From the doorway we watched her go. She walked stiffly across the road to the car, got into the back seat beside Millicent. I tried to find Millicent's eyes, to let her know that I loved her, that we would fight this, but she was too far away and the street was too dark.

Max had gone to bed, palely, quietly, had asked no questions; he had meekly turned on his side and fallen asleep, his arms wound tightly around his pillow. I wondered what he understood of what had just happened. I didn't know myself. Should I have kept him up? Asked what he was feeling?

What do you do?

I went back into our room and looked for Max's book, but he must have taken it back before he went to bed. I wondered if Dr Å had encouraged him to get his feelings down on to paper. Did it help him, to draw those angry pictures and write those angry words, or did it just make everything miserably vivid?

I decided to spend what was left of the night on the landing, my back to the banister, watching my son as he slept. *We'll fight this, Max.* That's what families do, isn't it, when bad things happen? They fight. But how?

What are we fighting?

At a little after five I opened the door to Millicent's office. There on the single mattress on the floor was Arla, naked, her cotton sheet half thrown off. *Don't look.* Her breasts were so small compared to Millicent's, and so high, and the last thing I should be thinking of. *Don't look.* Her nipples were lighter than Millicent's in colour, despite the deep Pacific Coast tan.

Held, I thought. I want to be held. *Perhaps you could hold me.* But as soon as I felt the thought I banished it from my mind. *At a time like this. What's wrong with me?*

'Arla,' I said quietly, crouching down beside the bed. 'Arla, wake up.'

Millicent had gone to meet her fate without shouting, without raising her voice; she had hardly even spoken. It had all been so very quiet, so very civilised. The police had been sober and respectful. No drama. Arla was the only one of us who didn't know. She had slept through her sister's arrest.

She sat up in bed. I could smell the sleep on her. 'Arla,' I said again. *Musky. Sweet.*

'Stupid douchey English birds. What in the world time do they wake up?' Then she looked at me, as if seeing me for the first time. She rearranged herself, pulled up the sheet to shield her breasts. 'Alex, this is not a good idea. You can not be in here.'

'I have to talk to you,' I said.

'Well, it's light, I guess. What time is it?'

'Five. The police have taken Millicent.'

'They arrested her?'

'In front of Max.'

She was silent.

How can I want you at a time like this, I thought. *I love her, and I know I love her now, and yet all I want to do is lie down beside you. Just hold me.*

'Oh, Alex,' she said. 'No.'

I want you to raise the sheet and let me lie down beside you. I mean, I know this has to be faced. And I will face it.

She was staring at me in utter disbelief. 'This is bad,' I said. 'I don't know what to do. What do I do, Arla?'

Just one hour. Max is asleep. We could pretend for one hour that this isn't happening. Just one hour, and I promise I'll face reality after that.

'I can't do what you want, Alex,' she said. 'Please stop.'

'What?'

'We can't pretend Millicent didn't get arrested,' she said, 'and I can not invite you into my bed. This is a bad situation, Alex. We have to figure out what to do.'

'What?' I stared back at her. 'What did you say?' I searched her eyes for some clue as to how she had divined my thoughts. 'How? I mean . . . yeah, how?'

'Alex,' she said. 'Your filter is not in place.'

'What?'

'I think maybe this is a shock reaction. You are not filtering your thoughts.'

'What do you mean?'

'You love Millicent, and you know you love her, and yet you want to lie down here beside me.'

'Did I say that aloud?' *Please, no.*

'Yeah,' she said. 'Yeah, you said that out loud.'

Oh please, no. I put my hand against the wall to steady myself. I looked down, and for the second time in a few hours was surprised by my nakedness. Why hadn't I dressed? When had I taken off my pants? *Christ on a bike.*

A thought struck me. 'Arla,' I said, 'did you hear me say "Please, no?"'

'Yeah,' she said. 'Yeah, I heard you say that. And "Christ on a bike." And that your penis looks weird.'

'Oh Jesus. Oh God. It's me, isn't it? I thought that was some weird echo from the arrest. It's me, Arla. We thought it would be Max, but it's me. I'm the one who's not coping with this. I'm the madman standing naked in front of you, with my inner censor switched off, sharing stuff that shouldn't be shared. I've become that man.'

'Alex,' she said, 'you're talking super-fast.'

'But I'm not.' *Everything is echoes.* 'Am I?'

'Yes, Alex, you are. I'm going to need you to slow down and breathe. Alex, look at me. You can *not* lose your shit.'

'I'm scared, Arla. I'm losing my mind.'

'We are not going to let that happen, Alex. You're in shock. We have got to get you to land your rocket ship on the right freakin' planet. And then we need to figure out how to help Millicent. Breathe.'

She got out of bed, stood naked in the middle of the floor, held me in her arms and counted with me as I breathed in for four beats, held my breath for four beats, and breathed out for four beats.

Breathe . . . two . . . three . . . four . . .

Hold . . . two . . . three . . . four . . .

Out . . . two . . . three . . . four . . .

'Wow,' she said after a time. 'Your pulse is really racing. Still. How we doing up there? Any closer to Planet Earth?'

'A little better,' I said. 'Thank you for holding me.'

I looked down at her. *Her skin against mine; her breasts crushed against my ribcage; her beautiful arms.*

She looked up at me, frowned. 'You guys sure have it tough.'

'You didn't hear my thought? When I looked down?'

'No,' she said. 'I think maybe your filter is back in place. You did not speak that thought.'

'I'm a mess. I'm ashamed of what I said to you.'

'No need, Alex.' Her voice was candy-store light, but there was a weariness in her eyes, a tightness around the edges of her mouth.

'I wasn't trying to sleep with you, Arla,' I said. 'I really wasn't. I think my mind was just trying to side-step reality.'

'Well, I guess you guys' reality really does suck right now.'

'And we've pulled you into it. I'm sorry.'

'Again, no need.'

'Max mustn't find us like this.'

'He won't, Alex,' she said. 'He won't.' Then she patted me on the back, brought the embrace to an end, and sent me back to my own bedroom.

21

I arrived at the police station at nine.

I had left Arla to sleep, called Fab5 and asked him if he could take Max to school. Max hadn't wanted to go, and we had argued furiously over this.

'Normality,' I said, over and over again. 'We need to keep things as normal for you as possible.'

'But this isn't normal, Dad.'

'I'm really sorry, but this is the nearest thing to normal I can provide.'

'But nothing's normal, Dad. Not even nearly.'

Max had eaten his cereal in angry silence, playing a game on my phone; he was dressed and sitting on the staircase when Fab5 rang the bell.

I sat waiting in a large room with white-painted brick walls. In the middle of the room were four blue plastic chairs and a small Formica table. One of the fluorescent tubes overhead was flickering its last, beating out a rhythm that my brain could not lock into. The ceiling was made of suspended plastic panels. There was no window.

Millicent entered with two uniformed officers. I wondered for a moment whether they were the two from the night before, but decided they couldn't have been. Union regulations. Millicent drew up a seat opposite me. We sat staring at each other across the table. She looked tired, but no worse than I was used to her looking these days.

'You look good,' I said.

'Thank you. I do not.'

I looked around at the officers, who were hovering by the door. What do you do in this situation? Do you kiss? Are you allowed to hug? I reached out and took Millicent's hand.

'Sir,' said one of the officers. Twenty-five. Fresh-faced. Whole career ahead of him. 'Sorry,' I said. I withdrew my hand.

The other officer, female, plump and cheerful, shook her head in mock approbation. I guessed she was a little older. She said something to her colleague and left the room.

The finality of that gentle metallic slam. Steel door in a steel frame. The young officer locked the door, then collected a chair from by the table, and went to sit in the corner of the room.

'So I'm in custody, but they didn't charge me yet,' said Millicent.

'They aren't going to charge you. You didn't do it. You have your alibi.'

'I don't know,' she said. 'I was never in this situation. And I was only at the radio station for an hour, max. What if they ring the radio station, and decide I lied to them? I never knew I was going to have to defend my alibi.'

'Have you called a lawyer?' I said.

Millicent shook her head. I took out a list of criminal defence solicitors that I had made from the internet and slid it across the table towards her.

'Just a moment, sir, ma'am,' said the officer in the corner. He walked to the table and looked down at the sheet of paper.

I caught Millicent's eye, mouthed 'I love you.'

The edges of her mouth twitched upwards. A parody of a smile. 'I guess I'm lucky you guys didn't cuff me to the table,' she said to the officer.

'Right,' he said. He picked up the sheet of paper.

'This is going to be OK,' I said.

'We don't know this is going to be OK, Alex.'

The officer turned the sheet of paper over, held it up to the light. What was he looking for?

'So far everyone has been really nice and polite. But they didn't really start to ask me questions yet. Who knows how that's going to go?'

The officer decided he was satisfied with the sheet of paper. He pushed it across the table towards her and went back to his chair.

'So,' she said, 'I guess at some level I deserve this, don't you think?'

I drew breath, made to speak, but she cut across me before I could begin. 'Because what I did to you and to our marriage was bad. I took something that was only a little broken, and broke it a whole lot more. But what I did to Max is worse: I can see that now. Only Max can't punish me by leaving me, so you will.'

'Millicent, shut up,' I said very quietly. 'Shut up and listen to me.' I took her hand, but she shook me off.

'Sir,' said the officer in the corner. 'Sir, please.'

'Sorry,' I said. I turned to Millicent. 'I'm sorry, Millicent. I shouldn't have done that.' I looked over at the officer in the corner. 'We need to talk about what you're going to do.'

'I'm going to ring a lawyer.'

'We need to formulate a plan. I don't know how long they're going to give us.'

'And I just told you the plan, so we're done with that. I'm going to ring a lawyer. Thank you for bringing me the information. You can go.'

'Millicent, you are not yourself.'

She looked up at the ceiling. The light was still advertising its own imminent death. I wondered if the flickering was making her nervous. It was certainly putting me on edge.

Millicent ran her thumb and middle finger over her eyebrow, then looked me directly in the eye.

'No. I mean this, Alex. I seriously breached the mother/son clause. And now Max hates me. Doesn't he?'

'OK, yes, he hates you.'

She was gulping air now; her nostrils flared; she was fighting not to cry. 'Well, look at that,' she said. 'I guess I was hoping you would contradict me, Alex. Stupid, no?'

'No, I think you're right. He does hate you. I hate you too, if I'm being honest.'

I could see the blood pulsing in her neck but the colour had drained from her face; she looked utterly undone. I glanced across at the police officer but he was looking at something on his phone.

'I hate you a bit, Millicent. Just at the moment.'

'What do you mean?'

'Look around you. Look where we are.' The gunmetal door, the painted brick walls, the police officer in the corner. He was staring at us now. I leaned in to Millicent and lowered my voice. 'It was hard to read what Max wrote. What he knows.' The door opened and the female officer appeared in the opening. She nodded to her colleague, who got up from his seat and put away his phone, staring all the while.

'Ms Weitzman, it's time to go.' It was the female officer. Millicent stood up. I stayed in my seat.

Millicent looked at me and swallowed hard, sniffed noisily.

'I hate you *now*, Millicent. I don't think it's for ever,' I said. 'I can pretty easily imagine a world where I don't hate you. Max will stop hating you too, although it might take him a little longer. It's a process, too.'

She considered this. When she spoke, it was in a very small voice, her face very close to mine. 'It's too late for us.'

'It's never too late. I love you, and no matter what you did, I will always love you. And I understand now that that means I have to forgive you.'

'Well, you're a bigger person than I am.'

'Ms Weitzman, now.' A hand in the small of Millicent's back, a uniformed arm, guiding her towards the door.

She stood in the doorway, the officers towering over her in her plain clothes and her flat shoes; I wanted to tell Millicent that everything would be OK, that we would fight this.

Instead I said, 'Do you think I could say goodbye to my wife?'

The officers exchanged a look. The WPC nodded at me. 'You do have that right.'

'Can I hold her?'

'I think that's more a question for your wife.'

I looked at Millicent. She nodded cautiously, stood stiffly as I held her in my arms.

'You're strong,' I said. 'You'll be out soon.'

'Yeah,' she said, 'maybe,' and stepped backwards out of the embrace.

The sadness in that tight little smile as they led her from the room.

I looked at the open door. I looked at my chair. Was I supposed to wait here? No one had said. I sat back down at the table. After five minutes the female officer returned and led me back through countless corridors towards the front desk.

'When can I collect her?'

'That depends, sir.'

'There's nothing to charge her with.' *Why have you stopped being cheerful?*

The officer came to a stop, and for a moment I thought

275

perhaps I had spoken my thought, but she simply said, 'Your wife is under arrest on suspicion of murder, sir.'

'When can I come for her?'

'The custody clock started at 03.00 hours.'

'So I come and get her at three tomorrow morning? You let her go after twenty-four hours, don't you?'

'That's not for me to say, sir. Really her lawyer should be advising you on that.'

I considered this. Perhaps I should have taken control. Perhaps it had been a mistake to expect Millicent to choose her own lawyer.

'Alex.' A hand on my arm. I turned and found myself eye to eye with the female detective. June.

'Oh.'

'I'll take this, Pamela,' she said.

The uniformed officer brightened. 'Cheers, mate.' She walked off along the corridor.

'Well,' I said, 'this is awkward.'

'What do you mean?'

'You arrested my wife. I was just leaving.'

We walked in silence to the door of the police station, stood on the top step, looking at each other's shoes. The sky was overcast and the humidity unbearable, as if London were projecting a hangover back on to me.

'Alex,' said June, 'have you ever come across the notion of the gendering of crime?'

'OK, June . . . What is the gendering of crime?'

'Men and women kill in different ways.'

'What, you mean men murder strangers they don't like the look of with knives and guns, and women murder lovers who mistreat them with poison, and smother babies they can't take care of with pillows?'

'Something like that, statistically speaking, yes.'

'Bit reductive. What's your point, *June*?'

'The iron.'

I laughed. I laughed as I had when I discovered the corpse of the neighbour, all rictus and dick and discordant limbs.

The detective looked consternated. 'Generally speaking, women use what's to hand in the home.'

'Really, June? That's your case?' I was laughing hard now. 'You think Millicent is the kind of woman who uses an iron? I mean, do we even look like the kind of couple that owns an iron? Because I promise you we don't. You really don't know my wife.'

Absurd. Completely absurd.

'It was a Black and Decker iron. Practically a tool. How much more manly can an iron get?'

'Alex,' she said. 'Listen to me . . .'

She looked so serious, standing there sweating in her pinstripes.

'No, June, you listen to me.' I composed myself for a moment. 'I mean, I suppose she could have stabbed him with her nail file, or beaten him about the head with her hairdryer, or tickled him to death with her makeup brush. Except, guess what, she doesn't own any of those either.'

Tears were filling my eyes now. I rubbed them away with the back of my hand, made myself tall, forced myself to stop laughing.

'Thanks,' I said. 'I really needed that.'

'Alex,' said the detective, 'I'm not sure you appreciate the seriousness of your situation.'

'Yes, June, if there's one thing I appreciate, it's the seriousness of my situation. And of Millicent's. You think I'm not gravely concerned? But – unlike you, it seems – I know the difference between serious and absurd. And this is – and I'm sorry, because I'm trying really hard to keep the swearing in check – this is fucking absurd. I mean, I don't want to tell you your job or anything, but *Ms Mercer? In the bathroom? With an iron?* Are you out of your mind?'

'Bottle of wine, wasn't it?' she said. There was no cruelty in the words, but the laughter froze on my lips.

My hand moved involuntarily towards my face. I stopped it before it could reach the subtle tracery of dried blood, all that now remained of the blow Millicent had dealt me in the kitchen.

'No,' I wanted to say. 'No, that's not the same thing.'

'Have you spoken to a DV team?' she said.

I nodded. 'At the hospital.'

'And have you considered whether to press charges?' The sympathetic look was back.

'I shouldn't have laughed,' I said. 'It's the stress of all this. I know you have a job to do.'

She nodded. 'You're dealing with an intolerable burden,' she said. 'You need to know that we already have a twelve-hour extension on your wife's custody. Approved by an inspector. But after that she's out.'

'What are you saying? That you want more time?'

'I'm telling you how things are.'

'I can't press charges against Millicent.'

Mr Sharpe wanted the meeting over as quickly as I did. Neither of us mentioned that he had seen me in the pub with Rose; nor did he ask where Millicent was, nor how things were at home. He knew we were having difficulties, he said. It was perhaps to be expected that Max was *acting out*. Had we spoken to Max about what he had done, about why he had punched Ravion Stamp?

Yes.

Ravion Stamp did not have a spectrum disorder, as Max appeared to believe. He was a normal little boy. He and Max did not like each other, but they would be going on to different secondary schools after the summer break.

All right.

Perhaps we should leave it at that, then?

Perhaps we should.

We shook hands and left it at that.

* * *

278

Caroline. I had completely forgotten about Caroline. Something – Norway? Arla? the arrest? – had erased her from my mind.

She rang me as I left the school, asked if I would meet her for lunch at a members' club near Manchester Square. And I went, although in truth I did not know why. It was Millicent who needed my help now, not I who needed Caroline's.

But I had asked to see Caroline; it had taken strength for her to ring me. She was waiting for me in the Welles dining room. It was just after half past twelve; the room was almost empty. She looked comfortable here in the club, in her elegantly expensive clothes, at this elegantly expensive table, with its lead crystal and its starched linen. She didn't stand up, and for a moment I wondered whether I should bend and kiss her. Then a waiter appeared, and I sat down and ordered a good whisky.

She smiled, and raised her water glass to me. She had grown her hair longer now and wore it drawn back, wound tight on to the crown of her head, where it was held with long pins. There were tiny lines around her mouth and eyes.

'I wanted to apologise to you,' I said. 'But I'm not sure where to start.'

'You don't have to apologise to me, Alex. You were very young.'

'Twenty-seven isn't young. Twenty-seven is should know better.'

'Perhaps,' she said.

From above the fireplace a muscular man in a military uniform leaned forwards from the back of his horse, his sword extending outwards into the room.

'Is he one of yours?'

'No,' she said, 'he's not *one of mine*. Mine are downstairs somewhere.'

A waiter appeared beside me with a large tumbler of whisky on a small tray. I took it and put it on the table in front of me. I dipped my finger into my water glass and let three drops fall into the whisky.

Caroline raised an eyebrow. 'How can you be so deft, and yet so gauche, Alex?'

'Sorry,' I said. 'But the whisky's too good not to. I didn't mean to embarrass you.'

'It's not as if anyone's going to judge me by your behaviour. They may, of course, judge you. But you haven't been my problem for a very long time, have you, Alex?'

I stared at her, uncertain of what to say. She called over a waiter, ordered a bottle of wine.

'Well,' she said, 'I hadn't planned to come here and be angry with you. It isn't as if I can't see that you've changed. You have a wife, and a son, and I'm sure you love them both very much. But then you needle me about where I come from, as if there's anything I can do about my family, and it's as if you haven't changed in the slightest. It's an accident of birth, Alex. Nothing more.'

'And yet we're here,' I wanted to say, looking at the portraits on the wall. 'Amongst *your* equals and *my* betters.'

She was right, though. Something in me still wanted to lash out at her, even now. *I have to stop rushing to judgment.*

'I have a temper,' I said at last. 'It attaches itself to the wrong targets. To the people I love. I don't know why. I can see it now, and now that I know about it, I don't behave as badly as I did to you. But it's still there, and sometimes I take it out on Millicent, or on Max.'

'I see.' A look of concern crossed her face.

'Never physically,' I said. 'I would never.'

'All right.'

'I think I learned it from my father.'

'From your father?'

'He came home angry from the Korean War. No one helped him. It got too much for him eventually. Although I always knew he loved me.'

At this she looked troubled.

'No,' I said. 'No, I'm not placing the blame for what I did to you at his door. I betrayed you, and when you asked me to leave you alone I harassed you.'

She made to speak. But the waiter arrived with the wine. I insisted she taste it. She ordered a goat's cheese salad, and I ordered the same.

'You don't have to accept my apology, Caroline. But I do have a need to apologise to you.'

'Alex,' she said, 'you said your anger attaches itself to the people you love.'

'Most strongly, yes.'

She took a swig of wine.

'How deliberate is your choice of words?'

'Deliberate.'

'You loved me, Alex.' Almost like Millicent on that day thirteen years ago. 'You loved me.' Almost an accusation. 'Well, I never knew.'

'Neither did I. Pathetic as that sounds.'

We picked at our salads. The whisky obliterated the flavour of the goat's cheese, made it flat and lifeless. We talked a little about our lives. She worked for a charity, and was often out of the country. She did not talk about men, except to say that she was single, by choice. She had never considered having children. Her parents were very understanding about the life she lived. She was their only child. Without a son they already knew, she said, that the line would not continue. 'Their little failure, not mine.'

'Strange,' I said. 'In my family we only produce boys. One a generation. Max, my son, is the only son of an only son of an only son.' She smiled at this, and for a moment I saw myself married to her, posed formally in the walled garden of her brick-built country house, boy-child in arms, smiling out at the world. Lord of the Manor; almost but not quite.

When we had finished eating she said to me, 'Alex, I have

281

long since destroyed any record of what you did. If the police did contact me I should be obliged to say what happened between us, but I should also feel an obligation to say that it is clear you have changed. For what that's worth. My old solicitor died years ago. I should be surprised if the firm kept a carbon copy – even more so if the police ever found out about the letter.'

'Thank you,' I said. I took her hand.

'No,' she said, drawing away. 'Alex, I would like you to stay away from me in future.'

She meant it.

'I'm confused, Caroline.'

'I forgive you, Alex. But I don't want you near me.'

'Well,' I said, 'this is humiliating.' I took a slug of wine. After the whisky it tasted thin, sharp, as nauseating as mould on bread.

Her voice softened. 'I can see that you're trying hard to be good; I think you *are* a better man now. A good man. But you still have that strange broken quality to you, and that makes you dangerous to women like me, who like to fix things.' She gave an embarrassed little gesture. 'There's a stupid little piece of me that still wants to fix you, Alex.'

'I'm sorry for what I did to you,' I said.

'Well,' she said, 'perhaps we should bring this to an end.'

'OK.'

'I do think you're right, Alex, by the way. I think you *have* inherited something of your father's shell shock. That anger doesn't just disappear. It gets handed down, father to son.'

'I wasn't claiming that,' I said.

'You wouldn't be the first man it happened to,' she said. 'It's very widespread. You don't experience combat. You don't see your friends killed. You don't take part in atrocities. But you inherit the psyche of a man who has.'

'That doesn't make sense.'

'Actually, it does. It's called transgenerational trauma.'

'And you know about that from one of your little charities, do you?'

'I work with refugees, if that's what you mean, Alex.' She said it quietly, and without anger. 'Their children, the ones born in the safety of London hospitals, develop the same scars as their parents. Same symptoms – outbursts of anger, panic attacks, a sense of something being permanently broken – but without the flashbacks to the traumatic trigger.'

She left an enquiring pause. I decided to say nothing.

'Most of them don't understand why they're traumatised, Alex, because they have never experienced the trauma that their parents lived through. But they live with their parents, whose disorder is untreated, and they inherit the disorder. Just being around someone with PTSD is enough.'

'You think I'm like them?' *I know I'm not like them.*

'At least your father knew the cause of his suffering. I don't think you do. And a part of you feels compelled to strike out at other people. Although I believe you when you say you're getting better.'

'I don't want your pity,' I said.

'I don't pity you, Alex.'

There was a warmth in her eyes. Empathy perhaps. Not pity. 'But now that you know what it might be, you could seek help.'

'I'm coping,' I said, 'but I'm going to go now.'

I thought for a while about trying to find work, but found myself watching television instead. I watched an early-afternoon programme about a maximum-security prison in Michigan for women. Everybody shouted. Not one of the women in the prison claimed to be innocent. Two of the inmates had smothered their children, one had poisoned her husband, and another had burned down an entire city block in downtown Detroit. 'Sure,' said the firebrand, 'sure

283

I have some regrets.' It was the narcotics that had made her do it. The programme showed an image of her, skeletal and out of hope. She looked better now; she worked in the prison library. But really it was all over for her: she was never getting out.

Once, in the days before Millicent, when I wasn't sleeping, a psychiatrist suggested I could have transgenerational trauma; he called it War-Related Intergenerational Post Traumatic Stress Disorder, though.

It seems to be a real thing, passed from returning soldiers to their families, from fathers to their sons. I looked it up.

I don't have it.

Rose rang. She wanted to know why I had missed Bryce's funeral. I told her that I had been in hospital over the weekend, that I had wanted to come. I didn't tell her about Millicent and the bottle.

'He was a better guy than I realised,' I said.

'How do you mean?'

'I mean, he was a good guy. He had it tough.'

'How do you mean?' she said again.

'The lost child. That must have been very hard for him.'

The line went very quiet.

'What do you mean by the lost child?' she said at last. 'What did he say to you, Alex?'

'He didn't say anything to me. But he told my wife about his little girl. About Lana.'

Again, Rose said nothing.

'Rose,' I said. 'You still there?'

'Yeah. I'm here.'

'He did well to rebuild his life after that.'

'Did he?' she said. 'Did he really?'

'What do you mean?'

'Alex,' she said, 'I think we should meet.'

'It's complicated,' I said. 'There's a lot on.'

I ended the call. I didn't tell her about the arrest.

When Max got home I tried to talk to him. How did he feel about Millicent being arrested? Fine, he said.

'Fine?' I asked. 'Really?'

'Yes.'

How did he feel about what he'd heard, about what he'd seen of the affair? Fine, and again fine.

'Max,' I said, 'are you sure you're OK?'

'Yeah.'

'When are you next seeing Dr Å?'

'I go three times a week.'

The reproach in his voice, in his eyes: *you should know that.*

I rang my mother and asked her about the arrangements for the funeral. 'Oh, son,' she said, 'it's all in hand.'

My mother was in no mood to speak about practicalities for once. Instead we spoke for a long time about my father. She had washed the last of his clothes now, although really she could see that there was no need; she had filled the house with pictures and music, had been playing his Serge Gainsbourg records – 'the *boulevardier* ones, mind, not the sexy ones' – over and over. She found herself talking to my father though she knew he was not there.

'Foolish, Alexander, is it not?'

'No, Mum, there's nothing foolish about that. I miss him too.'

'Right enough, son,' she said. 'Aye. Thank you,' as though there were something to thank me for.

When at last she asked after Millicent, as I knew she would, I told her that Millicent was OK. Busy, though. And sent her love.

'Send her my love back, will you not? Tell her that I miss our little chats.'

*　　*　　*

Arla came home at eight and we ate pizza and drank wine in the kitchen as if nothing was wrong. Max took himself off to bed early, and Arla and I carried on drinking. Anyone looking in through the back door would have thought we were man and wife.

22

'Dad! Dad!'

'Max.' No light through the curtains. 'Max, are you OK?'

'I'm fine, Dad.'

I switched on the light. 'What time is it?'

'Half past two.' He was dressed. Red t-shirt, dark blue jeans. 'Dad, can you find the neighbour's key?'

'Max, what's going on?'

'Can you, though?'

'No, Max, get back to bed.'

Max left the bedroom. I turned off the light. I wondered if Millicent was awake, lying on a bed in a police holding cell, thinking about the fact that she wasn't being released. I had spoken to the lawyer she had chosen from the list, a young woman who sounded far too delicate to be a criminal defence solicitor.

Millicent's solicitor had confirmed what the detective had told me, that the police would hold Millicent for another twelve hours. Surely they couldn't do that, I had asked. Yes, she was afraid the police could extend Millicent's custody, as long as the request was approved by an inspector. If it was of any comfort, she didn't think they had very much on Millicent; she suspected they were simply trying to frighten her into a confession. She expected Millicent to be released without charge.

Sound of a footstep on a loose board. Someone downstairs.

I pulled on a pair of pants and a t-shirt. Max's room was empty. As I stood on the landing I heard the back door open. I went back into Max's bedroom, pulled the curtain away from the window, looked down.

There in the garden was Max. He looked up at me, then turned and walked deliberately towards the love seat by the wall.

No!

I pulled on a pair of trousers, slipped on a pair of trainers and headed downstairs.

As I reached the kitchen I saw Max disappear over the wall into the neighbour's garden.

Please God, no!

I looked around. There was no light in any of the houses except ours. What was he up to? What the hell was he up to?

As soon as I stepped on to the love seat I saw him, standing at the neighbour's back door.

'Max, come back here.' My voice was quiet, but he must have heard me. 'Max.' Still he paid me no attention. I jumped up on to the wall, and down into the neighbour's garden. I listened. Distant traffic. The slam of a car door. An engine starting.

Max had the neighbour's back door open now, had pulled it as far back as the hinges would let it go. Then he crouched down, seemed to be waiting for something. I saw a faint beam of light fall on to the varnished floor. Car headlights in the street, I thought. The door to the neighbour's front room must be open. I could hear the change of gear, see the beam from the headlights pass across the floor.

Panic like a hand across my throat. *If someone sees us now . . .*

'Max,' I said, 'close the door.' But he stayed crouched where he was, looking into the house, listening. What was he doing? What was he waiting for?

I went to him and stood behind him for a while, looking in. I could see nothing.

'What is this, Max?'

'Shh, Dad, wait.'

'We're going home, Max.'

But Max simply shook his head.

'Max,' I said. 'Max.' *Don't let him take charge.*

At the sound of a car engine in the street Max tensed. As the light from the car swung through the room the edges of the furniture lit up, eerily familiar. That better, cleaner version of our kitchen, the lines sharper and straighter somehow, the paintwork immaculate, every gap in the floor filled.

The light intensified, and Max crouched lower, his head almost level with the floor.

'Max,' I said, 'Max, what are you looking at?'

'You're too high up, Dad,' he said, as if speaking to a cretin. 'You're going to have to wait for the next one.'

'For the next car?'

'Yeah.'

'What am I looking for, Max?'

'You have to see it, Dad. But you have to get down.' I looked around. I was fairly certain no one was watching. Somewhere nearby I could hear a helicopter; somewhere, a siren. In the street beyond a couple was arguing, voices raised. The woman's voice chided; the man's pleaded. On the main road a dustcart collected refuse from the chickenshops: paper and card, bones and fat. A night like any other night in our part of town.

The voices grew distant. A car engine approached.

Max looked up at me. 'Dad, you're too high up.'

'What am I looking for?'

'You'll see.'

I crouched down beside him, stared across the floor. And

289

then I saw it. There in the light of the car headlights was a layer of dust as thin as the bloom on a new plum. And as the light swept across the floor I saw what Max had seen.

Two sets of footprints. One led through the door and into the front room, and the other led from the front room towards the back door.

'Did you see it, Dad?'

'Yes, Max, yes, I saw it.'

I didn't need to see it a second time, but I waited with Max anyway, afraid perhaps that what I had seen was a trick, the product of fatigue and of fear. And the next passing car confirmed it. Two sets of footprints. The same women's shoes. The strange, hour-glass shape of them. Wedged soles, I guessed. How could Millicent have been so stupid?

We drank milk and ate biscuits in our own kitchen, me at the table, Max on the worktop.

'Dad, were those the shoes that Mum has?'

I looked at Max. I didn't want to have this discussion.

'I don't know. And how did you open the door, Max?'

He picked something from the ticket pocket of his trousers. 'Catch.'

A slick metallic parabola. I fumbled the catch, and something fell to the floor near the foot of my chair. I reached down and picked up a key. It looked like one of Bryce's. We sat there, the two of us, staring at it, and at each other.

'The neighbour thought Mum lost it. I heard him shouting at her for a very long time. He said he wouldn't give her another one, even though he did. He was really shouting. When do you think she went in there?'

'Max,' I said, 'we don't know that it was Mum.'

'But when do you think it was?'

'I don't know.'

I did know, of course. It had happened the night I was in Edinburgh. That night Millicent had abandoned Max. It had to have happened then. I believed what she had told me: that she had sat in the park, in the rain; that the mud had ruined her shoes. That much was probably true. Although, I wondered now, had she actually told me she had sat in the rain in the middle of the park, or had she simply implied it? In any case, she was in the neighbour's house before her shoes were covered in mud.

Those shoes were in our bin.

'Are those footprints why the police arrested Mum?'

'I don't think they can be, Max.'

'Why not?'

Because the police searched the bin and didn't take the shoes.

'I don't know.'

'But what do you *think*, Dad?'

'Back to bed.'

'But it's almost time to get up.'

'It's four o'clock, Max.'

I was sure that the footprints weren't the reason, that the police had been acting on a hunch. Unless there had been another forensic team in the house, shining lights at low angles across the floor, the police could not have seen Millicent's footprints in daylight.

When Max was asleep I went to the front door. There was light in the sky now. I brought in the grey composite dustbin that stood jammed in front of the bay window, stood it in the middle of the floor in the front room.

I began to take out the bags one by one. I wasn't completely sure what I was looking for. The smell of rot was over-powering, and it was all I could do to keep from retching. Serve us right for mixing food waste in with the recyclables. Everything was covered in a fine blue-green powder. I forced myself not to gag, tried to hold my breath.

Near the bottom of the bin I found what I was looking

for: a tied Sainsbury's bag through which I could feel Millicent's shoes. I put the other bags carefully back into the bin, and wheeled it outside again.

I untied the bag. Inside were two more bags. In one were Millicent's dress, bra and pants, the ones the rain had ruined on the night she abandoned Max. In the other were the shoes she had worn when she had returned to Bryce's house. If she had been telling me the truth, if she had thrown her clothes away that night, she had gone to the trouble of removing them from the bin again before the police had searched the house. Otherwise, surely – *surely* – the police would have found these bags, and when they had found them they would have wanted to know what they were doing there. My wife had waited until after the police search to dispose of her evidence.

Then I found something else: inside one of the shoes was a small pair of soft leather gloves; inside one of the gloves was a small piece of heavy black adhesive tape, compressed into a ball.

23

Back in the white windowless room I waited, staring at the gunmetal door. The room was airless, and the dying fluorescent tube flicked uselessly on and off, waking some animal instinct in me for flight. There was nothing to look at, so I took out my phone. 11.06. No signal.

Millicent arrived, flanked by two officers I didn't recognise. She was wearing the same clothes as yesterday; the tendons in her neck were drawn tight, and the corners of her mouth were dry and cracked.

'Hey,' she said.

She sat down, tried to smile, reached out for my hand.

I let her hold it for a moment, then drew away from her.

Your footprints in the neighbour's house.

'Well,' she said, 'everybody's still really polite, but this was a long night. It got so I started wishing I had something I could confess to. Kind of like you said. But I think they started to realise I don't.'

The door opened, and a uniformed officer showed in a young woman, pressed white blouse and knee-length twill skirt, tall and perilously thin. She introduced herself to me, her voice tremulous: Millicent's lawyer. She was nervous behind her wire-rimmed glasses. I forget her name.

'Millicent has been doing brilliantly, Alex.' The young woman sat down beside Millicent, rubbed her hand encouragingly, looked expectantly at me. I said nothing, so she spoke again, as if to fill the silence. 'We'll have you out soon, Millicent. Won't we, Alex? You can go home, have a little sleep, a nice long bath, and be fresh in time for your radio show this evening.'

What were you thinking?

I must have grimaced, because something stopped the lawyer in her tracks. Everyone in the room was looking at me.

'I'm sorry,' I said.

'You're sorry?' said Millicent. The young lawyer looked puzzled.

The abandonment of Max.

'Millicent,' I said, 'I can't do this.'

'What do you mean?'

'I'm pressing charges.'

'Alex, wait. What?'

The bottle arcing towards me through the air.

'I can't do this any more. I don't know who you are.' I looked at Millicent, pale in her crumpled shirt, the lines in her face etched deep by lack of sleep.

I leaned in to her, spoke softly so that only she could hear. 'Your footprints. I found your footprints in the dust on the floor of Bryce's house.'

'Alex,' said Millicent. 'Alex, I'm going to need you to put our family first.' She was trying to keep the pleading tone out of her voice, but to anyone who knew her, it was there.

I leaned in again. 'I won't tell the police what I found, Millicent. But I *would* like to know what they learn from you.'

I had given her the gloves as a present, years before, after a filming trip to Italy. Soft brown Florentine leather. They had cost a fortune; I had never seen her wearing them.

'Alex,' said the lawyer, 'I wonder if we might go somewhere and talk this through.'

'I'm sorry,' I said, 'it's already done.'

'Good man,' the detective had said when I told her of my decision. 'Give us a little time to have a look at what's going on here. Break down the resistance. Maybe see if my colleagues can't get a little confession out of her.'

Was it Max's book? Was it the footprints in the dust? Was it the gloves in the dustbin? Or was it just the grinding, gut-wringing exhaustion that came with each new discovery?

'They won't threaten her, will they?'

'Alex, mate,' said June, 'this is all about what emerges through dialogue. We all need to know the truth about your wife.'

'And you're not pressing charges against me? I'm no longer helping you with your enquiries?'

'Our focus is now on your wife.'

Some wiser inner voice told me that pressing charges against my wife was like sleeping with her sister, that I was becoming a colder, crueller version of myself. But I pushed the thought away. I wanted to know the truth.

Although, as my wiser inner voice reasonably pointed out, if I was on a mission of truth then why wasn't I telling the police about the footprints, or about Max's book?

The police did not let Millicent ring the radio station. I found out later that her lawyer rang and spoke to someone who worked in sales. The lawyer did what she could, without explaining that Millicent was under arrest, said that her client could not appear on the radio that evening due to circumstances beyond her control. The radio station must have read between the lines.

An hour later the station manager returned the lawyer's call, made it clear that the station would not be inviting

Millicent back. The police had rung the manager, and the manager had told them Millicent had been there for no longer than forty minutes on the night of Bryce's death. Millicent's alibi had collapsed.

Still, said the lawyer, she didn't think the police had much to work with; Millicent hadn't directly lied to them.

I searched those parts of the house where I thought Millicent might have hidden something. I found nothing in her wardrobe, or in the backs of the cupboards in the kitchen, or under the sink. On top of our cigarette cupboard I found an old pack of Marlboro. I sniffed at it, felt the pull of nicotine, but threw it away, along with the rest of the rubbish.

There was nothing in the outhouse, as far as I could tell, and nothing in any of the drawers in the front room. I found nothing in Millicent's office. I opened books, riffled through stacks, even opened the paper drawer of her printer. Nothing. What was I expecting to find that the police hadn't found? I didn't know.

I stared at the sofa bed, made up for Arla, and wondered for a moment whether Millicent might have slipped something in there; it seemed unlikely. A lustful, greed-driven voice deep within me whispered that I should search Arla's bed, run my hands across her possessions, delve into her bags the better to know her, but I silenced the voice. Arla was a mistake. Arla must not happen again.

A low chirrup. The cat was on the banister outside Max's room, looking up at me, eyes full of adoration. I hesitated at the door, wondered for a moment whether Millicent might have hidden something there. But to use her son to shield herself? Whatever she had done, I could not see Millicent deliberately betraying Max. And Max was organised enough himself that he would notice the slightest object out of place. We had long since stopped tidying his room for him.

The cat tapped gently at my elbow with her paw. I held out my hand to her, and she rubbed one cheek against me, then the other. She did not follow me downstairs, but sat chirruping on the banister, watching me go.

It occurred to me that Millicent might have buried something in the garden, but I could not think what. I looked around, wondering if I could spot newly dug earth – surely it would be darker? – but nothing seemed out of place. Our lawn, what there was of it, was yellowed and scorched from the remorseless London summer. The garden was uniformly unkempt. I looked under a few bushes, but felt foolish, and decided that Millicent would have felt foolish too. And besides, who knew who was watching?

For the third time in recent days I trailed the stepladder after me up the stairs.

The loft was dark as the grave, the heat oppressive.

An impression of shadows as I flicked the switch; something out of place; then nothing. The lightbulb had glowed orange for some small fraction of a second. Then it had failed. I retained the shapes, the moment stretching out through my brain. Persistence of vision. Something had changed. Something was out of place.

I stood in the dark for a moment. I was certain that Max had at least one torch, but I didn't want to give myself away by taking something from his room. I would be sure to replace it wrongly. I went downstairs and found my phone.

The flashlight on the telephone was useless up here, really, if you didn't know what you were looking for. But something was definitely out of place. I had seen it at once, in that first orange flash, some change in the silhouette of one of the piles. It was small, but I was sure of it. An edge that seemed to have hardened and shifted.

She had moved a box. There, on the right, near the bottom of a formless pile near the hatch. It was close enough to the ladder that she could reach it without stepping into the loft. I tracked the light beam across the floor, saw only my own footprints. She must have assumed that I wouldn't look up here, or that if I did, I would find nothing. If she stood on the ladder, she could come and go without leaving a trace.

I shone the light around the edges of the box. A ream of budget paper. The box was made of stiff cardboard, bright blue and white. *VALUE PACK*. I ran the light around the top edge of it. There were boxes above it, but they didn't fully cover it. I put the torch in my left hand and I reached out with my right. I hooked my fingers around the furthest edge of the box, and nudged it gently. It moved easily. It did not seem to be carrying the weight of the boxes above it. I shone the torch in front of the box, and saw from the path in the dust that it had recently been moved.

I drew the box towards me; the boxes above it teetered, like a child's tower. Perhaps it was part of this pile. Perhaps it had always been a part of this pile. But my hands were shaking, and I guessed that I had knocked it slightly against the boxes above as I pulled against it.

I stood at the top of the ladder, swaying slightly, holding the box in two hands, my phone clamped in my left; I hoped the tower of boxes in front of me would not fall. I didn't want Max to find me surrounded by debris on the landing below; I didn't want to have to explain myself.

After ten seconds I decided that the boxes would not fall. With my left hand I slid my phone up the side of the box I was holding and on to the top of it. Something inside clinked. Glass?

I climbed carefully down, put the box on the bed in our room. Then I went back up the ladder and carefully fetched the envelope from on top of the beam. I closed the hatch on the way down, and carried the ladder out to the back garden.

I burned Caroline's letter and the non-molestation order

in the grate in the living room. I went back upstairs. I was no longer the one with something to hide.

Baubles. Hand-blown baubles that my mother had given Millicent shortly after we had married. Edwardian glass for our little Edwardian house. They had belonged to her own mother. I had been sceptical, but Millicent had treasured them, had seen in them a transmission of something important, a contract between my mother and her. We had never hung them on a tree – people like us don't decorate like that at Christmas – and I had never given them a thought, never wondered what had happened to them. They were carefully arranged in even rows, with little balls of red tissue paper separating them from each other. I lifted each one carefully out on to the duvet of our bed. It was the imperfections that made them beautiful; they refracted tiny rainbows across the room, splitting the sunlight. If you held them to your eye, you could see tiny bubbles, minute variations in the thickness of the walls. They were far too exquisite for people like us.

Fifteen of them, then a layer of red tissue paper, then another fifteen. I lifted out the second row of tissue paper. There, underneath, was what Millicent had hidden from me.

I shook the box out on to the bed. Envelopes: some were curled, their hard edges frayed, their creams and whites softened and greyed by the years; the addresses seemed to dissolve a little where the old ink had edged imperceptibly outwards from the crisp clean strokes of the fountain pen. Others were stiff, bowed outwards by the paper inside, full of the promise of news and love.

We had that in common, then. We had each kept a stack of letters from our past.

Except. I looked at the names and addresses.

Paul Weitzman
Vera Weitzman
Arla Weitzman
Thaddeus Ackerman

All in Millicent's beautiful, flowing copperplate. Letters to the people she loved. I wondered for a moment why they had given the letters back to her, before realising that I wasn't thinking clearly. The letters were stamped, but not one of them had been sent. I turned over a few of the envelopes. They were sealed.

Sarah Mercer

She had written to our unborn child. This envelope did not carry an address. Write a letter, they tell you. OK, you say, I will *try* to write what I think. No, not what you think, what you *feel*, they tell you. What would you say if you could speak without consequence?

I turned the letter over, wondering when Millicent had written it, wondering what she had said to our little daughter, to little Sarah who never was. I wondered if opening the envelope would teach me anything I didn't know, whether to know what she had written – believing that it would never be read – would bring me closer to my wife. Or would it just leave me empty and full of regret, knowing once and for all that Sarah's death had opened up a gulf that could not be bridged? Two parents, divided from each other by grief.

Bryce

Two letters to Bryce. I turned them over. These were different from the others. They had been torn open, and doubtless read by Bryce. Funny that he hadn't used a letter knife. I put them on the pillow on Millicent's side of the bed, then began slowly to repack the box.

Rosie

I hadn't noticed the card at first. It had been trapped in a corner seam, and hadn't fallen out when I had shaken the box. The envelope was stiff, smaller and lighter than the others. It looked new: the ink on the front was crisp and dark. I turned the card over. It had not been opened. I put it with the letters to Bryce and repacked the box. I took great care with the placement of the baubles; I didn't want them to break, and my hands were shaking.

I thought about fetching the ladder and replacing the box at the bottom of the pile, but Max would be home soon. Instead I put the box at the back of my wardrobe. I could worry about what to do with it later. Then I put the three envelopes into the inner pocket of my rucksack, and began to pack for Edinburgh.

Max accepted without question that the police were extending Millicent's custody, that she would not make it to the funeral. I didn't tell him that I had pressed charges. He didn't need to know.

The staff on the sleeper had unlocked the door between the two tiny compartments for us. 'Do I get my own room, Dad?' said Max.

'Yes, if you want it.'

'Cool.' He pushed open the door between the compartments till it clicked into place, then threw himself down on the lower bunk. I sat on the lower bunk in my own compartment.

'Can I choose which one I want to sleep in?'

'Of course, Max.'

He stood up and pulled the aluminium ladder away from the wall. For a moment he disappeared out of sight, and then he was sitting there on the top bunk, smiling down at me.

'If Mum was here, would she have had one room for herself, so you and I had the other one?'

'I don't know, Max. Maybe.'

'Do you hate her?'

'No, Max. This is just a very difficult time for your mother and me right now.'

'And for me.' An abject, dejected look clouded his features, then was gone. 'It's like, now it's you and me against Mum.'

'I'm sorry, Max. I do know it's very hard for you. But I want you to try not to take sides.'

'OK,' said Max. 'But did you tell the police what was in my book? Is that why they arrested her?'

'No, Max, and the police don't arrest people for having sex.'

'I know that really. They probably should, though.' He laughed a sad little laugh, then brightened a little. 'Did you think my pictures were funny, Dad?'

The train lurched; metal ground against metal. Old rolling stock. I looked around the cabin. First class, they called this. Dirt in the windows, and fading purple decor. Still, the bed linen was clean, and Max seemed pleased to have his own cabin. He was standing on the ladder now, looking around.

'Max,' I said, 'why did you make those pictures?'

'I don't know. Like, I thought it would be better if he wasn't really doing Mum when he said those things. Because I didn't want him to do her. It was horrible, Dad. So I thought what it would be like if he wasn't doing her when he said those things.'

'I can see that makes sense. But don't say doing her.' *Not about your mother, at least.*

'OK,' said Max. He jumped to the floor of his compartment and disappeared from view again.

'Is it better if I say boning?'

'Max, what are you doing?'

'Opening the blind.' He reappeared in the door opening. 'Do you want me to open your blind, Dad?'

'No thanks, Max.'

'Dad, please? Can I?'

'All right,' I said. He carefully drew the bottom of the blind down, then guided it upwards. Warehouses and pumping stations, canals and brown-field sites, high-rise blocks and low-slung housing schemes.

'Will we see our house?' said Max.

'I don't think so.'

We sat on the bunk, looking out of the window. After a

while we hit the suburbs. Order and planning, red brick and green space, two cars on every drive.

Max got up and went back into his compartment. Something creaked, then clicked into position. I could hear Max brushing his teeth. 'You found the sink, then?' I called.

'Yeah, and the toothbrush. And the soap. Dad, do I have to wash my face?'

'You can choose, Max.'

'Do I have to wear pyjamas? Or can I wear my pants?'

'Pants is fine, Max.'

His skinny angularity on the ladder. Red pants. Narrow shoulders. He pulled the sheets aside and got carefully into bed. Then he found the light switch and the night light came on in his compartment. I got up to kiss him good night.

'Good night, my beautiful boy.'

'Do I have to go straight to sleep? I mean, I might not be able to.'

He was excited. This funeral trip was an adventure to him. I held him to me. 'Just lie quietly,' I said. 'Enjoy the journey.'

I turned off my own light, lay back on my bunk.

'Dad,' said Max after a while, 'Dad, did you like my pictures?'

'Just rest, Max.'

'No, but did you?' He turned round in his bunk, put his head over the side, stared down at me through the narrow doorway. 'Did you like the last one?'

'The one in the bedroom? I mean, it was well-drawn, and everything, Max, and you know I really like the way you draw, but it's hard for me to say that I *like* any of those pictures. It was upsetting for me to know what you'd heard, you know?'

'But Dad, that's not the last picture. You stopped before you got to the end.' He sighed heavily, then said, 'Can you give me my bag please, Dad?'

'I don't think I need to see any more pictures, Max.' I didn't want to go back into that world. 'And it's night time.'

'Please, Dad. I won't be able to sleep if you don't. Please?'

'OK,' I said, exasperated. 'All right.'

I stood up, handed him his rucksack through the door, leaned back against the top bunk in my own compartment. Max turned on his reading light, then he unzipped the top pocket of the rucksack and took out his book. He flicked through until it was open at the double page of Bryce, hanged, in the bedroom. 'There,' he said, and handed it back through the door to me. Then he carefully lowered his rucksack as far as he could and let it drop to the floor.

I sat back on my bunk, turned on the reading light. Bryce's broken body against the bedroom door. I felt a queasy sense of foreboding.

'Turn the page, Dad,' said Max. He was watching me keenly from his bunk again now. I turned the page.

Another double-page spread. The scene was domestic: Bryce in the bath, listening to a radio on the side of the bathtub. Bryce was completely recognisable, and this time he was completely alive and completely at peace. There were no ropes, no animals; no lolling tongue or popping eye.

The bathroom was perfect in every detail: the pattern of the tiles on the wall, the moulded plastic scroll at the top of the tub, the expensively pretentious fittings, the monogrammed motifs on the towels. Bryce wore an expression of contentment and calm, as he washed his back using a long-handled brush. Soap suds dripped across his shoulders down the side of the tub and on to the floor. On the floor was an open bottle of red wine, and a glass was carefully positioned on a little protruding shelf halfway along the wall.

Another of Millicent's paperbacks lay spine up on a bath rack above Bryce's groin; on the rack there were also candles, and two bars of soap. Bryce looked tired but contented, fulfilled. He was smiling a jovial, unthreatening smile. Max had recorded the grown man reading in the bath, the glass of wine at the end of the working day.

'It's a good picture, Max,' I said. 'A very good picture.'

Maybe he had worked through his animus towards the neighbour. Maybe we were reaching the end of the drawings, the end of the process: the end of Max's anger. I tried to hand the book back to him through the door. 'Thanks for letting me see this, Max.'

The tiniest shake of the head. He was alert, his gaze sharp, all wakeful anticipation.

I turned the page and everything went cold.

The same patterns in the tiles, the same scrolling at the top of the bath, the same monogrammed towels. It was the same image, but changed. The body in the bath was the same, but changed. It was still Bryce, but the sinews in the neck and arms and thighs were taut, the torso rigid, suspended slightly above the water. The legs were kicking out, hard. The hands gripped the side of the bath. The wineglass had been knocked over, as had the bottle on the floor.

Max had drawn the neighbour at the moment of his death.

Still my son watched me. I could read nothing in his expression.

I turned back a page. Everything was the same size, in the same place, yet Max could not have traced one image on to the other; the paper was too thick for that. I compared the drawings for a while, flipping backwards and forwards between them. There was no doubt about it – they were designed to be seen together. A before-and-after pair, from a smile of contentment to a rictus of absolute, unendurable pain. Backwards and forwards, like a gruesome flick-book.

Seconds separated the two pictures, separated the living Bryce from the dying Bryce. Alive – dead – alive – dead. Wineglass up, wineglass down. Bottle up, bottle down. The emotion in the turn of the page, like a flash cut. Like television.

It was all there. The biting of the tongue. The kicking of the legs that must have cracked the fibreglass and plastic of the bathtub. The blood gathering at the nostril. All so much more dramatic thanks to the serenity of the scene before. Like television, calming things down before the climax. Then bang, dead. This wasn't just a document, a record of what Max had experienced. This was cleverer, and more upsetting. Max wasn't just sharing the facts of what he had experienced, he was sharing a cold bolt of adrenaline, the cruel horror of the neighbour's death. These pictures were designed to be seen. *He wants us to understand what he felt.*

Think, I thought. *Breathe.*

The iron in the bath between Bryce's legs: the electric iron that Bryce must have sat carefully on its end, so that it didn't melt the plastic of the tub before he pulled it carefully in on top of himself. A cord ran out of the bath, and out to the edge of the image. There was no iron in the first image. It appeared as if from nowhere in the second.

'Max,' I said, 'was it important for you to show me these pictures?'

'Yes,' he said. 'Dr Å says just because I draw bad things, it doesn't make me bad. She says it's like a process, or something.'

That word again. *Process.*

'Are the cartoons the way you felt about the neighbour?' I said.

'I suppose. It was horrible, Dad. Really, really horrible.'

'And the other pictures, are they about the shock of finding the neighbour?'

'I don't know. I mean, I didn't draw the boner.' He sniffed loudly, twice. 'Yeah, maybe. A bit.'

'Then I'm glad you showed them to me.' But really, who could be glad about something like this? And yet . . . And yet Millicent's predication had not come true. The drawings might be gruesome, the feeling expressed might be terrifying, but Max was *working through*, and he was OK. He really seemed to be OK. He wasn't falling. He wasn't unravelling. This was a process.

306

Max was *moving on*.

Thank God, really. We were neither of us in any state to catch our son, to put him back on his feet, so thank God he wasn't falling. Thank God, I thought, for Dr Å. And thank God for Millicent's foresight. By predicting Max's fall, she had prevented it.

I thought of Millicent then, wondered whether she was lying in her own narrow bed in her narrow police cell. Probably not. June's colleagues would be politely depriving her of sleep, kindly bringing her coffee and sparkling water, and subtly, ever so gently – incremental question by incremental question – pushing her closer to the edge. The police are not what they once were, I thought. They have the measure of people like us now.

Millicent was alone at the police station. There would be no one to catch her if she fell.

What have we done?

I woke with a jolt from a dream I could not remember, breathing hard, frightened.

Frightened because I had remembered what the other thing was, that truth I had been pushing below the surface in the hope that it would drown, or dissolve, or merge with something else. Because it was not a good truth.

I realised that I had been deceiving myself. Because what I wanted wasn't truth; what I wanted was to love Millicent with the intensity and the certainty that I once had. I was worried that that might no longer be possible. I was worried that the truth might be getting in the way.

For a moment in Norway I knew: it was there in front of me when she swam upwards and away from me; I knew that I would find her at the surface. That felt like truth, and for a moment that was all I wanted. The anticipation of her, the knowledge that love was waiting above me, real and vital, sunlight and air.

But we were home now. There were whole swathes of my wife's life that were unknowable to me: her parents; baby Sarah; the neighbour: I knew next to nothing about what she felt about any of these. I could do nothing more than guess because Millicent didn't give me much to go on. And all I knew was that the things that caused Millicent hurt, or stress, or humiliation, were the things that Millicent buried deep, engulfed in strata of silence and pain.

And so we gave each other 'space', and we got by; and isn't that how marriages work? Give and take, they say. Respect for boundaries, they say. Intimacy without *enmeshment*.

But not now. Not any longer. Something was coming to an end. There was a truth coming to the surface now, and I didn't think there was much I could do about it. Not any more.

I told Millicent that someone had replaced the fuse in Bryce's iron with a steel bolt. She must have known that Bryce didn't own an iron.

Yet she said nothing.

I read the letters that Millicent wrote to Bryce. They were both very short. The first said:

> *Well, you sure unscrolled me, Bryce. Can't eat for*
> *thinking about that.*
>   *Unscroll me again.*
>   *Ever,*
>   *M*

It spoke of a certain kind of sexual obsession, but there was no mention of love, and in that I took some comfort. No one who truly loves signs off with the word *Ever*. It's a reflex, a platitude. It's American for *Best wishes*. It's *Cordially yours*.

Millicent's second letter to Bryce was dated two weeks before his death:

Bryce,

I cannot help you, and I will not be party to this. I did not ask for it, and I do not seek it.

Leave me alone. Confess to what you have done.

'Dad.'

I slid the letters under my pillow.

'Go back to sleep, Max.'

'What are you reading?'

'Nothing.'

'But I *saw* you.'

'Go back to sleep.'

'Are those Mum's?'

'No.'

'They are. You're reading the letters Mum went to get from the neighbour's house.'

My mind raced. How could Max possibly know? Had he found the box? He could probably have reached it from the stepladder. He wasn't much smaller than Millicent. I thought of his thin arms dragging the ladder up the stairs while Millicent and I were out. What did he know?

'You might be right,' I said at last, 'I think Mum might have gone to get her letters from his house.' Strange, then, that the police hadn't found them first.

Max switched on his reading light. 'Why did you lie, Dad?'

'I wasn't sure that was how they came to be there.'

'You found them in that box in the attic.'

'Yes,' I said. 'Yes, I did.'

'Did you read the other ones?'

'They were sealed.'

'So?'

'What do you mean, Max?'

Max shrugged, rolled his eyes.

'Max,' I said, 'Max, have you been reading your mother's private correspondence?'

'Obviously.'

'How?' I said.

'Scissors and glue. It's easy.'

'You've been opening your mum's letters?'

'You would if you could.'

I was tired, and couldn't find an answer that wasn't going to make a hypocrite of me.

'You should read the one she wrote to her dad,' said Max. 'Do you want to know what she said?'

'No, Max. No, I don't.'

'She said, like, "Let me refresh your memory, Dad: Thaddeus took his own life. I was 3,000 miles away."' Max was running the words together, but the angry syntax was Millicent's.

'"Know too that for as long as you think his choice was my fault we shall remain estranged. Whatever you think I did, I did not do. Send no more checks. You will have realised by now that I get by without them. Sincerely, Millicent."'

I could think of nothing to say.

'Who was Thaddeus, Dad?'

'Someone your mum was once close to.'

'Who died?'

'Yes.'

'Did American Grandpa think Mum did it?'

'I'm sure he didn't think that, Max. Not really.'

'Why didn't she send the letter, then, Dad?'

I was still awake at five. Max was asleep, snoring quietly to himself. He had left his reading light on, and I had not turned it off for fear of waking him, though I had long since switched off my own. I slid the letters out from under the pillow. There was just enough light in the cabin to find my way down the ladder and locate my rucksack on the lower bunk. I opened the rucksack and slid the letters back into the zipped pocket, beside the card addressed to *Rosie*. I sat for a while, the rucksack between my legs, then slid my hand in again and drew out the card. I turned on the reading light in the lower bunk, and looked at the envelope, turning it over and over.

The address on the card was somewhere in Surrey, and although Millicent had not used a surname I was sure it was to the same Rose. The seal looked good, and for a moment I decided Max could not have opened it. But then I noticed a tiny triangular cut. The bottom right corner was missing. I compared the two edges. The right-hand edge was a little thicker than the left. I ran my finger along it. It was very slightly uneven.

By rubbing my thumb and forefinger across the seam I found I could loosen the glue at the side of the envelope. I started at the bottom near the tiny missing corner, and began to work my way up. The most effective thing seemed to be to keep my movements tiny, almost imperceptible. My finger hardly moved against my thumb. And yet. Tiny flakes of yellow-grey glue began to fall out through the gap and on to the pillow. After five minutes I had opened the seam halfway up. I tried very gently to draw it open by pulling it apart, but the glue was good, and I was worried that I might tear the paper.

When I had the side of the envelope fully open I carefully drew out the card inside.

It wasn't a card of condolence. Not exactly. It was a work by Georges Braque, a print in yellow and blue of a bird in flight, simple and very beautiful. Inside Millicent had written:

Rosie,

Your brother is gone: a devastating loss, and one in which I feel implicated. Know, however, that I could never have foreseen the consequences of our affair.

Precisely because it was an affair, Rosie, and nothing more. I was unhappy, I made a bad choice, and for that I am truly sorry.

311

Please understand: what he wanted was impossible.
Please do not contact me. And please, leave my
husband alone.
Ever,
M

My wife, I thought. Severing ties.

Millicent knew Rose.

If I had gone to Bryce's funeral I might have discovered that.

24

My mother met us at the station, dressed for the cremation in a light suit of black wool, fully made up. It was twenty past seven.

'You didn't have to come, Mum,' I said.

'Aye, I did,' she said. She kissed me gently on the cheek, then crouched down, spry in the dust and the fumes. 'Hello, young man,' she said to Max. 'And where's your mother? Not off the train yet? She's never still asleep, is she?'

Max looked pointedly at me.

'Millicent's not with us, Mum. She's sorry.'

'Aye,' she said. 'I've not heard from her since you were last here, Alex.' She left a pause, which I chose not to fill. What was there to say?

By twenty to eight we were sitting in my mother's kitchen. Max ate Coco Pops and Frosties from a selection of mini-cereals, while my mother and I drank coffee. I said no to toast, but ate half a sugared grapefruit that she had prepared before she had left the flat, the segments painstakingly separated from the skin with a knife she owned for precisely that purpose. My mother had risen early.

I had considered shaving on the train, but had decided I could do a better job in my mother's bathroom. By the time

I was out of the shower, a towel around my waist, Max was wearing the jacket and trousers he had brought with him, and a white cotton shirt straight from the packet.

'Is he not smart, son?' my mother said, her voice pregnant with emotion. 'I've a tie set aside for you, Max.' She picked from the dresser a dark blue tie with a regimental motif and handed it to him. 'There's one for your dad too.'

'Mum,' I said, 'there's really no need. I have a tie with me.'

'I just thought, you know, your father . . . Well, anyway, Max, put it on, then.'

He raised his collar, then draped the tie carefully around his neck.

'Well then,' said my mother. 'Knot it, darling.'

'Erm,' said Max. He sent me an imploring look.

'Oh,' said my mother. 'Oh.' A look of amused disappointment. 'Alex, does your wee man not know how to tie a tie? What about his uniform?'

'We don't wear ties at school.'

'Come here, Max,' I said.

'Aye, maybe just get dressed in the bathroom, Alex, and I'll help the boy with his tie.'

My mother had arranged for the hearse carrying my father's body to meet us at the crematorium, and the taxi came to collect us at twenty past eight.

'Your father could not abide a funeral cortège, son,' she said, as we drew away from the building. 'It's all so solemn and so slow. Stops folk going about their business, because they'll not overtake you. Terrible waste of time and energy for everyone else.'

'People just want to show their respect, Mum.'

'Aye. Maybe. He'd not like the fuss, though.'

She wanted to talk about practical arrangements. There would be a cold buffet back at the flat. The girl would let herself in. Did I think I would like to say a few words at the chapel? And perhaps Max could read some words from the Bible?

'OK,' said Max. 'But I don't really know the Bible.'

She passed him a sheet of paper with the passage printed out in large text. 'Just say it slowly, son,' she said. 'It'll be fine.'

Had we really not talked about any of this before now? I wrote a few notes on the back of a piece of paper I found in my jacket pocket. There wasn't time to think much about my father, but perhaps that was in his spirit.

Max sat between my mother and me in the front pew on the left-hand side, looking down at his piece of paper, quietly mouthing to himself the words of the reading. The chapel was modern, starkly beautiful: angular stained glass, white pillars, a minimum of iconography.

The minister made no pretence: he hadn't known my father and had no stories to tell about him. I suspected my mother had hired him for his honesty. He told a few gentle jokes, was briskly efficient, spoke reassuringly about God.

When my turn came I spoke for ten minutes. I spoke about the love that I felt for my father, about how he had always let me know that I was loved, about how unusual that was for a man of his generation. I wanted, I said, to take the best of him, and pass it on to my own son.

Perhaps I should have spoken about my father's war record. There were old men there in uniform, comrades-in-arms. But I didn't know what to say about his time in Korea, didn't want to think about that version of my father, didn't want the image of the dead Korean soldier anywhere near me and my memories – much less the beatings.

The chapel was full, far more friends than family, and people listened closely, nodded in recognition as I spoke about his ambition, his honesty, and the oddness of his sense of humour.

I began to tell my father's favourite joke: a Scotsman, an Englishman and an Irishman; a bee-keeping competition and a television presenter. The joke built slowly towards its obscene punchline; my father would leave the longest of pauses after the feed line: 'Isn't that a very small hive for such a large number of bees?' He would look around the room from face to face, giddy with the anticipation of what was to come, take a theatrical heave on his pipe, start coughing and have to lay it on the table beside him.

I could feel my mother tensing as she recognised the joke, stiff of back in her spare wooden pew, mortified by what I was going to say.

I stopped speaking, sought her eye. My mother looked away, said something to Max.

'Mum,' I said aloud.

'Aye,' she said, very quietly.

She looked at me very directly then, and for a moment I knew the truth, that losing my father was unbearable to her, that she would give anything not to be sitting here, in front of these people; I could feel for a moment the anxiety and the grief that she buried beneath her implacable surface. *Sandwiches at ten fifteen. The catering girl has a key.* My father was gone, and with it her world.

The chapel was silent. No one so much as coughed. I tried to send her a thought: *This will be OK, Mum. Trust me.*

I could see my mother biting back tears. Max leaned into her, put his arm on her back. She nodded, looked down at her hands for a moment, then looked up again and half-smiled. I continued the joke, but cut out before the punchline.

'My mother and I would like you to join us for coffee and a light lunch after the service. And by the way, and I'm sorry, padre, but . . .' I nodded in the minister's direction, then mouthed the words '. . . Fuck the bees.'

The minister looked discomfited. Here and there people suppressed laughs.

'You heard me, ladies and gentlemen. Fight the bees.'

It wasn't funny, but it broke the ice. People laughed far more than the joke deserved. Even my mother laughed a little.

Everyone in the chapel had heard my father tell the bee

316

joke. Even Max. No one ever found it remotely funny, but my father would sit in his smoking chair, his pipe upturned on the occasional table, crying with laughter for minutes on end until eventually you would start laughing too. ('It's the bees, you see, son. He just doesn't care. *Fuck them!* He just wants to win the competition.')

I spoke then about regret, about how sorry I was that I had not always shown my father the love that he deserved, about how sorry my wife Millicent was that she could not be there. My voice faltered slightly as I explained that Millicent had been detained by a pressing personal issue; I implied, without lying, that it was medical, said we were all hoping for a positive outcome.

Max, I said, had asked me to talk about fishing. I had many happy memories of fishing with my father, I said, and I would forever miss sitting with a rod and line and talking about not very much. I hoped to create many more memories fishing with my son. I spoke about how fishing linked my father and the family's past with my son and the family's future.

It wasn't strictly true: my father and I had not fished together. But it was a funeral, and it seemed like the right thing to say, and when my voice caught and it seemed for a moment as if I could not go on, I looked up and discovered that people were crying. It contained a truth, of sorts.

The minister asked Max to come to the front, and he stood beside me at the lectern and looked at the expectant faces.

'Love suffers long and is kind love . . .' he read, his voice loud and clear.

He stopped for a moment. 'Is that slow enough, Dad?'

I bent down beside him, whispered, 'That's brilliant, Max. You're doing brilliantly.'

'Does not envy love does not . . .' he said, '. . . parade itself is not puffed up.'

He turned to me.

'Dad,' he whispered, 'everyone's looking.'

317

'I know, love,' I whispered. 'Just look back over the tops of their heads. That way they think you're looking at them, but you don't get distracted by their eyes. They're all on your side. Everyone's on your side.'

'OK.' He turned back towards the ranked pews. 'Love does not behave rudely love does not seek its own is not . . . provoked love thinks no evil.' He paused again. 'Is that what you mean, Dad?'

'Yes,' I whispered, 'no one can tell.'

'OK. Does not . . . rejoice in . . . in-iqu-ity but . . . rejoices in the truth bears all things . . . believes all things hopes all things . . . end-ures all things.'

My mother was mouthing the words under her breath as Max read them; she was composed now, regal almost. Wasn't this a passage you normally heard at weddings? Still, it made sense at a funeral.

'Love never fails but whether . . . there are . . . pro-phe-cies . . . they will fail whether there are tongues . . . they will cease; whether there is knowledge . . . it will vanish away.'

We went back to our pew. Someone – an army comrade of my father's, I think – said, 'Good boy, Max.' I wondered if he, too, had suffered from untreated trauma. How many more were there like my father?

We stood to sing the twenty-third psalm. *The Lord's my shepherd, I'll not want.* Max didn't know the words, but my mother handed him a hymn book turned to the correct page. I thought about school assembly, and laughed inwardly. Our bald head teacher in his black suit and umbrella, his compensatory moustache and his sadistic punishments. He liked to belt seven-year-old boys found snickering during the service. By the age of eight I was a confirmed atheist. The Lord was not my shepherd.

It had been easier to hate our head teacher than my father. My father had not been a sadist. He had not enjoyed hurting me. And he had stopped: he deserved credit for that.

318

Max sang sweetly, if a little loudly; my mother gave him an approving little smile and patted his hand. Two women in the row behind were singing a descant, high above the main melody. Max looked around, then mimed putting his fingers in his ears. I realised suddenly that I was struggling, that I had started the song too low; I tried to go up an octave, missed several notes, then finally found the key again.

The organ cut out for the third verse, leaving our voices starkly exposed, reflecting back at us from the white-painted stone.

Yea, though I walk through death's dark vale
Yet will I fear none ill

I don't know why the tears came then. Perhaps it was the defiance of the words, the idea of a soul, unbearably alone, refusing to be afraid. Perhaps it was the chapel full of people. We were thinking one thought, it seemed to me then.

My father was gone.

I managed to sing as I cried, the other voices bearing me along as I struggled to get the words out. When I looked round my mother was weeping into her cotton handkerchief. I pulled her tightly to me, held Max close with my other arm, forced myself to keep forming the words.

For thou art with me, and thy rod
And staff me comfort still

I felt only the lack of my father. He was gone.

25

When the guests had left my mother drove Max and me to Blackford Hill. We walked up past the observatory, stood looking out at the city below us, none of us saying much. We watched handsome women throw plastic balls with fearsome efficiency, saw lurchers and deerhounds launch themselves down the hill in pursuit, tumbling as their teeth made contact with their quarry, giddy with the chase.

Max found a tennis ball in the gorse and offered it to a sun-dazed retriever. The dog nuzzled his hand, sat at his feet panting, eager and exhausted in the heat.

'Well then, laddie,' said my mother. 'Throw it.'

'Won't the owner mind?'

'Throw the ball, son.'

The ball arced high, took a bad bounce and landed again in the gorse at the side of the path. The retriever stood up, looked down the hill after it, then ambled off in another direction, tail high.

The catering girl had tidied up while we were out. My mother set out the rest of my father's fishing equipment on a bed in the spare room so that Max could choose the pieces that he liked, while she and I sat in the kitchen and ate chocolate cake with silver forks. I offered to stay, but she shook her head, helped herself to another slice of cake.

'What is it, Mum?'

She waved the question away.

'Mum?'

'When your father and I had problems, we overcame them, Alexander.'

'You did well for yourselves, Mum.'

'Jesus Christ.' She said it very quietly, and for a moment I thought I had misheard. But she said it again, and I realised I had not misheard. 'Jesus Christ, give me strength.' It was louder this time, half-prayer, half-curse.

'Alexander,' she said, with great deliberation, 'son, where is your wife?'

Had the police broken Millicent yet? Had she confessed to killing the neighbour? *You need to know, Alex.*

'Alexander?' said my mother again. 'She's not written for weeks. I know you are having difficulties. You're not yourself. Neither's Max. Will you not speak to me about what's wrong?'

A second breakdown, I thought. My mother knew about the first, because Millicent had told her. ('Although,' she had said, 'it was not technically a breakdown.') My mother might believe a second breakdown.

'I can't really say, Mum.'

My mother poured tea, sat eyeing me sceptically. Then she took a forkful of cake, chewed it slowly, swallowed it carefully down. She dabbed at the edges of her mouth with a napkin. She put the fork on the tablecloth beside her plate, took a sip of tea, and dabbed again at her mouth with the napkin.

'Whatever may have happened, son, your wife is the glue that holds what's left of this family together.'

'I don't know, Mum. I don't think I know who she is any more. She has never – never, Mum – taken Max and me to meet her parents. I mean, I know it's a ten-hour flight, but come *on*. What does that say to you?'

'People break with their past for all kinds of reasons, son. Look at your father.'

It was true. I had never met my father's parents.

'Alexander,' said my mother, 'you know how you were before you met her. You were a wretch. All those English girls, and never content.'

'I wasn't a wretch, Mum.'

'Aye, well.' A slight tilt of the head. 'You and your wife make each other happy. I've seen it, son.'

'We don't, Mum,' I said as quietly as I could. 'Not any more.'

'Well,' she said, 'you must see to it that you do.'

Max filled a grey metal tool box with fishing equipment. Then he selected a long canvas bag with two rods in it.

My father had made the rods from tank aerials. He had spent hours in his workshop retooling them, cutting them down, fitting locking joints, binding ceramic eyelets on to the metal with industrial adhesive. They were heavy and old-fashioned, but Max liked them.

While my mother made sandwiches in the kitchen I found a roll of tape in a drawer in the hall. I taped up the side of the envelope that Millicent had addressed to Rose, and as we walked to the station I slipped the card into a post box.

Leave my husband alone.

I rang the custody sergeant from the train corridor and told him I wanted to withdraw the assault charge against Millicent. June rang me shortly after, asked me to reconsider.

'We need a little more time, Alex.'

'If you haven't charged her with murder, you're going to have to let her go.'

'We're not there yet.'

'Good,' I said. 'Because she has nothing to confess. She didn't do it. It's a suicide.'

Of course Millicent wouldn't have confessed. She was no killer. Why had I let them persuade me to press charges? *What's wrong with me? What would I be without Millicent?*

'Alex, don't you want to know the truth?'

'It's bullshit, you know, June,' I said, 'using an assault charge to try to get Millicent to confess to murder. I should never have gone with it.'

The line went dead.

I rang Millicent's lawyer and told her I was dropping charges. 'Oh,' she said, 'oh, they really should have rung and told me that by now.'

I told her about the conversation with the detective.

'Alex,' she said, 'you do know that that woman is not your friend? Anyway, Millicent's basically OK. Or she was last time I checked in. June's colleagues have been very professional, at least.'

'Do you think she did it?' I said. 'I mean, no one could really believe that, could they?'

'Alex,' she said, 'I'm your wife's lawyer. You pressed charges against Millicent. That puts you and me on opposite sides of the table. I'm sorry.'

'Please,' I said, 'please, I'm all at sea here.'

'You did the right thing, Alex.' She ended the conversation.

Millicent was sleeping when we got home. Max didn't ask to see her. He went willingly upstairs to bed, and by eleven he was asleep too.

Arla and I ate a tomato salad and shared a pork pie from the delicatessen. Something in Arla's demeanour told me she knew, that Millicent had told her I had pressed charges.

We made careful, precise smalltalk about things that didn't matter: we spoke of Israel and of Palestine; we spoke of racism, and homophobia, and we spoke of the Russian

Federation; we spoke of the impoverishment of Britain, and we spoke of the national debt. On any other day these subjects would have mattered. But today we made other people's suffering the subject of our smalltalk. The most important thing was not to disagree.

I spent some time wondering whether I should give my side of the story, explain to Arla how I had come to press charges against her sister. In the end I decided not to. I could read in her eyes exactly what she thought of me.

Then Arla asked me why Millicent and I seemed to have so few friends these days.

'Do we?' I said.

'Yeah, remember your wedding? It was a cumulonimbus of awesome. You guys were stratospherically popular. So question: where are all your friends these days, Alex?'

I explained that life seemed to have become largely about survival since Sarah's death.

'Are you saying that's some sort of trigger, Alex?' she said.

'No,' I said, 'but it makes you more discerning about your friendship.'

'So, Millicent has – who, Alex?'

'Me,' I said. 'Millicent has me. And Max.'

'Sounds like she's kind of lonely. Max is lonely, which has to be the only reason he hangs out with his aunt. And you have?'

'Fab5.'

'About that,' she said. 'He came round. Asked me out.'

'Really?' I said. 'Wow.'

'Hope that won't be a problem,' said Arla.

'No, Arla. No, it's not a problem.'

'You know,' she said, 'two promiscuous people in a big city, finding each other.'

On any other day that might have stung. But right now it didn't matter at all. Right now it was smalltalk.

26

Arla went to bed at two. At three I went upstairs. I found Millicent lying on top of the covers, her fingers curled around Max's book. He must have put it there before he had gone to bed. What was he trying to achieve?

I tried to pull the book from Millicent's hand, but her fingers clung to it stiffly and instead she woke. She looked at me, then looked down at the book.

'Yep,' she said, 'well, my son still hates me. Hello, Alex.'

'Hello, Millicent.'

'How was it?'

'How was what?'

Cold disbelief in her eyes. 'Your father's funeral, Alex?'

'OK,' I said. 'It was OK.'

She was shaking her head now, her eyes fixed on mine. 'I guess really I'm asking you about Max, and not whether you thought the funeral was *OK*.'

'Max is fine,' I said. 'He did well. He read, and it was very moving. I think it helped him. You would have been proud.'

She smiled, and for a moment her coldness lifted. I could take you in my arms, I thought. I could hold you and talk to you about our beautiful son. Then the coldness descended again, and I knew that I could not.

'Here's where you ask me about my last two days, Alex.'

'Millicent,' I said, 'Millicent, I'm so sorry.'

'Really?' she said. 'You're sorry? Not a problem, Alex.'

'I did a terrible thing.'

At this she looked almost amused.

'Let me condense the experience for you, Alex. Four main questions. Did I have an affair with the neighbour? Did I have a business relationship with the neighbour? Did I kill the neighbour? Why did I withhold information? To which my answers were, consistently, *yes, no, no*, and *I'm sorry I withheld information, detective, but I did a stupid thing and was scared of what everyone would think*. Over and over and over again, till they ran out of time and had to release me.'

'Millicent, I was out of my mind. I believe you. I know you didn't kill the neighbour.'

'Huh. Interesting. So I didn't really get the chance to tell you,' she said, her voice level, matter-of-fact. 'I won't contest the divorce. You're free to leave me, Alex. You actually have to. For your own sake, and for Max.'

'Millicent,' I said. 'Stop.'

'In fact, you should really throw me out. You can have my share of the house. How's that for an incentive?'

'I'm not going to throw you out.'

'No, you should. It's your job to protect Max from bad things. You're his father. And I guess I have to accept that I'm one of the bad things you need to protect him from.'

'We lost our way, Millicent. That's all.'

She was shaking her head. 'I'm a horrible mother, and a horrible wife. And you both believe in vengeance, but only you can punish me. Because there's this bond between you and Max, and you have to do what he can't.'

'I'm not divorcing you, Millicent.'

'You will. We need to get this started.' Still that matter-of-fact tone. 'For me as well as you. It's the next logical step in the process.'

326

'Drop the cynical act, Millicent. You can't walk away from this. I know you won't walk away from Max. For the first time in your life you can't simply jump ship.'

She shook her head. 'The problem is I hate you too, Alex. I'm trying not to, because I know it makes me less of a person, but really I do.'

'OK,' I said, 'I should never have brought charges against you.'

'Oh.' She looked almost amused by this. 'Alex,' she said, 'Alex, how could you think I wouldn't know?'

'Know what?' I said.

'Seriously? You're really going to do this?' She looked at me for an instant, then looked away again. 'Max saw you,' she said.

'Saw me doing what?' I wanted to ask. But I guessed, of course, what Max had seen, and what he had told Millicent about what he had seen.

What have I done?

Again Millicent turned and looked at me, and again she looked away. 'I guess at least he let us have Norway. Though that kind of magnified the impact of the blow. He told me the night we came back. He's a smart kid. I guess he knew it would destroy me.'

'Max doesn't want to destroy you,' I said. 'You're his mother.'

'He's a tiny traumatised child, Alex. And the person he wants to spend time with right now is the woman he knows you fucked. You revenge-fucked his aunt, who also happens to be my sister. She's actually the most stable influence on his life.' Again that matter-of-fact tone, dangerously brittle. 'And of course, you knew that all the time we were away. And then we come back here, and there's a closeness between you and Arla that I can't explain. It's like you're secret friends or something. And then Max tells me why, and it all makes sense.'

'I wasn't thinking about Arla when we were away,' I said.

'That's a cute variant on the *it-meant-nothing* defence, I guess. Anyway, you don't have to apologise. I deserve that you slept with my sister, really I do. I get that I caused it by sleeping with Bryce. Intellectually I get that. It's just that there will never be a day when I am comfortable with that fact. Not now, and not in some imagined future where none of us hate each other. I know that's very *black-and-white* of me, Alex. But I can't accept your apology, and I can't forgive you, and I can't forgive her, and I want her to leave.'

'I'm done betraying you now, Millicent. It won't happen again.'

The disbelief in her eyes was clouded by pain now. 'You think *that* brings us back to some sort of Day Zero? You seduce my sister and you think you can *press reset* on me?'

'Millicent,' I said, 'if you force the end of our marriage, Max *will* end up hating you like you say. Forever. Please don't walk out of this.'

'Are you trying to break me, Alex?'

She cried then for the longest time. I lay beside her, but she would not let me touch her. Then she stopped crying; she went out to the bathroom and ran all the taps; when she came back into the bedroom her clothes were wet and she had a towel wrapped around her head. She threw herself down on the bed and picked up Max's diary.

'I mean, you win, Alex,' she said after a while. 'Morally, you win. My humiliation is complete. I surrender. I'm sure you and Max will be very happy together, without me. Arla can stay for as long as she wants. I'm going to gracefully withdraw from your lives. We're done.'

'No,' I wanted to say, 'I'm going to fight for the family, for you, for us. This time you don't get to walk out on trouble. This time we face things together.'

I lay on my front for a while, wondering what to say that wouldn't make things worse, struggling against sleep. When

I felt its weight descend upon me I shook it off, then lay on my back, staring upwards, tensing the muscles in my legs and in my arms. I knew that to give in would only make Millicent hate me more. But presently I also knew that there was no fighting it, that sleep had me in its loving embrace, was pinning me down, gently pressing against my limbs, easing them downwards; soon it suffused me; it was in my spine now, and there was no hope for me; sleep had me; it would not let me go.

Millicent came into the bathroom while I was shaving and peed matter-of-factly. For a moment I wondered whether this was a sign of forgiveness, or at least a suggestion of forgiveness. But when I smiled at her and she smiled back, there was an emptiness behind her eyes that told me everything.

In the kitchen Millicent and I drank coffee and ate nothing. Arla and Max drank orange juice and ate Pop Tarts; they spoke only to each other.

'So,' said Arla, 'last day of school. Wanna play hookey with me?'

Max looked over at me, then at Millicent. We smiled our smiles. Max looked unnerved.

'I should probably go to school.'

'I could call your head teacher.'

'No,' he said, 'I actually want to.'

'You do?'

'Thanks, though.'

He got up and put another Pop Tart in the toaster.

'Max,' I said.

'What?'

I looked at Millicent, who flashed me another eviscerating smile.

'Nothing,' I said. Let him have his Pop Tart. This was not a time for a talk about sugar.

Max sat down. Then he stood up and went into the front

329

room. Millicent, Arla and I sat in silence, the air heavy between us. Max came back in and sat down again.

'I get off at one, though. Do you want to come and get me?'

'Sure,' said Arla. 'Want to put a Pop Tart in the toaster for me?'

'Why aren't you my mum?' said Max. 'You're so much better at it than *Millicent*.'

Millicent's smile was gone. Then it was back.

'Max,' I said.

'What?'

'Just . . .'

'It's what you think too, Dad.'

Millicent's smile was very broad now. 'Good idea, honey. Would you *like* to be his mother, Arla?'

Arla's own smile flickered out. She could feel the anger in her sister, but she didn't yet know what Millicent knew. She looked at Millicent, then at me, then at Max. Then the California smile was back, warmer than ever. Breezes and cotton candy, bodies in the surf.

Millicent knows, Arla.

But Arla only smiled back at me.

'Shh,' said Max. 'Listen.'

The timer on the toaster. Traffic and birds through the back door. Nothing more.

Max stood up, very deliberately, and went to the back door. He opened it wide, and went out into the garden. He came back, carrying one end of the stepladder, dragging the other across the lawn.

'Max, the grass.'

'You don't care about the grass,' he said.

He dragged the ladder into the kitchen and past the table, and out through the door into the front room.

'Aren't you going to help him, honey?'

'He can do it,' I said. 'I'm sure he's done it before.'

Whatever Millicent's true reaction was, she quickly masked

it behind a smile. But the anger behind the eyes was no longer there. There was something else. Fear, perhaps?

Sound of the ladder being dragged up the staircase, hard and metallic against the softness of the wood. Then everything was very still.

Part of me wanted to say, 'Arla, Millicent knows.' Someone was going to have to say those words, in one form or another, and soon. But it couldn't be now.

I could hear Max's bare feet on the stepladder. Then nothing. I thought for a moment about the loft, and wondered if I should tell him to be careful. *Only beams and plasterboard.* Then I could hear Max's voice, speaking softly, then his feet on the stepladder again.

In the kitchen we made a play of shrugging at each other. Arla shrugged at Millicent. Millicent shrugged at me. I shrugged first at Arla, then at Millicent. Everyone smiled. Only Arla smiled with any warmth.

She knows, Arla.

Max was padding down the stairs. His voice was small, soothing, and coaxing: not words so much as sounds. I did not hear him cross the floor of the front room. He entered, carrying the cat. He put her down on the work surface and turned on the tap. She lapped at the water.

'Dad shut her into the loft.' The reproach in his voice, in his angry stare. The cat must have slipped up the ladder behind me when I had taken Millicent's letters. I had closed the hatch and shut her in. She had been there for two days. Why had she not mewed, or scratched?

'It's OK now, Foxxa,' he said. 'It's OK, girl.'

'It's good that your hearing is so sharp, Max,' I said.

'Yeah,' he said. 'Yeah, it is.'

Arla took Max to school.

I was almost relieved when Millicent stopped smiling. I tried to speak to her as she stood in the front room putting on her shoes, leaning against the banister for support. All she would tell me was that she was going 'out, Alex. I have a *lot* of thinking to do.' She flashed one last smile at me, then closed the door delicately behind her to emphasise her point.

The cat, however, was kind to me. She sat in my lap, washing herself, contented after water and food. She nuzzled against my hand, arched her back as I stroked her. Then she got off my lap, and sat down beside a piece of string that was lying on the floor. She stared at the piece of string, then stared at me, chirruping.

'No, cat,' I said.

She patted at the piece of string, then looked at me, eyes wide.

'OK,' I said.

I got up and picked up the piece of string; she leapt at the end of it, turned a backflip in the air as the tip flicked out of reach, her body level with my ribs. Flexion and torsion: first her chest, then her stomach. Now her front paws pointed downwards, now her rear paws. She landed almost without a sound; made herself low, ready for the next jump. I drew figures-of-eight in the air, and she turned backflip after backflip, supple and young in the sunlight, predator and imaginary prey. A tiny pool of undeserved calm; everything else was maelstrom.

'No!'

Shouting in the street.

'No, you can't! It's not yours to effing sell.'

It was very close. I went up the stairs and into Millicent's office. I drew back the curtains. Arla had left the window open.

There was a man, angry, outside the neighbour's house. That much I had understood from the shouting. He was tall, bearded, with short black hair and dark olive skin. His light-grey suit looked expensive and cool. He kept walking away, hands folded tight into his chest; then he would turn, throwing out his arms as if pleading, and walking back towards the open door. I could not see who was on the other side of the door, but I could hear a female voice that I did not know urging him to be calm.

'Jesus,' I heard the man shout. 'Tell me this isn't true!'

The man did not look dangerous. As I stood and wondered whether to intervene, Mr Ashani came out into the street, walked purposefully past our house and over to Bryce's front door.

'All right, my dear?' I heard him say to the woman who stood hidden there. He took the man by the arm. 'This lady is not the source of your troubles, sir. She is here at my request.'

'You brought in an effing estate agent? Effing unbelievable.'

Mr Ashani released the man's arm. 'I am the owner. Perhaps you wish to address yourself to me?' Mr Ashani led the man across the street and away from the argument. I heard Bryce's door close.

From this angle I could see the man's features better. Indian, I thought. Handsome. Tall. Thin. Mid-thirties. I saw Mr Ashani and the man pointing over at our house, and wondered whether they could see me in the upstairs window. There was no point in pretending I wasn't watching and listening.

I went to check my appearance in the bathroom. I looked tired, and my hair was a mess. I splashed water on to my face; I tried to do something about my hair; I went down the stairs and out into the street. The man was on his way, was about to disappear round the corner. I would have caught up with him if I wanted to; instead I hung back.

A hand on my arm. 'That poor girl,' said Mr Ashani. 'He wanted to give her a piece of his mind! When it is *I* who own the house; yet he did not dare to shout at *me*. He simply made his excuses and left, like a coward. Tell me, Alex, sir, do I inspire fear in *you*? Do I ever make *you* uneasy?'

'Who was that?'

Mr Ashani reached into his cream slacks and produced a crisp business card, which he handed to me.

Mann and Bryce
Architectural Project Management

There was a telephone number on it. Nothing more.
'You may keep the card.'
Mr Ashani went into his house. I stood for a while, blinking into the sunlight and the dust, then went back into mine. Then a thought occurred to me. I went outside and rang Mr Ashani's bell.
'Emmanuel,' I said when he answered, 'Emmanuel, have the police told you you can sell that house?'
'No,' he said, 'but they have yet to tell me that I may not.'

By early afternoon I was sitting in the office of Ravinder S. Mann, architect. He was having, he said, a new sign delivered. The old one was still on the door; the old one still said Mann and Bryce.

The table in the boardroom was white. Everything was streamlined; everything looked new. There were eight white chairs, two red chairs; two purple chairs. I sat in one of the red chairs. Ravinder Mann ('Call me Ravi, Alex') sat in one of the white chairs in his cool grey woollen suit, looking detached and handsome, fingertips pressed lightly together. There were five books in the large bookshelf. One was grey; one was pink; three were black.

He seemed at first to think I was there on business. An assistant brought pastries and an assortment of teas. Out of the window was a garden of raked white gravel. I thought of Bryce's house, and wondered whether it was Bryce who had designed the office.

'So,' he said, 'personal recommendation, right?'
Expensively educated, I thought. Something about his

bearing, his manner, his diction. That thing Oxford people often do: trying to convince you that they're less posh than they are.

'I lived next door to Bryce,' I said. 'I mean, I still live there.'

A look of intense grief passed across his face, and immediately I felt like an idiot for judging him.

'I'm sorry for your loss,' I said.

'Not a personal recommendation, then,' he said.

'No.'

'You're Alex.' It wasn't a question. He knew who I was.

'I'm Alex. Yeah.'

'I wish I knew what to say. I'm so sorry . . .' he said.

That your friend seduced my wife.

'You don't have to be sorry,' I said.

He made to pour the tea. His hand shook, and he spilled quite a lot of it over the surface of the boardroom table. We sat looking at the puddle as it spread slowly outwards, enveloping the bottoms of the cups. Perfectly level, I thought. *Architects*.

'Alex,' he said, 'shall we go to the pub instead?'

I looked back at the pooling tea as it inched towards the edge of the table.

'What about this?'

'Screw it,' he said. 'It's all screwed, anyway.'

We spent the first pint talking about football. We both had our reasons for hating it. He had been an overweight child. At school he had worn glasses and an eye patch; his mother had written notes to his teachers excusing him from gym. Hard to imagine now that no one wanted him on their team.

At my school, I told him, football was Hibs or Hearts, Fenian or Protestant, knife fights down the Grassmarket on a Friday night.

'Scourge of religion,' he said with a wry smile, rubbing his beard.

'You're . . .'

'A Sikh,' he said.

'Practising?'

'Ish.'

He told me again how sorry he was about what Bryce had done. It wasn't like him, he wanted me to know. He was a good man at heart. The old Bryce would have been appalled at what the new Bryce had done. He was sure of it.

'You don't have to apologise for your friend.'

'You think you know someone,' he said. 'But you don't. You don't know them at all.'

He said nothing when I handed him his second beer. I asked him if he was OK.

'He was clever,' he said. 'He didn't empty the client account, so I didn't know. Everything else, though. Everything else he screwed.'

I took a long swig of beer, waited for him to continue.

He looked up, and the edges of his mouth tightened. 'I don't even know how much is missing. He dismissed the bookkeeper. All I know is, we're effing screwed. Well, he's dead. *I'm* screwed. Cheers.'

He tapped his glass against mine, a little too hard.

'Cheers,' I said, reflexively.

'What am I going to do, Alex?'

In other circumstances I would have liked the man. In other circumstances we could have been friends, I thought.

'Do you want me to tell you what he was doing, Alex?'

'OK.'

'Sorry,' he said, 'that's just my way of telling you I'm *going* to tell you what he was doing. Because I have to tell you; because I'm scared to tell my wife, and I have to tell *someone*. You look like a good guy.'

'OK . . .'

'Three of our clients have now told me he asked for payment in cash. The wonder is that any of them would do it because they're none of them fools, but yes, they paid him in cash, because he was a persuasive little beggar, and they did.'

I thought sadly about Millicent; he had certainly persuaded her. 'A scaffolder came to our door,' I said. 'Bryce gave him our address.'

'Oh, Lord, no,' he said.

'He was trading from our address,' I said. 'Although I don't think he was ever in our house. Sorry. I'm not trying to make things worse.'

'No, I need to know,' he said. 'How much this time?'

'Twenty-three thousand? Twenty-four?'

'Do you have any idea how long it takes before a creditor comes knocking at your door, Alex?' I made to speak, but he carried on. 'Again, I'm going to tell you. In my line of work, four or five months. Minimum. They know how long it takes to get paid, and they trust us, because they know it takes *us* time to get paid by our creditors, and because this business is founded on trust. And now we've effed that trust, haven't we? Or at least, Bryce has. I'm finished.'

There was despair in him now.

'I heard you outside Bryce's house,' I said. 'Saw you.'

'Oh,' he said. 'Yes. Yes, I shouldn't have shouted at her. Not her fault. Not her fault at all.' He looked at me pleadingly, pulled at my sleeve, as if there was something I could do to help him. 'I thought at least I might have some sort of claim against the estate. That was my last hope. And I'm ashamed of it, but I thought he owed me that, at least. And then I find out there's no effing house to sell, and I am completely – not to say utterly – effed.'

I didn't know what to say, so I offered to go to the bar again.

'I'll send the girl some flowers,' he said, 'while I still have a bank account.'

'Have you told the police?' I asked.

'Not yet,' he said. 'Do you think I should? I mean, I know I should. I will, I promise. I will.'

'That sounds like a good idea,' I said. 'I'm sorry.'

'Do you know the weird thing?' he said. 'Do you know what the absolute weirdest thing is? Do you, Alex? The weirdest thing is, is that . . . is that . . . is that everything's still how it was. It's like, there's this massive cliff of ice at the end of a glacier. I mean, I'm standing here in a boat on the ocean just in front of it and it's got to fall, yes, but nothing has come crashing down yet, and it all still looks perfect. I know it will start to break up. It has to. But it hasn't yet. Everything still looks as if it could remain intact.'

I looked towards the door of the pub.

It was then that I saw Rose. She was sitting, reading a book, at a table by the front door. In front of her was a small glass of white wine. Had she followed me here, I wondered, or had she been there all along?

Ravi smiled bitterly. 'What are you thinking right now, Alex?'

I smiled defensively back and he carried on talking. 'You're thinking that we don't even make buildings, Alex, that really we offer a kind of management service, and that I'm being pretentious and architecty. You're thinking that I'm over-working the metaphor of the ice wall, and that I should shut the eff up and play the hand I've been dealt.'

Rose was looking at me now, and for a moment my gaze met hers.

Stay away.

'No,' I said. 'That is not what I'm thinking.'

'You are,' he said. He drained the rest of the beer in his glass. 'I would.'

I went to the bar again, wondered whether the pub had another way out, wondered how soon I could decently leave. Perhaps the easiest thing would be to walk straight past Rose. Send a clear message.

Did Ravi know Rose? He gave no sign of having seen her, but he was lost in his own misery. I was certain he was about

338

to tell me that the ice wall above him would break apart, that it would fall into the sea, that a wall of water would sink his boat.

'Alex, the bank still loves us, you know,' he said as I gave him his third pint. 'We still have seventy grand in the client account; we still have a reputation. I mean, it's beginning to get a bit frayed around the edges, but on paper we're a legitimate operation. We are standing in a beautiful new boat with a group of high-value individuals watching a pristine cliff of unbroken ice. That is where we are. We are in the great Antarctic Ocean, and it's a glorious day. And no one can see the fissures and the cracks, *no* one. But *I* can hear the ice moving on itself, and *I* know that cliff is going to fall, and when it does the wave will sink our boat. And I'm the captain of the boat, and I will be the last man off and it will take me down with it. *That's* why it's a good metaphor.'

He drank down half of the new pint. I looked at the ceiling.

'You know, Alex, I still go to work as if nothing has happened, knowing I can't rescue this, but still sort of believing I can. Do you know what I spent the rest of the morning doing, Alex? After I'd humiliated myself by shouting outside your house? Pitching for new work. And do you know why? Because you called and asked to meet me. Your telephone call gave me hope. It got me thinking about new clients. New possibilities. First time in weeks. And then *you* come into the office, and I can see that you're not a new client, and that everything is going down.'

'I'm sorry,' I said. I thought of the business he and Bryce had built up. I thought of the tea he had spilled, and wondered whether it was still pooled there on the level surface of his perfect white table.

'I'm sorry,' I said again, and meant it. The man was ruined, and he knew it. Friends in another life, perhaps, but in this life there was nothing I could do to save him. It would be

339

as much as I could do to rescue what was left of my own family.

I did not see Rose slip from the pub as I left, but I heard footsteps in the street behind me, and turned to find her there at my side.

'You know Ravinder,' she said.

'You followed me here.'

'He's a good guy.'

'I love my wife, Rose,' I said.

'Yes,' she said, 'and I need to speak to you about that. Please listen to what I have to tell you.'

'I'm sorry,' I said. 'I really need to be at home. Please don't follow me.'

She followed me. Five minutes of my time she wanted. She had to speak to me. No, I said, and walked on. She wasn't going to take no for an answer, she said, not on this. It was too important. I needed to know, she said. Millicent needed to know. For the sake of our future happiness. This is insane, I said. No, she said, this is not insane, Alex. If there is one thing this is not, it's insane.

'This *is* insane,' I said.

'Hear me out,' she said.

I walked on. The streets grew dirty and the air grew bad. She matched me step for step.

She didn't look insane. She looked determined.

I relented.

Coffee.

I took her to The Cheeseria! The Cheeseria! smelled of other people's babies, of soured milks, of some nameless rot, topped by a shrill note of ammonia. The Cheeseria!, with its capital T and its exclamation mark; with its two tiny tables, and its unpasteurised cheeses. Essence of fucking cheese.

I ordered double espressos. The last thing The Cheeseria! made you want was milk in any form.

'I need to clear something up with you, Alex. And Millicent won't speak to me.'

At the other table a girl of twenty-five sat talking loudly at a mobile phone, held six inches from the side of her head. 'He's an obligate carnivore, Mum. Yeah, so no brown rice.'

'What do you want to clear up with me, Rose?'

She was looking levelly back at me. She didn't look insane or predatory. She wasn't holding my gaze for longer than she should, or touching my hand by accident, or arranging her body to draw my gaze. There was nothing aggressive or frightening about her.

'Alex,' she said at last, 'Alex, what did my brother tell Millicent about Lana?'

'That she was his little girl. That she died when she was one. That his marriage fell apart after that.'

'That's what I thought you said. Christ.'

I could see the pain in her, though she tried to blink it away. Then she frowned and made a point of looking at the girl at the other table.

'Mum, we love him too,' the girl was saying, 'but he's a cat. Yeah. So no brown rice.' She must have realised that we were staring at her then because she gave a silent 'oops' and went outside to finish her call.

'Lana was my daughter,' said Rose at last.

The stain of incest. That most ancient of crimes. It made a horrible kind of sense.

Rose must have caught the look that crossed my face.

'No, she was *my* daughter. Not Bryce's. God, the thought.' She smiled for a moment, then pain erased the smile from her face. She rested her elbows on the table, pressed the tips of her fingers into her forehead.

'He told Millicent she died when she was a year old,' I said. 'Viral meningitis.'

'She was less than a year old. Ten months. And they call it meningitis. Just meningitis. But otherwise he got it about right.'

She bent over, dug into her bag, and produced a photograph of herself sitting in a blue plastic chair, breastfeeding a baby in the middle of a hospital ward.

'I debated whether to show you this. Long and hard. Forgive me if this is the wrong decision.'

In the middle of the baby's forehead was a colourless plastic tube with a red screw valve, held neatly in place by surgical tape. A thinner tube ran directly under the baby's translucent skin.

'I'm not a fan of melodrama, Alex,' she said, 'despite what you think of me.'

'God, Rose.'

There was nothing insane about Rose – I could see that now – though she looked tired and disarrayed.

'Towards the end they started running out of veins. Hence the cannula on the forehead.' She gave a little laugh, making light of her suffering. How alike she and Millicent were in that. As if it embarrassed them that their grief showed.

The photograph had been taken by Lana's father. Yes, they had been married. He was a good man but they were no longer together. The strain of losing Lana had pushed them in different directions. Suffering had coldly worked its fingers between them and drawn them apart. And no, Bryce had never been married. And no, Bryce had never come close to losing a child.

Rose had coped: barely at first, then increasingly well. Lana's father had not. Rose had left, had found a new career in a new town, but it had taken her some years to get back on her feet.

'If I've behaved in any way inappropriately, Alex, it has never been intentional.'

'Please,' I said. 'I should be apologising to you. I misread you. I should have listened.'

That attraction, that sense of a secret shared: it was Rose's secret, and we did not share it. She had done what neither Millicent nor I could.

How do you move on? If there was a part of Rose that I wanted, it was her answer to that question.

'What, Alex?'

I was staring at her. 'I feel terrible, Rose.' I should stop staring at her. I forced myself to look away. 'What happened to you was worse than what happened to us,' I said. 'Worse than I can imagine. And you dealt with it so much better. I feel ashamed that I misread you.'

'It isn't a competition, Alex.'

'You did though. You coped.'

And then Bryce took her story and told it to Millicent as his own. How did it feel, I wondered, to be used in that way by your brother? To have your pain repackaged and sold on to someone else?

She must have guessed at my thought. 'He wasn't a sociopath, Alex,' she said. 'He was a lonely man who envied what other people had, and never understood how they had got to where they had got. Anyway, I thought you should know.'

'He told Millicent your story,' I said. 'He pretended it was his.'

'Yes,' she said. 'Yes, he did.'

Bryce used Millicent's grief over Sarah as the means of her seduction. He lied to and humiliated her.

Of course she killed him.

Millicent wasn't home in time for supper. I ate with Arla and Max. Arla and Max talked to each other; I didn't say very much. Then Max looked meaningfully at Arla, and Arla looked meaningfully at Max, and Max nodded, and Arla nodded. Then Arla asked if she could take Max to the cinema to celebrate his last day of primary school. Some kind of sci-fi all-nighter. 'Planet of the Apes', or something. The good ones, said Max, not the crap ones. Sure, I said. If she could get him in, why not? It really *was* kind of an all-nighter, said Arla. OK, I said. Really? said Max, was I sure? Yes, I said, I was sure.

I gave Arla £80. 'Too much,' she said.

'Take it,' I said.

I sat in the front room waiting for Millicent. After a time I realised that the sun had gone down and that I was sitting there in the dark. The streetlight shone orange through the window. Most of the time, nothing happened. Cars passed; silhouetted figures slouched home from the pub.

Some time after one she opened the door. She turned on the light, and saw me at once. She smiled her empty smile.

'Home alone?'

'Yes.' I smiled back. 'Last day of school. Arla wanted to treat him.'

'OK.'

She took off her shoes, placed them with more than usual care by the front door, then began to walk upstairs. 'I'm super-tired,' she said, as if that explained where she had been. Still that smile.

I heard her close the bathroom door behind her, heard her slide home the lock, heard the sound of water running down the outside of the building. She was brushing her teeth.

I went upstairs. I made a dip in the bedclothes, and fetched the box from the back of my wardrobe; I tipped the baubles and the letters gently from the box, left them in a pile in the middle of our bed. I closed the bedroom door, felt the latch click. I went back downstairs.

I heard Millicent unlock the bathroom door. Then she opened it very slowly and walked towards the bedroom. There was a measured quality to her movements, a deliberateness that was meant to signify something – what?

I heard her open our bedroom door, then stop at the threshold. The house breathed.

'Alex,' she said.

I said nothing.

'Alex,' she said again. I sat where I was. After a while, I heard her feet on the floorboards again.

'Yes?' I said.

She was halfway downstairs. She wasn't smiling now.

I stood up. She came and stood before me in the living room.

'You were going to go to sleep,' I said.

'Yes,' she said, 'yes, I was.'

'And we need to talk.'

'What in the world kind of a weird statement was that up there?' she said.

'You were going to go to sleep,' I said again.

'Aren't you tired, Alex?'

'Millicent,' I said. 'I know.'

'What do you know, Alex?' she said. 'What do you think you know?'

'I know what you did. I half-know why you did it.'

'No,' she said. 'No, I don't think that you do. I don't think you know the half of it.'

I tried to take her in my arms, but she was standing so stiffly that it was impossible. She pushed her arms down and away, a gesture of rejection, stepped away from me slightly.

'Don't leave us, Millicent.'

'Please don't use Max against me.'

'Then don't leave me, Millicent. We can sell the house and slip quietly away. Together.'

'Oh my God,' she said. 'Oh my God, Alex.' She was looking at me properly, her eyes searching mine. 'Jesus. You think . . .'

'Yes,' I said, 'I think that now.'

'How can you think that, Alex?'

I went upstairs and fetched the other letters, the ones that she had retrieved from Bryce's house. They were still in the inside pocket of my rucksack. Then I took the Florentine leather gloves from the back of one of the shelves in my wardrobe.

She was standing where I had left her, looking smaller than ever. I handed her the letters, and the gloves.

'I intruded into your privacy,' I said. 'I needed to know.'

She nodded.

'Why didn't the police find them?'

'He hid them in his bookshelf,' she said, 'in the spine of one of my books, in case that detail amuses you. *Marriage for Cynics*. In plain sight.'

'But you'd think they would . . .'

'I don't *know* how they missed them, Alex. But they did.'

We stood in silence for the longest time. Eventually I went into the kitchen to find wine. When I came back into the living room, Millicent was sitting on the sofa.

'What was he threatening you with?' I said.

'Alex,' she said. 'You are wrong.'

'You asked him to leave you alone,' I said. 'It's there in your letter. What was he threatening you with?'

She took a long swig of wine. 'The usual thing,' she said. 'He was going to tell everyone everything. Isn't that the usual thing?'

'And what would you not be party to?'

'He wanted me to go away with him. Like, we would elope. It was ridiculous. So fricking juvenile. And then he starts having his mail sent here. Like, we were part of something together. Like, I was party to his fraud or something.'

'Millicent,' I said, 'what was he going to tell?'

'Alex,' she said, 'please don't force me to tell you what you already know.'

'I don't know, Millicent. I really don't know.'

'I think you do know, Alex,' she said. 'I mean, it's all there, spread across our marital bed.'

'I haven't read your letters,' I said. 'Max has. He has this technique with scissors and glue. It's not invisible, but it's pretty close.'

'Shit,' she said. 'Well, I guess he would get a fairly consistent theme.'

'What theme?'

'Abandonment. Like I run from my problems, or something, and leave other people behind to *deal*.'

'What's in the letters?'

'I just told you. And, kind of, I guess, apologies. Or explanations. Or something. Only I didn't send any of them, because I don't like to . . .'

'You don't like to *share*?'

'Yeah, you get to laugh at me, Alex. Good for you. But the truth is that I get ashamed, and I try to explain, and what I have to say sounds so lame, that I *can't*. And yeah, I get that it's laughable.'

'I'm not laughing at you.'

'And then I try to explain myself, and I even suck at that. And because of that I have no one left except you and Max. And Arla. Arla has pretty consistently refused to let me abandon her. I don't deserve her as a sister, and I don't deserve you as a husband.'

I reached out towards her. She shook her head.

'You and Arla sure exacted your revenge on me, didn't you? I get it. I'm laughable.'

'You aren't,' I said.

'Oh, I am. And I can't even send her away, because right now she's the most stable family member Max has.'

Voices in the street. Max and Arla. I picked up the gloves and the letters, and was already at the top of the stairs when I heard the key in the lock. I tossed the letters and the gloves on to the bed with the other letters, then pulled the bedroom door closed behind me and stepped back on to the landing.

'Hey,' said everyone, all at the same time.

The next half hour was excruciating. Millicent and I made hot chocolate for Max and Arla, and saw them both safely into bed, smiling all the while. When we were sure they were both safely asleep, we stopped smiling. We spent the next half hour sitting on the sofa, not daring to speak. You killed him, I thought. *You killed him.* Yet I said nothing, and nor did Millicent.

At length we went out, leaving a note in case Arla or Max woke up again. We found an all-night café that served undrinkable coffee in Styrofoam cups. Millicent took a mouthful and spat it out into her palm. Then she reached for a serviette and knocked over her cup. We apologised to the man behind the counter, borrowed a cloth, ordered large mugs of tea instead.

At a table by an open fire escape, a young couple sat smoking cigarettes and French kissing. Like us, I thought. *Like us before it all went wrong.* Millicent watched them for a while, then turned to face me.

'Are we always going to make each other unhappy, Alex,' she said.

'We don't,' I said. 'Not normally.'

We ordered full English breakfasts and more mugs of tea, then watched each other as we ate in silence. The couple by the fire escape paid and left, laughing.

'Millicent,' I said, 'Arla told me this weird story about you giving birth in a beetroot field.'

'There was no beet field,' she said. 'There *was* a miscarriage, though. Quite a late miscarriage, it turned out.'

She let me take her hand.

'Sarah wasn't the first,' she said. 'I suck at getting pregnant. Or I suck at staying pregnant. Max was the exception. Sarah was the rule.'

The lightness of the words.

'It happened at high school. At ten thirty a.m. on a Tuesday. During English class.'

'Not prom night?'

'That was the night I skipped town. The miscarriage happened the week before.'

She had not known she was pregnant. The stomach cramps had continued all morning. They had started on the way to school. The bleeding had begun as she stood at her desk reading out an essay. The class had gone very quiet, and it had taken her some time to realise. Then she had run from her class to the girls' toilet block, knowing only that something was badly wrong. She had scooped that tiny, rigid body into her sweater and carried it to the school nurse, humiliated and fearful, desperate for help.

'I guess I thought there must be procedures. But she took it next door, and it sounded like she dropped it into some sort of metal container.' Her voice became very small. 'I think she incinerated it, Alex.'

Word had got out. There had been blood on the floor of the English classroom; she suspected the nurse had said something careless. She had skipped the last few days of school, but they let her graduate all the same. She really had planned to go to the prom, but her nerves had overcome her.

'And if I read the letters that you wrote to your parents?' I said.

'I guess those letters were kind of angry. Like I thought they thought it was all my fault. Not that they ever said it.'

'And to your boyfriend?'

'I thought you could write letters to the dead. Did you never do that?'

'No,' I said. 'No, I never did.'

'You would have hated the eighteen-year-old version of me,' she said. 'Real superstitious. I sucked.'

'You could post those letters,' I said. 'It might give you . . .'

'What? *Closure*?' she said. 'You don't believe in closure, Alex. There's no such thing. I wrote those letters when I was eighteen. What does an eighteen-year-old girl know about anything? How do you even send a letter to a guy who took his own life?'

349

She looked so small, sitting there on the other side of the table from me, arms folded angrily across her chest.

'Why did you never tell me, at least?' I said, after a time.

'It was an earlier version of me. I mean, I *thought* it was. Maybe it's still me.'

I sat back in my chair, and took a long, hard look at my wife. 'Millicent,' I said, 'were you pregnant again this time?'

'Briefly.'

'And Bryce knew?'

She nodded. *Christ.*

'Was it his?'

She made a helpless little gesture. 'He decided it was.'

'And you lost the baby?'

'No,' she said, 'no, Alex, this time I took measures.'

'You had . . .'

'. . . a termination,' she said, in words I could hardly hear. 'Eight weeks.'

The man behind the counter glanced up at us. *Leave us alone.* I stared at him and he stared back. *Let us be.*

'Were you going to leave with him?'

'He was crazy,' she said.

'Is that a no?'

'That would be a no, Alex. A very firm no.'

I was scared, sitting there. I was trying so hard not to judge; trying so hard to keep my own anger from bursting through.

'Just how much money did he steal, Millicent? For your new life together?'

Millicent sat there, shaking her head slowly from side to side.

'It was thousands, wasn't it? Tens of thousands?'

'I never wanted any of that, Alex. Look, I know you think I'm a bolter. And I know I cemented that by talking about divorce. And sure, part of me still wants to bolt. But I know I can't this time. I always knew that. There's Max. And there's you.'

'I believe you, Millicent.' I looked over at the man behind the counter. He was pretending to read a magazine now, still listening to our conversation. 'What about the gloves?'

We stared at each other. Millicent's eyes registered something like shock. I leaned in towards her again.

'I know you went to get the gloves, along with the letters. And that weird little piece of tape.'

This time she looked puzzled. She leaned forward, and I turned my ear towards her mouth.

'I don't know how he came to have my gloves, Alex. I never once wore them. But yes, I found them in a drawer beside my letters, and yes, I took them back.'

'And the piece of tape?' I said.

'I don't know anything about a piece of tape.'

We sat back in our chairs. Millicent looked tiny, and exhausted. But there was an angry defiance to her, as well.

'Was he in our house? Is that how he got them?'

'No, Alex, I swear to you – he was never in our house. Please give me a little credit. I maintained *some* boundaries.'

The man at the counter pretended not to hear. I could see him react. But we were just another couple arguing over an affair; the police already knew about the affair.

I leaned over and spoke directly into her ear again. 'So, what were you doing in *his* house, when I was in Edinburgh?'

She pressed her fingers hard against her temples for a moment, then blinked twice. Then she brought her mouth close to my ear.

'I wanted to be less strongly linked to him, Alex, nothing more.'

'You should have handed the gloves and the tape to the police.'

'No, Alex,' she said, her voice a tiny whisper, 'I really should *not*.'

I leaned in, closer still. 'You killed him,' I said.

Millicent stiffened. I straightened up a little. Millicent's eyes blazed – anger, and something that looked almost like insolence. The bravado of the eighteen-year-old girl.

'Didn't you?' I said.

She leaned her mouth towards me, and I turned my ear to meet it.

'No, Alex, I did not kill him.'

Again we looked at each other. I leaned in towards her, again brought my mouth very close to her ear.

'I know why you did it now.' I sat back in my seat. 'Rose told me.'

'What, Alex? What did Rose tell you?'

'About Lana.'

'What about her?'

'Come on, Millicent. I know.'

'What about Lana, Alex?'

'She wasn't Bryce's daughter. Bryce never had a child.'

'No,' she said. 'No, Alex, you are mistaken.' That same matter-of-fact tone as the night I told her Bryce was dead. As if she were refuting a badly constructed argument.

'It's true. Rose had a daughter called Lana, who died.'

'No,' she said again, but I could see that she believed me.

'You didn't know,' I said. 'I thought you knew.'

'No, Alex,' she said. 'I didn't know.'

Relief flooded my body. 'You didn't do it. Thank God. Thank God, Millicent. Thank God.'

I tried to take her in my arms but she pushed back her chair and stood up, walked to the counter. She exchanged words with the man behind the counter, and he showed her to a room in the back. I heard taps running. I heard water in the pipes. And I heard Millicent's keening sobs, loud above the running of the water. Neither of us spoke. The man behind the counter could hear Millicent crying too. I could feel his eyes upon me, but I avoided eye contact. I couldn't bear one of *those* conversations.

Women, eh?

Ah, yeah. Women!

Bryce had fooled Millicent, as he had fooled so many other people. My beautiful Millicent, so sharp, so funny and so clever. And he had duped her; even she had been seduced by the lies of the lonely little man in the next-door house.

From the counter the man came to the table with two more mugs of tea.

'I didn't order this,' I said.

'Sounds like you need it, though.'

'Yes,' I said. 'Yes we do. Thanks.'

'Are you two all right?'

'I don't know,' I said. 'I really don't know.'

The sun was up, and already you could feel the heat building in the dirty streets. It was six o'clock.

The neighbour's house had been emptied. The blinds were gone from the windows, the furniture cleared from the front room. 'Huh,' said Millicent, her forehead pressed against the glass. 'Looks smaller.'

Is that all you have to say? I thought, but did not ask.

Her footprints would be gone, more or less, hidden amongst the prints of the removal men. If you didn't know what you were looking for, you'd never see them now. Would the police rearrest her if I rang and told them what to look for? Or were they done with us?

Why did she go back into his house? Why was she lying to me? Why the gloves? Why the tape?

Let it go, I thought. Millicent was telling the truth about the most important fact: she didn't kill Bryce, I was sure of that now. *Let it go.* I put my hand on the small of Millicent's back and guided her towards our little house.

Forgive.

Still, though: the gloves; the tape.

27

Max's book was on our bed again, on the hollow where a few hours before Millicent's letters had lain.

'We have to talk about this with the shrink, don't we?' said Millicent.

'The drawings?' I said. 'Probably.'

I opened the door to Max's bedroom, and we stood there on the threshold for a moment, watching him. Calm rise and fall of his chest; body completely given over to sleep.

'Max,' I said, experimentally; he did not react.

Millicent put a hand on my chest. 'I noticed something weird through my embarrassment and shame and humiliation,' she said. 'Because I did read Max's book pretty thoroughly, hard though that was. And the sex stuff, it's a description of what he heard, right?'

How small our son looked, and how perfect, arms thrown outwards, pyjamaed legs kicking away the covers: bare-chested, brave and very small.

'I don't want to have this discussion here,' I said.

'Sure.' She closed Max's door; we went back into our own room and pulled the door shut behind us.

'Sorry,' said Millicent. 'Super-strung out.'

'Yeah.'

'But you know, Alex, the last description he wrote was the day *before* you guys found Bryce. How come he didn't write any description of finding him?'

'The pictures are the description,' I said. 'And he was dead, so he didn't make any noise.'

'Then how come he didn't date the last two pictures?'

'He's eleven,' I said.

'You keep saying that. You'd think he would draw the erection.'

'He's an eleven-year-old boy who's trying to understand your affair, and Bryce's suicide, and why everything in his life got turned over by that. He's like someone who's read the instruction manual but has never actually seen a car.'

'Yeah,' she said. 'I guess.' She was not convinced. 'He lifted the rest of the pages out. Look.'

It was true. The last four or five sheets of paper had been cut from the book with a scalpel. Almost invisible.

'What do you think?' she said.

'I think Max has a sense of drama. Anything he wrote or drew after this would be an anti-climax.'

'I guess,' she said. 'Yeah, you're probably right.'

At six fifteen Millicent mailed Dr Å from her phone asking for an appointment. The cat appeared from nowhere, lay beside us on the bed, purring musically. Eventually the purring stopped and the cat slept.

At seven thirty Millicent woke me in panic. Dr Å had sent an SMS. She would see us at eight thirty.

We arrived seven minutes late for our appointment. The door to Dr Å's consulting room was open. She had placed coffee cups on the floor by two of the chairs, and on the floor beside Max's chair was a glass of water.

Some slight imbalance as I sat down. I ran my hand across the top of my right thigh. Something about my wallet was wrong, I thought. The weight, perhaps. Strange that you even notice.

'Can I have juice, Dr No?' said Max.

'You have water, Max,' she said simply.

'OK,' he said. He sat on his chair and smiled. I was surprised at how lightly he took being summoned to see the shrink, how willingly he deferred to her.

'You asked to see me urgently,' said Dr Å. 'And here we are.'

'Yes,' said Millicent. 'I wasn't expecting you to see us so soon.'

'Max, did you feel the same sense of urgency about this session?'

'Not really.'

'So,' said Dr Å brightly, 'something couldn't wait.' She looked at me. I looked at Millicent. Millicent looked at Dr Å, then at Max, then at me.

The clock marked time: almost ten minutes down, and nothing to show for it. Max picked up his glass and blew bubbles into his water.

'Max, don't,' I said.

'I can do what I like in here,' said Max. He put down his water. 'Can't I, Dr No?'

All three of us looked at Dr Å.

'And I would only say that such behaviour is unusual from you in my experience, Max. Are you trying to provoke a reaction in your parents?'

'Sorry, Dr Å.'

'We're all a little frazzled,' said Millicent.

'I'm not,' said Max. 'Not really.'

'Perhaps I can ask you, Millicent,' said Dr Å. 'Why are we here?'

'Max has a notebook,' she said.

'His diary?'

'He told you about it?' she said.

'I am familiar with it. He left it with me at the start of his course of therapy.'

356

Of course, I thought. That's why the police didn't find it.

'Well, I don't think I understood how much my son hates me until I read it.'

'It's not about you,' said Max. 'It's about him. The neighbour.'

Millicent got up; she drew her chair across the floor away from Max and towards Dr Å.

'So,' said Dr Å, 'what is it about Max's diary that brings you all here?'

Millicent carried on speaking very quietly. 'There's such hatred in those drawings. They're like a sort of revenge fantasy of all the things that Max wanted to happen to Bryce. I never thought my son would be capable of such hate.'

'You interpret this as hate,' said Dr Å simply. 'I'm not certain that it is.'

'It is a little bit, though,' said Max. 'Because it's like, when you're at school, and someone says "your mother" and there's a fight, because it means your mum lets other men do her. Can I go in the garden?'

'I'm agreeable to that,' said Dr Å. 'If your parents are. Perhaps Max could come back in twenty minutes?'

Millicent nodded. Dr Å looked at me. 'Yes,' I said. 'Fine.'

Max got to his feet and went out, leaving the door open.

'Millicent,' said Dr Å, 'Max needs to be enabled to express his legitimate anger.'

'Well, wow, you sure *enabled* him.'

'You did not see the pain in what Max just said?' Millicent gave a sad little grimace. 'First he expresses anger, then he cries. In this room, that is permitted. The crying is the second half of the equation, if you will. Your son is a very sensitive little boy. In this room he cries a lot. Perhaps he does not feel he can do this at home?'

I said nothing. Maybe she was right.

'So how do I stop him hating me?' said Millicent.

'Show him that things can be repaired.'

'That's it?'

'It takes time and hard work.' She turned to me. 'Alex, it's your job to show Max what a man can be. And Millicent, it's your job to show him that what Alex is, what Max will become – that that is completely acceptable. To be a man is something good, something to be accepted, and to be cherished.'

Millicent rolled her eyes. She did not return my smile.

Dr Å turned to me. 'It's also Alex's job to show Max where he's *wrong*. You have both experienced, I think, how harshly boys judge their mothers for what they see as their sexual failings?' I nodded. Millicent nodded. 'That can seem very unfair, Millicent, I know, but it seems to be a fundamental part of how small boys are wired. The Madonna/whore complex is very real to them. It's something I expect adult men to have got past.' She smiled at me. A joke, I thought, I really hope that's a joke. 'So in this case it's Alex's job to show that bad things can be forgiven, no matter how raw they feel. For you to split up would be a cataclysm for Max, however angry he is. Your son needs to learn how to forgive.' She paused, clearly expecting me to say something.

'I've already told Max that,' I said. 'He doesn't want me to forgive Millicent.'

'It's not what you say, Alex. It's what you do. He will take his cues from you. There is, I think, a lot of unresolved anger in your little family.'

'You think I preach forgiveness and practise wrath?'

'It isn't what I think that's important, Alex,' she said simply. 'And you are not the only one whose anger is unresolved.' She flashed Millicent a significant look.

'What?' said Millicent. Dr Å simply smiled.

'Do you think we need therapy?' I asked her.

'Again, that really isn't for me to decide. But I don't think I need to see Max again. Unless he wants to see me.'

Millicent and I got up to go. Max had not returned. He

would be waiting for us outside, I thought. We paid Dr Å, and agreed that we would contact her if any of us felt the need.

Max wasn't outside. He wasn't at the bus stop, and he wasn't in any of the shops near the bus stop.

'Should we be worried by this?' said Millicent.

'It's nine thirty,' I said. 'I don't think he's been kidnapped.'

'Yeah, he probably went home,' she said.

She texted Arla:

Max with you?

Shortly after, Arla replied:

Yep.

We walked home along the bus route, hardly speaking. North London was already unbearably hot, and I could feel the threat of a headache behind my eyes, a gentle throbbing in my left temple.

The neighbour's front door was open. A woman in a suit was attaching an estate agent's board to the pillar by the front door. She went inside, leaving the door ajar.

We paused at the front door, looking at each other.

'Go on,' I said. 'Knock.'

'You'd be OK with that?'

'I'd like to see it again too.'

Millicent opened the door. 'Hello?' she called.

The estate agent was shockingly young. But there was a firmness in her handshake, and a confidence in her bearing: all direct eye contact and good posture, bright teeth and immaculate shoes.

'We live next door,' said Millicent. 'Could we take a look around?'

'Of course,' said the agent. 'It's a beautiful property, really nicely presented. Although really, to achieve the best price, they should have left the furniture in it.'

I wondered if Mr Ashani had sold Bryce's furniture.

We looked around the living room. Those perfect walls, that perfect wooden floor. There was no sign of damage to the ceiling, and I guessed from the smell that the room had been repainted. No trace here of Millicent's affair. Except, of course, for that stain on the floor. There was a slight darkening where the sofa had been, where the water that had dripped through the ceiling had gathered.

'You aren't thinking of selling, are you?' said the agent.

'No,' said Millicent.

'We'd be more than happy to advise you if you do. These houses are doing really well at the moment. Especially if you've extended into the loft.'

'We have not extended into the loft,' said Millicent, a little sharply, I thought. 'But that's good to know.'

We hovered at the foot of the stairs. Millicent looked shaky. I put my hand on the crook of her arm. 'It's OK,' I said under my breath. 'This is OK.' She nodded, uncertain. I went upstairs; she followed.

There was a plain new bath in the bathroom, and Mr Ashani's workmen seemed to have tiled over the old tiles and touched up the paintwork. Everything was crisp and white; no trace of blood on porous ceramic, no reminder of Bryce's violent end. Simple and cost-effective.

I turned and knocked into Millicent, who had been standing behind me. I held her shoulders, turned her slightly as I squeezed past her, left her standing illuminated by the light that streamed in through the window. How far away she seemed.

Let her have this moment.

As I watched, Millicent sat stiffly on the edge of the bathtub. She raised her hand, pinched the bridge of her nose. She

360

doesn't want me to see her crying, I thought. She doesn't want me to know that she's mourning him.

Be the bigger man.

I stood alone in the middle of Bryce's bedroom. There were four light patches on the dark wooden floor where the legs of the bed had stood. I wondered how much the bed had rocked under Bryce and Millicent; how much of the scraped varnish was down to my wife's infidelity? Enough for Max to have heard, that much was sure.

I walked across the floor to the window. A board creaked underfoot. I looked out at the garden. Mr Ashani had razed Bryce's love bower. He had removed the trellises and unmercifully cut the rose plants back to their roots. There was nothing left of the scene of Millicent's seduction.

'Hey,' said Millicent from the doorway.

'Hey,' I said. 'You OK?'

Millicent nodded. 'Pretty much.'

She walked hesitantly towards me across the wooden floor. Again a board creaked.

'Look,' I said as Millicent reached the window. 'It's all gone.'

'Huh,' said Millicent.

I left her looking out of the window and located the loose floorboard with my foot. It was small, no more than ten centimetres wide and fifty long. I crouched down beside the board. When I placed the tip of my shoe on it, I could slide it slightly from right to left. I pulled out my keys.

'What are you doing, Alex?' said Millicent.

'It's OK,' I said quietly. 'She's downstairs.'

I selected a key that was long and flat, and slid it into the gap at the side. The board lifted easily.

The money was arranged in five rolls, each one fifteen centimetres in diameter. The rolls were held together with thick rubber bands. None of the notes on the outside was bigger than a twenty, yet I was sure this was far more than £70,000.

361

'Millicent,' I said, under my breath. 'Millicent.'

Then she was at my side, crouching down beside me, looking into the floor space. I could feel her breath on my ear, an uneven staccato.

I kept expecting to hear feet on the stairs.

I looked at Millicent. *We can't, can we?*

No, she thought back at me. *No, we can not.*

We stayed there for a moment, both shaking our heads. *No. No, absolutely not.*

There was nothing to see in the second bedroom, nothing in the tiny featureless study. I went down the kitchen. Bryce's expensive stove was still there, but the room had been stripped of the little soul it had once had.

'Funny,' I said to the agent, who was standing in the open back door. 'Seeing it like this.'

'People say they want character,' she said, 'but what they really want is smooth walls and stripped floors. It's a slightly depressing lesson, I suppose. These houses were never supposed to be turned into white boxes.'

'It's like seeing ours with the life drained from it.'

'The market's insane at the moment,' said the agent. 'We've valued this place twice in the last month. Once for the owner, and once for his lawyers. It's jumped up twenty thousand in four weeks. Four weeks. And it'll sell like that. Whoever buys it can move right in.'

I thought of Mr Ashani scheduling a meeting, carefully selecting a time when his tenant was at work, and cheerfully escorting a valuer through the house: the embodiment of moral certainty.

'We're incredibly untidy. We're not very saleable,' I said.

She tilted her head at me, amused. 'I'm sure yours is much nicer.'

I smiled at her, and went out into the garden. The lawn had been cut short again. I looked around, positioned myself

362

between the roots of the rose bushes, and stopped there. I thought I could see indented earth where Millicent and Bryce had lain, heard but not seen inside the bower. A flash of self-pity, an imagined moan, and for a moment I could feel Millicent's betrayal: the presence of Bryce, and the absence of me. I took three deep breaths and pushed the thought aside.

I found Millicent in the kitchen talking to the estate agent.

'Want to see any more?' I said.

'No,' she said. 'No . . . It's . . . I'm done.'

We thanked the agent, and took her card.

We rested against the low wall in front of our house, neither of us wanting to go in. I was aware again of my wallet, of something not quite right.

'Scary,' said Millicent.

'What?' I said.

'That girl. So young, so smart, and *so* fricking confident.'

'It's an immoral profession,' I said.

'Is it?' she said. 'What do we do that's so much better than that? What do I do? I'm not exactly a force for good.'

'You help people.' I slid an arm around her waist.

'Do I?' she said.

'You get letters,' I said.

'Doesn't everybody?' she said.

'Do you know what my mother said? When I told her that we didn't make each other happy?'

'What?'

'She said, "see to it that you do".'

She weighed this for a moment. 'Interesting,' she said. 'Not necessarily wrong.'

'So let's cut each other some slack. And try to be good to each other. And wait for life to get better, because it will.'

'So for you it all boils down to that?' she said.

'It does.'

'You've got to admit it's kind of a passive philosophy. Maybe you need to stop just letting things happen to you.'

I kept noticing my wallet: it felt a fraction too thick, a fraction too heavy against my thigh. *Something isn't right.*

I trailed my right hand across the top of my thigh. There was something very wrong about the feel of my pocket. I hooked my thumb inside and felt. Smooth, slick almost, jammed in under my wallet. I stood up slightly, slid in my hand. Drew it out again. *Alex Mercer Esquire.* Copperplate handwriting. A tiny square envelope. I turned it distractedly over and over in my hand.

My unconscious mind understood what my conscious mind did not. I felt the blood pounding in my ears, though I did not yet know why.

'Not from you, I'm guessing?' I said at last, holding it up to Millicent.

'Nope.'

Max, then. Obviously. 'What does he think he can tell me that's going to stop me from forgiving you?'

Millicent shook her head. *Surely there's nothing more.*

'You should open it,' I said, giving her the envelope. 'I'm the passive one.'

I'm calm, I thought. This is over. This is done. *Breathe.*

She ran her thumbnail along the gummed edge of the envelope, breaking the seal. Five sheets of paper, each with a pencil drawing on one side: the missing pages from Max's book. She handed them to me, one by one.

On the first was a radio very like Bryce's, drawn with great accuracy, as if from life. In red ink Max had drawn a heavy forward-sloping line over the radio. On the next page was an old-fashioned electric fire. Max had coloured the heating element of the fire in red ink. The fire, like the radio, was obliterated by a red slash.

I could taste blood in my mouth now. I knew before I saw it what was coming.

On the next page, Max had drawn the Black and Decker iron that we had found in Bryce's bath. Then he had painstakingly drawn a large green tick that overlapped its lower right corner.

Fuck.

I looked at Millicent, saw the panic rising in her. I wondered if she could read the same panic in me.

On the next page was a three-pin plug, dismantled. The fuse had been removed, and replaced with something made of metal. How skilfully Max had drawn the metallic surface; it seemed to shine dully from the paper.

'No,' said Millicent, as if speaking to herself. 'Please God, no, Max.'

The last page showed the circuit breakers from a fuse box. Bryce's fuse box, I guessed, drawn in fetishistic detail. Over the breaker on the right Max had stuck a small piece of industrial tape. I ran my finger over the raised edge.

I looked at Millicent. Millicent looked at me, then looked away. She put the drawings into the envelope and handed it to me. She leaned back on to the wall, put the tips of her fingers to her temples, screwed her eyes shut, exhaled heavily. 'Jesus,' she said, as if to herself. 'Please, no.' She took a very deliberate deep breath, then exhaled noisily again.

'Wait here,' I said. I got to my feet, rang the bell of the next-door house.

'Hello again.' The agent was surprised to see me. 'Have you and your wife reconsidered?'

I shook my head. 'I wonder,' I said.

'Yes?'

'I wonder, would it be OK to look in the electric cupboard?'

'Of course. That's why I'm here.'

She led me to the area under the stairs. Four panels, flush with each other. She leaned gently in against one of the panels, and it opened. It was dark in the cupboard, but I could see a line of breakers just as Max had drawn.

'I wonder,' I said. 'Do you have a torch?'

'Just a sec.'

She produced a tiny two-cell flashlight from her inside breast pocket.

'Thanks,' I said. 'Impressive.'

'Tool of the trade.' She twisted it on and handed it to me.

These were the breakers in the drawing. There could be no doubt. I held the flashlight to the final breaker on the right. It looked a little different from the others, its surface a little rougher. I looked round at the agent, who was watching me attentively. *What to say?*

'I wonder . . . What would it cost for us to do this, do you think?'

'The box? A couple of hundred? But if you mean a full rewire, well, it's a bit of a piece of string.'

Please, I thought. Turn away.

'Do you know a good electrician?'

'I might do.' She looked at me expectantly, her expression open and friendly.

Please, I thought, look it up on your phone.

'I could probably ring you with the information. I mean, we aren't allowed to recommend, but I can pass on details.'

'OK,' I said.

Someone knocked. The agent turned towards the front door.

I turned the torch around. I tamped the end of it gently against the breaker on the right. Some slight softening of the blow, almost imperceptible. I felt a resistance too as I drew it away from the breaker. I closed the cupboard, took two steps away. Then I turned the torch over and looked at the base. A tiny smear of adhesive. That was when I knew.

The gloves. The ball of tape.

Millicent was standing at the front door, frowning in at me.

I handed the torch back to the agent, apologised and said that we had to go. My wife and I had a lot of talking to do about the house.

'What is it, Alex?' said Millicent, as the neighbour's door closed on us.

'We need to go inside, Millicent. We can't talk about this in the street.'

Millicent nodded.

Arla was drinking orange juice in the kitchen. 'Hey,' she said as we came in. 'Coffee?'

'Arla, do you know where Max is?'

'Upstairs. In his bedroom.'

'Would you check that for me?' said Millicent.

Arla looked from Millicent to me, and back to Millicent. 'Want me to ask what's up?'

Millicent shook her head. Arla shrugged and went upstairs.

'Those pictures,' said Millicent, a half-whisper.

I shook my head. 'Wait.'

'Then I'm going to fix coffee,' she said.

'No,' I said. 'Wait.'

Arla came back downstairs. 'OK,' she said, 'Max is in his room, reading.'

Millicent and I looked at each other. 'Would you ask him to please come downstairs?' she said.

'OK,' Arla said. 'Whatever you need.' She went back upstairs.

'We can't talk to him about this, Millicent,' I said. 'Not yet.'

'I know,' she said.

We looked at each other. Millicent looked emptied, exhausted. I badly wanted a cigarette. I wondered if she felt the same creeping nausea that I felt.

'You and I have to talk,' I said. 'Before anything, you and I have to talk.'

'I know, Alex.'

Millicent went back to making coffee. She didn't turn to look at Max when he entered the room.

'Max,' I said.

'I came straight home, Dad,' he said.

'You were supposed to come back to Dr Å's,' I said.

'I didn't *say* I would.' His body was upright, his stance active. He was looking me directly in the eye.

I stifled the urge to run at him, to hold him by his bony shoulders and shake the swagger from him. Instead I turned away.

'Arla,' I said, 'I want you to take Max out for exactly one hour.'

'All good, Alex. Sure,' said Arla, sounding anything but sure.

'Sixty minutes,' I said. 'Go now, please.'

Max sloped from the kitchen into the living room. Arla closed the living-room door and said very softly, 'What's up, people?'

I looked at Millicent but she carried on making coffee, didn't turn round.

'Wait,' I said. 'Later.'

'OK. All good,' Arla said.

'Yes. All good,' I said. 'Thank you very much. All good.'

When the front door had slammed shut I went into the living room and looked through the curtain. Max and Arla were walking down the street. Max's stance was erect and alert, like a terrier on a rat-hunt. I thought Arla looked a little stooped, a little more stressed, a little more *British* than she had when she had arrived. But I was watching her from behind; I could have been imagining it.

I went back into the kitchen.

'So,' said Millicent.

'So?'

'So it's kind of a witness statement,' she said. 'He's saying the police were right. That it isn't suicide.'

'Hmm,' I said.

'What?'

'It isn't a witness statement,' I said.

'Not strictly,' she said.

'Not at all.'

'What do you mean, Alex?'

'Millicent, look at me.'

'I'm looking,' she said.

368

'It's a confession.'

'This is no confession.'

'Millicent . . .'

'Max is my son, Alex.'

'He's *our* son. And this is his confession to the murder of Bryce.'

'No. No, you are quite wrong.'

'Millicent,' I said, 'listen to me. I found tape adhesive on the breaker switch in Bryce's house.'

Millicent stared at me. Then she looked at the floor for a moment, then towards the window. Her eyes flicked as if she were watching a landscape pass by the window of a high-speed train. She looked back at me, looked away for a second, then locked her eyes on mine, searching for something. Finally she looked away and nodded.

There was something broken about her now, something unreachably, unfathomably sad.

28

For the longest time neither of us spoke. On the stove the water bubbled up through the coffee. Millicent poured us both a cup; then she opened the door into the garden. I followed her out and sat beside her on the love seat under the ivy by the wall.

We drank our coffee silently, watched a flock of starlings mobbing a crow in the sky above our heads. I thought about Max, and wondered what he would be thinking now. I was starting to realise how little I really knew about my son.

Little Max, who had put an end to Millicent's affair, brutally and with great precision. Max had, I thought, been trying to tell me so for a very long time. *He takes his cues from you.* What did he think of me, that he should do such a thing?

The crow tumbled through the air, dropping to escape the starlings that massed around it, antibodies around a virus.

I watched Millicent as she watched the crow, her dark eyes tracking the predator, the desecrator of nests, as it rose and dipped far above. Her eyes flicked to me for a moment, then flicked back to the birdmass following the crow. 'What, Alex?'

'I suppose I was just wondering what your thoughts were.'

'I have no thoughts right now,' she said. 'Although the birds are kind of beautiful. Like a living cloud of anger. You wouldn't want to be that crow, right?'

'I suppose.'

I thought of the time Max had found me at the open back door of the neighbour's house. I remembered what he had said. 'The fucking fucker's fucking fucked.' Bryce was the *fucking fucker*. Bryce was *fucking fucked*.

He had spoken with such relish; he must have believed he had done the right thing, believed that the death of the neighbour would make things right between Millicent and me, that we could return to being the little tribe we had once been. I looked over at Millicent.

'Do you know what Max said to me, *before* we found Bryce?' I said.

Millicent said nothing, her eyes tracking the cloud of birds, dark eddies against the flawless sky.

'He said, "Come and see". And then he took me to see Bryce, dead in the bath.'

Above us the starlings shrieked in outrage, grouped and regrouped around the crow, wave on wave.

'I know you're right about Max,' said Millicent after a time. She looked down, and touched my hand.

'I don't want to be right about Max.'

'I know you don't, Alex. You're a good father.'

'You're a good mother, Millicent.'

Millicent's nostril flared. She shook her head. 'Not so much, not lately.'

The angry cloud shrank to a denser black, and the shrieking intensified. For a moment the crow disappeared.

'We should go in,' I said. 'We really have to talk.'

'Do you think that crow's going to be OK?' said Millicent.

'It's a crow,' I said. 'So, yes.'

'I know it's a crow,' she said. 'It's not like I'm trying to make it a symbol for anything.'

The kitchen was jarringly tidy. We put Max's notebook and

the envelope with the extra pages on the table; then we sat drinking more coffee and staring blankly at the drawings. Radio, fire, iron, plug, breaker. The thought process was so clear, so confidently expressed. Max had made them in the expectation that they would be seen: there could be no doubt about that.

How to kill the neighbour? With a radio? No. With an electric fire? No. With an iron? Yes, perfect. But first I shall have to bypass the fuse in the plug, and disable the breaker circuit.

I picked up the book and looked at the pages that showed the neighbour in the bath. Bryce alive; Bryce dead. The space between was nothing more than a page turn, a second at most.

'There's something I don't understand,' I said. 'The pages in the envelope were never wet.'

'Huh,' said Millicent. 'Weird.'

She sat there at the table, radiating brittle intensity, eyes darting, while she uselessly reshuffled the five small pieces of paper from the envelope, as if seeking some alternative reading. How small she looked, I thought, how very small and lost.

I apologised to Arla when she came back with Max, and asked her to go out for the rest of the day. She asked me what the hell was going on; then she asked Millicent what the hell was going on. When neither of us said anything she asked Max if he was OK.

'I'm fine, thank you, Aunt Arla,' he said.

'Well, if every*thing*'s peachy and every*body*'s peachy then that's just peachy,' said Arla. She smiled her Pacific-Ocean smile, but I could read the anger in her eyes.

'You guys should ring me when you're on top of your *stuff*. Tomorrow I go home. I sort of kind of thought maybe we could go get some Chinese food later?'

'Mum knows Dad did you,' said Max. 'Would it be OK to have pizza instead?'

'What?' said Arla. She looked at me. I nodded. *She knows.*

'Seriously?' she said. 'I mean, really, Alex? Really? What is it with you and your need for revenge? It's sophomoric, you know that?'

Millicent stood up. 'It wasn't Alex who told me.'

Arla looked from me, to Millicent, to Max. Max looked suddenly uncomfortable, as if caught stealing sweets. 'Oh,' said Arla. 'OK.' She swallowed, rocked on her heels; then she drew breath, raised her chin and met Millicent's gaze. I looked at Millicent's right hand, clenching and unclenching, her eyes locked on Arla's.

The back door was still open, but I could no longer hear the starlings harrying the crow.

Arla was the first to drop her gaze. 'OK. Millicent . . . I guess the truth is that it was what it looks like, and that I can't explain why it happened. I don't know where to begin. I did a really terrible thing.'

'You were always such a follow-the-script second child, Arla.' Still Millicent hadn't dropped her gaze.

'And I guess I deserve that right now. Millicent, if there was some way . . .'

'. . . that you could unmake this?' said Millicent. Arla gave a sad little nod. Millicent exhaled sharply, rubbed her hands across her forehead and down her cheeks to her chin, held her lips between her clenched forefingers.

'Aunt Arla,' said Max. 'Aunt Arla, do you think maybe Dad did you because the neighbour did Mum?' There was no malice in the question. It sounded as if Max genuinely wanted to know what she thought. But I couldn't help myself.

'Shut up, you manipulative little shit.' I was on my feet, my face very close to his. Max crumpled and took a half-step backwards.

Arla and Millicent stared at me. I could hear no traffic

373

noise, but somewhere in the street a fightdog gave voice. Millicent put a warning hand on my arm, reached her other hand out to Max.

'Sorry,' I said. 'I'm sorry, Max. And I'm sorry, Arla. Max should never have spoken to you like that. You're sorry, aren't you, Max?' Max nodded, the picture of small-child contrition. I put a hand on his shoulder. 'He's been under a lot of stress. More than any boy should have to cope with. We'll see you later.'

Arla backed slowly out of the kitchen. I heard her footfalls on the living-room floor. She opened the front door and slid it quietly shut behind her.

'Sit down, Max,' Millicent said gently. 'We need to talk to you.'

'OK,' said Max. 'I want Ribena.'

'All right,' said Millicent. 'You can fix yourself some Ribena.'

'Can't you make the Ribena for me?' said Max.

'I think you can do it yourself,' I said.

Max sighed a theatrical sigh, and got up. He turned on the tap and left it running while he fetched a glass from the cupboard, located the Ribena bottle on the kitchen work surface. God, the thinness of his shoulders; the fragile angularity of him. Was he really capable of murder?

Max poured a large measure of Ribena into the bottom of the glass, then looked enquiringly first at me, then at Millicent. 'Is that too much?'

Neither of us responded. Max emptied the Ribena bottle into his glass. He topped up the glass with water and sat down, left the tap running.

I turned off the tap and sat down at the end of the table.

'So,' said Millicent.

'So-o-oo,' said Max, a valley-girl parody of her accent. Millicent rubbed a hand across her eyes.

'Did you do it, Max?' I said.

'Did *you* do it?' He was looking me straight in the eye. Was he challenging me?

374

'I expect you to answer my question, Max.'

'Alex, wait,' said Millicent. 'I would like that you not make this a confrontation, OK?'

'OK,' I said. 'All right. But Max, I do need you to answer my question. We need to know what happened.'

'I *don't* need you to answer my question, Dad, because I know the answer already. You didn't kill the neighbour, even though he was doing Mum, and you never would have killed him, either, even though he was a fuckingbastardingcunt, because you're much too scared and you're much too nice.'

He sniffed hard. His breathing was laboured. He was close to tears. I could see that now, could see in him Millicent's defiant fragility.

'Max,' said Millicent softly, 'honey, slow down a minute. Just stop for a moment. Take time to breathe.'

Max shrugged. 'OK.' He gulped at the air, inhaled and exhaled, three times. Then he drank down half of his Ribena, put the glass carefully back on the table in front of him.

'OK, honey,' said Millicent, 'so why don't you start by telling us, how did your book get wet?'

'The neighbour dropped it in the bath.'

'What was Bryce doing with your book, Max?'

'He was in the bath. I gave him the book, and he dropped it in. I had to dry it really carefully and write over it in pen again. It took a really long time.'

'Max, my beautiful child,' said Millicent with a tenderness that surprised me, 'you are going to have to explain to us what happened. In small steps. From the start.'

'When I made the book? Or when the neighbour dropped it in the bath?'

'When he dropped it in the bath.'

'I knew you meant that.' Max sipped his Ribena, looked at his mother, then back at me. He's pausing for dramatic effect, I thought.

A sharp look from Millicent – *do not rise to this.*

She was right. The defiance was a front. Perhaps he needed it to be able to say what he had to say.

'Anyway,' said Max, 'I knew that the neighbour was going to have a bath, because I could hear the water running in the pipes.

'And so I got some tape, and I waited until I could hear the neighbour getting into the bath, and then I went downstairs and Dad was working and you weren't here, and I went out into the garden and climbed over the wall.

'And then I opened the neighbour's back door with my key and went in and then I went into the sitting room and opened his fuse cupboard and I taped over the breaker switch.

'Also, I already knew it was the right breaker switch because one day when the neighbour wasn't at home I plugged in a light on the landing and the breaker turned it off. Like, I know about electricity and stuff.'

'Max,' I said, 'did you plan this?'

Max nodded. Of course he had planned it.

'Anyway,' said Max, 'I had to walk really carefully and it took me quite a long time to go up the stairs so the neighbour wouldn't hear me. And the bathroom door was open and you could see the neighbour in the bath, but he wasn't looking at me because he was reading his book, so I went really quietly past the door, and I went to the cupboard in the landing and I got out the iron. And even though it made a little bit of noise I don't think he heard anything.'

You're eleven, I thought. *How is any of this even possible?*

'I had to do the plug before, when the neighbour wasn't at home, so I came home early one day from school because I told Mr Sharpe I wasn't feeling well, and he believed me because normally I don't tell lies. Really I don't.'

That conviction: the child who knows right from wrong; the irony of it.

I wanted to put my arms around him, draw him back to a time before all of this. I wanted Max to be ten once more;

I wanted Millicent to be undefiled by the neighbour. A year, that's all it would take; give us a year and a little insight and we could side-step this.

A month even. A month back, the neighbour would still have seduced Millicent, but he wouldn't be dead. There must be other possible outcomes. There must be something I could have done to head this off.

'I wore gloves, though,' said Max, 'because I know about fingerprints.'

'You took your mum's gloves?'

'She never wore them anyway.'

I looked at my son. A little boy, asking for his father's approval, wanting me to know he'd thought of everything. *Why can't you be ten again, Max?*

Max drank down the rest of the Ribena, held the glass a few centimetres above the surface of the table, and dropped it on to its end.

'I think Arla's been drinking the Ribena.'

'So, fix yourself something else, honey,' said Millicent.

'Please may I have Ribena?'

Millicent looked meaningfully at me. 'What?' I said. Her eyes flicked towards the door. 'Are you seriously suggesting I go to the shop?' I said. 'Now?' Millicent nodded.

'Crisps too,' said Max. 'Please, Dad.'

I remember nothing about walking down the street, I remember nothing about entering the shop, and I remember nothing about the walk home. But I remember my thoughts, in precise and frightening detail.

I wondered how Max would get on as a ward of the British state, skirting the walls of some secure institution, trading phone cards with other terrified souls, trying to stay a step ahead of the big kids with their shanks and their shivs.

How would my sensitive little son measure up? Not well, I thought, not well at all.

The evidence must be destroyed. *Truth be damned*. What kind of man would willingly see his eleven-year-old son face justice?

Another visit to the neighbour's house, a little white spirit on a cloth, and a wipe of the breaker switch while the agent's back was turned. That would do it. Anything else, any other prints to emerge unexpectedly, could be explained by the fact that it was Max and I who found the body. You know small boys, don't you, June? They touch everything.

I was calmer when I walked back into the house.

Millicent and Max were sitting together at the kitchen table. Max looked like an eleven-year-old boy with cuts on his knees. Millicent looked like a concerned mother.

I put the bottle of Ribena on the countertop and dropped a large packet of Monster Munch on to the table in front of Max.

Millicent got up. She broke the seal on the bottle, poured a generous serving of Ribena, topped it up with water from the tap.

'Have we got any ice?' said Max.

'I don't know,' she said, putting the glass down in front of him. 'Go check for yourself, honey.'

'No, it's OK.'

My son, and my wife. It all looked so normal, so very North London. I sat down at the table. Millicent sat down. Father, mother and child at our little table in our little kitchen in our little overpriced house.

'It's OK, Dad,' said Max. 'I didn't tell her anything while you were out.' I said nothing in reply. Max opened the Monster Munch and placed a stack on the table in front of himself. Then he poked his pinkie through the maw of an extruded potato monster and raised it meditatively to his lips. He can't read us, I thought. It's almost as if he expects us to reward him. He still thinks he did the right thing.

378

'Dad,' said Max.

'Sorry, Max. Go on.'

'So, anyway, the neighbour was in the bath and I think he heard me plugging in the iron, because he shouted, "Who's there?" and I shouted, "Max", and then I went into the bathroom, but I left the iron outside so he wouldn't see it. I think he was quite surprised to see me, and maybe a bit cross, but I don't think he was frightened. And he asked me what I was doing and how I got in but I didn't answer that, but I took out my notebook and opened it at the first of the drawings with all the ropes and he started to read it.'

I could think of nothing to say, so I took a handful of Monster Munch and made a small pile of them in front of me. I put one in my mouth. Horrible – both cloyingly sweet and saltily moreish, like a dilute memory of bad drugs.

'Don't take them if you don't like them, Dad.' Max eyed me diffidently. He threw a Monster Munch into the air, made a show of catching it in his mouth.

'Anyway,' he said, 'I think maybe the neighbour was embarrassed or something, because he covered up his *penis* with one hand, except he couldn't really, because he was reading the book and he kept having to turn the page. And he was getting water on my drawings because his hand was wet, but I didn't say anything. And I took Mum's gloves out of my pocket and put them on, but I went out of the bathroom to do it, and then I went and got the iron and put it on the floor in the bathroom but he didn't see because he was looking at the pictures.'

'Max,' I said, 'where did you get the iron?'

Max looked confused. 'It was his iron. The neighbour's.'

'He didn't own an iron.'

'He did.'

'Max, don't lie to me.'

'I'm not. I'm not a liar.'

A man of expensive tastes. 'He had his clothes dry-cleaned, Max.'

Millicent's hand was on my arm. 'Alex,' she said, 'he owned an iron.'

'The police told me . . .'

Millicent's gaze did not waver.

'Oh.'

If indeed you owned an iron . . . June had not lied to me either. She had simply suggested a possibility. I was a dolt.

'I'm sorry, Max.'

'It's OK. Anyway, he asked me how I knew what his bathroom looked like and I told him I had Mum's key and I had been in his house before. And he looked quite angry, like he wanted to get out of the bath, but I wasn't sure if that was because of the drawings or just because I was in his house.

'And he asked me if it was him in the bath, and I said, "Yes, it's you now." And then he looked at the next picture and I think he was a *bit* frightened but he was trying not to show me that he was, even though he was covering up his *penis*.'

I thought of Bryce hiding his penis from the little boy from next door; the little boy who knew Bryce had *done* his mother; the little boy who was standing there proudly in his t-shirt and his mother's brown leather gloves, the iron on the floor beside him.

'And he was looking backwards and forwards between the two pictures like I wanted him to do.' Max was speaking very softly now. 'And then he said, "Is that also me?" and I could hear that he was trying to sound all calm and grown-up but really he wasn't.'

When did Bryce first see the iron? *When did he know?*

'And I said, "Yes, it's you, soon." And he said, "What do you mean, soon?" and I said, "About seven seconds." And he asked me what I meant again and he didn't sound calm any more and he started trying to get out of the bath but he slipped. And I did feel a bit sorry then, but I thought about how he did Mum and I picked up the iron even though it was really hot and I threw it into the bath.'

380

Millicent looked utterly stricken.

'Then the neighbour started to kick, and his face went all red, and he dropped my book into the bath, which is how it got wet. And I think he was dead then.'

The brokenness of Bryce's body. The redness of those lips. The agony of the scene. An eleven-year-old boy's idea of justice. I looked at Millicent. Millicent looked blankly back at me. *What do we do?*

'Do you think he was dead, Dad?'

'I don't know, Max.'

'But do you think he probably was? Like straight away?' There was a pleading note in his voice now.

'Max, I'm sorry, I really don't know.'

'I went out of the room for a while just in case he wasn't, and then I counted to three hundred slowly, like one hippopotamus, two hippopotamus, three hippopotamus, and then I went downstairs and took the tape off the switch. Because they wait five minutes in America. Like if it's an execution, or something. Although probably they're already dead.'

'Max,' said Millicent. 'Max, can't you see?'

'What, Mum?'

Millicent wrapped her arms very tightly around herself. She sat rocking backwards and forwards in her chair.

'But I didn't know there would be a boner. And anyway I checked afterwards on the internet and it's normal. Like when they kill murderers in America. Murderers get boners, even though they're dead.'

'Jesus, Max,' said Millicent. 'What the fuck?'

'You shouldn't swear at me, Mum,' said Max. 'You *asked* me how my notebook got wet. I just told you what you asked me to tell you.'

'Alex,' said Millicent. 'I'm going to need you to engage.'

'Max killed the neighbour. He threw the iron into the bath. He clearly doesn't understand the implications of what he did.'

381

'Alex,' said Millicent, 'let him tell us himself. Don't pre-empt.'

'OK,' I said. 'Why, Max?'

'Why what?'

'Max, I think you understand what I'm asking you.'

'Can I have a cigarette, Dad?' he said. I shook my head. Max turned to Millicent. 'Can I, Mum?'

'Honey,' said Millicent, 'we need for you to answer the question. Why would you do this?'

'Can I have a cigarette then?'

I shook my head again.

Insolent fury, immediate and raw. 'I want a cigarette.'

'You don't smoke, Max,' I said. 'And there aren't any.' My voice sounded weak, defensive.

Max took a Marlboro ten-pack from his trouser pocket. An old one of ours. Red, black and white. He knocked it experimentally on the table, then opened it, and offered it to me. The cigarettes inside had been gently curved, the packet edges frayed, from the inside of Max's pocket. The tobacco smelled stale.

Max flicked the bottom of the packet with a finger. A cigarette loosed itself from the others. He held the packet closer to me, full of challenge and bravado. But the tremor in his hand told a different story: a child, knocking at the door of the adult world.

'Put those down, Max,' I said, as gently as I could.

'Don't you want to know why I killed the neighbour?'

I swallowed the urge to shout at him. My blood was up: the cigarette in my face, the call of the old Marlboro packet, the extended arm, the floppy hair and the bright blue eye. *Do not rise to this.*

'I did it for you, Dad,' he said. He took a cigarette from the pack and put it in his mouth. 'Can I have a light please, Dad?' His body was poised, now, cocksure: had he practised this move before? I could taste the exhilaration on him, the dangerous thrill as he dared us to make him stop. But behind his eyes was something altogether less certain.

'Take the cigarette out of your mouth, Max.'

'I know you want one.' Max's eyes did not leave mine. 'Why do you always think you have to pretend?' But he took the cigarette from his mouth and put it behind his ear. Then he turned to Millicent.

'Even though Dad's angry and he swears a lot, he wouldn't kill someone. He never would. But I know he wishes he'd done what I've done, because he hated the neighbour when he found out about how he did you and everything, and now he's glad he's dead.'

'Max,' I said. 'Max, stop. That's not true.'

'You're only saying that because you found out he was doing Mum *after* he was dead.' He turned back towards Millicent. 'But even though he hates the neighbour he would just have forgiven *you*, because he thinks those are the rules or something. You shouldn't just forgive her, Dad. *Please, Dad*. You shouldn't make it so easy for her.'

Millicent's eyes locked on to mine.

'Max,' I said, 'listen to me. I would have wanted your mother back anyway.'

'But Dad, she didn't *want* to come back. Why won't you listen to me?' He was exasperated now. 'Didn't you read any of her letters?'

'No, Max, I didn't.'

'She wasn't *going* to come back. She always just runs away and never goes back.'

I didn't look at Millicent but I felt her put a hand on my forearm. I put my hand over hers. I didn't dare look at her for fear that what Max was saying was true.

'Max,' I said, trying to slow my breathing, 'I really, genuinely don't know what would have happened. Maybe your mum would have left me. But this is a terrible, terrible thing. You don't take away people's choices because you think they're going to make the wrong choices.' Millicent's hand tensed on my arm.

Max sniffed hard. His voice was tremulous. 'You just say what you think you have to say,' said Max. 'It's like, you're just politically correct, or something. If you could say what you really thought, you would thank me.'

'*Thank* you?'

'I just wanted us all to be together. Like you did.'

'You took a man's life, Max.' I had shouted these last words.

'But Dad,' said Max, his voice tiny, 'why is killing worse than fucking?'

'It just is.' *Control your voice.* 'It's worse. You've taken a life, and ruined the lives of all the people who loved Bryce.'

'But *why* is it worse? *Why* is what *I* did worse than what *he* did?'

'People sleep with the wrong people all the time. I slept with Arla.'

'You wanted to get back at Mum for what she did to you.'

'No, Max,' I said, 'I don't know why I did it.'

Max hesitated, thrown off balance. He looked first at me, then at Millicent.

'How can you not know why, Dad?'

'Max, I genuinely don't know why I slept with Arla.'

'But you told Mum you weren't sorry.'

'How do you even know that?' I said. Max blinked at me. 'Anyway, Max, I don't know why I did it. People sleep with the wrong people for all sorts of complicated reasons. Like your mum did. Like I did. And for what it's worth, I am sorry for sleeping with Arla. I shouldn't have done it.'

Millicent stared at me, appraising.

'I'm truly sorry, Millicent,' I said. 'It's the worst thing I have ever done, and I will be sorry for doing it for as long as I live.' She nodded then, and turned her attention back to Max.

'No,' said Max, desperation in his voice now. 'You're telling lies. It was because you thought she was sexy and pretty and you wanted to get back at Mum.' He was almost shouting, but I could feel the panic in him. The ground beneath him was leaching away.

'Max,' I said. 'You're eleven.'

'I know about sex.'

'You're clever, but you're a literalist.'

That stopped him. 'What?'

'Literalist means you don't – you can't – understand how untidy and imprecise the adult world is. You can't hope to, because you haven't felt these things yourself yet.'

'I did know what it meant,' he said softly. 'And I've done something you've never done.'

A spike of cold rage, and I was on my feet.

'You're right, Max,' I said. 'You're absolutely right.' I looked at Millicent. *Are we going to let this pass?* Millicent gave the tiniest of frowns. The stricken look had left her now. There was something harder and more determined about her demeanour. She nodded. Her eyes flicked to Max, and back to me. Allies.

'Your mother would never do what you've done either, would you, Millicent?'

'No,' said Millicent, 'I never would.'

'You're a child, Max,' I said. 'You are nothing but a child. You don't understand what you've taken from that man.'

Max stood up, pushed back his chair.

'Sit down, Max,' said Millicent.

'You two can't tell me what to do any more,' he said, his voice tremulous.

'Or what?' I said. 'Sit down.'

'No,' he said. He straightened his tiny frame, forced himself to look me directly in the eye. 'You know what I did.'

Again, the certainty of his words, undercut by something that sounded very like fear.

'Are you threatening me, Max?' I said. 'Sit down.'

'You know what I did.'

I leaned forwards in my chair and brought my face very close to his. 'You really don't want to do this.'

'I killed a man.'

'And you're full of murderous rage, Max. I get it. Doesn't *make* you a man. Sit down.'

Max looked up at me, fists tight, eyes vibrating in resentful fury.

'Alex,' said Millicent. 'I think that's enough. You're frightening him now.'

'Not enough, clearly,' I said and stood up. 'Do you have any idea how little you are to me right now, Max?'

Max leaned backwards for a moment, then threw himself at me. The first blow was harder than I expected. The tiny fist struck my chin with a force that astonished me, throwing me off balance. *Control.* I looked down at him and laughed.

'You can't hit me back, Dad,' he said.

'That's OK, Max,' I said. 'That's fine.'

He struck me twice more, but I was ready for him now. The blows glanced uselessly off my left shoulder, off my right arm.

'Is that really the best you've got?' I said.

'Alex, don't,' said Millicent.

'Hit me again, Max,' I said, but I saw that the fight had gone from him. Tears were welling in the edges of his eyes.

'I thought you'd be proud of me, Dad. And you're not.'

'I am,' I said. 'And I always will be. Just not of this terrible, terrible thing you've done.'

Max stood there, gulping air. Heavy tears drew paths down the side of his nose, skirted the edge of his mouth, pooled at the tip of his chin, then dropped through dark space. I put a hand on his shoulder. He tried to shake me off, but I drew him gently to me and held him as he sobbed.

We stood for perhaps twenty minutes, my arms wrapped tightly around my son's fragile frame. Then I sat quietly down and guided him on to my lap. Millicent reached for his hand, and Max let her take it.

386

No one spoke for more than an hour. I saw the minutes tick over on the clock on the stove. My thoughts were disordered, fleeting and half-formed.

We would leave.

We would fight this.

We would unburden ourselves and face the consequences.

We would deny everything.

Mostly I simply saw Max in extreme close-up: the tear-soaked tips of the lashes of his left eye, where the long London summer had bleached them white; the tension in his left hand, where the nail of his forefinger was cutting into the quick of his thumb.

We did this, I kept thinking. Your mother's infidelity and your father's rage. Millicent and I had brought this upon the world, had caused our son to take a life. He had done, he thought, what I would have done if only I could, if I had known what he had known. We made him what he is, I thought. *We* did this to our son.

A sharp crack. The cat at the feeding bowl, eating dry food. Max looked up, but said nothing. The cat ate her fill, then jumped up on to the work surface, licked the open end of the tap, wanting water. No one moved.

It was Max who spoke first. 'Tarek doesn't want to be my friend any more. He said I've been acting like I'm spectrum.'

'Does Tarek know, Max?' I said.

Max bit the edge of his mouth. 'I never said anything. I swear.'

'Who else knows?'

'Just you and me and Mum. I never told Arla.'

'Not Dr Å?'

'Dr Å says you have to be *grandiose* if you think you can decide if someone should live or die. I didn't want her to stop liking me.'

'OK, Max,' said Millicent, 'here's what we're going to do. From now on this isn't your problem. It's our problem.'

'But they'll take me away from you,' said Max.

'No, Max,' she said. 'They aren't going to take you away from us, honey. I promise you. But you have to let your dad and me steer this, and you have to do what we say. Everything we say.'

'It hasn't gone the way I thought it would, anyway.' He looked completely and utterly undone.

'No, honey,' she said. 'Of course it didn't go the way you planned it. You can't solve this. We can.'

'Dr Å said lots of murderers are a bit mad, but that doesn't make them insane. She says they should still go to prison.'

'Max,' said Millicent, 'Max, my sweet, sweet child, it's not because you're insane, or because you're bad. You made a wrong choice because you were behaving like a much bigger person.'

'But that's what grandiose *means*, Mum.'

'I know that, Max, honey,' she said. 'My sweet little child.'

But I saw how she shivered, even as she tenderly held him to her breast.

At two, Max went into the living room to watch cartoons. Ten minutes later I found him asleep on the sofa, face down. The cat had stretched herself out along Max's spine. She raised her head and chirruped softly at me. Then she blinked twice and rested her head in the nape of Max's neck.

I went back into the kitchen. 'Millicent,' I said, 'are you sure that we can protect Max?'

'It's our job,' she said simply. 'We're his parents.'

'Those kids who killed Jamie Bulger were the same age as Max, weren't they? They weren't protected by their parents,' I said. 'I mean, having parents didn't stop them from going to prison. They were tried as adults.'

'That was an experimental killing of a child. This is not at all the same thing. In the absence of better evidence, it's a suicide. We can protect Max.'

I picked up a cigarette from Max's packet, rolled it exploratively between forefinger and thumb. Fine threads of tobacco dropped from the tip. I looked over at the gas cooker. I would lower my head to light it in the flame, suck the smoke greedily down, stand up dizzy with the thrill of nicotine in my yearning veins. *Old friend.*

I looked back down at the cigarette. 'How many of these do you think he has?'

'I don't know. All of them, I guess. We lost a *lot* of cigarettes.'

I held the cigarette out to her. 'You want it?'

'More than you would know.' She pushed it gently away. I put it back in the packet. Then I got up and went out into the garden, faced the wall on the opposite side from Bryce's house, and threw it as hard as I could. It spun high. Three gardens at least, I reckoned, before I lost sight of it. Five, maybe.

Voices from Mr Ashani's garden.

'Sir, please remain calm.'

'I am perfectly calm, young lady, but what you are suggesting is an outrage.'

'I suggested nothing, Mr Ashani.'

'You know perfectly well that you are drawing an inference.'

The voices were raised, but sounded distant. Perhaps they weren't in the garden after all. I pulled myself up and looked over the wall. Mr Ashani's garden was empty of people, but his kitchen window was open.

'It's no more than an informal conversation at this stage, sir.'

'And yet you wish to search my house? You call this informal?'

'If you would like me to formalise the situation, sir, that can be arranged.'

I dropped back down into my own garden. Shortly afterwards I heard Mr Ashani's window slam shut.

The kitchen was dark after the searing summer light outside. I closed the door carefully behind me. 'Alex,' said Millicent, 'what's up?'

I walked through to the front room, pushed the curtain aside. There he was, being led to a marked police car. Mr Ashani must have seen me open the curtain, because he stopped.

He turned towards me. His eyes met mine.

He looked utterly humiliated.

Millicent was standing by the door to the garden, heavily backlit, waiting for me. 'Is Max telling the truth?' I said. 'Were you going to leave me?'

She walked past me and out of the room. *House, marriage and children.* So small, in my case, and so imperfect. A tiny house, a marriage that didn't look much like a marriage, and one single child. Still my only real achievement, though, because my television career was probably gone.

She was going to leave you. I heard Millicent's feet on the stairs. She hadn't taken off her shoes. I thought about the rot in the floorboards, now spreading from the bathroom to the bedroom, of the window frames that barely fitted, of the pathological mess of the life we lived: God, but the *neglect* of it. The house was tidy now, but give it a week. Coming in through the front door, the neglect would be the first thing that hit you.

House, marriage and child. *She was going to leave you.*

Had we neglected each other as we'd neglected the house? I didn't think so, but how do you *know*? Only the very naive believe that love is all you need; but the other stuff, the boundaries and the fights, the sex and the food? Hadn't we been good at that?

Perhaps Millicent had truly loved the neighbour. Perhaps she had seen in him a man who would not neglect her as I had done. Perhaps his tidy little house represented something else to her: a cleaner, better version of what a marriage could be.

Millicent returned. She was carrying the letter from Bryce.

'I know that you loved him,' I said. The fight was gone from me now. 'Max knew too. That's why he was so afraid.'

'Oh, Alex.'

'Didn't you?'

'Yes,' she said, 'for a time I did.' She nodded sadly to herself.

'And you didn't want me to know.'

'And now you know,' she said.

'Were you going to leave me?'

She handed Bryce's letter to me. 'You forgot this,' she said. 'You forgot that I told him no.'

'So it's husband before lover,' I read to myself, 'duty before passion, routine before LIFE.'

'Poor guy,' I said. 'He never guessed what was coming.'

'I see the envy in his words,' she said. 'I didn't see it then, but I see it now.'

'He envied me?'

'Yes, Alex, he really did.'

'He thought I had it all?'

She nodded.

'Do I?' I said.

'Alex, that is not a question I can answer for you.'

It was then that someone knocked at the front door.

29

I went through to the front room. Max was lying on his side now, the cat cradled in his arms.

Another knock. Max stirred slightly, but did not wake.

I looked through the eyehole. There was something familiar about the man standing on our front step, but his shape was so distorted by the lens of the eyehole, and my thoughts so disordered, that I could not at first discern who it was. *Breathe.*

'Ms Weitzman?' He had seen the movement at the eyehole. 'Ms Weitzman, it's the police.'

I considered for a moment. I didn't have to let him in, I thought.

The policeman knocked a third time. 'Mr Mercer?'

I opened the door. The policeman who had interviewed Millicent in the garden. June's boss. He looked past me into the front room.

'Alex, is your wife at home?'

I considered this for a moment. On balance, I decided, Millicent wasn't. Not for the police. Not right now.

'Not really,' I said.

I stepped out past him on to the street and pulled the door closed behind me. The lock clicked into place. I folded my arms across my chest. *Where's the warrant, porco?*

'My son,' I said, as if that explained it. We stood looking at each other for a moment. He was as smart as I was dishevelled, pinstriped in the afternoon daze. I wondered what sort of house he lived in.

He produced a small envelope from his inside jacket pocket. Windowed. Addressed to Millicent.

'Well, this is weird,' I said.

'How so, Mr Mercer?'

'My day's been all about little envelopes today. I'll give this to Millicent.'

He handed me a business card, then wished me goodbye.

'Who was that?' said Millicent, as I walked back into the kitchen.

'The officer who interviewed you. The man.'

'You really never got his name? Jeez. What did he want?'

'Derek. His name's Derek. I really don't know what he wanted. Polite as ever, mind. He didn't offer me counselling this time. But he did give me this.' I handed her the envelope.

'Huh,' said Millicent.

'They're interviewing Mr Ashani. I think they implied they thought he had done it.'

'Wow,' she said, 'that's kind of desperate.'

I sucked at my nail. 'If they're going to accuse Mr Ashani, do you think one of us should do the noble thing?'

'What in the world are you talking about?'

'We can't let him go down for our crime.'

'He won't.'

'He had motive, and he had opportunity. He had his own keys, for God's sake. And an iron.'

'And he didn't do it.' Millicent was staring at me, slowly shaking her head.

'Millicent, I think maybe I need to confess to the murder of Bryce so that some sort of justice could be done.'

'No, Alex.'

'If Max can't take the consequences, I can. We *did* this to him.'

'Again, no. What is it with you? No one is going to jail.'

'But someone should, and Max mustn't, and Mr Ashani can't take the fall for that.'

'They'll interview him under caution. He'll be out in hours.'

'You're sure of that?'

'I'm sure of that.'

Millicent held the corners of the envelope between the thumb and middle finger of her right hand. She tipped it experimentally one way, then the next. 'Alex, did the police ever ask you about the tape adhesive on the breaker switch?'

'No.'

'That's a little curious, right? If they think it's a homicide? And they are kind of clutching at straws if they're accusing Mr Ashani.' She was shaking the envelope gently.

'What do you mean?'

'Alex, it's a suicide. That's what we have to think. That's what we have to teach Max to think. That's what the police are going to have to think, once they're through accusing the neighbours. Don't go screwing with a version of the truth that works. For everyone. Look.'

'Oh.' Dulled a little by the opacity of the paper in the envelope's window was a clean metal edge. White gold and sapphires. My grandmother's bracelet.

'I think they closed our file.'

'He didn't tell me that.'

'Yeah, Alex, I think he just did.' She opened the envelope with great care and slid the bracelet out into her left hand. Then she dropped it into my right hand. 'Look.'

I cupped the bracelet in both hands. 'If I hadn't been so angry, none of this would have happened.'

'Alex, you *have* to get real. No one is going to prison. We are not *that* family, and you are not *that* man.'

'What do you mean?'

'You sweet, confused fuck.' She laughed. 'I mean, *you*? In prison? That just isn't going to work, for you, or for us. Like you wouldn't go to pieces. Get serious, Alex. I can't do this alone, and Max can't do it without a father.'

'Maybe not.'

Then she became very formal. 'Alex, there is something I would like for you to do for me.' She raised her right arm, and I opened the tiny gold catch, slipped the bracelet on to her wrist.

Millicent's eyes were shining. I laughed.

'I know,' she said. 'Stupid, right?'

'No,' I said. 'Not stupid at all.' The catch slid into place. MW.

Millicent Weitzman.

My wife.

We spent two hours constructing the big lie. Mostly it was Millicent who spoke, and mostly I agreed. The lie had one major flaw. If Max ever confessed to someone outside the family he was finished; and then we, as a family, would be finished too. The truth was our enemy now; the truth would not set us free.

Max could not now reach adulthood as the untroubled soul we wanted him to be. 'That train left,' Millicent said matter-of-factly, and of course she was right. We would never now be the classic *good-enough* parents you read about in books. We would neurotically police his friends and, when the time came, his girlfriends. There would be no more shrinks, no one to whom Max could unburden himself: from now on he had only us. But the alternative was so much worse.

Millicent burned Max's book. She had dried the sink thoroughly with an old pair of pants from the laundry basket, and crushed the pages into balls, making a loose pyramid on the bottom. Then she lit the pyramid at the four corners with a lighter that Max had hidden on top of a high cupboard.

I passed her the five pages that Max had cut from the book; she made balls of them and added them to the fire in the sink. Tiny angry fires reflected back at me from Millicent's dark irises; highlights in her hair burned red. There was a strange calm about her now. She knew what she had to do. When there was nothing left but brittle balls of ash she turned on the tap and we watched them collapse and fleck into the steel sink, carried by the water in tiny flakes out of our house and out of our lives.

Only then did she let me take her in my arms. Only then did she cry for what was lost.

The rest of the day ran with delicate precision. Millicent rang Arla at four and told her we would meet her in town at six. We had woken Max and explained to him what was going to happen to him, and what he had to do and to say. He listened to what we told him; he did not ask a single question.

Millicent embraced Arla when we met. Then she held out to Arla the letter she had written her when she arrived in Rhode Island.

'Half a lifetime away,' she said. 'Here.'

Arla took the letter, and tried to apologise to Millicent. It was all good, Millicent said. There was nothing to discuss and no more apologies needed.

We drank overpriced beer at a Chinese restaurant with worn carpets and spectacular food. Arla half-filled Max's tea cup with beer, and Max sipped delicately at it throughout the meal. I remember looking around, and thinking how happy we all looked, how like a family.

Soon I shall be gone. Bryce had been planning to move – that was the worst of it. If Max had not acted, his mother's seducer would have melted from our lives. Millicent's decision had been made and so too had Bryce's. Max, I thought, why couldn't you just wait?

Still, it was good to have a plan.

30

Arla was gone. Her flight left Heathrow at ten; she had woken Max at six to say goodbye; she had not woken Millicent and me.

Millicent and I got up at eight. Max was on the couch in the living room watching cartoons. Not hungry, he said, so Millicent and I drank our coffee and ate our toast without him.

When we had finished eating Millicent went upstairs and returned with her old letters. Full disclosure, she said. After all, Max had already read them. No, I had said, no, I don't want to play policeman with my wife. How much do I really need to know? And if I felt a sadness that some parts of her past would remain unknown to me, at least that thought has been spoken now.

At half past nine Millicent went to the post office. She took with her new letters that she'd written to her parents, bought new stamps for the envelopes, and posted them: she was certain I wouldn't much like her father or her mother when I met them.

'As certain as I was that you wouldn't like my mother?' I said.

'Yeah, OK,' she said. 'Who knew?'

She met Mr Ashani in the street on her way home; he was red-eyed and angry after an eighteen-hour interrogation. Mr Ashani had paid a high price for his religious views. Someone had heard him in the street; someone had come forward; some unseen neighbour had reported him for saying, 'We must hope that this is murder.'

The police had interviewed Mr Ashani under caution; they had spent those eighteen hours effectively asking him the same two questions again and again: how much money did the neighbour owe him? Why did he want him dead?

Later that evening, Mr Ashani would find the loose board in the bedroom of the house he was selling. I had replaced it so that one end extended slightly above the level of the floor.

Being an observant man, Mr Ashani knew at once that something was out of place. Being a moral man, he took no more than was due to him from his tenant Mr Bryce (plus a small consideration for his trouble); being an excellent judge of character, he trusted that Mr Ravinder S. Mann would distribute what was due to his creditors from the brown-paper parcel that Mr Ashani carefully placed at the door of his office.

Neither of them cared to involve the police.

Four days later Millicent and I agreed the sale on our house. The offer was below the asking price, but the estate agent didn't object when we accepted it.

In October a coroner's court returned a verdict of suicide.

31

We trekked out across the ice, my son and I, the snow brittle beneath our skis.

In the middle of the bay I strained at the ice drill; a perfect cylinder of frozen seawater rose slowly above the giant bit. I felt the drill loosen as it reached the water below. Max picked up the spade and shovelled slush from the hole. We dropped in our lines and waited.

'Morten's dad once drove all the way to Denmark,' said Max. 'Over the ice.'

'Does it go that far?' I said.

'Not normally. It used to though.'

The ocean creaked as ice moved slowly against ice: unseen forces, ancient and terrifying. The sun was low. There was no wind. I wondered for a moment if we were putting ourselves in danger, but saw skaters far out beyond us and put the thought from my mind.

It was Max who had drawn up the first cod. It had lain there on the ice, thrashing uselessly, gulping air. An alien creature, too large, too alive.

'Can I have the knife, Dad?'

He killed the cod with a single efficient cut behind the head, cleaned it and threw the guts back down the hole. Then he dropped his line back through the ice after it. Controlled aggression, I thought. Isn't *that* what separates man from boy?

Of course I have wondered about that weekend of water and unreal light. Did Millicent bring me to Oslo to scout out the territory? Did she want to see for herself a country that would not deport our son? But my wife has the soul of a romantic; there was no cynical intent behind the visit. Millicent has sworn to me that she never once suspected Max; I believe her.

She researched the country before we came back, though; she read countless journals and books at her computer; she pored over translations, mouthed strange words to herself, all *K*s and *S*s and Øs. She made phone calls, anonymised through servers in the Far East, to public prosecutors in Bergen and Trondheim, to heads of Child Protection Services in Oslo. She was an English journalist with a London accent and a few theoretical questions. Everyone was very kind, and very professional. She was certain no one suspected a thing. She learned that at the very worst Max would face a light sentence in comfortable surroundings. He was, after all, eleven when he killed the neighbour. Most likely he would not be removed from his family, if the murder should ever come to light.

'The justice system is rational and humane there,' Millicent said to me one evening. 'You guys have European passports. And I'll get leave to remain because of you. We really have no other choice.'

Yes, I know. But what kind of father would risk his son being tried and sentenced as an adult? Max was not a Freak of Nature. He had not led a Life of Depravity. He was not The Monster Next Door.

Millicent and I were damaged people. That's why we fitted, of course: any two-dollar shrink would say so. And like so many damaged people of our generation, we masked our pain behind alcohol and easy cynicism. Which worked well until we had Max.

Our cynicism confused our son. It masked the line between pain and cruelty. But Max saw the contradiction too – that I never acted on my anger, that I did nothing to change my circumstances. He saw this as my tragic flaw and he killed Bryce because he knew that I would not.

His mother and I were certain that Max wouldn't make the same choice a second time. He had learned from his terrible mistake.

Now that Max had time to reflect on what it meant to take a life he was truly sorry for what he did. Our only-begotten son killed from the very purest of motives, which is love, and from the very oldest, which is revenge.

When Max is a little older he will come to understand this as his own tragic flaw. For now it must be enough that he is sorry.

I did read the letter Millicent wrote to Sarah. I read it first on my own, and then again with Max. It was beautiful, and simple, and very raw indeed. We read the letter with Millicent's permission, and it made us both cry.

I looked at my boy, beautiful in the low sun, backlit and self-assured. You knew, I thought.

'What, Dad?'

His bearing had changed: he was fitter now, more poised. A little taller.

'Dad, you're staring at me.'

'I was thinking . . . Are you OK, Max? You seem to be OK.'

'I'm fine, Dad.'

You knew, I thought. You're the only one of us who knew, Max. Millicent couldn't explain how she had wandered from the path. Nor could I. But you knew exactly why you killed Bryce. You wanted to keep the family together, thought that was what it took. Your crime ruined your life, as it did ours, but you knew why you committed it.

What Max had wanted, in short, was this: father and son, fish and ice. Love expressed through the doing of stuff.

'You're fine, Max? You're sure you're fine?'

'I like it here, *for faen.*'

'What?'

'Nothing.'

In an hour there were five cod. Max threaded an orange cord through their gills and carried them in a gloved hand as we skied slowly back across the ice to where Millicent stood waiting on the shore.

Acknowledgements

My agent Judith Murray and my editor Julia Wisdom both saw something in my manuscript, and made me rewrite and rewrite until we were all happy with it. To them and to everyone else listed here I am extremely grateful. Tim Lott, Eleanor Moran, Kate Stephenson, John Tague, Thorgeir Kolshus, Charles Boyle and Tor Øverbø read and advised on drafts. Johnny Acton, Phil Wiget and Jeremy Drysdale read early chapters and encouraged me to keep writing. Kathy O'Donnell, Lucinda Acton, Fiona McLaney, Dominic Edmonds, Leslie O'Neill, Gabrielle Osrin, Francis McPherson and Satnam Virdi helped me with the research. Dehra Mitchell, Oliver James, Davinder Virdi, Thomas Bjørnflaten and Simon Aylwin gave specialist professional advice. Ida von Hanno Bast, Signe and Stein Lundgren, the staff of Kaffebrenneriet on Frognerveien, and the House of Literature in Oslo all – in one way or another – gave me a place to write. And Charlotte Lundgren did every one of these things, and more.